SUMAC

CHARLES NEAL

FLAME GRAPE PRESS

FOR MY MOTHER AND FATHER

FLAME GRAPE PRESS

Copyright 1993 by Charles Neal

LIBRARY OF CONGRESS CATALOG CARD NUMBER:
93-73293

ISBN: 0-9638727-0-2

Printed in the United States of America

PART ONE

1

Ethel Turner was trying to remove a hair that sprouted from a mole on her chin when she heard the telephone ring. Taking her eyes away from the mirror, she focused on the kitchen clock, suspecting that it was her friend Miriam calling with a report about one of the early morning cable soap operas or some other juicy gossip. Smiling at that, she struggled off the chair and plodded heavily toward the phone.

"Hi there, honey," she drawled into the receiver. "Tell me what I missed."

"Can I speak with Mr. Wayne Turner, please," an unknown voice surprised her.

Ethel paused, knowing that her husband was sleeping and that it was not wise to wake him before he got up of his own accord. "He's not in right now," she finally bluffed. "But this is his wife."

The man on the other end cleared his throat. "Well I'm calling from Greenwood's TV and Hi-Fi in Westport because it seems that no payments have been made on your 25-inch RCA television for over three months."

Ethel reached for her pack of cigarettes on the kitchen table. "Well I just don't understand," she said. "My husband didn't mention anything to me about not payin' the bill. It must've just slipped his mind or somethin'."

"I don't think that's possible," the man stated coldly. "We've been in contact through the mail a number of times, but we still haven't even received a partial payment."

"Well I'll tell my husband as soon as he gets up," Ethel said, quickly adding, "I mean as soon as he gets *home*. I'm sure there must just be some kind of mistake that you've made or somethin' like..."

The man on the other end cut her off. "No, we haven't made any mistake here," he said assuredly. "And according to the contract that your husband signed when he took out the lease on the television sixteen months ago, we have the legal power to remove any appliance we rent for which no payment is received after a period of three months."

Ethel nervously jetted out some smoke from her heavy lungs. "What do you mean the 'legal right'?" she snarled. "We almost got that thing paid off!"

"Power of attorney," he stated confidently. "You seem to forget that until the actual appliance is paid off, it remains Greenwood's property."

"You can't do that!" Ethel insisted, raising her voice. "We've already paid a lot of money to your stupid store. I'm sure that contract gives us some rights too."

"Excuse me, Mrs. Turner," the man interrupted her, raising his voice to her level. "But our 'Rent to Own' policy doesn't mean 'Borrow to Own'. And I'm telling you right now—if we don't see the money that's due on that set within forty-eight hours, someone from our store will be coming out to remove it."

"Well I just don't think you can do that," Ethel said quickly. "We've done a lot of..."

"Forty-eight hours," the man said, ignoring her statement and reinforcing his own. "That's Friday at twelve o'clock noon."

"I mean we've done a lot of business together," Ethel persisted. "And we've paid a lot of money to your store..."

"We hope to be hearing from you within that period, Mrs. Turner," the man said. "Have a nice day."

Ethel chattered into the phone for several seconds before realizing that the man on the other end had hung up. She slammed down the receiver, then stared at the dirty dishes piled in the sink and shook her head. What a nerve those stores had, she thought; always offering deals with their leasing programs and practically begging you to sign a contract by giving things away for free. But as soon as you fell a little bit behind on your payment, their fake, friendly attitude left and they were all over your back.

Hadn't they already paid off a refrigerator and microwave oven from that same store, she wondered, and been only late twice with those payments? Hadn't the manager smiled and told them he understood their financial situation, and said that the back payments were no big deal when they had later agreed to sign another contract for the television?

She wished that she had mentioned those things before the snotty bastard had terminated their conversation, figuring the creep was just lucky he'd caught her off guard.

Ethel noticed that her foot was tapping nervously, and she breathed in and out rapidly several times in a feeble attempt to get herself together. Here it was only twelve noon and she felt like a nervous wreck.

4

Her day had begun so hopefully too. As with every other day, she got up at seven o'clock and made breakfast for her two teenage children. She was careful not to make any noise that might wake her husband, who continued to snore noisily in their queen-sized bed.

After the kids had left the house, she had made her way to the tiny bathroom, where she removed the pink polyester robe, stood on the scale and noticed that she had lost another half-pound—and now weighed in at two-hundred-and-six even.

She felt delighted with that number because it proved that her latest diet was working. It was one she had read about in the *Weekly World News* called "The Caffeine Diet," that had been developed by some doctor in Brazil. It called for the consumption of twenty cups of coffee a day and supposedly had worked for millions of housewives around the world. The theory was simple: The coffee filled your stomach with calorie-free liquid and took away the need for food. Since beginning her regime five-and-a-half weeks earlier, she had managed to shed a total of one-and-a-half pounds.

But even though the diet was proving to be a minor success, she didn't really feel any slimmer: If anything, she just felt a little bit more edgy, for which she had taken more Valium tablets than usual to calm her nerves. The phone call she just received did nothing to help them. And what was worse was that even though she had eaten a full breakfast with two eggs, toast, hash browns and grits, and eaten the remaining items on her kids' plates after they had left for school, she still felt hungry. Her nerves always ignited her appetite, she thought, forcing her to consume anything that was within reach without even thinking about it.

She knew the root of her anxiety lay in the fear that the television would be taken away, leaving her out of touch with events occurring on her favorite shows. In all her life, she had never been without a screen to stare at, and the thought of its imminent absence frightened her. As she mindlessly dumped four heaping tablespoons of sugar into a fresh mug of coffee, she just hoped that they had enough money to pay the bill before such a nightmare became reality.

Which was actually something she wasn't sure about, as when it came to the family budget, Ethel was completely in the dark—her husband Wayne was always the one who dealt with every aspect of their finances. And in a way, it pleased her because it took some responsibility off her shoulders. After all, whenever she looked at the bills that arrived at the house—with all the figures for estimated units spent and cost approximations—she had great difficulty in figuring out what the actual due price was, let alone whether it was correct of not. It all just seemed so technical, like Greenwood's "Rent to Own" program.

Ethel lit a cigarette and wrapped her stubby fingers around the coffee mug. The worst thing, she felt, was that there were a lot of other things that she still wanted: a dishwasher, a VCR, a clothes dryer, and maybe even a satellite dish. But now, the salesman who had once smiled and joked and promised and acted like a friend, instead called on the phone and complained, made snide remarks, and threatened to take away things she felt were her property.

She was doing her best, she thought: After all, it wasn't easy to feed a family of four with the money that her husband brought home, especially now that he was only working one job. Before, when Wayne had put in additional hours, she had even had money to buy a few extra things that had brightened up their home a little—things like plastic flowers for the kitchen table or air freshener for the bathroom. Now the money that Wayne gave her at the beginning of the week was only spent on food and absolute necessities. Why, just the other day she couldn't even afford to buy a box of girl scout cookies that some youngster had been peddling in front of the grocery store.

Deciding to divert her attention from such unpleasant business, Ethel swallowed what remained of the sugary coffee, poured the rest of the pot into a jumbo, insulated cup, and then shuffled her feet across the floor toward the family room. Its walls were covered in white, plastic paneling, fashioned to look like real wood, including painted knotholes. She sat down on the sofa, atop the shedded dog hair of Ivy, their white-and-brown boxer. Ivy was now licking herself in the opposite corner, digging into her loin so hard that the skin was actually bleeding.

"Stop that, Ivy!" Ethel yelled at her.

The dog paused momentarily and stared at her with a confused expression, and then drove her mouth toward the sore point again. Reaching toward the coffee table, Ethel grabbed the first thing she could reach—a battery—and hurled it toward the animal. She missed, but the battery bounced off the wall with enough force to send the dog hurriedly toward the other corner.

After yelling at the dog again, Ethel reached for the remote control, quickly realizing that the object she had just hurled had been its source of energy. Hoisting herself from the sofa, she loafed over to the corner and forced it within the little plastic device, breaking a copper spring as she did.

"Goddamn it!" she snarled, throwing the remote control back onto the floor and crushing it under the weight of her heel. She turned on the set manually instead, and then settled back into the chair to watch her favorite soap opera, which she invariably followed by watching her third, second and fourth favorites, in that order.

It was the part of the day she enjoyed the most, a relaxing period before going off to work, when she could see the lives of others and escape into their world without the interruptions of the rest of her family. She glued her eyes to the set and observed the beautiful, tanned characters, and wondered what it would be like to live in a California coastal town where the sun danced along the shifting tide. Or to have a rich husband with a pleasant demeanor, or a young handsome boyfriend who complimented her on her attributes. Fantasizing even further, she imagined having clothes from a designer store and a skinny body to squeeze into them, expensive cologne to bathe in, and a pretty face to apply make-up to.

As some commercials interrupted the action, she closed her eyes and felt the additional Valium she had swallowed begin to take effect. A sales pitch for detergent gave way to a more pleasant tone within her empty mind, and she gradually felt herself moving away, as if being transported to another planet.

Floating swiftly from the musty confines of her own sitting room, Ethel gradually saw herself in a convertible—a big convertible with a long hood. Next to her sat an attractive stranger. They were driving next to the ocean, because off in the distance she could see waves crashing down against the rocky coast. There were palm trees swaying along the sides of the road, and the moon reflected off the automobile's shiny hood. She wasn't sure where they were going, but she guessed it might be a place like heaven. As she leaned her head back against the soft, cool leather seat, the wind whistled past, as if her ear were next to a giant conch shell. She could almost make out words, like the shell was calling her.

"Ethel," the wind whispered. "Ethel."

Suddenly a pillow crashed against the side of he head, knocking her oversized, tinted glasses off and forcefully returning her to her familiar, dull surroundings, although all she could make out were its blurred, colorless forms. After reaching absently for her glasses for several moments, she finally found them and looked toward the kitchen opening,

Ethel focused slowly on her husband Wayne. He was dressed only in boxer shorts, standing with one arm resting against the door jamb and shaking his head. From her angle, his pale, hair-covered potbelly looked unusually large.

"Who was that on the phone before?" he grumbled.

Ethel looked toward the television and noticed that a different program was on. She wondered how long she had been asleep.

"The TV store," she finally said. "We have to pay for the television in the next two days or they're gonna take it away. He said we haven't paid for three months." She reached for her cigarettes and then added, "Haven't you been payin' the bill?"

Wayne fiddled with his balls a little and then walked out of view and opened the refrigerator.

Ethel inhaled her cigarette deeply. "He said, 'Rent to Own' doesn't mean 'Borrow to Own'," she yelled, trying to get some sort of response out of him. "And that if we didn't pay the bill in forty eight hours, they'd come out here and take it away."

"What else did he say?" Wayne grunted, returning to the doorway with a container of milk. He drank it directly from the carton and spilled most of it down his front.

She didn't think she had forgotten any details. "Nothin'," she said. "But those guys really piss me off."

Wayne tilted the carton toward his mouth again and finished it with a loud gulp. "I'm gonna go to town and buy some oil for the car," he finally said, seemingly unconcerned with the repossession threat. "Make me somethin' to eat, all right?"

Ethel shifted her weight on the seat and stared at her chipped nails. "How about callin' the security company and seein' if they have anything else?" she added hesitantly as he departed.

Ethel waited for a response to her suggestion but got none. So she lit another cigarette, pried herself from the comfortable chair, and shuffled out to the kitchen.

As she was preparing some food for her husband, she began brewing more coffee because she knew that the hot food in front of her would tempt her to eat again. She figured some more coffee would prevent her from recklessly abandoning her diet. Wayne's disregard of the TV problem didn't help matters at all. So she reached into the kitchen cabinet and splashed a shot of whiskey into the remaining lukewarm coffee.

In the bedroom, Wayne pulled a checked shirt off the coat hanger in the closet and hummed along to a country song coming from the clock/radio. He had heard Ethel's question clearly, but had intentionally ignored it. After all, this was his day off from work, and the last thing he wanted to do was think about his job or what extra scrambling he could do to make a few extra bucks to pay off the TV. All he wanted to do was take care of a few things around the house that needed attending to, and not think about some little pipsqueak from the rental company bitching because one of their payments was a little bit behind. He was pissed off enough as it was that his day had already been partially ruined by this outside intrusion, and knew he needed to put it behind him. He figured his silence would get the impression across to his wife that he would deal with the problem later.

"Hey Wayne," Ethel said when he returned to the kitchen. "How about callin' up the security company and seein' if they can give you a few more hours?"

Wayne sighed and mumbled an obscenity. "I'm tellin' you right now Ethel!" he yelled in his typical high-pitched tone, one that bore his Appalachian upbringing, "I don't ever want to hear you make a suggestion like that again, because the job I got now isn't like the one before. I need more concentration for it and also more rest, so there's no way I'm gonna moonlight on my day off. I need it to recuperate and prepare my mind for the next week."

"Well you heard me say that they're gonna come out here in a couple of days, didn't you?"

"Yeah I heard!" he shot back while wrapping a belt around his thick girth. "And I'm gonna go down there. So shut the hell up and don't pester me anymore about it!"

"But the guy said he was only gonna give us forty..."

"If I said I'll take care of it, I'll take care of it, goddamn it!" Wayne screamed. "I'll get the money tomorrow and throw it right in that little jerk's face. Don't worry about it!"

"OK," she said, putting butter on a couple of Eggo waffles that had just popped out of the toaster. "I just don't want that TV bein' taken away."

Wayne stared across the room at his wife and sighed. She knew he didn't like butter on his waffles, yet here she was caking it on. How many times would he have to tell her that before she finally figured it out, he wondered. "Are you gonna eat again?" he asked sarcastically.

Ethel turned around and stared at him through her glassy eyes, unsure of what he was talking about.

"Eggos already have a buttery taste, goddamn it!" he snarled, picking up the colorful box and waving it in her face. "So they don't need anymore goddamn butter! If you do that one more time, nobody here is gonna eat waffles again!"

That comment worried Ethel, because she loved waffles, especially when the melted butter nearly bubbled from the ridges. She also knew that when Wayne said something, he meant business, and that if he decided to forbid waffles in the house, she wouldn't be able to enjoy the sensation of the crisp, golden pastry gliding down her throat on a layer of maple syrup anymore.

"I'm sorry," she said, annoyed by her own stupidity. "It's just that that repo man worried me and I forgot. You know how me and the kids all love butter on our waffles. I just wasn't thinking straight, that's all."

"Yeah, well I'm not you or one of the kids," he hissed loudly, grabbing her by the arm. "I'm your husband, Wayne. You know, the guy who works and worries about the financial problems of the family, includin' all the bills. And you are Ethel, his wife, who takes care of things inside the house. Do I have to remind you of that agreement we made again?"

"Jesus Christ!" she yelled, pushing him away. "So I put butter on your waffles. Big deal!"

Wayne blew some steam from his nostrils and turned his back on her.

"Anyway, it isn't even butter," she continued. "It's margarine! So don't scream at me like that!" She quickly grabbed a knife and began cleaning the waffles with exaggerated gestures. "Here, I'll scrape it off if you want."

"Forget it!" he snarled, turning toward her with disgust and then moving toward the TV room. "You eat 'em."

Ethel threw the knife into the sink and silently cursed her husband, and then stared down at the plate of waffles. They looked so good, just the way she liked them actually. The margarine that she hadn't scraped off was now fully melted into the square ridges. She closed her eyes and imagined their presence inside her mouth, the rich flavor melting into her tongue. Quivering at the thought, she quickly reached for another cigarette.

In the other room, Wayne flipped around the channels and then turned the set off. "What a load of shit," he complained, coming back into the kitchen.

"Look Wayne," Ethel addressed him, sensing her two inch height advantage somehow lessened. "I don't want you gettin' upset about this stupid little thing. How about if I make you some pancakes or somethin'?"

"Forget it," he said, hocking up some mucus loudly and then swallowing it again. "I can't waste anymore time around here. I'm gonna get me somethin' to eat in town."

He pushed her out of the way and pulled his coat over his shoulder. "And by the way," he added, just before exiting. "Maybe you should think

10

about workin' full-time at McDonalds to pay for some of these stupid things around the house, instead of sitting on your fat ass and dozin' off half the mornin'."

Ethel looked through the window and watched his chubby figure plod down the wooden steps and make its way toward his car.

"Screw you," she drawled, pulling the Valium bottle from her robe pocket again and casually popping the top.

2

Standing in the tiny bathroom in only his boxer shorts and a t-shirt, Wayne Turner regarded himself in the mirror. Even though he had just waken up a few minutes before, his face bore no signs of drowsiness, and he felt energetic and fully in control of his senses. What he saw was the image of a man beaming with confidence and pride, a man who could handle whatever task was placed before him.

He nodded his head and smiled contentedly at his reflection. What he saw was a winner.

Wayne bent over the sink and ran some tepid water on his hands. Then he splashed some on his face before patting it dry with a fresh towel. Grabbing a can of shaving cream, he squirted some on his hand and rubbed it across his round, pink cheeks and into his chin and neck. He washed his hands and picked up a disposable razor.

Wayne drew slowly through the shaving cream, rinsing it off under the running water after every stroke. He was careful to cut a straight edge along the base of his sideburns, which hung about an inch below his ears, and especially careful while shaving his neck.

It was a sensitive area for him, made doubly complicated by the fact that he had to shave it all the way down to his collar where his thick chest hair began. When he finished, he rinsed off his face and rubbed it with a towel again, pleased with his ruddy glow that seemed to display an additional sense of exuberance.

Next he reached for a small pair of scissors and trimmed the hair of his sideburns, clipping them to a uniform length and around the edges. He rubbed his fingertips through them gently, feeling the hairs and twisting them. They were nice sideburns, he thought, and even though they didn't stand out because of their color, they were well shaped. He admired them in the mirror and touched them some more.

One of the reasons he liked his sideburns so much was because they were so full, in contrast to what remained of the strawberry blond hair on his head that, even though cut quite short, was still dense on the sides. He still had healthy roots around the crown that he let grow a bit longer, but the top of his head was completely bald.

It wasn't something that necessarily bothered him, because he knew that the majority of men over age forty normally experienced some sort of hair loss. His had started about twenty years ago, however, when he was about twenty, and at that time it had bothered him because it made him look so much older than he actually was. But with the passing of time, as he began to have narrow lines around his eyes and the creases in his face deepened somewhat, he began to think he looked better without hair on the top of his head, and couldn't even envision how he would look with a patch of hair hanging over his forehead, like his fourteen-year-old son Junior.

There was a knock on the door and he heard the voice of his daughter Darlene from the other side. "Daddy!" she yelled. "Hurry up! The bus is gonna come in twenty minutes!"

Darlene, who was in her sophomore year at high school, normally occupied the bathroom for a half-hour or so every morning, spending an eternity in the shower and frequently forcing him to take a piss outside. "Well that's too bad!" he yelled back through the door. "Now you'll know how I feel sometimes!"

Wayne reached for the jar of hair tonic and rubbed some into the hair on his sides. He pulled a comb through it quickly, staring glumly at the number of strands caught in its teeth, and then rubbed his greasy hands on his scalp to give it a healthy radiance. He washed his hands again under hot water, grabbed his towel, and dried them off. He exited quickly from the bathroom, flipping off the light as he went. As he rounded the corner, he almost collided with his plump daughter, who murmured, "It's about time" and then slammed the door shut behind her.

"Hey Wayne!" came another voice bellowing down the hallway—this time his wife Ethel. "You shouldn't take so long in the bathroom. The kids have to go to school, you know."

Wayne let her voice sail in one ear and out the other, then closed their bedroom door behind him. He didn't yell back at Ethel because, this morning, he was too involved in honing his look, something his wife obviously didn't understand was of utmost importance to a policeman.

And even though Wayne wasn't actually a police officer as recognized by the state, he knew he could have been one if he had realized when he was younger how cut out he was for that type of work. Instead, he had to think about the rest of his family all the time and wasted his youth with countless other jobs.

As it was, he was a registered security guard, which was *just about* the same as a policeman, he figured. He even had a diploma to prove his qualification, something some correspondence school had sent him in the mail when he had completed its course.

Besides, in his current employment, he had all the trimmings of a cop; the blue uniform, nightstick, handcuffs, pistol—everything. And like the state troopers, he enforced the law and held disdain for the bad guys. The way he saw it, he and they basically served the same function, but operated in different units—something like the air force and the marines, or the army and the navy. Their general purpose and goals were exactly the same, and the fact that the badge he now carried read "Security Officer" rather than "Police Officer" didn't bother him either, because he viewed it as just a minor thing, a mere one-word technicality that didn't mean jack-shit in the line of duty.

Wayne had worked for the Vanguard Security Company for over six years. He was hired shortly after the family had arrived in Indiana. Because of the outstanding marks and references he received through the Security Training Course, he believed (although he had never actually been told as much), he had been assigned to the armored car division at Vanguard. These trucks drove from bank to bank collecting and transferring the nation's legal tender.

The company had a fleet of eight trucks, each lined with three-inch iron walls and equipped with bullet-proof glass. Each truck had a team of three men: a driver, a shotgun guard who rode in the front, and another guard in the back who kept a solitary watch over the money.

This latter position had been Wayne's post since he had begun, and the person who undertook it, at Vanguard anyway, was known as the "clerk," because when the truck stopped it was he who loaded and transferred the heavy bags of paper money and coins from the compartments within the truck and placed them in the drawer for the driver to carry in. Meanwhile, "shotgun" surveyed the area, secured a path, and protected it.

Wayne had liked the "clerk" job to begin with because there were elements of danger and secrecy that went along with it. When people saw the truck, they knew something important was passing by. They knew there were stacks of money inside it and that at any moment, somebody could make an attempt to steal or hijack it, perhaps causing a shootout. And they knew that the man in the back—who they could only see through tiny slit windows—was equipped with a powerful rifle and would do anything he could to protect the money inside.

But whereas Wayne was fully aware that he was the last man

14

between the would-be thieves and the currency, he also knew the loneliness that this essential duty entailed. There was no contact with the other guards except by way of a microphone and, because of the thick armored walls, the only sounds you could hear were the sounds which came out of your own body. You were aware of motion and could see the street passing by through the small windows at the side, but you had no idea of the route you were taking. The clerk, in short, was an integral part of the security team, but an invisible necessity with no public eye.

So when one of the shotgun guards put in for his retirement the month before and Wayne was offered the job that required more interaction with the public, he didn't hesitate to accept it. Of course it had entailed taking several classes at night at the security school, but his natural interest with anything regarding law enforcement had actually made the extra training enjoyable. Most of the things he had to know for the examination he had already learned in his spare time anyway. Even the shooting test proved to be no problem—Wayne had been a good shot since his days with the National Guard years before.

He knew that the job of "Shotgun" was the most important position within the security team, because at the end of the day, that person was responsible for the welfare of the others. The driver had to watch the road and keep the vehicle moving, and the clerk had to keep track of the money, but the shotgun rider had to keep a peeled eye on the lookout for any suspicious-looking individuals or movements that might endanger the contents of the armored truck. This duty entailed intense concentration and a keen eye for detail.

When he worked the clerk's job, Wayne hadn't spent very much time between rising and leaving the house—after all, at work he was locked within six steel walls all the time. He shaved quickly, threw on his clothes, and grabbed a doughnut or something on the way to work. He was never fully seen by the public, and therefore his "look" wasn't that important. He had the rifle in the back, but it was really more of a silent threat than an obvious tool of intimidation.

While he worked Shotgun for the past week, however, the public had seen plenty of him, and Wayne always made certain that he looked right. He'd begun going to bed earlier than before, intending to be thoroughly rested before exerting himself for the demands of his post. As if partaking in a solitary ritual, he dressed himself slowly and deliberately, somewhat like an established actor practices before taking the stage.

Wayne tucked his white shirt into his dark blue trousers and wrapped a navy blue tie around his neck, re-threading it several times before getting the knot just right. Sitting on the bed, he pulled on his socks and then slipped into his shoes, which had been shined so thoroughly the night before that his reflection was visible in them. From a drawer he took his gun belt and, after making sure all the bullet slips were full, he drew it around his waist and fastened it. He removed his bulletproof vest from his closet, and slipped it over his head, securing the back and front pads at the side. From another drawer he removed his gun, a .38 caliber service revolver, and thrust it into his holster after making sure the safety was on. Finally, he took his protective helmet from the corner of the room and placed it on his head, careful to pull the padded neck flap over his collar.

Wayne raised the protective, shaded glass that covered his eyes and proudly strutted over to the full-length mirror, where he inspected his reflection. He adjusted the gun belt slightly, then pulled the vest a little bit forward and smiled again. Before him was an armed guard—ready for action.

The door burst open and broke his concentration, and as he turned his head toward it, he saw his wife Ethel, her fat figure barely squeezed into the pink bathrobe.

"I've been callin' you for the past ten minutes!" she yelled nasally. "Your breakfast has been sittin' on the table and gettin' cold!" She pursed her mouth and then suddenly made a strange face. "And what the hell are you wearin' that helmet in the bedroom for?" she gasped.

"I was just tryin' it on to make sure if fit right," came Wayne's muffled voice through the helmet as he struggled to get it off.

"Well OK," she said, looking at him slightly annoyed. "But can't you do that after you've eaten?"

"Listen Ethel," he corrected her when the helmet was off. "If I wanna try on my helmet now, I'll do it now! Don't tell me when I should do things! I'm riskin' my life out there and my preparation is important. I would think you would understand that."

"All right," she said, holding up her hands as if apologizing. "I can just stick the stuff in the microwave, that's no big deal. But I'd prefer to serve you your food straight from the fryin' pan like you always tell me to do it."

He clipped the helmet onto his belt and looked at himself sideways in the mirror, slicking down his displaced hair around the edges and trying to get it back in place.

Ethel rested her weight on one foot and looked at her husband

16

admiringly. "You sure do look handsome in your uniform," she purred in a low voice. "And you know how much I like to press your pants and iron your shirt so you look good out there."

She approached him slowly and began feeling the material of his shirt and then his skin underneath it. "Darlene and Junior have gone off to school," she whispered, pressing her body toward his. "And we're all alone here now, you know?"

Wayne stared down past her head and viewed her deep cleavage above her bathrobe, and felt her huge breasts squeezing against his body. He knew what she was insinuating but, just as a professional boxer negated the pleasures of sex before the big fight, Wayne also avoided it before work. He didn't want anything to distract him from the job in front of him.

But the next thing he knew, Ethel was pushing him backwards, and he suddenly lost his balance as his calves connected with the bed. He fell on the mattress and felt the dangling helmet sink into the small of his back, and then the immense weight of Ethel's form sandwiching him. He let out a grunt of pain and threw her off, bending over on the side of the bed and grabbing his back.

"Did I hurt you?" came Ethel's distraught voice over his shoulder.

"What the hell are you tryin' to do?" he yelled, looking at his wife's sprawling form atop the bed. One of her breasts had sagged out of her bathrobe. "You knew my helmet was on my belt!" he added.

"I didn't mean to hurt you," she said apologetically, getting up quickly and covering herself.

"I'm all right," he said, rubbing his back. "But you know I got to go to work," he added loudly. "And for all technical purposes, when I put on this uniform in the mornin' and until I take it off at night, I am on duty. And you know what that means."

"I'm sorry already!", Ethel said, annoyed at his insistence. "You just looked so good I wanted to eat you. I am your wife, you know? And that's my right!"

"Just forget about it," Wayne said, straightening out his clothes and looking in the mirror again.

"Well come and eat your breakfast already!" Ethel shouted as she walked down the hallway. "I got to get ready for work too, you know."

"OK," Wayne said automatically, beaming at his reflection. But with his shift due to begin in less than an hour, food was the furthest thing from his mind.

17

3

With a curious grin etched across her acne-scarred face, Ethel stared down at a Kleenex and examined the snot she had just blown from her nose. The mustard colored mucus was thicker than it had been earlier that morning, and she wondered if the differences between day and night temperatures and the huge amount of rain they had gotten recently had proven too much for her delicate body to bear. Figuring that was the reason, she made a mental note to pick up some Minute Maid orange soda at the store—a great source of vitamin C—and then stuffed the tissue in her pocket, just above the pill bottle.

Realizing she still had to put the clothes outside on the line, Ethel walked over to the washing machine. After wiping her nose with her sleeve, she grabbed the laundry basket and took the damp clothes out of the machine before loading the pile of dirty ones back in. Lighting a cigarette, she kicked open the screen door and walked outside.

The hazy March sky was too thick to allow any hint of the sun, and a slight breeze seemed to carry the final memories of winter away, bringing with it the refreshing clearness of spring. As Ethel crossed the yard, she was met by Ivy, who jumped at her legs and nearly sent her sprawling on the ground. She yelled and threw her leg out in the dog's direction while continuing to stumble toward the clothes line. Before pegging up the clothes, Ethel looked at her watch and mumbled an obscenity. She'd have to leave the house in just over an hour to be on time for her shift at McDonalds.

Working outside her own home had really thrown a wrench into Ethel's routine. She hadn't done anything of the sort since marrying her husband more than sixteen years earlier. Since that day, she had occupied herself with the full-time duties of homemaker instead. She was still committed to the duties of that job, but having to spend a good chunk of the day away from her home now gave her much less time to accomplish all the tasks she had taken care of before.

She started working at McDonalds several months earlier, partially because of Wayne's insistence, but mostly because of her desire for the household necessities that she'd grown tired of waiting for. Ethel figured that the only way she was going to get them was by finding more money than Wayne gave her—to find a job of her own. She was upset that she didn't have as much time to sit down and relax during the day anymore but, then again, she was sick of not having the things she felt a middle-aged woman was entitled to.

After checking a few places around town, she decided that her best bet was at McDonalds because they broke their working day into four-hour shifts (instead of the normal six-or eight). The job wasn't very difficult, and except for the manager and the full-time guys who worked the grill, Ethel found that she was the youngest person on her crew. The other women all had children who were now grown, and had taken the job more out of boredom than financial need. They were nice enough, but their talk about grandchildren or their recent times spent meandering around Florida in an RV got on her nerves a little. After all, she was there because her husband couldn't provide enough for their small family, not because she didn't have anything better to do.

Even so, her little job did have its benefits. Each week when she received her pay, she put some of the money in a jar. The week before she had gotten Wayne to rent a VCR from one of Greenwood's competitors that was having a special promotion. The machine was particularly handy because she was able to record her favorite soap operas while she was at work and keep abreast of their occurences when she got home. She'd already come up with an extensive list of other things that she desired, and had placed a second-hand dishwasher at the top.

Wayne was thrilled that she was finally doing some real work rather than "piddling around the house all day," as he put it. But even so, Ethel still had great reservations about working for somebody else. After all, cooking, cleaning, and caring for a family of four was a full-time job in itself, she felt. The McDonalds job was convenient because the kids were normally at school during her shift, but still she just wasn't as happy as she had been when she had made her own hours. She sneezed again and wondered if it could be the added pressure of outside work that had begun breaking her body down. Was a little extra money worth that consequence?

Ethel finished pegging the clothes to the line, then walked out into the yard to an area Wayne had dug up with a rototiller the week before. The upturned soil was dark and fertile, and Ethel paused at its edge, breathing in its deep mineral pungency. Wayne planted his first garden the year after they moved in, and over the past couple of years had expanded it gradually, so that now it was about the size of their mobile home. In it he grew corn,

19

tomatoes, string beans, peas, some lettuce, squash, carrots and eggplant; and this year, he had claimed he was going to give cauliflower a try.

Ethel looked at the uncultivated ground and knew that in just a few months it would breed full-grown, ripe vegetables. She shook her head, amazed at how things could change and become something completely different so rapidly, and then was reminded of the extra time she would have to spend getting them ready for the table. That thought triggered her hand to move toward her pocket and extract another cigarette.

While tightening her robe around her body, Ethel observed their mobile home from a distance. When they moved to Indiana from Kentucky, they bought just over two acres of cheap land that hadn't been used for much before, apart from perhaps some hunting, or maybe the dumping of old appliances and garbage. Almost immediately afterwards, they also got a good deal on a second-hand mobile home—an old model, but in good shape and very spacious—and placed it about a hundred-and-fifty feet from the road, where the incline stopped and the ground leveled off.

The first thing Wayne did once the trailer was stabilized was build an extension. He knocked a hole through the kitchen wall and constructed another large room behind it. That now served as their family room. Afterwards, he redesigned the inside of the trailer by moving a couple of walls around, so that Darlene and Junior could have bedrooms to themselves for the first time in their lives.

After settling into his first job, he took on a new project every year or so to improve the place. He built some chicken coops out back that he tended for a while before losing interest; a brick barbecue pit; a concrete wall out front that helped block the view from the road below; and, most recently, a small, wooden porch by the door just outside the kitchen. But whereas inside their home Ethel had decorated the new rooms so that they now looked as if they had always been there, the outside still looked to be under construction, as Wayne had simply covered the addition with black tarpaper instead of painting it.

Whenever Ethel suggested that he finish the job, he'd shoot back, "What's the point on spending money on the outside of the house when you live on the inside?" Recently she had mentioned its unsightliness again, and he had counseled her to send the VCR back and buy the paint with that money—his current resources were now directed toward the garden. His suggestion seemed absurd to her because it meant that she wouldn't be able to watch the recorded soaps, and since then she had decided to shut up about it and simply get used to the fact that from the outside, their trailer looked like a God-forsaken dump.

After crossing the brown, barren lawn, she followed the dog into the kitchen. Normally she did some housecleaning at this hour, but feeling as worn down as she did, she thought she'd take it easy and just tidy up a little. She picked up a few magazines from the floor, stacked them on the coffee table in the family room, straightened out the cushions, and emptied the two small ashtrays into the big one. Afterwards she took a package of chicken from the freezer to fix that evening for dinner.

Ethel walked down the hallway to the bedroom and squeezed into a pair of black polyester pants and a floral print shirt. After inserting a pair of hoop earings, she took off her wig, sat down at the make-up table and lit another cigarette. Surveying the five other wigs resting upon styrofoam heads, she tried to think which style would go with her outfit. She knew she wanted to look good, because after work she was due to play cards with her friends and she hoped to impress them a little. Unable to decide which one to wear, she decided to apply her face first and choose afterwards.

While unscrewing the top of a foundation tube, Ethel stared at her image in the mirror and frowned. Even though she had slept eight hours the night before, she looked like she'd been up half the night. The discolored whites of her eyes bore countless blood vessels that even her morning dose of Visine had failed to soothe, and the bags under her eyes looked as if they'd been painted there by an amateur make-up artist attempting to make a young actress look old. Her cheeks and nose were tainted a slightly darker red than her eyes—almost making her resemble an old alcoholic—and her chin hung down onto her neck in a few rough folds. Encompassing it all was dark hair in such horrendous condition that it almost looked diseased.

Running her short fingers through the clumped mass, she loosened the oil that had collected underneath the wig she had just removed. Her scalp itched and as she scratched it, she watched the dandruff emerge and fall gently, like fresh snow, onto her shoulders. On the outside, her hair appeared oily, but when she touched it, the sensation was more like that of brittle straw, and a couple of times she even thought she heard it crack. Examining it more closely by bringing its ends nearer to her face, she noticed that just about every strand was split at the end and in a seemingly irreparable state.

Ethel had owned a couple of wigs for years and had always worn them periodically, but she had never had to depend on them. Over the past year, however, she had made such a mess with her own hair that she now

21

had to wear them even at home. It all started the previous summer, when she got it into her head that she was going to go blonde. She had been a brunette all her life and for many years had wondered what she'd look like with lighter hair, and if indeed she might have more fun; women like that always looked so good in the magazines—so carefree and relaxed. But even more importantly, she thought that dark hair made her face look bigger, and reckoned that surrounding her round face with blond hair would at least conceal its true shape.

After buying some dyes and rinses at the local drug store, she began changing her color. Over the weeks, she went through several boxes of blonde dye, but noticed no change in the color of her hair. It wasn't until she read the instructions carefully on the fourth box before she finally learned that you needed to remove the natural pigment before changing to a lighter color.

Ethel was miffed at her own stupidity but eager to rectify her mistakes, so she bought some bleach and applied that to her hair. But after leaving it on for an hour, she was shocked to discover that her hair was painted with three colors! The hair at the roots had taken the bleach and turned white, but moving outward from the crown, the color turned yellow, while the bulk of her hair had changed to a very unnatural shade of bright orange. It was at that point that she began wearing a wig full time to hide her embarrassment.

A few days later she had repeated the bleaching process with the same results, and the following week she tried once again—but this time she left the bleach on her head for two hours instead of the suggested thirty minutes. Afterwards, the only change she noticed was that her scalp had gone from pink to red and hurt like hell, as a result of the bleach burns and peeling.

Frustrated with her hair's failure, Ethel knew that the only way she would be able to become a platinum blonde—like a movie star or one of the game-show girls—would be to cut her hair. But if she did that, she also realized there wouldn't be any length left to do what she wanted with it. Concluding that she'd have to settle with a lighter shade of blond, Ethel then went through numerous boxes of various shades, beginning with the Swedish blonde, then the Helsinki blonde, and finally the Hollywood blonde. Each time she was optimistic that she'd arrive at something she liked. But she was repeatedly disillusioned when, afterwards, she'd shower and watch all the color she'd just applied form puddles of dirty water at her feet, finally disappearing down the drain pipe.

After a couple more weeks, she finally found a color that stuck and convincingly covered up the orange underneath. Unfortunately, after examining it in the mirror when it had dried, she realized that her new hair color was now darker than her hair had been originally, making her face seem even more massive than before.

Ethel was now completely frustrated with trying to cover up such an ill-looking face with cosmetics as well, and she knew she was already late for work. She hastily threw the blusher on the table and reached for a short, curled wig. After slipping on some shoes, she shuffled into the kitchen and grabbed her glasses from the shelf above the sink, noticing a bottle of diet pills that had been pushed behind them. Unable to remember if she had taken her dosage earlier, Ethel reached for the bottle and shook two pills into her fleshy palm and, while chewing on them as if they were candy, propelled her weighty mass toward her green AMC Gremlin and sped off to work.

4

The Vanguard Security truck pulled through the iron gates of the Indiana National Bank and slowly rolled past the two armed guards. It was the truck's first stop of the morning and, like every day of the week, the place where they would collect the money that other banks had ordered. Once the gates were closed and secured, the team exited from the truck and made their way inside. There they were met by a bank official who gave them a printed manifest listing the drops and pick-ups they would be making that morning, along with the deadlines they had to meet. The official then led them to a safe, where they were given the fifty-odd bags of paper money and coins, each marked with its bank destination. Working together, they carried the bags to the truck and locked them within individual compartments.

Their clerk that morning, a young guy named Spears, had recently finished his training course and had only been on a few runs—never with Wayne or Maxwell, the driver, a fifty-year-old retired cop. Before sealing Spears in the back of the truck, Wayne—assuming the leadership position—had a few words with the new man. "We have six stops to make this mornin'," he told him. "And it looks like we're gonna be exchangin' a quarter ton of silver. So when I inform you that we've reached the drop, you get your helmet on and your shield pulled down and be ready to go. Got it?"

"You just give me the signal and I'll be there waitin'," Spears said confidently. "Cash in hand."

With an uninterested look on his face, Maxwell told Wayne they had to head out, but Wayne continued. "And as soon as those doors are open, you just move it into the bank like a rat's tryin' to crawl up your asshole. Understand?"

"You just give me the signal," Spears responded.

Wayne locked Spears in the the back of the truck, and then climbed in the front next to Maxwell, who already had the engine running. "You think he's gonna be OK back there?" Wayne asked him.

Maxwell gazed at him with a puzzled look on his face. "Yeah. Why wouldn't he be?" he asked.

"Well, because he's new and all," Wayne said.

Maxwell shook his head and rolled his eyes. "Don't worry about it," he advised, pulling the truck back through the open gates.

The portable safe moved up the road steadily, dwarfing the other cars around it so that at first glance it almost looked like a tank. You couldn't see the driver or his companion because of the tinted bulletproof glass. But, despite the truck's size, most people walking on the sidewalk or passing in other vehicles paid no attention to it.

Inside, however, Wayne Turner had settled into the shotgun position and was in a state of steady alert. His face was up close to the glass and his hands rested on the dashboard, while his ass was perched on the seat like a hawk ready to take off and attack its prey.

"There it is up there on the right. Bank One," Wayne said, motioning to the driver.

"I know," Maxwell said coldly. "I've been drivin' this same route for five years. You don't need to tell me. Why don't you tell the kid in the back instead."

"Right," Wayne said, sitting back and grabbing the microphone. "Spears!" he barked. "Do you read me?"

"Yeah," came his clear voice through a speaker in the dashboard.

"We're pulling in front of the bank now. Unlock the Bank One box, put the money on the floor and get ready to move."

Wayne pulled his helmet over his head while Maxwell parked the truck in front of the bank. "Ready to roll?" Wayne asked him.

"Easy does it," Maxwell responded holding up his hand. "Lemme get my helmet on first."

"Prepared Spears?" Wayne barked back into the microphone.

"Yeah," Spears said, over the sound of money bags being dropped on the floor.

"OK," Wayne barked, seeing Maxwell's helmet was in place. "Let's go!"

They exited the front of the truck and Wayne hustled toward the back to assess any possible danger. Seeing none among the few people who walked the streets, he waited for Maxwell. When he arrived carrying the sign sheet, Wayne signaled to Spears through the side window to open the door. Wayne took a few steps back and continued his observation while the other men carried out their duties. After several minutes, Maxwell appeared again, immediately followed by Spears and the outgoing cash. They threw it in the back of the truck. Wayne took another quick look around, locked

Spears in, and then nodded toward Maxwell.

Back on the road, Wayne noticed that he was sweating, but it wasn't because it was hot outdoors or inside the truck. It wasn't a nervous sweat either, he felt. After all, he was certainly in control and felt no fear. What it was, he reckoned, was his own form of natural lubrication, his body's oil so to speak. He liked that, because it told him that he was subconsciously warming up, like an athlete before a big match.

They continued their route without incident, stopping at four more banks. Wayne, as usual, was pleased with his handiwork. Not only had he performed his job flawlessly, but he'd also instructed the kid in the back, kind of shown him the way. Maxwell hadn't made much conversation with him, but Wayne took it as a compliment. When two people were experienced at their jobs, he thought, they needed to concentrate. One slip-up could be a fatal error for any of them, and they were both professional enough to know that.

As the truck pulled into downtown Columbus, Wayne checked his watch against the time they were scheduled to arrive at their last and biggest bank; The Indiana State Savings And Loan Company. He saw they were right on time and rubbed his palms together with anticipation.

The sun was beginning to peak through the fluffy clouds overhead. It was lunch time, so many people were taking advantage of the weather by taking a walk during their breaks or eating their food on the side of the street. The street was lined with cars, and the truck inched down the main street at a snail's pace through the traffic and the red lights. Not noticing any suspicious looking movements, Wayne took off his mirror glasses, blew out some hot air and rubbed them with a handkerchief before placing them back over his eyes.

"How you doin' back there Spears?" he called into the microphone.

"Just fine boss," was the muffled answer.

Wayne liked the way Spears referred to him as *boss*. It showed that he respected him. "Seems like he's gonna work out all right, don't he?" Wayne said to the driver.

"Seems OK," Maxwell answered, not caring much one way or the other.

Just ahead on the corner of the busiest section of town stood the bank, a large, fortress-like building with four marble columns and heavy, brass doors.

"OK Spears," Wayne barked suddenly. "We're movin' in."

Maxwell pulled the truck in front of the doors, and after Wayne and he secured their helmets, they lowered themselves from the truck. Before Wayne's foot even touched the ground, he had the gun out of its holster. He began waving it around to clear a path on the sidewalk through the people between the truck and the bank. "Move aside and keep this area clear!" he yelled at them.

Maxwell went into the bank in search of the guard inside, who would assist them with carrying the money bags. Wayne stayed on the street looking for any sign of foul play. To his right, a bearded man in a two-tone leisure suit had stopped next to the truck and seemed to be eyeing it suspiciously.

"Let's move along!" Wayne commanded him, shaking the gun suggestively in a direction away from the truck.

"I'm just watching," the guy said.

"Not here you're not," Wayne shook his helmeted head. "Let's go!"

Maxwell came out with a guard and opened the flap on the side of the truck. He handed two bags to the other guard and then grabbed two himself. Wayne hustled behind him and closed the door, being careful to keep his back to it and his eyes on anyone coming close.

Moving back toward the sidewalk, Wayne once again stood between the truck and the bank, motioning people to stay out of the way. They seemed surprised to see the solitary padded form with a drawn gun on the city sidewalk, and hurried in another direction immediately after being signaled, obeying his commands without question.

Looking good and feeling good, Wayne Turner was in his prime.

5

Ethel was unfolding a Happy Meal box for a customer when she looked at her watch and saw that it was five minutes past two. Her shift was officially over and she was already late for her lunch date at Tina Copenhaver's house. She looked behind her and saw one of the new high school kids—who was supposed to relieve her—flirting with one of the guys at the grill.

"Hey Dawn!" she yelled for the second time, annoyed at having to repeat herself to get the girl's attention. "Do you think you can come over here and start your shift?"

The girl made an annoyed face at the grill boy and shuffled over. "What do you need?" she asked.

Ethel handed her the box and motioned to the order on the register. "That," she said. "I've got an appointment that I'm already late for and I'm supposed to be off now. I've been waitin' for you to stop gabbin' over there."

The girl looked down at her watch and rolled her eyes. "Well you should of said somethin' then."

Ethel put her hands on her hips and glared at the girl. "I just did," she snarled before striding away and silently cursing the girl, who surely knew damn well that her shift finished at two o'clock. The stupid high school kids had begun filling up the summer posts, and they had to be constantly reminded of what their jobs were.

Ethel hadn't liked working with the old women that much either, but at least they did what they had to do energetically. If there was a customer at the counter, they'd rush to it, which meant she could rest a bit more on the sidelines herself. Now it was different; the new kids were always talking amongst themselves and leaving her to pull up the slack, so that she even had to rush her employee meal.

She normally liked to eat her lunch at a table without hurrying, but since she was running late, she decided to eat while driving. She gave the manager her order and ran into the staff room to change. But upon bending down to tie her shoes, she suddenly felt a little bit dizzy and braced herself against a chair. She often felt like that before she smoked her first cigarette, but never afterwards; confused by the sensation, she breathed in deeply a few times until she felt stabilized. When she opened her eyes, her head felt clearer, although now she felt a little sick to her stomach. She figured it was just a combination of her nerves and hunger.

Rushing out of the staff room, she picked up the bag at the counter and shuffled quickly out to her car. Screeching out of the lot, she drove with her left hand and maneuvered her right between the bag and her mouth, scarfing down the cheeseburger, small fries, and Coke she was permitted. She stopped at a grocery store to buy a big bottle of Pepsi and a bag of chips, and then continued her route, weaving her way along the calm suburban streets lined with single-story houses. She drove as she had eaten—as if on a mission—applying the brake briefly as she approached a stop sign and then rapidly shooting the car through the empty intersection. While she was making a turn, the plastic lid popped off the Coke, sending half the cup's sticky contents onto her black polyester pants.

"That stupid bitch!" she screamed, thinking of Dawn's dumb teenage face. She grabbed a napkin to dry the mess as she swerved up the road. She reckoned she'd have to sit down quickly or her friends would think she'd pissed in her pants.

Ethel pulled the car down a narrow gravel road, speeding across the potholes and past the weatherbeaten two-family houses that lined one side. She drew to a grinding halt across from one whose paint had held out for longer than the other homes it otherwise resembled.

In front of her, the vinyl roof of an orange Plymouth Satellite peeled under the sun's heat. It belonged to Miriam Tanner, a tall, slender, twice-divorced redhead. She had moved back in with her mother and supported herself and three kids on the money she collected from her ex-husband's child support. Across the street, in a tiny driveway, a green Dodge Dart was parked. It's owner was Tina Copenhaver, a short and pudgy mother of a ten-year-old son named Jason. She rented the left-hand side of the house along with her boyfriend Roy, a factory worker nearly a dozen years her junior. Since he was away during the day, the girls normally got together once a week or so at Ray and Tina's place to watch some television, have a couple of drinks, eat a few snacks, gab, and play some cards. Occasionally, when another friend stopped by, they played some games like rook or euchre, although because of their odd number, they were normally limited to poker or crazy-eights.

Ethel slammed the car door and wiped her stain a few more times with a dirty napkin. She kept on across the patchy lawn to the screen door. Without knocking, she swung it open and barged into the living room, where

29

her two friends were engrossed in an afternoon soap opera. Each one held in her lap a paper plate loaded with macaroni salad.

"I didn't hear you pull up your car," Miriam said, looking up and grabbing Ethel's attention for a moment. "We didn't know if you were gonna get here at all, so we already started in with the macaroni salad."

"Ethel looked down at her watch and realized she was nearly an hour late. "Yeah, well I had to stop at the store to pick up some pop and there was a big line, and also some stupid kid at McDonalds was late and I had to stick around a little longer than usual."

"I thought you were gonna be quittin' that job," Tina said.

"I want to," Ethel responded, sitting down and quickly filling her plate high. "But I want to get that damn dishwasher I been talkin' 'bout before I do."

"Well with that new promotion Wayne got, you should get him to buy it for you," Miriam said, matter-of-factly.

"Yeah maybe," Ethel said, driving a large spoonful of pasta toward her mouth. "But I'll proba'ly end up payin' for it myself."

As Ethel ate and focused in on the show, she couldn't help thinking what she really wanted to do was leave her job. After all, she was tired of the time she spent away from home, and had recently begun thinking seriously about becoming a full-time housewife again. She hated dressing in that stupid blue McDonalds uniform anyway, and she no longer had time to wash out the fast-food smell that seeped into her hair and skin. The only thing she liked about the job was the food, and fortunately her hours ensured that she could eat both breakfast and lunch. But it was still time away from the home, time she knew could be better spent away from the Golden Arches. In a month or so, she figured, she might have the money to buy a second-hand dishwasher. She told herself when that purchase was made, she'd throw in the towel at Mickey D's as well. Her only problem was Wayne's imminent disapproval of her quitting, and she knew she'd have to come up with a really good excuse.

"What did Robin say to her husband anyway?" she wondered aloud, suddenly confused by the events occurring on the screen.

"Ain't sure yet," Tina drawled, between bites of the heavy salad. "Should be comin' up after the next commercial."

As Ethel pushed spoonful after spoonful of the macaroni salad between her lips, she gradually began to feel the nausea creep its way back into her system and weigh down her belly. She wondered if it had something to do with her period, which was due in a few days. She often felt a slight discomfort and bloating around that time of the month, but usually only a day or two before. Trying to take her mind off the matter, she reached for the salad bowl and refilled her plate.

"Goddamn it, they do this all the time!" Miriam said. The show's credits had begun rolling, interrupting their rapture with Robin's growing dilemma. "We're gonna have to wait 'til tomorrow to see if she gets off with that handsome doctor."

"Yeah, they piss me off with that shit," Tina echoed, reaching for a smoke. "But I don't think she should. I don't think her husband's all that bad."

"What are you talkin' 'bout?" Miriam gasped. "He's goin' off with that girl at the tennis club all the time."

"Yeah, but I think he still loves his wife," Tina continued.

"I hate that girl," Ethel complained flatly, spewing out a chunk of food as she did. "And I don't really care what happens to her one way or another. I don't see why Franklin ever went off with that bitch anyway."

"Why do you think?" Miriam said, reaching for a cigarette. "You see the way she fills out that tennis dress."

Tina frowned and flipped some ashes toward her paper plate. "Exactly."

"Well, maybe she's got a good body," Ethel followed. "But who wouldn't if all they had to do was play tennis every day and spend the rest of the time buyin' new clothes to show off their figure?" Ethel paused and smiled slyly. "I mean, if I didn't have a family to worry about and look after, I could proba'ly do the same thing."

The others laughed in unison. "Well if you think about it," Miriam finally cut in, "she proba'ly don't have that great of a time anyway. She proba'ly hardly ever eats, don't drink, and is thinkin' about how she looks all day long. And for me, that just ain't very much fun."

"Although I suppose it wouldn't be that bad," Tina murmured.

Ethel tweaked one of her stomach rolls and frowned. "I don't even wanna talk 'bout her anymore," she said. "You got a can of beer Tina? My stomach ain't feelin' that good and I think it might help my digestion."

"Yeah, there's another quart in the fridge," she answered, eyeing a similar-sized empty bottle on the table. "Miriam brought 'em over. I think there might be a little rum left in the bottle out there too, if you want that. They say that's supposed to be good for movin' stuff through your system."

"I'll get 'em," Miriam said, collecting the paper plates and plastic spoons. "I wouldn't mind havin' a rum and Coke myself."

31

"Should be some ice out there in the freezer too," Tina called after her. "Grab a few glasses while you're at it. I think there's a few clean ones."

"How's Roy doin'?" Ethel asked, tapping a cigarette on her nail and then lighting it. "Been giving you any more headaches?"

Tina made a sour face and propped herself up in the chair. "Just the usual little ones," she responded. "You know, comin' back late when his supper's cold, or bringin' his friends back here and gettin' a bit rowdy in front of Jason. No real big deal. He ain't missin' work and gettin' his pay docked at least."

"I sometimes think a man's purpose on earth is to give his woman problems," Miriam stated, placing a couple of bottles on the table. "Been like that with my husbands, although I suppose I can't really blame 'em all that much. But I think Roy's actually beginnin' to come around. You remember how he was when he first moved in here?"

"Yeah," Tina said. "But that was a lot different then. I mean, we weren't goin' out together or nothin' like that. He was just rentin' out the spare bedroom."

Miriam splashed a generous measure of rum into a glass and dropped some ice into it. "Well I think that's a sign of true love, when a man changes his ways for his woman. Unfortunately, it wasn't like that with either of my husbands."

"Well I sure wish it was like that with my husband," Ethel said, knocking back a quick shot and immediately pouring another in her glass. "When I first met Wayne, he wouldn't hear of havin' me work outside the home. He brought home the money and I did all the rest. None of this double duty business like now."

Tina flipped the channel on the TV until it landed on a game show and then turned down the volume. "How'd you meet a guy like Wayne anyway?" she asked.

Ethel held the smoke in her lungs and thought momentarily. "I met Wayne back in Kentucky," she finally said while exhaling. "I was takin' a couple of classes at this technical school in Keavy, where I grew up. I guess I was about seventeen, and at that time wanted to be a dental hygienist. And one day he came in to have a tooth pulled or somethin', I can't remember exactly, but I had to clean his teeth first, I think. You know, it was like one of those reduced-price things like you get at hair salons with apprentices."

"How romantic!" Tina said, dropping another ice cube into her drink.

Ethel frowned at another memory. "Not really," she said. "He

32

actually complained about me to the teacher 'cause I'd cut his gum with that little tool you get the crud from between the teeth with.''

"So he was still a leather-lung back then?" Miriam said, exhaling a burst of smoke while rolling her eyes.

"Well, I guess he had some reason," Ethel temporarily defended him while opening the bag of cheese puffs. "Seeing that he was bleedin' and all. But the next time he came in, a couple of weeks later to get a couple fillings, who was there all alone again to do the preparin' work but me! Of course, he wanted no part of it, but seein' he had no choice, I cleaned his teeth again, makin' sure I was gentle about it. And that time I did a pretty good job, and I guess he was sorry or somethin' for reacting the way he did before and ended up takin' me out for doughnuts or somethin' afterwards.''

"I never knew you were a dental hygienist," Miriam said, as if impressed.

"Well I never actually became a full-fledged one," Ethel said, reaching for a cigarette. "Cause after that, we started seein' each other some and uh, one thing led to another, and before I knew it, Darlene was beginnin' to grow inside me.''

"How did Wayne take to that?" Tina asked, smiling slyly.

Ethel paused for a moment, trying to remember. "He was a bit pissed off, I think," she said, biting a nail, "seein' he couldn't continue with his studies. But in a way, I don't think he was that into whatever class he was takin' anyway, and us gettin' married gave him a good reason to leave—although he never told me that. But he did treat me real well back then. Had me stay at home all day relaxin' while he went out and worked.'' She sighed and shifted her body, allowing room for a silent fart to escape. "A lot different from the situation now.''

"Hey! Change it to channel seven!" Miriam interrupted while consulting her watch. "*Enter The Daylight* should be on, and I wanna see what happens to those gorgeous Kirkwood brothers and that lawsuit they got goin'. I tell you, those two are the most suave guys on television.''

Tina landed on the channel whose theme music was just ending. "Can't disagree with you there," she said, adding a bit more Coke to her drink. "If one of them came along, I'm afraid I'd just have to tell Roy to spend the night elsewhere.''

Ethel jammed a load of cheese puffs toward her mouth and reclined in the easy chair. "No kiddin'," she muttered, momentarily forgetting her own life while contentedly immersing herself in the ludicrous lives of imaginary others.

6

The sound of the lawnmower wavered as it attempted to chop through the crabgrass, dandelions, poison sumac, and other assorted weeds surrounding the mobile home before spewing out the mulch in an uneven row to the side. Every now and then the blade would catch a rock, sending a loud clack above the sound of the muddled engine, and it was during those times when Wayne would look over from where he was working in the garden and attempt to yell above the noise of the machine. He had been forced to buy a new blade the month before, and he didn't want to pay for another costly repair on account of someone else's negligence.

Muscling it through the dense foliage was his son, Wayne Junior, who couldn't hear him because of his proximity to the machine. Whereas Darlene took more after her mother, Junior looked more like his dad, with short light red hair that he parted on the side. At fourteen, he was already about Wayne's height and, although certainly not fat, he was a little chubby. He had a small pot belly and his chest was fleshy, almost like that of an adolescent girl. He wore only a pair of white gym shorts and sneakers and, because of his work outside that morning, his normally pale skin was beginning to turn a painful shade of pink on the back of his body.

"Hey Junior!" Wayne yelled several times before finally getting his attention. "Turn that thing off for a while and let it rest! And go put your shirt on! You're gettin' a sunburn!"

The boy turned off the machine and then walked over to his father, breathing a little heavily. "Hey Dad," he said. "Can't I do the rest of this tomorrow? I'm tired of it."

Wayne lowered his head and shook it, looking at the boy's grass-stained sneakers. "N-O," he said, spelling out the word for good measure while staring at his son's pink, sun-freckled face. "You still haven't done out in the back there. And you know I got to train later on."

"Yeah, but I was gonna go over to John's house this afternoon," he whined. "We were gonna ride our bikes."

"I don't care what you were gonna do," Wayne answered, annoyed with his son's obstinacy. "You haven't had to mow the lawn for three weeks and you knew you had to do it today. So you just go into the house now and tell Mom to make you lunch. And then I want you out here to finish the job!''

"But I don't wanna do it anymore today," Junior protested.

"Well sometimes we have to do things we don't want to," Wayne said, taking off his work gloves. "I been doin' things I didn't want to do all my life, and it's just somethin' you're gonna have to get used to, too."

"But can't I do it tomorrow?" Junior continued, digging his heel into the ground.

"No you can't, damn it!" Wayne yelled. "So just do what I told you to do and get the rest of what I assigned you done!"

Junior spit on the ground and looked at him angrily. "I already been out here for two hours," he hissed.

"I don't care if you've been out here for ten hours," Wayne responded, hustling his balls. "The job's not done, and until it is, I don't want to hear anything else about it. Now move it!"

Junior exhaled loudly and began walking dejectedly toward the trailer. Wayne watched him for several seconds and then headed back toward the garden, pleased with his command of the situation but a little worried at the lazy character his son was beginning to demonstrate. It seemed that more and more Junior just wanted to ride his bicycle or watch TV without doing any of the chores expected of him around the house. It was a problem with all the kids today, he thought. The boys just wanted to play all day, and the girls just wanted to sit around on their asses inside, glued to the TV screen. Ethel had allowed Darlene to become like that, but he'd be damned if Junior was going to follow in her footsteps.

Overall, his son was really a decent worker, he reasoned, but like any kid his age just needed to be pushed a little. There would be other days when he could ride his bike, and he knew it was important that the boy learned the principle that work comes before pleasure. One day he figured he'd thank him for it, but it was Wayne's duty now as a father to instruct him in that regard. What the kid needed was to sweat a little outside before he went and played, just like he did when the banks closed at midday on Saturday afternoon and he came home early. He didn't whittle away his time like so many other people, but used the time to take care of things around the house that needed attention.

At this time of the year, he gave his attention to the garden, whose plants had sprouted the month before and some of which were now nearly a foot in height. It was something that he was proud of and consequently cared for fastidiously. Not only were the vegetables better than the ones they used to buy at the store, but he also knew that the hands that picked them were raised in America.

More importantly, he knew that growing his own vegetables saved the family a lot of money. And it wasn't just around the time when he harvested them, but all year long. The things could be frozen or put in jars and be kept for months. So in addition to never having to buy produce at the supermarket, they could also avoid the spaghetti sauce section, the canned vegetables and a good portion of the frozen foods. Looking down at the raspberry vines creeping against the fertile soil, he figured soon they would be able to avoid the jam and jelly section as well.

After burying a pole next to each of his tomato plants, Wayne cut several lengths of string and began tying their stems to the pieces of wood. When he finished, he cleared the ground of any weed that had begun to push its way up next to the plants. He then lightly tilled the ground with a small rake so that water might seep in better, and finally checked the onions' progress by pulling one out of the ground. After observing it, he decided that he'd dig the rest of them up the following weekend.

As he walked back toward the house, he saw his pink-tinged son pound down the steps and reluctantly march toward the lawnmower. The boy glared at him angrily, and then yanked at the cord several times until the engine finally kicked over.

"Hey Junior!" Wayne yelled, shaking his head. "Easy with that thing! You know how much it costs to replace?"

"Don't worry!" the boy yelled back. "I'm not gonna break it!"

"And listen," Wayne said, pointing to the large pieces of particle board standing on end near the far corner of their property. "I want you to mow back there first before anything else. And don't forget," he added. "That area has to be raked afterwards."

Without responding, the boy wrestled the machine past Wayne and out toward the back, kicking up a trail of dust in his wake that blew directly into Wayne's face.

Wayne yelled something else toward him but could hardly hear his own voice above the racket of the lawnmower. Shaking his head while dusting himself off, he walked toward the trailer. When he swung open the screen door, he expected to see some food on the stove waiting for him, but all he saw were a few dirty dishes and pots in the sink. He heard the loud blare of the TV in the family room and moved toward it. Ethel and Darlene were sprawled out across the chairs and watching a game show she had recorded.

"Hey Ethel," Wayne said, staring down at his wife. "How's about fixin' me some lunch."

"There's some franks and beans out there on the stove," she said absently, her eyes fixed on the screen. "Junior just heated 'em up so they still should be warm."

"Yeah, well the pot's now in the sink," Wayne said, raising his voice a little.

Ethel looked at him briefly before returning her eyes to the screen. "Well he must of eaten 'em all," she responded, concentrating on the sound of bells and lights flashing before her. "Lemme just see the end of this first."

"Goddamn it!" Wayne shouted as he stepped into the room. "I've got things to do this afternoon and you two have all day to watch that. Don't make me turn it off!"

Ethel sighed loudly. "All right!" she said, shifting her bulk to an upright position and grabbing the remote control beside her. "And don't shout," she added, putting the show on pause. "I've already got a headache."

"From what?" Wayne grunted. "Watchin' too much of that shit?"

Ethel hoisted herself from the chair with difficulty and grimaced at her husband. "You wouldn't understand unless you were a woman," she said, reaching into her pocket for another cigarette and then staggering toward the kitchen.

After wolfing down the fish sticks and fries his wife had fixed him, Wayne walked toward the sand piles in the back yard. He was dressed in his security uniform and carried a shoulder bag that contained various targets, a snub-nosed revolver, and a box of about fifty pellets. As the hot sun pounded down on his torso, Wayne felt the familiar anxiety pump through his nervous system, brought on by his anticipation of what he referred to as "training."

Specifically for this activity, he had constructed a small training ground with several sheets of wood propped next to each other. The boards stood about seven feet high and served as the backstop for the multiple rounds of pellets he shot every week at a number of homemade targets he tacked along their front. He knew his own private shooting range was necessary, because it was important for all law officers to continue improving their already-superior levels of physical agility and marksmanship.

37

Unfortunately, because his economic situation demanded it, he was forced to use imitation hardware rather than the actual piece he carried on duty, as the bullets for that weapon were priced far beyond his means.

He had bought the semi-automatic target pistol from a sporting goods store in Columbus. It cost him less than fifty bucks (including 200 pellets), and it looked and felt pretty much like the real thing. It didn't handle as well as the service revolver he wore to work and barely carried a kick, but it at least afforded him something to practice with within his budget.

He normally began his routine with a number of stretches and exercises he had learned during his time in the military service. So after laying his bag on the ground, Wayne sat next to it and spread his legs in front of him, leaning his face forward in an attempt to touch his nose to his knees. He told himself that he could have made the connection if it wasn't for his sprawling gut which stood between them. But as the sweat began seeping from his pores, he could feel his taut hamstring muscles begin to loosen anyway.

Rolling over onto his stomach, he began a set of push-ups next. Wayne was unaware that his body was not flat as it should be, but instead bent at a forty-five degree angle so that his ass sailed high in the air while his arms bent only slightly before his small, upturned nose met the ground. Thinking he did the set of twenty with perfect form, however, he was content to move on to another exercise.

Laying on his back next, he attempted to raise his bent legs a few inches off the ground and hold them for ten seconds, but after only about five, they rapidly sunk back to the earth. He did the ten brief, strained reps in that manner anyway, gradually lessening the time until he merely kicked his legs into the air before letting them crash to the ground.

After resting for a few minutes, he stood up and did fifty jumping jacks and then thirty twists with his hands on his hips. Afterwards, he swung his arms around for about thirty seconds and rolled his neck for about ten. The final exercise in his routine was twenty-five sit-ups, but because he felt he had been bending over and working his stomach muscles in the garden, he decided to skip them. He figured that his abdomen had already endured enough punishment, disregarding the fact that they were his least favorite exercise and the one set that he had never been able to finish.

Breathing heavily, Wayne wiped the sweat from his brow and walked to a point about fifty yards away from the backdrop. Turning suddenly, he pumped his short legs in its direction, propelled by the added momentum of his gut bobbing beneath him. When he finally reached it, he collapsed to the ground.

When he regained his breath several minutes later, he walked briskly back to his starting point and repeated the exercise three more times. His body moved and recovered more slowly with each successive run. By the time he reached the final sprint, his short figure appeared to be power-walking.

Feeling that he deserved some rest after performing his exercises so well, Wayne laid down on the ground a while longer and prepared himself for the next phase. He hated the physical part of his training and was glad it was over, but he also knew that it was important to keep the body limber—a sound body was home to a sound mind.

He readily admitted there were other guys who had been blessed with more agile bodies but, deep down, he was also aware that the most important thing for a lawman was how well his trigger-finger functioned under pressure. And in that respect, he knew he was a champion. He even had several trophies on the family room windowsill from his days with the National Guard in Kentucky to prove it.

Wayne brushed some grass clippings from his sweaty forearms and noticed a slight rash developing on his forearms. He figured it came from the poison sumac he cleared earlier from the wall near the front of the house. The stuff was a real pain in the ass, he thought, because each spring he tried to get rid of its roots, but the next year it just grew back stronger and in more directions, giving him a nasty reminder of his failure to rid his life of it every year.

He considered returning to the house and rubbing some pink ointment on his arms to halt the irritation and spread of the rash. But, since he was already involved with another chore, he decided to take care of his skin later.

Instead, he took out a number of homemade targets and tacked them to the boards. A couple of them were very simple, marked only with a bull's-eye, while others depicted various sections of the human body, such as the head, chest, or groin. He walked back to where he had begun his sprints, placed the bag back on the freshly mown grass, and removed the pellet revolver.

Although he had a couple of other guns on his property—like a hunting rifle and a .22-caliber handgun he kept in his dresser drawer for the family's protection—Wayne certainly wasn't a gun nut. He had done his hitch with military and was a paid member of the National Rifle Association, whose policy of upholding the Second Amendment of the Constitution he supported. But he also felt that the men who collected an arsenal of weapons, and converted their semi-automatics into fully automatic machine guns or bought powerful assault rifles like the imported AK-47 were a dangerous, radical faction of society.

Wayne had no interest in paramilitary groups who liked to go out on the weekend and play soldier with their buddies. It seemed that about every month, one of them would take his arsenal out on the street and blow off a little steam by turning his firepower on a bunch of strangers. They made up a hazardous fringe element who took their guaranteed right too seriously, Wayne felt, without respecting their arms or the rights of others—as those who were required to carry a weapon did. They were people who had to be to be watched carefully, and who just seemed to interfere with the surveillance of actual criminals.

After dropping more pellets into the snub-nosed pistol, Wayne lay on the ground, aimed carefully, and fired six rapid shots at the first target. He reloaded, moved in front of the next target and, resting his weight on one knee, proceeded to empty the gun's ammunition into the second target as he had done with the first. Filling the revolver again, he moved sideways to the another target and assumed a squatting position, firing the weapon's contents into the image depicting the head. He repeated the process with the last two targets, standing upright with the fourth and drawing the gun from his holster with the fifth, creating new holes in the paper as he had done with the previous shots.

When he had finished, he approached the targets and walked slowly between them. He had scored direct hits with nearly all his shots, slightly missing the mark with only a few shots while positioned on one knee. It didn't bother him much, as that position was a bit antiquated nowadays, and a position used more in competitions than on the street.

Pleased with his accuracy, he removed the used targets and tacked up three new ones, each depicting the male torso. As he attached the final one, he heard the distant hum of the lawnmower burp and slowly cut off. He looked over and saw that Junior had finally finished the lawn and was now moving toward the trailer, his red body contrasting sharply with the green field surrounding him. The area was now quiet, calm— tranquil even. It made him more aware of his home's isolation, and he liked that. No cars driving past, no boisterous neighbors, no disagreements from his family members, no sounds. It was one of the reasons he had chosen the site in the first place: It was real peaceful.

Concentrating on the targets again, Wayne prepared himself for the final and perhaps most strenuous phase of his training. Walking casually to the far right hand side of the shooting zone, he reloaded the gun and placed it in his holster and then stood nonchalantly. Pretending he was being taken by surprise, he suddenly began running to his left before pulling his gun and firing it at the target. From there he ran the opposite way and fired again. After pulling the trigger a few more times while in motion, he stopped to regain his breath and reload.

The last six shots he fired after rolling on the ground and assuming the position on his stomach. It was the most difficult exercise to shoot acurately from, but the most likely position he might be forced to shoot from if the situation presented itself while in the line of duty. He'd run, roll, and then shoot before getting up, finally dusting himself off and repeating the process. The first five shots went smoothly, but as he was about to make his roll for the final one, he tripped on a tuft of grass and didn't quite get set before firing. Immediately after popping the shot, he heard it ricochet off a rock to the right of the boards and then heard the sound of shattered glass. From the ground, he saw that one of his bedroom windows had been shattered.

Cursing himself, he holstered his gun and pulled the leather strap across it, then walked over to the target board to check his results. He noticed that he had made contact against some part of the torsos with all the other shots, but he still hadn't pegged them in the exact center, where the heart would be. Still, he reckoned, except for the last misfire, he would have immediately incapacitated any perpetrator of a crime.

Smiling smugly, he felt that his hard work was paying off with real progress. Within a short amount of time, he figured while scratching his discolored forearms, every bullet would be meeting its mark.

7

Ethel crouched over the toilet in the bathroom and balanced herself precariously over the commode. She attempted to urinate into a jar she held directly beneath her and, after squirting onto her hand, she finally got the receptacle into the right position and began feeling the warmth of her piss rapidly rising through the glass. When it began to overflow, she balanced the jar on the rim of the bathtub and sat down to finish releasing.

Without washing her hands, she picked up the urine sample and examined it. It was pale yellow, almost like beer, and clear, without any cloudiness or floating particles. That pleased her, as she remembered reading somewhere that those latter qualities were signs that the kidneys were not functioning properly.

After lighting a cigarette, Ethel grabbed a small box from the medicine cabinet and rapidly read the instructions again. She quickly pulled the cover off the box, then took out a colored stick and removed the plastic around it before dropping it into the jar of urine. Placing it in the medicine cabinet where it was out of view, she pulled down the toilet seat and nervously plopped down on top of it. She looked at her watch and noted the time, and then began to wait.

It was three o'clock in the morning, and Ethel felt tired and drained of all her energy, although it wasn't just the late hour that fatigued her. She had begun feeling that way constantly a few weeks before, when the summer had officially begun and the pleasant hot weather had slipped into long hours filled with thick, unpleasant humidity. It made her sweat more than usual, and consequently slowed her actions around the house. The only thing that made her feel better was her new second-hand dishwasher, an appliace she had wanted for months and which her earnings from McDonalds had paid for.

With that finally out of the way, she had flatly told Wayne she wanted to quit her job, but he had insisted that she stick with it. Since it was summer, he reasoned, she could still put in four hours a day at work and take care of things around the house, especially since the kids didn't have to go to school. He had told her that Darlene would be at home all day and could give her a hand with the women's work, which would help her take care of her own duties. He even added that the extra money she made could be used to buy some paint or even be put in the bank, where it might come in handy someday.

She had to admit that a little extra money always came in handy, but now that Wayne had settled into the "shotgun" position and was bringing home a larger pay check, she also felt she had no need to work outside her home anymore. She had the things she wanted the most, and that had been her purpose in seeking a temporary job in the first place. She had never set out to take on her job as a permanent thing, but it almost seemed as if that was what Wayne now planned for it to be. Worst of all, he had started asking for the money she normally put aside for herself, claiming that he had plans to buy some fishing equipment. She reluctantly handed most of it over, pissed off that the fruits of her labor simply had to go to her husband's recreation, rather than something that might make the house look a little bit nicer.

Besides, in Ethel's eyes, her stupid minimum-wage job was becoming more and more unbearable. She was constantly surrounded by high school kids on their summer break, whose immaturity and inefficiency made the tedious conversations with the old bags almost a joy by comparison. Her time there had become a chore and a bore, and it began reaching a point where not even the food was very appetizing to her anymore—something she never would have thought possible.

Fortunately on the home front, Darlene now helped her out a bit with the cleaning. But with the produce from Wayne's initial harvests beginning to fill the kitchen and Darlene unsure what to do with it all, Ethel found that she had more work than ever—and because of it felt more and more run down. She was tired all the time, and seemed to be yawning continually. But even with her exhaustion, she also began to find that she was having difficulty getting to sleep at night, which just left her more worn out the following day.

Because of her extra exertion, she had paid a visit to a doctor, who had prescribed medium-strength Valium to be taken shortly before she went to bed. Initially, it had worked and she felt better. But soon afterwards, she began getting stomachaches and experiencing brief spells of nausea. So she had decided to make another appointment with the physician to get a different prescription—one that might be gentler toward her sensitive body.

Yet even when she had begun taking the weaker dosage he had suggested, she still didn't feel much better. In fact, she felt a bit worse, because the weaker pill didn't always achieve her desired effect. She often tossed and turned for an hour or more before finally seeking relief with another dose—which only left her feeling drowsier than ever in the morning.

As she began nearing the time of her period shortly thereafter, she felt none of the usual bloating and discomfort leading up to it, and when she was due, she had hardly bled. It hadn't caused her much concern, though: She knew that the chances of her being pregnant were very slim because she and Wayne only had sex about twice a month—and she always used her diaphragm. It wasn't that unnatural for her barely to moisten her Modess pad anyway, because her menstrual discharge varied greatly from month to month.

But as the next month passed, she began to experience prolonged spells of nausea—not very often but at times so intense that she'd have to sit down for a few minutes. This time, she figured, it was probably a chemical imbalance or some stress-related illness. It wouldn't have been surprising to her either, because with all her work, she didn't even have time to watch her videotaped soap operas anymore.

But when she had missed her period again the weekend before, she began to question more deeply the sensations she had been bearing recently. She had been pregnant a few times and certainly knew the sensations that a pregnant woman felt, but that was during simpler times, when not as many extraneous factors, such as her stress and high tension, were at play. However, after another week passed, she finally began to get the message that her periods of nausea probably didn't have anything to do with her nerves or the pills she had been taking. And that's when she had finally decided to pick up the test at the drug store and find out if what she had begun to suspect was actually true.

She looked at her watch and saw that it was time to find out, for better or worse. After wiping her sweaty palms, she stood up and walked over to the sink. Picking up the color chart from the test in one hand and the urine-filled jar in the other, she put them together in front of the light and saw the stick had turned navy blue. Moving the stick down the color chart slowly, she stopped when the two shades matched. She shifted her eyes to the word written underneath the color: "POSITIVE."

The letters blurred in front of her and she suddenly felt another spell of nausea overtaking her. At that moment, the jar slipped from her hand and smashed to the floor, shooting a splatter of her lukewarm piddle and jagged glass in myriad directions and completely drenching her bare feet.

Stepping quickly to the commode, she released a thick stream of vomit straight into the hole. After retching several times, she finally regained her breath and stood up, steadying herself in front of the mirror and staring at her reflection until it finally began to come into focus. She frowned at her image, then cleaned up the mess beneath her with a sponge and mindlessly threw it into the laundry hamper.

Feeling slightly more stable, she walked out to the kitchen and sat down, resting her elbows on the sticky table. She lit another cigarette and inhaled quickly several times, attempting to come to terms with the test result that insured that something was growing inside her, getting slightly larger every time her heart beat blood through its tiny body.

It had been eight years since Ethel had last conceived a child, although that final time, Wayne had not been the father. The pregnancy occurred on one of his extended periods away from home, when she had drunkedly fallen for the advances of one of her sister's friends, and paid the price for believing that he would pull out. It had been a big mistake, but Wayne never found out about it—she had an abortion without his knowledge as soon as she missed her period—and the consummation of her foolish act had ended up in a rusted dish somewhere in the backwoods of Kentucky.

This time, however, she was certain Wayne was the father, but she still had the sinking feeling it was another mistake. Thinking about it more, she was almost certain of the night it must've happened. It was almost two months before, she recalled. Wayne had gone night-fishing down at some river; tired as usual, she took advantage of his absence by going to sleep shortly after he had left.

A number of hours later, she was awakened by her husband, who flipped on the light and noisily threw his fishing boots on the floor. He was obviously drunk and she pretended to be asleep; she hoped that she could return quickly to her dreams after being unpleasantly jostled into such an ugly reality. But when he sat down to remove his rubber pants and landed right on one of her legs, she had bolted up in bed and groggily admonished him for his carelessness. They spoke a little bit—probably about his prowess as a fisherman—and once he was naked, he crawled into bed and pushed his unshowered body next to hers.

Wayne had never been the most gentle and romantic person in bed, but she normally welcomed any sort of opportunity at having an orgasm, even though he rarely gave her time to achieve it. So in spite of the stale smell of beer on his breath and the repulsive odor of fish on the hands which probed her body parts roughly, she finally surrendered herself to his demands.

When Wayne had grunted for the last time, he rolled off her and, as usual, began snoring immediately. And as she lay looking around the room unable to get back to sleep, she realized she had forgotten to cover her diaphragm with spermacide as she normally did before their relations. Her doctor had told her that the jelly was not absolutely essential, but to be used as an extra precaution. She normally followed his instructions, except when she wasn't given the time to remember, like that night. It wasn't a big deal, she recalled thinking, and when she finally drifted off to sleep, the doctor's advice and her own thoughts sailed away with her consciousness.

Until now, sitting at the kitchen table and remembering again. And as she continued thinking, she began to tell herself that the pregnancy had been entirely her husband's fault. He had awakened her in the middle of the night and forced himself upon her while she was still half asleep. He hadn't even mentioned the spermacide as he sometimes did, and precautionary sex was obviously a two-way street. He was just going to have to wake up and smell the coffee.

She stood up and hastily grabbed a can of Hamm's from the refrigerator. She already felt drunk, but she figured another beer might make her think more clearly.

She was pregnant—that was a fact—and really, she supposed, it wasn't that big a deal. After all, she was only thirty-six years old—young still.

Maybe this child was even the seed that would bring Wayne and her closer together, she continued thinking, and give them some sort of focus as they moved on through the years. Within five years or so, she imagined, Darlene and Junior would be off on their own and she'd be in her early forties and lonely, and have to begin acting like some sort of grandmother or one of the retired women at the Golden Arches, a vision that seemed more like a nightmare.

She also realized that by having a child, she would be writing her ticket away from Mickey-D's and back into the home. Perhaps her condition was a signal for her to assume a real middle-aged woman's duty—cooking, cleaning, and bringing up kids—and not working with that stupid McDonalds uniform on for a few extra bucks a week.

She tried to imagine a little blob floating around inside her and, as she did, slowly began to wonder if her pregnancy had been an accident at all, or if she may have meant for it to happen in the first place. She sat looking at the beer can wondering if she could have been that desperate or that stupid or both.

46

And when she finally drained the can several minutes later, she still didn't know the answer.

But she had a pretty good idea.

8

The oscillating fan on the kitchen counter hummed gently from side to side and blew the hot air around the room, but from her position on the floor, Ethel was unable to enjoy even its minimal relief. She was on all fours, crawling around the linoleum and attempting to remove some grease stains with an old toothbrush. Her knees stuck against the dirty surface and sweat seeped out of her pores, dropping in large beads in front of her so that she hardly needed the bucket of soapy water to aid her with her cleaning.

Ethel exhaled loudly and tossed the brush on the kitchen table, deciding to finish the job later. She hadn't slept all night: Instead, since the sun had first illuminated the horizon during the wee hours of the morning, she had pondered what she had begun to view as her two options. One was to discuss her pregnancy with Wayne, and then perhaps reach a mutual decision that an abortion would be the best thing for the family's welfare. That would mean she'd be back at work, with her wages going toward the removal of the fetus. Or the second, where they would decide to keep the baby, and she'd assume the role of a pregnant mother—something that would certainly exclude work outside the home in the near future.

Ethel knew the second option suited her intentions best, yet she was worried about how Wayne was going to react to that choice. Nearly certain that he'd throw a fit, she figured she'd tell him right before he went to work so that she could let the cat out of the bag before he had time to react. Then she could be away from him for the rest of the day, when he could view the situation reasonably.

There was a reason for her being somewhat fearful; after all, the news of her first pregnancy caught Wayne completely off guard. She remembered that night clearly. They had seen *Billy Jack* at the Keavy Drive-In Theater earlier in the evening, and afterwards parked in front of her apartment. He had drawn her close.

"I love you," he told her for the first time.

"I love you too," she said, echoing his sentiment.

They kissed briefly and hugged each other warmly. She felt closer to Wayne than she ever had. Then she sprang the news.

The look that came across his face was like none she had ever seen on a person before—and, fortunately, not since. It was a look of anger bent by a hate so tightly intertwined that it suffocated them both. It seemed to fuse the present and the past together and then destroy the two slowly, ending the chance for his future by choking all he had achieved to obtain it, twisting and draining so rapidly that a putrid puss, thick like molasses, seemed to leak out of his soul.

And at the time it had scared the shit out of her.

Fortunately, Wayne regained his composure several minutes later.

"All right," he finally said. "I'm gonna drive you back home and I'll stop by tommorrow. But first, I got to cancel my classes and then I got to find a job. And after that, we got to make some arrangements for marriage."

In contrast, a couple of years later when Junior came into the world, Wayne was so thrilled that she had given him a son that he had actually cried for joy. Shortly thereafter, they had mutually agreed that they would stop having children and concentrate on the two that they already had, unlike so many of their kinfolk, who just got more and more bogged down with every additional child. That was fourteen years ago, and they had been successful in their pact.

But now, she had no idea how he might react.

She looked at the clock and knew that Wayne would be leaving shortly. He had stopped eating breakfast at home, claiming that a full stomach made him a little drowsy and therefore inattentive to his duties. Nowadays he simply grabbed a doughnut and a mug of coffee before shooting out the door.

Ethel took a deep breath. She knew she'd better hurry if she wanted to get this out of the way once and for all.

After searching around the ashtray and lighting the end of a cigarette, Ethel walked down the hall and pushed the door open gently. Wayne was bent over on a chair and tying the laces of his shoes. "Hey Wayne," she said nervously, standing in the doorway. "I got your coffee and doughnut all ready for you."

"Yeah, OK," he said, making sure the bows on his shoes were even. "Just put 'em by the door."

Ethel shifted her weight uneasily. "But they didn't have the jelly ones like you like, so I had to get honey-dipped."

"That's all right," he said, looking at himself in the mirror and then at her reflection. "Just try to get the jelly ones the next time."

"OK," she said, taking a step into the room. She paused, trying to get her wording right. "Wayne," she began. "I got a confession to make."

"Confessions are for Catholics and their priests," he blurted out, smirking at his wit while searching around the closet. "Where did my shoe-shine kit go?" he muttered.

"I've decided to stop workin' pretty soon," Ethel began, speaking toward his back, "'cause I don't think it's too good for my physical condition."

"What are you talkin' about?" he asked, shaking one of the coats in the closet away from his head and emerging from behind it with the kit. "What physical condition? Your stomach?"

"Yes actually," Ethel said, annoyed at the crack and feeling her adrenaline begin to pump. "That's exactly what it has to do with."

"Well just because they allow you to eat at work," Wayne said, opening the wooden box, "doesn't mean you have to have hamburgers and french fries every day. Why don't you get one of them salads for a change, or somethin' with less calories?"

"You don't seem to understand me Wayne," Ethel said. "Even if I went on a bread and water diet for the next six months, my stomach would still be gettin' bigger."

Wayne put his shoe up on the box and began dabbing some black polish on it, not really listening to her. "Or maybe you should do a bit of exercise out in the back if you're so concerned about your stomach. This heat'll sure shed more pounds off than those stupid pills you take sometimes."

"Don't you understand anything?" Ethel screamed. "I'm not talkin' about the food at work or some exercise or any pills! I'm talkin' about bein' pregnant!"

Wayne stopped himself and looked up at her with a confused expression while placing his shoe on the carpet, inadvertently staining it with wet polish. "What did you just say?"

"That I'm pregnant, stupid!" she yelled, looking down angrily.

Wayne stared at her intently, then shook his head, and finally began to buff his shoe with the brush. "C'mon Ethel, don't joke around with me," he said. "I'm gonna be guardin' over two million dollars today."

"It wasn't a joke!" Ethel said, annoyed by his lack of concern and sucking on her cigarette hard. She almost wanted an argument now, a little fight that might get everything out.

"You're pregnant?" he mouthed, looking at her dumbly.

"That's right," she responded. "And I took the test to prove it."

He was silent for a moment as he tried to think clearly.

"Am I the father?" he finally asked suspiciously.

"Of course you are!" she hissed, raising her head abruptly. "What the hell kind of a question is that?"

He was silent again, looking around for something, although he wasn't sure what. "Well if you got pregnant," he said, trying to keep his cool while heedlessly tracking the black polish around the room, "you're gonna have to have it."

"What do you mean, 'if *I* got pregnant'," she said sarcastically. "It takes two to tango, Mister!"

"Yeah, well that's the woman's job to look out for those things," he responded. "With the Trojan it was my problem. But you know you didn't like when I used 'em. You said they got you all dried out."

Ethel wanted to scream at him, but she knew he had a point. Wayne had used rubbers until a few years ago. But she had decided to switch to the diaphragm, hoping to get a bit more enjoyment out of sex by experiencing the sensation of flesh upon flesh. It hadn't worked though.

"You can't pin this all on me!" she finally shouted. "I won't let you! And if that's the way you feel about it," she added, "there's still time left to make an appointment down at the health clinic to get rid of it."

"An abortion?" Wayne said, surprised at the suggestion.

"That's right," she said defiantly. "If you don't want me to keep it."

"Oh no!" Wayne said facing her. "I never said I didn't want you to keep it. I just said it was your fault." He pointed his finger at her and added, "And I never want to hear you suggest somethin' like that again. One thing I would never allow is for my wife to have an abortion, because abortion is murder." He stopped himself and searched around the room for a rag. "In fact, it's worse than murder," he added, "because it's killin' somethin' that hasn't even done anything to deserve it yet."

"Well, quit being so gloomy then, for Christ's sake!" she said, tipping some ashes into her weathered palm. "You should be happy that we're gonna bring another life into the world."

"Listen Ethel!" Wayne said while polishing his other shoe forcefully. "You've told me the situation and I've accepted it. But you don't need to tell me how I should feel about it, because frankly, that's none of your business. Now if you could just move out of my way, I've got to get to work. I'm already late as it is and I don't want this unexpected news to affect my

51

performance.''

"And how about my job?'' Ethel said, running down the hallway after him. "A pregnant woman shouldn't be workin' under all that tension!''

"Look Ethel,'' Wayne said while filling his plastic mug with coffee. "If you just found out you're pregnant, there's no reason why you can't work for a few more months. We're sure as hell gonna need that money when the kid comes.'' He snapped the lid on the coffe mug and grabbed his bag with the doughnut. "So I don't wanna hear anymore shit about your job,'' he added, pushing open the door. "And in the meantime, I don't want you spendin' the money you make on anything foolish neither.''

Walking out onto the porch, Ethel watched him get into his car and then kick up some gravel with a quick exit. She felt relieved, and told herself that a couple more months at McDonalds would pass quickly now that she knew she had an out.

She returned to the kitchen, knowing that she had to get ready for another shift. But first, she stopped herself, pulled the bourbon bottle from the top shelf, and poured herself a shot.

She wasn't sure if she wanted to go through all the shit of having another child, but she did know that before long, she'd be back home all day, doing things her way.

And because of that, she sure as hell felt like celebrating.

9

Wayne leaned back in a yellow-corded beach chair, whose rusted aluminum legs creaked loudly as his weight balanced delicately over its two rickety points. In front of him was a hundred-foot-square hole that had been bulldozed several years earlier and filled with rocks and spring water, as well as a few trash cans full of fish from the state hatchery. For ten bucks a day, anyone could prop himself along its edges and keep whatever they pulled in that weighed over a pound, with a five-fish maximum. It had drawn a steady stream of customers since its opening. But as time went on, no one had bothered to replenish the stock, so it was getting harder and harder to catch any fish in the pond.

Most of the people who used it were retired men who didn't have anything better to do—certainly not the type of fisherman that Wayne considered himself to be. He saw himself more as he saw the men in *Field and Stream* magazine—sportsmen serious about their craft, not armchair fishermen who simply went down to the lake to chew the fat with others. He usually angled down at the Quayle river, getting out in the middle of the stream and fighting the current, scientifically approaching the fish as if they were game. But once in a while he came to the pay lake simply because he liked the taste of catfish.

That afternoon was no different than the other afternoons during the recent months, apart from the fact that today he caught five fish within a few hours. It was surprising, since the other men, sitting close to each other on the opposite side of the small body of water, hadn't seemed to catch even that many between them.

He recognized the other guys but had never talked to them much. There had been many opportunities to do that over the summer but, fact was, Wayne wasn't interested in talk. He came to the lake to relax and be on his own after a busy week of policing, not to discuss trivial things like church reunions or the weather with strangers. If they wanted to whittle away their time in such dumb ways, Wayne felt it was their business: But he did not go in for social clubs of any sort, a conviction he had silently maintained by seating himself as far away from them as possible.

The cool blue sky overhead was softened by a thin layer of wispy clouds. Wayne adjusted the red-and-white baseball cap on his head, grabbed his pole from the cup beside him, and sent the line into the lake again. Reclining back in his chair, he finished off a can of beer and then sent the can over his shoulder. He closed his eyes and burped, and as he did he relished the flavor of the brew mixed with an egg salad sandwich he ate earlier. The sounds of the birds overhead filled his unusually quiet mind.

The rumbling of a red pick-up truck suddenly ended his brief peace. It made its way up the gravel driveway and stopped near the half-dozen or so parked cars to the right of the other men. It belonged to the owner of the lake, a retired farmer around seventy years old nicknamed Smiley, for the obvious reason. Wayne only knew him because it was he who collected the money, but he had never exchanged more than a couple of sentences with him beyond the necessary pleasantries. He knew that before long he'd be coming over to collect the fishing fee.

After making sure his line was secure, Wayne walked toward the woods, kicking some pine cones as he moved along and inhaling the sweet pine sap that covered the trees' coarse trunks with a glossy sheen. When he reached a secluded spot, he squatted down amidst the thick evergreens and felt his bowels slowly begin to shift outwards. He'd be making his way home soon, he thought, and was pleased with the catch he had made. He figured he'd have Ethel grill up a few of the fish tonight. They could save the others for another meal, and wouldn't have to buy as much meat as usual. The prospect of saved money made him feel good.

Wayne knew things like that were more necessary than ever, now that Ethel was pregnant. Her confession had, of course, thrown him for a loop. But what had irritated him even more was that he finally felt that they were getting to a point where they could begin saving some money for their future, with both of them working and the two kids well into adolescence. Yet he also knew that mistakes occasionally happened. After all, that's how Ethel had become pregnant with Darlene. That accident had forced him to give up his classes at the community college and get some money together by going to work in a factory making deodorant cakes for urinals.

Fortunately, he thought, he had a steady, decent-paying, highly enjoyable vocation that he wouldn't have to give up this time because of an unexpected child. He guessed he could just about make ends meet, as long as the rest of his family helped out. They'd have to do without things that weren't completely necessary, and just spend more time in productive ways. He'd already sent the VCR back to Greenwood's, and switched the television to a smaller, more affordable model. He figured he'd be getting a pay raise before too long anyway, so at least he'd be able to keep up with the medical insurance payments. He could deal with the costs of one other baby, he supposed, but he told Ethel that after the kid's birth, they would take some one-hundred-percent reliable methods to prevent another pregnancy.

Wayne wiped his ass with some dry ferns and backhanded some flies before fastening his trousers. After returning to his chair, he slowly reeled in his line, baited the hook again, and then cast it toward the center of the small lake. Easing himself back into his chair, he unscrewed a thermos of iced tea and took a long pull. To his left, he saw Smiley making his way over, walking along the edge of his lake while wedging another chunk of tobacco into his cheek. He stopped several yards from Wayne.

"How they bitin' today, pal?"

Wayne lowered the thermos to his knee and stared straight ahead glumly. He resented Smiley calling him *pal*—he certainly was not—and he also resented Smiley's question, because he was sure that the other men had told Smiley what a good day Wayne had had. When he finally looked up at the gaunt pond owner, he saw Smiley staring down into the bucket, utterly amazed that somebody had pulled in so many.

"Pretty good," Wayne finally said while picking up a magazine, adding more forcefully, "for a change."

Smiley faked a laugh and then became more studied. "You know we got a limit here of five fish," he said, adjusting his hat.

Wayne flipped a page of the magazine and read one of the headlines. "What's that?" he asked, looking up.

Smiley spit a steam of brown juice into the lake and then gestured with his head toward the bucket. "How many you pulled in today?" he asked, smiling.

"Well, you know I didn't take any away last week," Wayne drawled.

Smiley grinned and readjusted his lump of tobacco. "Rules is rules," he drawled, shaking his head consolingly.

Suddenly Wayne's line jerked taut. He threw down the magazine and grabbed the pole, immediately knowing by its tension that he had a fairly large one at the other end, probably bigger than the others laying mouth-up in the bucket. He turned away anxiously and ignored the lake owner.

"If we didn't have no rules, there wouldn't be no fish left for anyone else," Smiley continued, just the same.

Wayne yanked on the pole and jerked the fish out of the water. Sure enough, it was the biggest he had caught that day by far. The men on the other side of the lake eyed him angrily as he pulled in another one.

"I'm sorry," Smiley went on. "But I'm gonna have to tell you to throw that one back in. You know what I said about the five fish limit here, and by the looks of it, you got more than that already. You just can't hold on to that thing."

The fish hit the ground with a slap and Wayne attempted unsuccessfully to pin it to the ground. Over his shoulder, Smiley continued whining about the stupid limit and how he was going to have to take it away. Wayne finally got ahold of the body of the fish, which squirmed maniacally in an effort to get free. He reached inside its mouth to remove the hook, but it wouldn't come.

"You already got five in the bucket," Smiley repeated himself.

Wayne continued trying to yank the hook out. He didn't want to cause undue pain to the stupid fish, but it kept twisting its head further and further onto the hook. He finally managed to get it out with a quick thrust but, in doing so, drove the hook into his own hand, its piercing stab stopped only by what looked to be the fish's mangled lower lip. He let out a grunt and finally yanked out the hook with a swift tug. As he did, he drew a deep gouge across his own palm and kicked over his bucket, spilling the rest of his catch.

"Hey! Don't hurt yourself!" Smiley blabbered.

Wayne stared at the blood seeping from his wound and suddenly grabbed the sputtering fish by its tail and pounded it against the ground as if it were a hammer. Its spine cracked and its gills collapsed, sending its entrails splattering across the dull, brown grass and leaving only the tail in his hand.

Smiley stood with his mouth open as Wayne spun around and hammered every other fish he had caught into the ground. When he had finished, his hands were sticky with scales and tainted with the crimson color of blood.

No longer smiling, Smiley stared down at the six abominations and shook his head. The other men had begun making their way over to the scene. "How 'bout the ten bucks for today?" Smiley stammered.

Wayne sneered at him and answered his question with a cold silence. Finally breaking the tension, he brushed around him, hastily folded his chair and grabbed his things before pivoting rapidly and hustling over to his car without looking back. Blood continued dripping off his hand as he jammed the key into the ignition.

So much for relaxation and a fish dinner on his day off, he thought angrily, slamming the car into gear and sending up a storm of stones toward the flabbergasted faces behind him.

10

Ethel and Wayne sat in the warm confines of their kitchen. The smell of grease and bottled gas surrounded them, adding to the room an air of comfort and security. They were alone together, for a change; Darlene was at the high school practicing with the marching band, and Junior was away on a Boy Scout camping trip. Wayne had just returned from his morning shift and was still dressed in his uniform, and Ethel wore her pink robe, whose dirty cuffs blended into the sticky wooden table they rested upon. In front of them was a plate of grilled cheese sandwiches, a bowl of macaroni salad, a bag of potato chips and a couple of cans of beer.

"How was work today anyway?" Ethel asked, biting into a sandwich.

"The same," Wayne muttered.

"I would've thought on Saturday there's not that much money to bring between the banks," she said, taking a sip of beer.

"Yeah, but everybody's out on the streets shoppin' and lots of people are around," he responded, as if the shoppers' presence annoyed him. "So you have to be on your toes constantly. All eyes."

Ethel stared out the window at the thinning branches. The cool autumn wind swirled some leaves recklessly along the ground. "I think the cold weather's beginnin' to set in for good," she said between bites.

"Yeah," Wayne muttered. "I'm gonna have to wrap some plastic around the windows next weekend. Give us a little extra insulation."

"Well I wouldn't mind you startin' with the TV room," she said. "I noticed a real draft comin' in the window there last night."

"I think the bedrooms are a little more important," Wayne said, shoving the last corner of the sandwich into his mouth. "You could do with a bit less TV anyway, so maybe I'll do that room after I finished all the others."

Ethel intentionally ignored his last comment. "Those sandwiches sure were good," she said.

"Well why don't you make us some more?" Wayne suggested, leaning back and tapping his stomach. "'Cause I'm still hungry."

"Yeah, me too," she said, running her hand across her own belly. "And I may as well use up the rest of the bread," she added with a smile while hoisting herself up. "Why don't you have some of the cole slaw. You haven't even touched it yet."

"No, I don't want any," Wayne grumbled. He gazed at a few papers scattered across the table—coupons Ethel had cut out, some old sections of the newspaper and other assorted pieces of junk mail.

"Why not?" she responded, spreading some margarine on the sides of the white bread and slicing a few pieces of Velveeta cheese to go with it.

"'Cause I tried some earlier and it tastes like the rest of the stuff in the refrigerator," he answered flatly while looking toward her wide back.

"I didn't notice that," she mumbled, dropping the sandwiches into the frying pan.

"Well that's probably 'cause you smoke too much," Wayne said, ripping several pieces of junk mail in half. "When you smoke, it kills your taste buds. You probably don't have any left anymore."

"Oh come off it," she said, turning around and grabbing a handful of potato chips.

"It's true," he said. "Anyway, you shouldn't be smokin' anymore, seein' how you're pregnant. If you don't watch it, that baby might drop out lookin' like my foot."

"Gimme a break, will you?" Ethel said, shaking her head. "I don't even smoke that much. I smoke less than a pack a day."

"Yeah, like one cigarette less," he snorted.

"Ha ha," she said sarcastically. "And anyway, for your information, I read the other day that if you're pregnant and you suddenly cut out somethin' like nicotine after your body's been used to it for years and years, that it can do the fetus more harm than if you keep up the normal levels. So there."

"I don't think a qualified doctor would say the same thing," Wayne huffed.

"Yeah, well a doctor happened to write that article," Ethel said, grabbing some more chips and returning to flip the sandwiches. "Besides, I was smokin' when I was carryin' Darlene and Junior and they sure came out all right," she added over her shoulder.

"Sure," Wayne said absently while glancing at an official looking letter written on school stationery. As he began to read it, a puzzled look crossed his face. "What's this thing here all about?" he called across the room.

"What's that?" Ethel mumbled through a slice of Velveeta she had snuck into her mouth.

"This thing about a school trip."

"Junior brought that home the other day," she responded, turning up the heat slightly and coming over to take a closer look. "His teacher is arrangin' some sort of trip up to Fairmont to visit the place where James Dean grew up. It's a permission slip and we're supposed to sign it and have Junior take it back to his teacher."

"But what's this thing down here at the bottom about money?" he said frowning.

"That's supposed to pay for rentin' the bus they're takin' up there, 'cause I think it's about a hundred miles away." She stared over his shoulder and squinted toward the sheet. "What does it say, ten bucks or somethin'?"

"Yeah, that's what it says," he responded, shaking his head. "And I'm not gonna sign it." He crumbled up the paper and threw it toward the garbage bin, and then cracked his knuckles in front of him.

"Oh for Christ's sake!" Ethel said, putting her hands on her hips. "It's only ten bucks!"

"The money doesn't have anything to do with it," Wayne voiced coolly while reaching for an old section of newspaper. "I've got other reasons why I don't approve of that trip. And you better get those sandwiches," he said looking up. "They smell like they're burnin'."

Ethel quickly turned around and saw the smoke rising from the pan. "Shit!" she hollered.

"You can give me the one that's the least burned," Wayne muttered, moving his gaze toward the comics.

"Don't worry about it, Wayne," she said as she grabbed a knife and scraped off the burned parts. "I was gonna do that anyway." She threw the frying pan into the sink and ran some water over it, blasting a cloud of warm steam into the air with a loud sizzle.

"Should I call the fire department?" Wayne added sarcastically.

"Put a lid on it Wayne!" Ethel retorted with an annoyed look on her face. "I just wanna know what you have against Junior makin' that trip," she added while placing the sandwiches on the table. "The guy's about the only famous person that ever came from this state."

"What are you talkin' about Ethel?" Wayne hissed as if she were stupid. "There are lots of famous people from Indiana. "Benjamin Harrison was from Indiana and he was a president of the United States. And Abraham

Lincoln lived here when he was around Junior's age. Even Dan Quayle is from Indiana for God's sake. They should go on a school trip to see their houses instead.''

"All right Wayne," Ethel said, nodding her head and holding up her hand. "So maybe they were from Indiana. How am I supposed to know? But don't change the subject. What in the world do you have against Junior goin' up to Fairmont?"

"Lots of things," Wayne replied without looking at her.

"I wouldn't mind goin' up there myself," she said. "We've never even been up there."

"And we're never gonna go," Wayne replied flatly.

"But James Dean is an American hero for God's sake," Ethel said, annoyed with his obstinacy.

Wayne dropped the paper suddenly and stared at her in disbelief. "James Dean was *not* an American hero," he snarled defiantly.

"What do you mean?" she said, biting into her sandwich. "Who doesn't know who James Dean is? The guy was the original 'rebel without a cause'."

"Exactly," Wayne said as if she had just proved his point. "The rebel *without* a cause. The guy was so screwed up himself that he didn't even know what he was rebellin' against. He was just a crazy, mixed up kid who tried turnin' everybody against their parents. He was a little punk, that's all, who preached rebellion. But before he could answer for any of his stupidities, he drove his car into a tree and killed himself and never lived up to his pose. Do you call somebody like that an 'American hero'?"

"You make the guy sound like he was a politician," Ethel said, reaching for some cole slaw with her fork. "He was a movie star, just like John Wayne for Pete's sake."

"Wait a minute!" Wayne said, putting his sandwich down on his plate and pointing his finger at her. "Don't go comparin' that little brat with John Wayne! The Duke commanded respect and was somebody to be looked up to. John Wayne was an adult who was in control at all times, and gave people some valuable guidance. He proved himself over decades and played a lot of roles in hundreds of movies. You never saw him yellin' at his mother or pushin' his father against a wall like that other brat. He had a sense of dignity about him."

"Well James Dean was a lot better lookin' than John Wayne," Ethel said dreamily, washing her sandwich down with some beer.

Wayne sighed and then addressed her seriously. "Ethel, why do

61

you say such stupid things sometimes?''

''Well he was!'' she retaliated, confident of her own judgment.

''Then that's exactly one of the problems,'' Wayne countered, staring at her and shaking his head. ''Just because the guy is good lookin'—which I would disagree with anyway—you think he's worth somethin'. The guy was nothin'. He was a confused little juvenile delinquent who understandably died young. That's the only thing that should be remembered about him. He's like that other guy that all the teenagers look up to, that singer Tim Morrison or whatever his name is, you know, the guy they had that TV special about the other night. He was the same, except he was a despicable drug addict as well who happened to make a lot of bad music. Subversives are what they both were. And personally, I don't approve of my son being conned by all that shit.''

''Well the teacher seems to think that it's worthwhile for the class to visit his town,'' she said, forcing the last corner of her sandwich into her already full mouth.

''Well I don't!'' he said, raising his voice. ''What I do approve of is what he's doin' this weekend off in the woods with the Boy Scouts. Out there he's learnin' to survive, not complain. He's learnin' how to discipline himself and work with other people around him, not how to buck the system. It's just like the army. You respect the other guys who are ranked above you and instruct the ones below you. Moody, unadjusted characters get straightened out—and in a hurry, believe me. Things like that are a good example for the boy and a hell of a lot more healthy than treatin' some outcast as a hero. Can't you understand that?''

''Well how's he gonna feel when he's the only one not goin' on the trip?'' Ethel muttered, forcing some more potato chips into her mouth.

''To be honest, I don't care,'' Wayne said. ''But I'm sure there are some other clear-thinkin' parents like myself who proba'ly think the same way as me. And if there aren't, I guess that I'll just have to set the example.''

''Well why don't you just think about it a little bit more?'' she said with a hint of optimism while lighting a cigarette. ''Maybe you'll see things differently.''

''Ethel!'' Wayne said, pushing his plate away from himself and grabbing the paper again. ''Why don't you just think about it a little bit less. Like never again!''

Annoyed, Ethel grabbed the plates from the table and carried them over to the counter. Her husband could sure be an asshole sometimes, she thought.

11

In the television room, Darlene blew hard into her saxophone, which hung chained around her neck. It shook with an off-key wail that wavered slightly as her short, stubby fingers slowly attempted to stretch toward the keys, rarely hitting the right notes.

"What the hell is that noise?" Wayne asked his wife, entering the house and laying a basket full of raspberries on the kitchen counter.

"Darlene practicin' her saxophone," Ethel said, putting a few blocks of wax into a double boiler fashioned with two pots.

"It sounds like an elephant fartin'," he said with a scowl on his face.

"I know," Ethel said, shaking her head. "But she's got to practice if she's gonna get better."

Darlene started to wail again, then stopped abruptly and emptied saliva from the mouthpiece onto the carpeted floor. Adjusting her glasses, she examined the music propped up on the mantelpiece more closely. She thought she spotted what was causing the problem, and blew into the horn again.

"Good God almighty!" Wayne blurted, grabbing the basket and heading for the door again. "If I were you I'd get a pair of damn earplugs. I don't know how you can take that."

"Lower your voice!" Ethel demanded. "She'll hear you for God's sake!"

"Don't worry!" he yelled over his shoulder going back out to the yard. "She ain't gonna hear me above that racket!"

Darlene was practicing her part for the high school marching band, which would be putting on a halftime show during the football game the following weekend. When she practiced with the rest of the group, it always sounded as if her parts were correct. But when she was by herself, she just couldn't duplicate the way she knew it was supposed to sound. Rubbing the narrow, chapped lips of her small mouth onto the reed, she took a deep breath and emptied her lungs through the winding brass tubes once more.

Ethel cringed as the screech assaulted her body. For the past couple of hours, she had been working hard in the kitchen, boiling and jarring raspberries and then pouring a layer of wax on top of them to preserve them for the upcoming months. She enjoyed preserving the raspberries; as the fruit of Wayne's garden had encircled her with its sweet, candied aroma, she rewarded herself for her labors with a large spoonful of the gooey jam with every jar she filled. She had lost herself in sweet-tooth heaven, but now, after filling a few dozen jars, the luscious pap was weighing heavily on her expanding stomach, playing uncomfortable games with her digestive tract.

Darlene's racket vibrated her body with another outburst. Turning the heat off under the double boiler, she reckoned she'd finish the job later after taking a short rest and letting her stomach recuperate. She walked into the TV room and saw her daughter's back expanding with oxygen for another go at the notes.

"Darlene!" she yelled, catching her before she let it go.

Her daughter turned around suddenly. "Yeah," she responded through shortened breath.

"Do you think you could go practice that in your room for a while with the door closed and give me some time to relax a little?"

"I'm sorry," Darlene said innocently. "I didn't know the noise was botherin' you."

Ethel plopped herself on the couch. "No, it's not that at all," she said, rubbing a hand across her stomach. "It's just that Momma's not feelin' too good. I think it's proba'ly the baby affectin' my system."

Darlene had a puzzled look on her face. "What's it feel like when your pregnant?" she asked.

"Oh, it's all right after a while," Ethel said, reaching for a cigarette. "But the first half is pretty wearin'. You feel nauseous a lot of the time, and it just takes a long time to get used to it. You've seen how I got to lay down a lot, 'cause if I don't, it's just a bit too much to bear."

Darlene seemed scared by the idea. "Can you feel it movin' around inside you and all?"

"Sometimes," Ethel said, lighting up. "But not too much right now. But when it starts kickin' some, I'll let you know and you can feel it. You didn't kick all that much, but when your brother started in, it was like he was tryin' to kick a football or somethin'."

Darlene grimaced. "Sounds awful painful," she mumbled.

"Oh, a little bit," Ethel said, adjusting herself slightly. "But it's more discomfort than anythin' else. And believe me, the reward in the end makes it all worthwhile. You'll see yourself some day."

"Well I hope so, I guess," she muttered uncertainly.

"No problem," Ethel added while exhaling.

Darlene paused. "Do you know if it's gonna be a boy or a girl?" she asked.

Ethel stared toward the end of her cigarette. Other people had asked her the same question, but she was completely unsure of the answer herself. Fact was, Ethel had stopped seeing Dr. Timson after three months of pregnancy because he kept hounding her about smoking and drinking, saying that it might affect the fetus—which she knew was absolute hogwash. After all, she smoked some and drank occassionally while pregnant with Darlene and Junior. They came out fine. So as far as she was concerned, the doctor could save his hot air, and she could save on some medical bills.

"I'm not sure, darlin'," Ethel said, moving the cigarette toward her mouth. "I prefer to let nature decide that."

Darlene nodded, then looked down at her saxophone with contempt. "Well I've just about had it with this baby," she said unhappily while unhooking its cord from her neck. "I just can't get it to sound the way it should."

"It sounded all right from the kitchen," Ethel lied. "I just don't know why you kept stoppin' all the time."

"Last week the band director told me that I had to play the rhythm instead of the melody," she said dejectedly. "And I can't do it 'cause I just can't hear the song correctly in my head."

"Well keep it up, honey," Ethel encouraged. "The rhythm's even more important than the melody sometimes. And harder. He proba'ly said that 'cause he sees your potential. You'll get it, don't worry."

"Yeah, I guess so," she said, taking apart the instrument and packing it in its case.

"Can you turn on the TV when you're finished with that sweetheart?" Ethel asked, stretching out on the sofa and lighting another cigarette. "I can hardly move. I think I'm just gonna lay here until I start to feel better."

Darlene flipped on the set and then carried the case into her room. Against one wall was a single bed covered with a pink comforter and assorted pillows and dolls. There was a small desk in one corner with a few school books and supplies on top of it, and some shelves her father had put up in another corner for her clothes. Beneath her were assorted rectangles of differing shag carpets that had been pieced together from remnants at a carpet store, covering most of the room but leaving the area under her bed

65

and desk bare. The lime green curtains over the bed were pulled back, illuminating the room with a dull light that made the white-paneled walls appear gray.

Looking out the window, she saw her father out in the garden cutting some vegetables from their stalks and placing them in a basket. Next to him, their dog Ivy was sitting on the ground, twisting her body and biting into her skin in an attempt to dislodge her fleas. Behind them, her brother was throwing a ball high up into the overcast sky, then running under its descending arc and attempting to catch it. At one point the ball landed right next to the vegetable basket and she saw her father turn angrily and yell something at Junior, before violently motioning to him to move further away from the garden.

She sat down at her desk and opened her English notebook, glancing over her notes from the past couple of weeks. The class had begun studying poetry, which until now she had always liked. She thought a poem was just like a story, but with rhyming words on each line—and fewer of them—just like a nursery story or the inside of a Christmas card.

But the poems Mr. Truman, her teacher, had recently read in class were like nothing she had ever heard before. The sentences didn't seem to relate to each other and there weren't even the same amount of words on each line. To make it all harder, Mr. Truman began talking about a bunch of weird things, like meters, and verse, and symbolism—things she just couldn't seem to grasp.

Staring down at a photocopy of a poem he had given her class, she scanned its contents, mouthing the words slowly. But when she had finished, it was as if she had just read something in a foreign language. She understood all the words—that wasn't the problem—but she just couldn't grasp the connection between them.

Earlier in the week, Mr. Truman gave an assignment to the class in which the students were supposed to write a short poem using some of these new ideas. He suggested that they write something about nature, and during her study hall earlier in the day she wrote something quickly that she planned to work on more at home that evening since it was due the following day. She found the page in the notebook and silently read her scribbled print.

''A flower starts as a sead
and each day grows slowly in the dirt
it moves up towards the sky
geting taller and taller
until nature tells it ''Stop!'

then it opens and is lots of colors
Pretty, oh so pretty
And everybody looks
and calls it Beautaful
We are happy
until someone cuts it
Or steps on it
or forgets to Water it
and then the petals fall off
the color fades away
And it dies''

She stared at the walls around her and wondered if there was anything she could add or change. But before she got very involved with her thoughts, she picked up the girl's magazine on the side of her desk and began leafing through it. It included lots of photo narratives of girls her own age and the problems they faced, all of which she had read earlier in the week. Turning the pages, she came to the advice section and concentrated on a letter from a girl seeking a solution to her acne problem.

The letter interested Darlene because she too was plagued by poor skin blotched with pimples. Every night before going to bed, she'd stare in the mirror and squeeze her blackheads, watching the thin tails of oil pinwheel out of her pores. But it seemed the more blackheads she managed to get rid of, the more whiteheads would begin appearing the next day. She had tried Clearasil and Oxy-5 and a number of other products on the market, but all they had done was either dry out her skin until it cracked, or left it looking as if she had smeared grease all over her face.

The magazine's skin specialist suggested a mixture of milk, lemon and vinegar smeared onto the face before bedtime. Writing the ingredients on a separate piece of paper, Darlene decided to give the recipe a try later that night.

She put the magazine away and temporarily forgot about the poem, picking up another textbook instead. She turned to the chapter she was supposed to read for her social studies class. She looked at the pictures of early Indian dwellings and the outfits the Indians wore, and was pleased to see that the chapter was fairly short. She counted the pages and then closed the book, figuring she could read them while she was watching television later on.

Her only assignment left was algebra. It was her least favorite class because there were all those numbers and formulas, the x's and y's—strange stuff that, frankly, perplexed her. It was like the symbolism in the poetry, difficult to understand because there were unknown elements to deal with. She grabbed a pencil, opened another notebook, and tried to work a few problems. The first couple were easy, but as she went on, her inability to find answers grew with nearly every problem.

She partially got around that problem by copying several solutions of the assigned questions from the answer key in the back of the book. But she knew she wouldn't have the work to back it up, however, and all she could hope was that the teacher would call on her to answer one of the simple questions. Or maybe she could ask one of her friends for the answers the next day. One thing for sure, she thought, was that she was wasting her time trying to solve those other problems on her own because they were just impossible. She folded the sheet of paper and tucked it into the book, saying, ''I hate math,'' out loud before tossing it on the floor.

Growing weary of her homework, she read her poem again and figured it was good enough. She grabbed another sheet of paper and, this time using a pen, copied it onto the fresh page. When she had finished, she thought for a moment and then wrote ''A Flowers Life'' at the top of the sheet and neatly printed her name at the bottom.

She placed the paper into her notebook and then returned to more interesting things—namely, her magazine. Flipping through the familiar pages, she finally landed on a number of drawings that displayed various kissing techniques. It was a subject that Darlene often wondered about. She had never had the opportunity to practice with a boy or man beyond a quick peck on her father's cheek on special occasions. It wasn't that she wasn't interested in boys her own age; they just didn't seem to be interested in her.

Figuring she could pick up a few tips that might prove beneficial when she was finally asked out on a date, she took a small mirror off the wall and held it in front of her. While consulting the diagrams, she attempted to form her lips into a suggested position, puckering her mouth until it was about the size of a large button. After moving her lips toward the mirror until they finally touched the cold surface, she gently eased her tongue in the direction of its reflection and moved it sloppily over its countless dried pimple stains.

Darlene pulled her head back and slowly opened her eyes, finding herself staring at her own plump face, barely contained within the mirror's dimensions. She smiled hesitantly at her image, and then checked another drawing before moving her lips close to the moist surface again.

It was the type of homework that was really necessary, she felt.

12

A gentle wind drifted across the land surrounding the Turner residence, bringing with it small clouds of powdered snow from the evergreen trees scattered around the yard. The first snowfall of the year had come earlier than people had expected and had lasted for four or five hours, finally stopping just after the sun had gone down and covering the ground to a height about an inch or so above the ankle. The clouds had moved away and a full moon now illuminated the snow across the bare branches of the larger trees, defining their crooked expanses with a velvety richness.

At the top of the driveway next to the house, Wayne leaned over the hood of his 1978 Plymouth Fury. He had turned on the engine a quarter of an hour earlier and, while the V-8 warmed up, had swept all the snow off the car's surface with a soft-bristled brush. Now he was removing any visible traces of moisture with a clean, white rag. It glided over the black surface effortlessly, as if the hood contained a charged field like a Ouija board, sliding one way and then the next and gradually spelling out a word. As he stepped back to admire the car under a spotlight attached to the side of his house, he imagined that if a word had in fact been spelled out, that word would have been R-E-S-P-E-C-T.

He bought the car the year before around the time when Ethel had begun working. She needed some transportation of her own, and he was tired of driving around in a small economy car. After all, since he wore a uniform and a badge, he wanted to get a car more appropriate to his occupation. And when he had first laid eyes upon the Fury at a used car lot, he immediately felt it was the vehicle that a man of his stature was entitled to. Hell, it looked just like a police cruiser.

He got a good deal on it because of its age, its size, and its high mileage. In fact, he was even been able to knock a couple hundred dollars off the figure soaped on the windshield when he offered to pay in cash. Its body was in nearly perfect condition, but he soon found out that it only got ten miles to the gallon and ran on parts that left something to be desired. He replaced what he could himself by buying used parts at a junkyard, and the more expensive faults he simply let ride. So now when he cruised up the road, the car made a lot of noise, but it didn't bother him all that much. He reckoned it sounded more powerful that way.

From the trunk, a huge antenna soared upwards. It provided better reception for his police scanner so that when he was driving, he could keep abreast of police events in the area. If there was a call in the vicinity where he happened to be, sometimes he'd shoot off and reach the scene of the crime before any of the county men even arrived. Of course, once he was there he couldn't do anything except watch, but the excitement of making the drive to a potential emergency sight at full speed thrilled him nonetheless.

Tonight, however, Wayne was planning to take advantage of the snow by training in another manner, this time while moving inside the vehicle. He planned to drive to the high school fifteen miles away and use its parking lot, which would be empty and well lit, to practice high speed skidding and accelerating during severe weather conditions. A couple of months earlier he had gone up to the same school during a thunderstorm and dug up one of its fields with his spinning tires, performing donut after donut as the grass of the disintegrating football field spit back behind him. But snow was something different, he knew, and as he pressed his sole into the ground beneath him and felt it slip over the gravel, he knew he'd also have to deal with a thin but potentially treacherous layer of ice already beginning to form.

His breath emerged from his mouth in short, regular bursts, disappearing almost immediately into the cold night air. Opening the door of the car and placing the rag underneath the black leather seat, a comfortable wave of warmth poured full-blast from the heater and struck him in the face. He unzipped the dark blue, thermal-lined, regulation police jacket he had picked up at a surplus store and dusted off the snow particles from its smooth plastic-knit surface. Then he slipped behind the wheel and closed the door behind him with a solid thud.

While he drove, he listened to the police scanner to monitor what was happening in the area. But after listening to several minutes of broadcasts requesting assistance for minor accidents, he turned the volume down until it was barely audible. In a way, he was relieved that he wasn't a county policeman—most of their working days were consumed by trivial occurrences like these. At least in his line of work, he told himself, he was in the firing line all day long. That way he never had to deal with the time-consuming negligence of everyday citizens, who more often than not made them serve rather than protect.

The car passed over some railroad tracks, and before long he viewed the high school on his right, its building completely darkened. It was a large, white-brick structure that now appeared gray against the snow surrounding it. It was, for the most part, only one story high, but it covered a substantial amount of territory, so that from afar it almost looked like a modern factory.

He drove slowly past, then turned into an entrance that led to a large parking lot, sandwiched between the auditorium and some classrooms. In the distance, he saw one of the county's technical schools that housed various workshops for the students who wanted to learn trades. When Wayne had bought his car, he had brought it to the mechanic's school, where they had done some work on the engine. They only charged for parts; labor was free, because the students who worked on the cars were learning the trade and therefore did the work to further their education. Wayne wasn't sure if they could be relied upon for major work, but they couldn't really screw up simple things like removing dents or minor maintenance. It was another way he'd learned to beat bills.

As he had hoped, the parking lot was empty except for a couple of pick-up trucks bearing the school district emblem on their sides, which were parked near the custodial area. The overhead lights illuminated the huge expanse of blacktop, which was filled during the week with the cars of students and teachers. But now, except for a few sets of tire tracks partially covered by the more recent snow, it was difficult to decipher where the tar ended and the grass fields began.

Leaving the headlights on, Wayne got out of the car and opened the trunk, taking out a number of cracked traffic cones he had found at the dump one day. He walked into the stream of light in front of him and placed the cones down in a straight line at regular intervals. He walked back to the car, slipped behind the wheel and pulled out slowly. Then he stopped at the far end of the lot, like a plane on the runway awaiting clearance for take off.

For the next hour and a half, Wayne ceaselessly shifted the automatic transmission between first and second, running a slalom course between the cones and then making a one-hundred-and-eighty-degree turn at full speed before running the course again. He occasionally readjusted the cones so that there was a fresh layer of ice in his path, or he accelerated into another part of the lot and practiced three-hundred-and-sixty-degree turns with both small and wide angles.

Alternatively, he raced the car toward a corner of the lot at full speed before slamming on the brakes, while attempting to skid in a straight line. When the car finally came to a halt, he'd throw open the door and, using it

71

to shield his body, assume a crouched "ready" position. Then he'd extend his gun toward some unknown object in the distance and pretend he was about to end the desperate life of some mad-dog criminal trying to make off with a bankroll.

When he finally decided that he'd had enough, Wayne collected the cones and returned them to the trunk. He wiped down the car with a rag, removing the slush that had stuck to its body. Even though the temperature outside hung just below the freezing point, the hood of the car was almost too hot to touch, and the heat rising out of the grating at the front was clearly visible, carrying in its waves the smell of burning metal. That didn't bother Wayne too much because he knew that V-8s were built to take such demanding punishment.

What bothered him more was when he saw that the gas meter inside the car was hovering near the "E" mark—just the day before, on the way home from work, he had put ten bucks in the tank. Fortunately, he thought, his snow training wasn't a weekly practice and, slamming the vehicle into drive, he cruised back to the main road and left his training ground. Behind him, the lot looked like it had been cleared by a snowplow.

Figuring that he'd get more fuel before returning home, he took another road that led to Westport, where he knew there would be a convenience store open that sold gas. A couple of miles along, he saw someone standing on the side of the road with a thumb extended. He didn't slow down—he normally refused to pick up hitchhikers—but as he passed by, he realized it was a girl. Taking his foot off the accelerator and applying pressure to the brake, he brought the car to a sudden halt on the shoulder. Looking in his rearview mirror, he saw the girl, bathed in the red illumination cast by the taillights, running toward the car.

She got in the car, slammed the door, and then looked over at the driver. "Hi," she said, slightly out of breath. "You goin' as far as Westport?"

"Yeah," Wayne replied, nodding his head and observing her. She was young, he figured about sixteen, although she looked older because of all the make-up she was wearing. She had long, dark hair partially covered by a yellow ski cap, and she was wearing a faded pair of tight jeans and a dark blue down jacket. A plaid scarf was wrapped around her neck. Even though she had only been in the car a few seconds, he could smell alcohol on her breath. He pulled the car back onto the road and they drove silently for a couple of miles.

When he was younger, he occasionally hitched rides when no other form of transportation was available to him. Back then, though, one could afford to trust other people and get in a stranger's car without thinking twice about it. Nowadays, however, he realized you couldn't even pick up a newspaper without reading about the disappearance of some young person who had been a little too naive.

He knew that it wasn't only the psychopaths behind the wheel who were now dangerous, but also the people who solicited rides as well. They were often thieves, rapists, queers, or escapees from a correctional facility. For this reason, Wayne normally didn't stop for people; in fact, he became frustrated when he saw other people stopping. He felt this only encouraged trouble on one side or the other.

It wasn't compassion that had compelled him to stop for the girl. He had stopped more out of anger, because he knew that she was, in the mind of a serial killer, like a huge neon sign blinking ''VICTIM.'' He had decided to stop only because he knew that she had put herself in grave danger, like a calf that has strayed away from its mother to find itself suddenly surrounded by wolves.

''How old are you?'' Wayne asked the girl, breaking their silence.

''Seventeen,'' she said, staring straight forward.

''Do your parents know you're hitchhikin'?'' he asked.

''I don't know,'' she responded blankly, turning toward him and trying to see his image in the dim light of the car's interior.

''Do you think they would approve if they did know?''

''Proba'ly not,'' the girl said. ''But if I want to see my friends, I don't have much of a choice.''

''Have you been over at a friend's house?''

''Yeah, right near where you picked me up,'' she said. ''But I got into a fight with my boyfriend and decided to leave without him.''

Wayne suddenly looked toward her. ''Have you been drinkin'?'' he asked.

''No,'' she said.

Wayne returned his eyes to the road and nodded his head knowingly. Not only was she a thrill-seeker—demonstrated by her hitchhiking—but she was also a liar. She obviously had been drinking alcohol which, besides being against the law, also made her more vulnerable. And with all that make-up she had on, Wayne figured, she was probably a little slut too. She'd probably let just about anyone feel her up just to spite her boyfriend. Somewhere along the line, it was obvious that her parents had failed to teach her a few important lessons.

73

Wayne glanced at her again. "Do you smoke?" he asked, suddenly becoming aware of the stale odor leaking from her down coat, an odor intensified by the heat blowing toward her.

"Once in a while," she said, staring at him suspiciously and then listening to the jargon blurting out of the scanner. She looked around the car quickly and then back to the radio before looking at the driver again. "Why are you asking me all these questions?" she asked with a puzzled look on her face. "Are you a cop or somethin'?"

"Do I look like a *police officer*?" Wayne asked.

"Yeah," she said, nodding her head.

Wayne was pleased with her response. "Well you're lucky I stopped for you," he said. "Because when you get in somebody's car that you don't know, you never know what might happen inside."

The girl looked over at him and smiled. "Yeah, but this is the country," she said, laughing a little. "It's not like we're in Indianapolis or anything. Nothin' ever happens out here."

"Well it's not like we're that far away, neither," Wayne said, becoming more serious. "Didn't you hear about that seventeen-year-old girl that disappeared a few months ago in Batesville? This is where things like that do happen. Lots of guys drive around hundreds of miles until they see someone like you, along the side of the road with their thumbs out...lookin' for it."

"Look, I'd prefer if you didn't talk about that stuff," the girl said. "It gives me the creeps."

"Well it should give you the creeps," Wayne said. "Because that kind of stuff happens all the time." He paused before continuing. "Now I carry a gun because my profession demands it. But a lot of people carry guns without being entitled to them. Now if I happened to be that type of person, what could you do about it?"

"Listen Officer," she said, annoyed with his lecture. "Maybe you just better let me out here."

Wayne smiled at her falsely. "You said I was a police officer," he said. "But then again, maybe I'm not."

"Stop the car!" the girl shouted suddenly, her collected manner slipping now into panicked uncertainty.

Wayne didn't respond, but sat quietly, thinking. Not only was the girl all the things he had thought earlier, but she was also defiant—and obviously needed to be corrected. "Just suppose I was the type of person who said 'no' to every little request you made," Wayne said, accelerating the car.

74

"What could you do about that?"

"I don't know," she said, searching for the door handle.

"You definitely couldn't do that," he said, smiling again and relocking the doors with the remote control. "Because I control the locks from over here," he added, slipping on the lock guard. "Some people even saw off the handles so that the doors are impossible to open from the inside."

"Look," she said, breathing more heavily and beginning to show signs of fear. "I was just hitch-hikin' on the side of the road because I wanted to get home. And I already asked you to stop talkin' about that stuff."

Wayne was silent for a few seconds. "Do you take dope?" he suddenly snapped.

"No!" she responded flatly.

"But you smoke cigarettes," he shot back.

"I already told you that," she answered, looking into the back seat as if suddenly expecting to find someone there.

"Do you get good grades in school?" Wayne addressed her after another pause.

"They're all right," she said, shaking her head and looking at him, perplexed. "What do you want from me anyway?"

"What do you think I want?" he questioned her further while turning toward her and smiling again.

"I don't know," she said. "I just don't want you to hurt me."

Wayne concentrated on the road briefly before turning to her again. "What would you do if I pulled out a knife right now?" he asked quickly.

"I guess I'd scream," she said, burying her face within her scarf.

"And who would hear you? Locked up inside a car in the middle of nowhere?"

"God, I guess," she muttered. "But I don't want..."

"And do you think God would stop an unstable person from rapin' you?" Wayne snickered. "And then slicin' your throat and throwin' you out all cut up and mutilated on the side of the road for the animals to eat? Because that's how it happens, you know."

"Stop the car!" the girl moaned. "Please!"

"No," he responded flatly, calmly ignoring her request. He drove on without talking for a couple of minutes, letting her continue to whimper. "What are you thinkin' of doin' after high school?" he finally asked.

The girl didn't respond.

"I just asked you a question," Wayne said, raising his voice. "Answer!"

"I want to get married," she finally whimpered.

"Married?" Wayne asked, as if not understanding.

She suddenly pointed to a house on the side of the road. "That's where I live!" she yelled enthusiastically. "Stop the car! Stop the car!"

Wayne responded to her request by stepping on the gas. "We're not even in Westport yet," he said, shaking his head and laughing. "I thought you told me you were goin' to Westport."

The girl didn't respond verbally, but began crying more, her sobs relayed intermittently between incoherent words that Wayne recognized as being those of a prayer. He drove on in silence, letting the girl think a little bit.

When the car finally entered Westport, he asked her calmly where she wanted him to drop her off. Her tear-filled face stared at him with a confused expression, and then a sense of life re-entered her gaze. She appeared relieved, as if her prayers had been answered. "Right up there at the light!" she blurted thankfully.

"If you want," Wayne said in a fatherly tone, "I can drive you right to your house."

"No, right here is fine!" she responded quickly, wiping the moisture from her face.

He stopped the Fury and hit the unlock switch, but as he prepared a final moralistic statement for the girl, she thrust her body outside and made a frantic dash from the car. Wayne waved to her, but could see in the rearview mirror that she was running as fast as she could in the snow covered distance.

Wayne smiled and nodded his head contentedly, pleased with his evening's work. He figured that, in the future, the girl would never be hitchhiking again. And, because of that, he may have just helped save her life.

13

As her husband searched for space for the car in the jammed shopping center parking lot, Ethel Turner stood near the sliding doors of the Wal-Mart. A gentle wave of warm air from within blew through the doors and toward her every time they opened. Looking at the blinking trees and gold-and-silver garland draped across the storefront, she thought that she was finally beginning to feel the Christmas spirit. It had been a long time coming, as her thoughts normally turned toward the Yuletide around the beginning of December. But because the child had been growing inside her—making her look larger in the mirror each day—and because she had continued to work at McDonalds, she just hadn't had the time to realize that the holiday season was already upon her.

She watched the snow fall gently past the glare of the spotlights illuminating the outside of the store, and listened to a group of kids at the other end of the shopping center singing Christmas carols, their high voices in the distance filling the area with good-spirited warmth. Between the children and her, a man from the Salvation Army stood outside the drug store and rang a bell, unobtrusively appealing to the good will of others.

Their presence and the multitudes of excited children with radiant expressions reminded her how much she loved this time of the year. The familiar songs, the lights blinking in brilliant colors against the white snow on the ground, and the anticipation of a family celebration normally put everyone in a good mood—and brought unaccustomed smiles to the faces of people who rarely displayed any sort of happiness.

It had always been a special time of the year for Ethel. When she was a girl, her father used to put up lights all around the outside of the house, while her mother took care of the inside, spraying artificial snow on the windows and putting candles in the windows. They always had a big Christmas tree covered in shiny tinsel, which gave the whole house the sweet scent of pine. She'd spend hours with her sister staring at the different-shaped bulbs on the tree and seeing their reflections in various colors, and revel in the secrecy and surprise of all the brightly wrapped boxes laying at the base of the tree. Night after night, they would try to guess what they contained.

When she became a mother herself, she tried to pass on some of the magic she had experienced as a kid to her own children by decorating the house and encouraging them to revel in its mystery. She covered the lawn with a blinking Frosty the Snowman and Santa with his sled and reindeer. She decorated the tree, and spent long hours in the kitchen making Christmas cookies and cakes. She played Christmas songs on the record player, told the kids stories, and watched the specials on TV with them every year. She drove around town with them at night to look at the ways other people had decorated their homes, and always took the children to the house where an old man sat in front dressed as Santa Claus and gave each child who visited a piece of candy.

When they moved to Indiana, however, all those lovely Christmas trappings became a thing of the past. Whereas they had always lived on streets where the houses were fairly close together and where people took pride in decorating them for the holiday season, the isolated trailer they now lived in was not even visible from the road. For the first Christmas in the mobile home, Wayne hadn't even taken the outdoor lights out of the box. He claimed that stringing them up outside the house and illuminating them would just be a waste of time and money, since nobody except they themselves could see them. And since they were inside, they couldn't enjoy them anyway.

He added that since the kids were now older and well aware that Santa Claus was, in fact, Wayne, they didn't have to make such a big deal out of the day like they had in times past. So instead of buying a natural tree, he bought an artificial one, telling her that it was a hell of a lot more practical and economical than searching for an overpriced real one every year. After all, he reasoned, they'd end up just throwing it into the backyard after its needles had all fallen onto the floor of the house.

She knew that some of what he said was true. But, even so, all of the magic that had once surrounded these days now seemed to blow away as quickly as the dust she removed from the plastic branches of the tree before assembling it every year.

As compensation for having to part with the traditions she had loved, Ethel simply became busier in the kitchen. She scanned recipe books for special holiday sweets and baked nearly every one she found. She found that she was eating her yield almost constantly as well, although she figured most of her additional weight was on behalf of the child growing inside her. Wayne could perhaps deny her some treats at Christmas, but damned if it was going to be the frosted cookies and cakes.

The kids at the other end of the shopping center were singing another song and the Salvation Army Santa continued to ring his bell. Ethel stared into the vastness of the snow-covered parking lot and saw her husband approaching in the distance. He walked briskly, with the collar of his jacket pulled up high to help protect his ears from the wind.

"Isn't it nice here?" Ethel beamed when he reached her.

"I'd say it's freezin'," Wayne responded bluntly, rubbing his hands together. "I had to park in the shoppin' center next door."

Ethel hooked her arm under his and directed him toward the choral group. "You wanna hear those kids down there sing a song?" she asked, smiling.

"No," he answered coldly, pulling her toward the warmth beyond the doors. "Let's just get this over with."

Once inside the Wal-Mart, the couple grabbed a shopping cart and slowly began moving up and down the aisles. Above the noise of the hundreds of shoppers, a Christmas tape played loudly over the intercom. Wayne looked at the Santa pictures pasted on every wall, the reindeer cutouts, and the models of little elves, and was reminded of all the reasons he hated the holiday season. It was all a big con, he felt, whose original purpose had been transformed into a giant commercial. Sale signs convinced shoppers to deplete their small savings on useless items—"gifts"—that he knew the recipients would soon outgrow or grow weary of.

He couldn't help thinking that nowadays the thought behind gifts didn't seem to matter as much as the number and expense of presents that people could impress each other with. It simply came down to money, he felt. Gone were the days when you could give a doll or a ball to a kid and be sure he would be entertained for weeks, even years, and be thankful for it. Now it was electronic this, computer that, with prices that soared to three digits and more. And kids didn't only ask for a couple of things. They made out huge lists of demands which they expected to be fulfilled! The whole holiday purpose was getting completely out of control.

As Wayne hunched over the shopping cart and trailed several yards behind his wife, he looked at the other shoppers struggling behind their overflowing buggies and shook his head. He had decided to go Christmas shopping with Ethel for one reason, and that was to prevent her from becoming one of them. He knew if she had gone alone he would have no way of keeping tabs of the money she spent or the presents she bought. He certainly didn't like being surrounded in the store by such unpleasant company, but knowing his wife's impulsiveness, he felt he had no choice.

Turning into the next aisle, he caught Ethel observing a display stacked on the floor. She picked up a box, read the information on it, and then looked at the price. "Hey Wayne," she called to him. "How about this for Darlene?"

"What is it?" he grumbled flatly.

"A hair dryer," she answered. "She told me that she wants one."

"Doesn't she already have one?" Wayne asked, cocking his head.

"Yeah," Ethel responded. "But every time she turns it on, she says it smells of burnin'."

"How much is it?" Wayne asked, pushing the cart closer.

Ethel looked back at the price. "$29.99," she said. "It's on sale."

Wayne hesitated, trying to thumb-scrape something out of his nostril. "You sure we can't get the other one fixed?" he finally drawled while working a piece of mucus between his fingers.

"Oh, come on Wayne. It'll cost more than that to fix it."

A frown crossed Wayne's face as he weighed the price in his head, but he finally motioned to the basket. "Well, I guess it's all right," he said. "Put it in."

As they proceeded up the next aisle, a message blared over the intercom announcing additional sales the store was offering. Wayne found the noise irritating and moved the cart faster.

"C'mon!" he said over his shoulder to his lulling wife behind him. "Lets hurry up and get the hell out of here. What else do you want?"

She stopped and took out a list from her pocketbook. "Let's see," she began. "Junior wants another video game that he can plug into the TV, and Darlene said she wanted a sweater. I also want to get Junior a new shirt for school, and a skirt for Darlene. And I wouldn't mind lookin' at..."

"Don't you think we could have gone to the Goodwill store to get the clothes?" Wayne interrupted her while moving forward. "They would have been a lot cheaper and just as good, maybe better. And in the winter, you can probably get shorts and other summer stuff for almost nothin' "

"It's Christmas, for God's sake!" Ethel whined, hurrying to catch up with him. "I get the kids their stuff at Goodwill during the year, but I would like to get them somethin' new to put under the tree. Is that such a big deal?"

"Well let's go to the clothes section then," Wayne yelled hastily, continuing to push forward, "and quit wastin' our time lookin' at all this other junk."

He increased his pace, weaving between the other carts and smashing into a couple that were unoccupied in order to get them out of his way. He didn't bother stopping to pick up the items he knocked off shelves in his haste.

When he finally reached the clothes racks, he turned around, but found Ethel nowhere in sight. He stood impatiently for a couple of minutes until she finally appeared carrying another box.

"Where the hell have you been?" he asked her, tapping his fingers impatiently on the cart handle against the rhythm of the jingle coming over the speaker.

"I saw a make-up kit along the way that I thought might make a good present," she said, pointing to the box in the cart. "It was really marked down, like twenty percent off."

"Is it for you?" Wayne asked.

"No, it's not," she responded, beginning to look at some of the clothes. "It's somethin' else for Darlene."

"Listen Ethel!" Wayne said, grabbing her by the arm. "The hair dryer for Darlene is all right 'cause I don't want the girl catchin' a cold by goin' to school with wet hair in the mornin'. But why in the world do you want to give her make-up? She's only sixteen, for God's sake. Don't you realize that a sixteen-year-old girl shouldn't be messin' with stuff like that?"

"What are you talkin' about?" Ethel said, astonished. "All the girls nowadays wear it."

"Well Darlene is not one of the other girls!" Wayne corrected. "She is our daughter. And I will not allow my daughter to do things like that 'til she's out of high school. So you're just gonna have to save that one for another year."

Ethel felt her blood pressure begin to mount. "Well she told me that's what she wanted!" she shouted.

"Look!" Wayne said pointing his finger toward her. "Since when do kids get everything they want for Christmas? You should have a bit more sense yourself!"

"Put it back in the basket Wayne!" Ethel hollered.

"Ethel, don't make me get mad in the store!" he yelled back louder. "Because if you want a scene, you'll sure as hell get one!"

Ethel huffed and noticed several customers had begun gawking at them. Trying to regain her calm, she looked back at her husband scornfully. "Let's look at clothes Wayne," she muttered through clenched teeth. "And we'll see about the other thing later."

81

"No, I've got a better idea," he snapped quickly. "You look at the clothes and pick them out, and I'll put this back on the shelf and find somethin' for Junior. All right?"

"All right!" she said hastily, moving out of the way of one customer and crashing into another. "But why the hell do you make such a big deal about a little make-up?"

Wayne marched away from her without responding. He just didn't understand why a girl Darlene's age should be painting her face like a little slut. Because that's what a lot of girls looked like nowadays, he thought. He saw them all the time walking around the town after school. They just asked for it, like that hitchhiker he'd picked up the month before.

"First comes make-up, then comes sex, and then comes problems in the baby carriage," he muttered to himself while breezing past the other customers in search of the cosmetics section. He grew impatient when he couldn't find it, however, so he tossed the box into a display for power tools and then walked over to the video game section.

It was in a corner of the store next to the toy section. The game display was laid out so that customers could play several of the games themselves on a number of television monitors. He had a hard time seeing the different games on the screens because the kids who had come with their parents were eagerly hunched in front of them, working the game controls and making it difficult for anyone else to get a glance.

The ones he could see all seemed to be of the futuristic genre, with space aliens trying to invade a planet, or some weird-looking creatures performing kung fu while attempting to escape from a lost temple or something. They all seemed like a bunch of junk to him. He saw nothing that might help to educate the boy as he was playing, the way he felt all children's games should. Staring down at some of the prices, he grimaced and shook his head, appalled that little disks of plastic should cost so much.

Prepared to look for another gift for the boy, he began moving away, but as he was about to leave the section, his eyes were drawn to the last game that was surprisingly unoccupied. The action on the screen appeared to him as if in a dream, and his eyes were transfixed immediately as he viewed a motorcycle mounted by a state trooper cruising up the road. Wayne stared open-mouthed at the khaki-clad figure with the polished helmet and mirror shades, high black riding boots, and shining badge mounted over his heart. He had a serious expression on his weathered face—one that didn't put up with any shit—and a high-powered, black-steel Harley Davidson adorned with polished chrome looming powerful between his legs.

But that wasn't all. As the officer glided along the tree-lined highway at high speed, a car suddenly appeared in the distance. It was swerving back and forth on the road, nearly hitting several cars that it passed. Suddenly the motorcycle accelerated and a pair of red lights began to flash at the front of the bike as he sped to catch up with the reckless driver. As he pulled alongside the car, his right hand came off the handlebars and moved up and down, commanding the lawbreaker to pull over to the side of the road. The profile of the officer was turned toward the car in an obvious expression of disapproval.

Smiling at the style displayed by the officer and intrigued by the game, Wayne stepped in front of the screen, grabbed the controls and hit pause. Pressing the different buttons and dials on the remote to see what they did, he quickly learned that there was a speed monitor, a light gauge, steering and arm controls and a final button that fired the officer's gun. Using the dial, he moved the officer's arm to his holster. The patrolman extracted what looked to be a service revolver, but bigger, possibly a .357 or something. Spinning the dial a bit more, he aimed the gun and pressed the firing button, hearing a loud, crisp shot immediately afterwards.

Laughing to himself and getting a better grip on the controls, he pushed the reset button and began moving the bike up the road, pulling in behind a billboard after a while to observe the traffic. Suddenly a car sped by, passed a truck on a double yellow line, and nearly hit an oncoming car. Wayne moved the Harley onto the road and gradually increased his speed while passing other motorists, some of whom turned abruptly and nearly forced him to fall. After dodging various road obstacles, he finally saw the vehicle he was pursuing. He hit the light control and moved up behind it but, as he did, several objects were lobbed at him from the car's interior, forcing him to slow down abruptly and almost crash.

As he regained his speed, he continued to dodge the bottles, grenades and whatever else they threw and finally reached down for the gun. He raised the arm's arc toward the car, hit the firing button, and saw the back wheel blow out. Aiming again, he shot out another tire. That caused the car to swerve but still enabled it to continue forward. Finally, he aimed for the back window and fired again. The window blew out with a loud blast and he saw the car lose control and smash into an oncoming vehicle. He smiled contentedly until he realized that he was unable to slow down himself, driving straight into the pile-up instead.

Deep down he felt he had to buy this and only this for Junior's Christmas gift. It was a video game, which he knew would please him, but more important was the fact that instead of watching some karate expert or science fiction spaceman fighting against aliens, he'd be seeing something realistic, whose action was an everyday occurrence. It might even help to steer Junior toward a career like his dad was involved in, Wayne thought. And what better present could you give your son than that?

A couple of kids had surrounded him and were watching the action, but Wayne did not give in to their occasional requests to play. Like a little boy himself, he reset the game again and again, and as the action passed quickly in front of him, he began seeing how complicated things could get. If you miscalculated your shots and happened to hit an innocent passerby, the screen would light up with the words "IMMEDIATE SUSPENSION." If you shot without foreseeing the possible consequences, you'd end up as he had earlier. Sometimes other drivers recklessly swerved to avoid a shootout and nearly killed you while doing so. And at other times, criminals armed with rifles would begin shooting at you from the back window. Its possibilities seemed endless and Wayne was absorbed in attempting to conquer them all.

Continuing to ignore the other kids' demands to play, Wayne inched closer and closer to the action until he could see his breath vaporizing on the screen. The shots fired and the cars crashed, and messages flashed in front of him in quick bursts of light. The noise jabbered intermittently from the machine, seemingly barking his name several times until he suddenly realized that he was being called from somewhere else.

He hit the pause button and left the video world. As he readjusted his eyes to the real world of the store, he saw Ethel waving her arm toward him in the distance, just outside the game area.

Staring back down at the game that now blurred in front of him, he absently handed the controls to a nearby kid and picked up a plastic-wrapped box containing the game. Checking the price, he frowned, but knew his decision had already been made—besides, the gift might pay off huge dividends in the end. With the game, his son would learn to respect the law, and the simple truth that messing with a man in a uniform always ended tragically.

"I've been lookin' for you for the past twenty minutes!" Ethel yelled over an announcement. "Have you been here the whole time?"

"Yeah," he said, handing her the box. "Junior is gonna love that."

"Great," she said, looking at it briefly before dropping it into the cart.

Wayne stared suspiciously at the other items in the cart below the box. "What's all that stuff?" he questioned.

"Oh, just some clothes for the kids," she said. "And a couple of other little things."

"Like what?" Wayne frowned, beginning to search through the basket, uncovering the layers of clothes. He suddenly stopped and extracted what looked to be a bra, although he wasn't sure because it had flaps over the cups. "What the hell is this?" he asked, holding it toward her.

"It's a maternity bra," she said, grabbing it from him hastily and throwing it back in the basket. "I thought that could be one of your gifts to me."

"Why in God's name would I want to give you that?" he asked.

"You know I don't have any of the special things a woman needs when she has a child," she said softly, but with a hint of annoyance. "After all it's been a long time. And that'll allow me to feed the child without having to uncover myself in public."

Wayne grunted and continued rifling through the other items.

"And how about these other boxes?" he asked suspiciously, blocking the cart which she attempted to move toward the check-out.

"Honestly Wayne," she said, shaking her head. "You spend so much time with your job or doin' things around the house that you have no idea what the kids need. I'm not pickin' out stupid things, like you might think. I'm gettin' 'em the essentials."

"I think I'd be a better judge about that than you, seein' how you thought that ridiculous make-up kit was an essential."

"Well if you want to know then," she snapped back, beginning to pull out various items and waving each one in front of him, "I'm gettin' a Timex watch for Darlene that was marked real low, as well as a skirt and some undergarments. And for Junior, I got a pair of slippers and a cheap clock radio, so he wakes up in time for school."

Wayne picked up the clock radio and examined the box. "What's wrong with one of those clocks with the two bells on top that you wind up? You could proba'ly get one of them for half the price."

Ethel grabbed the box from him and threw it back into the cart. "For your information, the clock with the bells is more expensive, and there's no radio that comes with it," she said. "They make this electonic stuff over in Japan or Korea or one of those countries, with computers that do all the work—at a fraction of the price that a person here could do it for. I read an article in *Women's Day* about that."

Wayne looked at her skeptically. "Yeah, maybe," he said. "But I'm sure it doesn't work as well as if some person had put it together with their own two hands."

"Please Wayne!" Ethel said, rolling her eyes. "Let's not argue about this anymore!"

Wayne stared toward the check-outs, packed with carts full of toys and other items. "OK," he said. "Let's hurry up and get the hell out of here."

About twenty minutes later, Wayne found himself signing the Visa receipt, frowning at the total but content that Christmas expenses were now out of the way.

"Hey Wayne," Ethel blurted as her husband scooped up the bags. "How about if you bring that stuff out, warm up the car and then pull it up here to the door. There was somethin' inside that I saw for you that I want to get, but I don't want you to see it."

"C'mon Ethel," he responded, impatient to leave. "I told you already that I didn't want anything."

"Yeah, but I know you're gonna love it," she said, winking. "You're gonna thank me a lot when you open it."

Wayne snorted and pursed his lips, staring at his smiling wife.

"All right," he finally said, handing over the charge card but flashing his disapproval. "But hurry up and don't spend too much money on it. Just because you made some money at your job doesn't mean it's only yours to spend."

Ethel nodded her head and then turned quickly, throwing herself back into the labyrinth of aisles and bouncing off an array of carts. She moved rapidly through the crowd, hauled several items for herself off the shelves, and juggled the large boxes back toward the check-out.

For such a stingy hard-ass, she smiled to herself, her husband sure was easy to fool sometimes.

PART TWO

14

Even though the holiday season was several weeks gone, the artificial Christmas tree remained in the corner of the family room. Its colored bulbs blinked intermittently, providing a cheerful contrast to the dull winter light outside. On the opposite side of the room, Ethel sat in front of the television, engrossed in an afternoon soap opera. Beside her, the dog slept peacefully. The plastic coverings that Wayne had taped around the small windows helped keep out the cold draft. But, even so, Ethel nestled under several layers of blankets in an attempt to fight off the chill, which permeated the walls her husband never got around to insulating.

Ethel glanced at her watch. She wondered what was keeping her friend Tina Copenhaver, whom she had expected nearly an hour earlier. Ethel had invited Tina over the week before, when Tina had mentioned that she was going to start selling Avon products. Tina spoke enthusiastically about her new enterprise because it would give her something to do in her free time and provide some extra money. She said she had been visited by the representative, who had given her a sales kit. In the kit were a lot of free samples and special discounts that she was allowed to offer to close friends.

Ethel recognized the quality guaranteed by the Avon name and knew that she had used and liked their products in the past. So she seized the opportunity by setting up an appointment with Tina at a time her husband wouldn't be at home. It was critical that Wayne not know about it because of what his reaction might be if he found out that she had bought anything he considered "non-essential." He laid down that law not long after the holiday season.

When the credit card bill arrived, it showed Ethel's excessive spending. In addition to the purchases Wayne and she made together, Ethel had also bought an electronic food scale, a couple of larger outfits, a small bottle of perfume, and an electric foot bath that heated the water and gently massaged her soles. She was sure to use them all quickly to render them non-returnable and then keep them out of his sight.

Not unexpectedly, the "amount due" figure caused a huge argument. But fortunately, Ethel had anticipated a fight and prepared a defense ahead of time—which was to be submissive. She let Wayne yell at her and then, to finally get him off her back, swore on the Bible that she wouldn't buy anything else unless he approved of it first.

Her oath had been believed.

But when she found out that her friend would have a huge selection of perfume at low prices, Ethel immediately decided to break her word. She didn't necessarily like having to do it behind Wayne's back, but there were certain things that she felt a woman needed and deserved—things her bull-headed husband obviously didn't understand. Delicate fragrances certainly fell into that category, and with an expert on the subject among her close friends, she figured she'd be an idiot not to take advantage of such an opportunity.

When the doorbell rang, Ethel instinctively reached for the remote control. When it didn't work, however, she remembered she had shattered it the day before when she accidently stepped on it. She shifted her weight to the edge of the chair and hoisted her lopsided body into a supine position, grunting loudly and readjusting her robe around her girth. As she watched the end of the current scene, she heard the doorbell ring again. Finally, she turned the set off and shuffled out to receive her caller.

Ethel opened the door and saw the rosy cheeks of Tina's face framed by the fur-lined hood of her parka. She let her in and closed the door behind her quickly, shutting out the cold wind that blew briskly outside.

"Is it snowin' out there again?" Ethel asked her.

"You can't really tell," Tina said, unzipping her jacket and placing a large suitcase on the floor. "It might just be the snow blowin' off the branches."

"Well let me make you a hot cup of cocoa and get you warmed up," Ethel smiled, taking her coat and putting it on a peg next to the door. "And take off your boots too," she added. "I'll get you a pair of slippers to put on."

"What a lovely little kitchen you have," Tina said after she sat down.

"Little is right," Ethel responded over her shoulder while putting a couple of extra marshmallows into the cups of Swiss Miss. "I suppose it's homey though," she added, placing the cups on the table. "I'd show you the rest of the trailer, but it's too much of a mess."

"Oh that's OK," Tina said. "It's always hard for a pregnant woman to do all that she'd like."

"You said it," Ethel said, nodding her head while lighting a cigarette. "I sure wish my husband saw things the same way."

89

"How is Wayne anyway?" she asked.

"He's OK," Ethel said without any enthusiasm. "Really involved with his work. He's supposed to have a meeting with his boss this afternoon, which he figures is gonna lead to another raise."

Ethel stared into her hot chocolate and bobbed the marshmallow up and down with her finger. "Darlene isn't home yet either," she said, changing the subject. "But I'm expectin' her soon. You know I told you I wanted to get her some make-up."

The two women chatted, and then Tina began talking about her new enterprise. She said that on account of the weather, things were pretty slow, but she had made a number of sales. She spoke about several of the people she'd met, described their houses and their behavior and told her exactly what they had bought. She complained that a couple of times she spent several hours in someone's home and they only bought one or two items. She mentioned that time-wasters like that made the job a little bit frustrating.

"Well you don't have to worry about that here," Ethel said, shaking her head and getting in the mood to smell pretty. "What about we start lookin' at some of what you brought over."

Smiling slyly, Tina opened the suitcase and began putting its contents onto the kitchen table. Before long, most of the table was covered with glass bottles, plastic compact cases, and small boxes, all bearing the Avon logo. It looked like an altar for the disciples of cosmetics to pray before.

Ethel's eyes widened at the sight. "They look beautiful," she said, flabbergasted.

"Well I've got samples of everything," Tina said with a smile. "I've got bath lotions, face creams, cosmetics, body oils, bath rinses, lots of different perfumes, bubble bath, lip balms, you name it. You just tell me what you wanna start with."

"I didn't know there was so much," Ethel said, perplexed by the choices before her. "How about some perfume that might be nice say...behind my ears."

"Okie-doke," Tina said, nodding her head. Tina scanned the array of perfumes, trying to decide where to begin. "Do you want scented waters, or essences? Essences are more concentrated."

Ethel thought hard. "Well, why don't you let me try 'em all," she finally said, "and we'll just see which ones I like best."

Tina thought briefly and then scanned the table. "I know," she said while reaching for a small bottle. "I'll start with the scented waters 'cause they're weaker. They're the kind of stuff you might want to splash on every

90

day after a bath." She squeezed the rubber bulb dangling from the bottle, and a fine mist sprayed onto Ethel's pudgy wrist.

Ethel inhaled the scent of her skin, closed her eyes, and smiled. "That smells just like a rose."

"They make it by diluting the liquid from pressed roses with distilled water," Tina said officially. "It's pretty, isn't it?"

"I'll say," Ethel responded. Her words were muffled by her fleshy arm, which she jammed up against her nostrils.

"This is lilac water," Tina continued, directing a squirt onto Ethel's other wrist. Ethel cooed with delight.

Ethel continued sampling the different waters, moving each squirt a bit further up her forearm each time. When they finished with the eight large bottles, Tina changed to the different essences housed in smaller containers, this time giving the samples in smaller doses.

"These are perfumes," she said and handed Ethel one of the bottles. "They're more concentrated, and also a little more expensive. But they're still very affordable, considerin' the quality of the Avon name."

After each scent was sampled, Tina shifted the used bottles to one side of the table so that before long the two sides began to balance. After half an hour and over a dozen more dabs, Ethel realized that she was beginning to confuse the different scents. They all smelled good, but they all smelled the same to her now.

As Tina kept spraying new samples, Ethel was also unsure whether the light-headed sensation she was beginning to feel was the result of aromatic ecstasy or the onset of nausea. The smells were becoming so overbearing she was beginning to sweat. When the front door swung open and a gust of cold air blew into the room behind her daughter, she sat back suddenly to regain her breath.

"It sure smells nice in here," Darlene said, closing out the cold. "Like a garden store or somethin'."

"Darlene," Ethel said, wiping her forehead and struggling to stand up. "This is a friend of mine, Tina Copenhaver. She's one of the women I play cards with, and she also sells Avon products. I told her to come over 'cause I wanted to treat you to some make-up. How does that grab you?"

Darlene smiled widely. "Really?" she said excitedly while tossing her books on the counter.

"That's right," Tina said. "And I brought lots of things over that are gonna make you look prettier than you already are."

Ethel began preparing more Swiss Miss. Darlene quickly took a seat at the table. Tina put a little bib over Darlene's ample chest and rubbed cleanser across her chubby, oily face. Then Tina applied foundation, eye shadow, blush, lipstick and mascara. She worked rapidly, picking up the various compact cases, combining a swipe of one color with a bit of another and then taking away the gloss with a puff of powder.

By the time Ethel placed the fresh mugs on the table, different colors were smeared across her daughter's face, transforming her into something resembling an artist's palette.

"Darlene honey," she said, exasperated, "you wouldn't believe how...how different you look."

"Just like a little lady," Tina said, stepping back to admire her work.

"Well get me a mirror!" Darlene said anxiously. "I wanna see!"

Tina opened her briefcase and took out a mirror. As she held it proudly in front of the girl, the front door swung open again.

Wayne burst in out of the cold. He froze in his steps, gazed down at the three females in the room one by one, and then glanced at the table covered with bottles. He didn't say a word, but his silence spoke his disdain loudly enough.

"Wayne," Ethel finally broke in. "I'd like you to meet one of my friends, Tina Copenhaver. She's one of the women I play cards with."

Wayne stared ahead, silent.

"Ethel's told us so much about you," Tina said uncomfortably.

Wayne moved his eyes slowly between the women before him, his face clenched with scorn. "This place smells like the bedroom of some cheap whore," he finally blurted before shifting his eyes to his daughter. "And what the hell does Darlene have all that shit over her face for? Did Halloween come early this year or somethin'?"

"Now wait just a minute, Wayne!" Ethel said, pointing her finger at him. "How dare you come in here and embarrass me like this in front of one of my friends!"

"Quiet Ethel!" Wayne said, raising his voice and pointing his finger back toward her. "You knew we went over this make-up thing before, and you know the way I feel about it. I told you it was prohibited!"

"Who said I was gonna buy any make-up for Darlene?" Ethel fought back.

"Darlene!" Wayne yelled, ignoring his wife and switching the finger to his daughter. "Get out of the room and wash that putty off your face. Now!"

Darlene glanced quickly between her parents and then sprang from the chair. She ran to the bathroom and slammed the door shut.

"Wayne, what the hell is wrong with you?" Ethel hollered. "Tina here sells Avon products and was givin' me some free samples. When Darlene came home, she asked if she could try a little bit. And Tina was nice enough to let her." She stamped out her cigarette and immediately reached for another while shaking her head. "And close the door for Christ' sake!" she hissed. "It's freezin' outside."

"I'll close the door," Wayne said calmly, "when you're friend Mrs. Copen-whatever packs all of her bottles into the case and walks back through it."

"Look Tina, I'm awful sorry about this," Ethel said, putting her arm around her embarrassed friend. "Wayne ain't normally like this. Maybe it's better if you get your stuff and we'll talk about the perfume next week at our card game."

"I think that's proba'ly a good idea," Tina said, looking spitefully over her shoulder at Wayne while placing the cases and bottles in the suitcase.

"I don't think that'll be necessary," Wayne retorted angrily, "'cause Ethel and me already have an understanding about that. And anyway, I think there's enough stink in the air to cover anyone who walks in here for the next year." He paused, and then pointed his finger toward Tina. "And I don't wanna see *you* around here ever again tryin' to peddle any more of this junk."

Ethel began helping Tina load her suitcase and repeatedly apologized for her husband's behavior. When they finished, Tina grabbed her coat and boots and hastily put them on, occasionally glancing at Ethel's husband. Wayne stared in the opposite direction and drummed his fingers impatiently on the top of the refrigerator.

"I'll help you out to the car," Ethel said, struggling with the suitcase and hustling to catch up with her friend, who was already outside. When she passed Wayne at the door, she stopped and eyed him spitefully. "I'm gonna get you back for this one!" she hissed.

Wayne looked away casually and tapped his fingers more rapidly.

Ethel grunted loudly and brushed her enlarged stomach past him. Clad only in her robe and slippers, she struggled down the snow covered steps toward Tina's car.

Wayne remained still for several seconds and then abruptly closed the door next to him, latching the deadbolt across it. The cold air outside would help his wife cool down a bit, he figured.

15

As the wind whipped past the bare limbs of the oak trees, its ominous howl was occasionally surpassed by the painful sound of limbs cracking. The fir of the evergreens was weighted heavily by layers of snow, while the frigid temperatures had added a thin layer of ice to the top of the powder on the ground. Its shining brilliance faded as the gray sky gradually became darker.

Breathing heavily, Wayne Turner broke through the virginal surface, crushing the thick undergrowth with his heavy rubber boots. He continued moving forward, leaving a solitary trail of human invasion behind. In the distance he could barely see another intrusion: his parked car, whose black silhouette was visible against the white blanket of snow that had blown onto it over the past ten hours. The Fury was parked along the vague outline of a service road, visible only by the wooden sticks along one edge that he had followed earlier in the day to a place he felt safe to hunt.

Staring at the bleak landscape between him and his goal, Wayne felt as if he had lost all sense of color, like the world had suddenly become a black-and-white movie. He paused for a minute, dropped his shotgun to his side, and readjusted his scarf around his collar in an effort to keep the relentless wind from permeating his chilled yet sweating body. Wayne's head felt like it was being compressed by a slowly turning vice. He pulled his hat down further so that it completely covered his ears with its frost-covered surface. Inside his boots, he could barely feel his toes shriveling within his wet socks. After clapping his hands together several times, he tucked his chin under the scarf and picked up the shotgun. With that, he pumped his short legs clumsily toward his goal again.

When Wayne finally reached the Fury, the light from the sky had completely disappeared so that even his path was no longer visible behind him. Once inside the car, he threw the shotgun on the back seat and huddled his body together in an effort to gain warmth. He rubbed his body parts briskly and jerked his legs against the cold seat. His heavy breath raced from his mouth and diffused in myriad directions upon contact with the frosted windows.

He shoved the key in the ignition and, after a number of false starts, the engine finally turned over. He pumped the accelerator rapidly and forced life into the frigid engine. As he began inching the car over the path's icy surface, the fan blew a constant stream of cold air toward him.

Wayne was depressed that he had spent another cold, exhausting, wasted Sunday in the woods. It was as if all the animals in the forest had turned against him and hidden themselves from the sights of his scope. He always hoped his luck would change, but it had been like that for years now. Indeed, his luck had been bad since he was busted on a damn poaching charge, shortly after the family had moved to Indiana.

Because the Turner family arrived after the applications for hunting permits were due, Wayne would have to wait until next year to hunt—legally, he was told by the sheriff. That disturbed him, as hunting had always been one of things that made the dreary months of winter tolerable. In addition—since the family had incurred a lot of debt as a result of their move—Wayne had also counted on the hundred or more pounds of meat that a decent-sized deer might yield.

He reluctantly complied with the law for a couple of months, but as the winter had wore on, he finally decided that his economic situation demanded an alternative to the grocery store meat department.

His first couple of attempts at jacklighting were fruitless. But as he drove home the third weekend, he had spotted a group of deer feeding about a hundred yards from the road.

No cars or houses were in sight and nightfall was rapidly approaching. Wayne parked his car on the side of the road, grabbed his rifle, and quietly worked his way into the woods. When he got within range, he leveled his sights on a small buck of four, maybe six points, and rapidly squeezed off three shots. His fire brought the animal to the ground immediately and sent the others scurrying for their lives in all directions.

Wayne hustled over to the animal and found it dead. He quickly tied one end of a rope around its hind legs, looped the other end around his upper body, then dragged the animal toward his car. But when he was nearly halfway there, he saw the headlights of a car slow down as it approached his vehicle, and finally stop. Abandoning his trophy temporarily in the middle of the darkened field, he ran off into the woods to hide.

When the car finally drove away, Wayne returned to his chore, pulling the animal over the frost-covered ground as fast as possible. Upon reaching his car, he managed to lift it onto the trunk and tie it down securely. Wayne wrapped a canvas tarp around his catch, and then congratulated himself for completing his clandestine operation.

Wayne's triumph was short-lived, however. Before he even started the car again, his form was illuminated by a pair of high-beams that rapidly emerged from a side road and skidded in front of his car. Before he knew what hit him, two uniformd men were hauling him out of the car and reading him his rights: "Poaching on federal property" was the charge they kept repeating.

At the trial, Wayne pleaded guilty to the charge, though he insisted he had been unaware that he killed the animal on the grounds of a protected National Reserve. He was given a stiff fine with a stipulation that made him ineligible for a hunting permit for the next ten years. The judges also warned him that a similar violation in the future would result in a jail sentence.

Since that incident, Wayne hadn't even looked at his shotgun. But lately, the urge to hunt had become so strong that he found it almost impossible to suppress. Consequently, he started going out again, being extra careful to stay as far away as possible from any roads or known hunting grounds. As he inched the car along the icy trail and struggled to see its edge, he cursed himself for taking such risks and coming away empty-handed.

Wayne finally reached the main road. After driving for about half an hour, he saw a bar amidst a small area of cleared ground. He pulled into the parking lot, thinking he could get a bottle of something inside that might begin to thaw out his insides. As he walked toward the entrance, he noticed a parked truck with a large buck sprawled out in the back. Its tongue hung out of its mouth and rested in a pool of congealed blood covering the truck's bed. Wayne counted the ten points of its antlers and felt envious of the marksman who had brought it down.

The bar was full of hunters with bright orange vests and hats. They made lots of noise as they recounted their stories of the big one that had gotten away. Wayne felt small and detached amongst them for some reason. He knew it was stupid to feel that way. But, to Wayne, the permit he lacked was like a membership card to a club that he was barred from. To be a non-member and attempt to mix in would obviously be frowned upon, in the same way anyone with a cop's badge naturally looked down on the rest of the world. Bearing this in mind, Wayne walked straight to the bar with his head lowered, bought a pint of whiskey, and then exited just as quickly.

Wayne slid back into his car, then unscrewed the cap, put the bottle to his lips, and swallowed a number of times before pulling it away. The sweet vapor of alcohol flowed past his lips and momentarily made him feel better. He watched another truck pull in. A couple of guys dressed in hunting gear got out and entered the bar, laughing and enjoying themselves. Wayne put the bottle to his lips and tipped it upwards again.

After emptying about a third of the bottle, he pulled out of the parking lot and steered the car along the ice-and-sand- covered road. The squeak of the windshield wipers occasionally broke through the rumble of the car's engine. As he stared blankly at the dim illumination his headlights cast in front of him, his mind began to drift away from hunting and toward his job with Vanguard Security. That was just another frustrating topic, because several weeks earlier he was demoted to the back of the bank truck—to the cashier's job he thought he had put behind him forever.

Wayne had received the news the same afternoon he kicked Ethel's friend out of the house. The reasons were simple enough. The recession was hitting the banks harder and harder and not as much money was being shifted between them. So the security company had been forced to take a couple of their trucks off the road and give some of its employees their walking papers. Fortunately, Wayne had been with the company for long enough to keep him from being laid off like some of the newer guys, like Spears. But because other shotgun riders had been there longer than him, his destiny was apparent. Instead of receiving the raise he expected, he found himself summoned back into the four claustrophobic, armored walls on wheels.

It certainly wasn't because his shotgun performance had been poor. In fact, when his boss at Vanguard gave him the news, he apologized profusely for the demotion. Wayne closed his eyes and could still hear the words from their meeting:

"If the job allotments went by technical ability alone Wayne, you'd be my number one man. But the company has to respect some of the other employees staying power..."

"But you just said I was your number one man..."

"Technically Wayne...you are...that's what I said...And I'm not saying the new assignments are justified...But I think they are fair. And believe me, as soon as the economy turns itself around, you'll be back where you belong. But respect my position. With times like they are, I have no choice in the matter."

A demotion, that's what it all came down to. And unfortunately, Wayne's salary was also reduced to its previous level. And with Ethel no longer working at McDonalds, all the little "extras" they had purchased became impossible to keep. Wayne deposited his rototiller and his wife's foot bath at a pawn shop in Columbus, and those sacrifices gave them a little

98

financial breathing room.

But what galled him even more than their shrinking finances was the fact that he was once again obliged to watch the world go by sideways through the little slit window in the back of the bank truck. Not only was it demeaning, it was also embarrassing, especially after working his beat on the street with the real world. Whereas before he lived and breathed his job, he now found he was bored even to think about it. He even began reading the newspaper to pass the time in between drops.

He was aware that it might take years for the economy to recover, and the thought of a man with his qualifications relegated to such a menial position during the prime of his law enforcement career infuriated him. He grabbed the bottle from beneath the seat and hastily took another slug before setting it between his legs. In the distance, he saw something bob up from the gulley on the side of the road, and as he turned on his high beams, two deer suddenly struggled out of the brush and rapidly attempted to cross the road. He immediately slammed on his brakes. As the car went into a skid, one deer leapt briskly back into the brush, but the other one froze in its steps, mesmerized by the oncoming lights.

The locked tires slid over the slick ice for several seconds before finally digging in. By that time, however, it was too late. As the car drew closer to the animal, Wayne watched the fear in the deer's eyes expand, its mouth opened helplessly. Then came the loud, sickening thud as his car smashed against its graceful body and sent its broken form flying through the air.

When he finally brought his vehicle to a halt, Wayne jumped out and ran back to the fallen deer. It was lying in the snow-covered brush on the side of the road, struggling for breath but unable to move its limbs. It was a small doe that he guessed was about a year old, if that. The one eye he could see was open but didn't blink. Off in the distance, Wayne could hear her partner crashing through the forest toward safety.

Wayne walked slowly back to his car, opened the door, and removed his shotgun. He loaded a shell into it as he returned, placed the barrel of the gun behind the animal's ear, and quickly pulled the trigger. The silence of the lonely road burst with the shell's explosion.

After he returned to the car, Wayne replaced the gun and then backed up next to the animal. He opened the trunk and spread out a piece of plastic to line its interior, and then grabbed a dirty blanket. He bent over, enveloped the corpse within it, and then struggled to hoist it into the area normally occupied by the spare tire.

99

Wayne bent the animal's legs so that they would fit, then slammed the trunk down and washed the blood off his hands with snow. He walked around to the front of his car and saw that the deer had left a permanent memento of its existence on the front of the hood. He mumbled an obscenity.

Wayne got back into the car and started the engine, then took another shot of whiskey before pulling back onto the road. In a way, the dent wasn't that big a deal, he thought as the car moved along the road. He could probably pull it out the next day with a plunger and leave no trace of the impact with the animal.

In fact, as Wayne moved closer and closer to home, he began considering that his family didn't have to know the exact circumstances in which the deer was killed, either. Just for the hell of it, he could tell them he shot it while he was out hunting, saying he'd tracked it for a few hours before finally pulling it down. They'd be impressed by the big hunter returning home with his catch, and he'd have Ethel make some sort of stew with the venison for everyone to enjoy.

Wayne smiled and pushed harder on the gas pedal.

His day off in the cold had paid off in the end, and he suddenly felt a little bit better.

16

Wayne and Junior were in the family room, watching the sports report on television. Darlene called them from the other room to tell them that their supper was ready. Neither of them responded or even acted as if they had heard her. They both continued staring straight at the TV screen as the highlights of NCAA basketball games flashed before them.

A minute or two later, Darlene appeared at the door and yelled loudly, "C'mon! The food's on the table already!"

Wayne held out his arm toward her without making eye contact, an unspoken signal that he often used meaning, "Be quiet." When the sportscaster appeared on the screen again, he looked at his son and said, "Indiana could have won that game if they had the coachin' they used to."

"No way," Junior said arrogantly, sitting back in his chair and shaking his head. "The coach isn't that important 'cause he just sits on the sidelines. The players are the ones who do the work. And Indiana's players suck this year."

Wayne glared at his son. Wayne knew that a team's players, acting on their own, amounted to nothing without someone to plan things and provide them with strategy.

It was the same with a family, he thought; they needed someone to look up to and receive guidance from. He knew that in the Turner household, he was that person. Junior, however, seemed to be warding off his advice. He had noticed it for a few months, and as time went on, their differing opinions were becoming more and more pronounced. Every time there was a job for Junior to do, he had to be reminded three or four times, and finally threatened, before he actually did it. Wayne figured some form of rebellion was natural in a teenage boy if his old man didn't provide an ideal role model. But Wayne was a cop, and what better image could he offer his son to look up to?

"Daddy!" Darlene interrupted his thoughts. "Will you come on? The stuff I made is gettin' all cold!"

"All right already!" he yelled, finally looking toward her and focusing on the folds between her chin and neck. His mouth hung open because, for a split second, he actually thought he saw his wife within her seventeen-year-old form, and somehow it made him pity her future. "Why don't you just bring the plates in here?" he finally said. "Your brother and me are watchin' somethin'."

"All right," she said, annoyed. "But I wish you would have told me that in the first place."

When the meteorologist began giving the details of the upcoming mild weather, Wayne began flipping around the stations, pausing a couple of seconds at each one before moving on. Darlene handed a plate to Junior and another one to her father. He turned back to the news and put the remote control on the floor.

"I sure hope the hospital calls soon," Darlene said, sitting down beside him and dumping a pool of ketchup on her french fries. "And I hope I have a new little sister."

"Well I have a feelin' it's gonna be a boy," Wayne said, taking the bottle from her. "And his name is gonna be Merle, just like the singer," he added proudly.

"That's such an ugly name," Darlene said, crunching a couple of her charred fries. "If it was a boy, I'd name him Jason or maybe Luke. And if it's a girl, I'd agree with Momma about Gladys."

"Gladys?" Junior quipped from his seat. "Are you kiddin' me? With all the names in the world, Gladys is about the last one I'd pick."

"What do you mean?" Darlene responded, chomping on her meat. "Gladys is a real pretty name. I'd love to have been named Gladys instead of Darlene."

"Well I don't really like the name Gladys either," Wayne said looking toward his son. "But your mother and I have already made an agreement that if it's a girl, she's gonna be named after her grandmother. And if it's a boy, his name is gonna be Merle Turner. So we just have to wait to see if the kid comes out with a tinkler or not."

Junior burped. "I wouldn't name my kid either of those things," he stated.

"Well it's not your kid," Wayne addressed him coldly, annoyed by his cocky tone.

Junior looked back at him and frowned. "Yeah, but it's gonna be my brother or sister for Christ's sake, and I'm gonna have to call 'em it for the rest of my life."

"Watch your language Junior!" Wayne barked.

Junior looked at his father and rolled his eyes. "Hey Darlene!" he yelled, diverting his gaze toward his sister. "Throw the remote control over here."

"What are you gonna put on?" she asked.

"I don't know," he answered, staring forward. "Just gimme it so I can see what's on."

"Well I wanna watch somethin' at seven o'clock," she said, throwing the device toward Junior. "So you can watch whatever you want now."

"Don't throw it! Hand it!" Wayne shouted. "I don't wanna have to pay to get that fixed again!"

Junior began changing the channels, pausing several seconds on each one before moving on to the next.

"Leave it on somethin' for God's sake!" Wayne hissed. "Or I'm gonna take the battery out of that stupid thing!"

"Don't jump my butt about it!" the boy said, flipping the station again. "I'm just tryin' to find somethin' good."

Wayne returned to his food and picked up a soggy french fry. "Don't you know you're supposed to drain the corn before you put it on the plate?" he grumbled to his daughter.

"Yeah, but I couldn't find the strainer," she answered, looking toward the TV. "So I tried to do it with a spoon."

"Well maybe you should try cream corn tomorrow night," he said, dumping some of the juice into the ashtray beside him. "Although this really ain't that far off."

"It's not that bad," she retorted. "I think it makes it almost like a sauce."

Wayne cleared his throat and continued with his meal, cutting through the meat with difficulty while knocking a few fries on the floor as his plate jerked. The dog, sitting at his feet and watching him attentively, quickly lapped them up, adding another chomping mouth to the room's noise. Shovelling a forkful of meat past his teeth, Wayne chewed the gristle for what seemed to him an eternity before swallowing the tough mass, which felt like a golf ball going down his throat. He washed down the few fries that weren't burnt with the rest of his beer. Then he put the plate on the floor for the dog to finish off.

"Hey Junior," Darlene said, looking at her watch. "It's time for that show I want to watch. Flip the channel."

As Junior reached for the remote control, the phone rang in the other room. The family looked at each other for several moments. Each one seemed to be waiting for one of the others to get it. Wayne breathed deeply and finally shuffled out of the room. Several seconds later he appeared in the room again, where the others stared at him anxiously.

"It's for you," he told Darlene. She jumped up and placed her plate on the chair, which the dog promptly knocked to the floor and began slopping at. Junior didn't even seem to notice.

Darlene grabbed the phone and began talking. Wayne pulled his jacket from a peg and another can of beer from the fridge and headed outside for some fresh air. As he opened the door, he hissed, "Keep it short. The hospital should be callin' any minute."

Walking across the soggy ground, he saw the small sliver of the moon above the tree tops. His breath was still visible, but there was no longer a harsh chill in the air. All that remained of the snow was just a few scattered patches, barely illuminated by the moon's weak glow.

Wayne let his mind roll back through the day's events. Earlier that morning, as he was about to leave for work, Ethel called him from the bedroom and told him to hurry. Running down the hallway, he found her reclining against the headboard of the bed, holding her stomach and breathing rapidly. She gasped that she thought the baby was on its way and for him to call the hospital and tell them to be expecting the delivery shortly. He propped her up with a few pillows and then hustled to the phone, where he called Vanguard Security and informed them that he wouldn't be coming in that day. Then he called the hospital. Moving quickly back to the bedroom, he stood his wife up, wrapped a coat around her, and struggled to support her weight as they walked down the steps and toward his car.

It was a situation he had envisioned for the past month or so, and he had gone over the situation enough times in his head to be completely prepared. After closing the door beside Ethel, he opened the trunk and took out a red "cherry" light that he borrowed from the security company specifically for the occasion. He attached the suction cup base on the roof over his door and plugged the cord into the cigarette lighter, which charged the light and made it revolve. Firing the car up, he skidded out of the driveway and fishtailed onto the road, turning on his emergency lights to inform other people to get out of the way...fast.

With the skill of an Indy 500 driver, he pressed the pedal to the metal and passed cars in front of him as if they were standing still. Ethel was moaning beside him and telling him to be careful. Yet he pushed on, screaming at her to relax and take deep breaths. Making the fifteen-mile trip in about ten minutes and having avoided several potentially fatal accidents by inches, Wayne finally swerved the car through the hospital entrance and accelerated to the emergency section, in front of where he brought the car to a skidding halt.

He rushed through the doors and called for assistance. A minute or so later, an orderly retrieved his wife with a wheel chair. As if he were working "shotgun" again, he ran several steps in front of them, clearing the path with silent expertise, completely confident that his blue uniform gave him the authority to take control of this situation.

Once Wayne was assured that his wife was in the proper hands, he casually walked back to his car with the aloofness of a professional. The hospital employees stared open-mouthed at him as he walked by—it was their way of showing respect. He removed the revolving cherry light and calmly drove the vehicle down to the parking lot, silently complimenting himself on a job well done.

Wayne spent the next few hours in the antiseptic-drenched confines of the waiting room, where he rubbed his moist palms together endlessly and nervously tapped his feet. He blindly flipped through various copies of old, crumpled magazines before tossing them aside. Several minutes later, he'd pick them up and leaf through them once more. Every time the door swung open and a nurse entered the room, he stood up and looked for the news which, to his chagrin, was never directed toward his looming figure.

Finally a nurse did speak to him. But she only informed him that his wife's contractions had slowed down, and that she probably wouldn't be giving birth until early that evening. Not wanting to spend the rest of the day in the hospital, which only reminded him of pain and suffering, he asked the nurse to call him at home as soon as the delivery was completed.

As the hours passed, he attempted to fill his time by doing some work around the house. But he made no real progress with anything he began. He knew it was his nerves because he had felt the same way when his first offspring had come into the world. He recalled that at that time, he refused to be in the operating room with his wife or take part in any birth assistance exercises, which he considered to be some weirdo trend that only caused confusion for the professional doctors. Ethel felt the same way. She didn't want to be involved in any sort of natural childbirth either because she believed it would be too painful. She was quite content to be given whatever drugs were necessary to diminish her suffering. And she made a point of telling Wayne that she thought his presence would only make her nervous and subject her to prolonged agony, anyway.

Crushing the beer can in his hand, Wayne began walking back to his brightly illuminated trailer. He hoped that his wife was not experiencing any unexpected difficulties. The wind blew gently through the thin fabric of his jacket, chilling his perspiring armpits. He filled the silent night air with a succession of loud burps, trying to ease some of the mounting pressure within himself, and threw the beer can underneath the front steps.

Upon entering the house, he was incensed to see Darlene still on the phone. He closed the door behind him and stared malevolently at her. She nodded to him knowingly, abruptly said goodbye to her friend and quickly hung up the phone.

"What the hell are you stayin' on the phone all that time for?" Wayne asked angrily.

"It wasn't that long," she said. "Only about twenty minutes."

"Well maybe the hospital has been tryin' to get through!" he said, raising his voice.

"Well I'm sorry," she responded, shaking her head. "They'll call back."

"Yeah, they'll call back all right," he said, eyeballing her. "But when the phone rings, I'm gonna be the only one talkin' on it from now on." He pointed his finger toward her and added, "Understood?"

"OK," she said, rolling her eyes the same way Ethel did when she was being scolded. "Nobody else is gonna call me anyway."

"They better not, 'cause if it's one of your friends, I'm just gonna tell 'em to..."

Wayne's voice was overwhelmed by the phone beside him, whose loud outburst made him flinch. He stared at it briefly, as if unsure what to do, and then suddenly reached for it before its noise sounded again. "Yeah!" he barked into the receiver.

Wayne regained his composure when he was told that the call was from the hospital. He listened attentively, smiled briefly, and nodded his head as he concentrated on the nurse's words.

"Wait a minute!" he said abruptly. "Can you repeat that last part? I don't think I heard you right."

He continued listening, and his expression changed from one of confusion to one of complete incomprehension. "Are you sure about that?" he gasped with difficulty.

Darlene was yelling to Junior in an attempt to draw him away from the television, and Wayne had difficulty hearing the nurse on the other end of the line. "Shhhh!" he hissed in his daughter's direction before directing his concentration to the call again. "And there were no complications?" he asked. "They're both OK?"

He shook his head up and down. "I see," he said vaguely, as if someone else were putting the words into his mouth.

He held the receiver to his ear a while longer and nodded his head several times while blandly mumbling a few more words into it. When he finally said goodbye, he lowered the phone from his ear and stared toward it for several seconds, as if wondering what it had just done to him.

"Well?" Darlene yelled anxiously in front of him.

He glanced at her face and then stared at the wallpaper behind her, noticing for the first time the smiley faces that comprised its design.

"What did they say?" Junior shouted, coming into the room.

Wayne continued staring blankly in front of him, watching the forms on the wall blur into unrecognizable shapes, and felt his heartbeat begin to accelerate and a cold sweat begin to seep through his pores. He swayed in the middle of the room, deaf to the repeated questions of his children, and felt a huge knot forming in his throat.

Suddenly, a disconnected signal blared from the phone and brought him back to reality. He stared at the receiver, completely unsure why it was still in his hand, and then handed it absently to his daughter.

"Is it a boy or a girl?" Junior asked again.

"Merle or Gladys?" Darlene repeated.

Wayne stared at one and then the other, but without uttering a word, marched straight to his bedroom and closed the door on the confusion behind him.

17

Ethel was almost asleep when the noise of her twin daughters drew her back into foggy consciousness. She slowly adjusted her eyes to the light of the late April sun, which poured through the bedroom window and cast a beam on the corner of the crib. The two girls within burped in short, disjointed gasps. It was time for their feeding, but Ethel decided to stay down a few minutes longer to get a little bit of the rest she had just been jarred from.

Ethel felt she deserved the rest. After all, the infants cried virtually non-stop the night before and into the small hours of the morning. She fed them and changed them, but they continued their racket, almost as if bent on gradually breaking her down. One created havoc while the other rested, then the other would pick up, and so it had gone. Wayne finally got up and wheeled their crib into the family room, dragging behind him one of the blankets from their bed.

When he returned, he told Ethel to spend the night on the sofa. He wanted to get a few hours sleep in peace without interruptions of any sort, he said, whether it was the kids' noise or her getting in and out of bed to tend to them. She succumbed to his demands and slept fitfully, and now—as the afternoon wore on—Ethel was wavering and paying the price.

With her head sinking into the pillow, Ethel's eyes roamed around the room to several pictures attached to the beige-paneled walls—a couple of cheap landscapes, an enlarged photo of the family taken a couple of years earlier next to the garden, and a watercolor of a vase of flowers she won at a county fair back in Kentucky. In a corner of the room, between the ceiling and the walls, she noticed the beginnings of a spider web. She stared at it for several seconds before slowly letting her eyes lose focus within the web's myriad spools of fine thread.

The day she gave birth, her contractions fluttered in the maternity ward into the early evening. The struggling baby caused her immense discomfort, and when the midwife finally informed her that it was time to begin the proceedings, she wondered if she had the strength to muscle the newborn child out.

Once in the operating room, she pushed and gasped for breath in harmony with the coaching of the medical team around her for hours. She felt the child gradually begin to move in the direction of her spread legs and continued to squeeze. She harnessed her pain by stretching her head back, closing her eyes, and concentrating on the sweat dripping from her pores. Finally, after several torturous hours, she was overcome by the sensation she hadn't experienced in nearly fifteen years: the slow, steady closing of her spread vagina, which oozed the jellied life out of her amidst a quivering, crimson mass of membrane.

Although she could see and hear the baby which just sprang from her pelvis, she knew that there was something else inside her insisting to get out as well. And when she heard voices around her telling her to keep her momentum going, she knew that the excess weight she had carried for three quarters of a year was not the bulk of one child alone.

She continued her contractions until she felt another mass begin to move again, easing its way out of her body and into the doctor's hands. When her groans finally began to wane, she became aware of a chorus of high-shrilled screams. She looked up and through tears saw two babies being held to her, each one a mirror image of the other. Ethel couldn't fully comprehend such an unexpected sight; she saw double images everywhere, then watched the multiple faces around her become distant. She even heard their moving lips lose their sound and sensed the bright lights above her rapidly fade.

Ethel keyed in again on the infants' cries. She opened her eyes, bringing back into focus the spider web in the corner of the room. She hoisted herself from the bed and attempted to stifle the sound of their bawling with the reassuring sound of her voice. She shoved her swollen feet into her soiled terry-cloth slippers and shuffled across the carpet to the crib. She stared down at the tiny pink profiles of the open-mouthed, bellowing identical twins.

The six-week old twins were named Gladys and Crystal (the latter at Wayne's insistence, after the country singer Crystal Gayle, since Merle wasn't possible), but Ethel still had trouble telling them apart. Consequently, she was never sure if she was calling each girl by her true name. But Ethel figured that as time went on and the twins got bigger and started growing more hair, she would be able to tell them apart more easily. They were cute and slightly big for their age, and Ethel certainly loved them, but she couldn't help feeling that she would have been happier with only one.

After all, that's what she had planned on: a little girl named Gladys, who would give her a reason to stay home and do chores during the day. Just one girl would have provided her with some entertainment when her favorite shows were not on TV. But nature threw a wrench in the works, and her plans for her middle age had been irreconcilably altered. Two mouths to feed, two diapers to change, and two screaming babies waking her up in the middle of the night, constantly demanding her attention, added up to simply too many problems.

Ethel lit a cigarette and slipped the robe off her shoulders. She unclipped her bra and felt her enlarged breasts slap down against her oval stomach. Since she had two infants to feed, Ethel couldn't alternate her breasts with each feeding like most mothers. Both milk ducts were painfully gummed and drained, and therefore needed extra special attention. She sat down on the cushioned metal chair in front of her dressing table, reached for the bottle of baby oil next to a vase of artificial flowers and unscrewed the cap. Staring at the monstrous images in the mirror, she poured some on one hand and supported a heavy breast with the other, gently rubbing the lotion into each tender mound in an attempt to moisturize their chafed skin.

Because of the excess milk Ethel's breasts held, they had expanded to even greater proportions than she had ever known. In a way, they looked to her like two regulation-size bowling balls obscenely connected to her thick torso. Their pale skin was pulled taut, revealing string-like blue veins that stretched crookedly across their surface. Her nipples appeared like huge circles of thin rubber, attached painfully to her front in crude stiches which seemed to be tearing at the seams. They had become much darker and extended so far to the sides that even her large hand gliding across their expanse failed to hide them. The points of the nipples themselves retreated into the chapped mass that surrounded them, as though trying to hide from their imminent suffering.

The light from the window reflected off her breasts and made them appear like two over-inflated balloons about to explode. Ethel finished with the lotion, took a last drag on her cigarette, and then hoisted one of the infants—Gladys she guessed—to her breast. She consoled the other by rocking the crib with her toe. Gladys gnawed on her nipple, trying to get a grip with her tiny gums before extracting some fluid. Her mouth moved furtively while her small eyes remained shut.

As the child became full, Ethel stared away from her reflection in the mirror and thought of other things. She was perturbed that her husband treated her cruelly the night before, instead of showing her the compassion and lending her the support she felt she deserved. After all, she didn't deliberately give birth to twins. Yet Wayne continually acted as if caring for them was her problem and hers alone. He claimed that his job was to provide

110

the material things they needed; that could only be achieved through extra paid work on his part. He had, in fact, picked up a few extra shifts at the security firm, but he still seemed able to find time for a little relaxation—something she felt she hadn't had much of since the birth of the twins.

Every night, she was forced to get up repeatedly during the wee hours to feed and change the twins. Then she had to get the food ready for the other kids. After that, the cycle continued relentlessly throughout the day. In between, she was expected to do the shopping, clean the house, scrub the floors, do the laundry, and monitor the children's activities in school. She was a strong woman—she knew that—but as each day passed and her drowsiness grew along with her discouragement, she felt as if she were sinking, dragged down by a bloated body, lead feet, and sore tits. Her breasts continually gave her the sensation that they were being twisted and pulled by a thick strand of course rope knotted around them.

Ethel pulled Gladys' quivering mouth away from her chest and placed her back in the crib, then lifted the other girl to the opposite breast. Crystal immediately clamped her mouth around the nipple and began draining what fluid remained.

Ethel put a cigarette between her lips and ignited it, exhaling the smoke in a large blue cloud that dispersed against her distorted image in the mirror. On the table top in front of her, she set her eyes upon her Polaroid camera. She'd already given several snapshots of the girls to her friends, and decided to take another one for her sister Becky in California as soon as she finished.

The two women hadn't seen each other in nearly six years. They had, however, exchanged letters every six months or so and spoke on the phone occasionally during most of that time. They were born nearly five years apart in Keavy, Kentucky and raised by caring parents.

Their father worked for the state, driving a steamroller over the freshly laid blacktop of the area's highways and byroads. He was a short, gaunt man whose face was almost triangular. His cheeks were drawn in and sunken, partially because of the four packs of cigarettes he smoked vigorously every day. He was reserved and easy-going, and normally spoke only after being spoken to, but he always worked hard to provide the family with the things they needed. He spent most of his non-working hours around the house. After dinner he would normally sit in front of the television and drink several glasses of strong homemade whiskey from his basement still. More often than not, he fell asleep in front of the set, suffocated in a thick cloud of spent smoke.

Their mother was a tall woman who grew up in central Louisiana and met her husband—six years her junior—while he was enlisted in the service at Fort Polk. After he was discharged, they got married and returned to his hometown in southeastern Kentucky. In contrast to her lanky husband, she was a heavyset woman who spent a great deal of time in the kitchen, frying up big meals whose leftovers always lined the refrigerator shelves and provided the family with an assortment of late night snacks. She occasionally made a bit of extra money sewing for various people in the area and was a member of several social clubs. But, unlike the man she married, she rarely touched alcohol. She didn't seem to mind the fact that he passively drank himself into submission every night; she just happened to be more attracted to sugar instead of alcohol.

As children, Ethel and her sister played together constantly. But as the years of their youth passed by, Becky began hanging around children more her age, and Ethel and she spent their free time doing different things. Physically, Becky was well-put-together and always had a number of boyfriends she stayed out late with. When she quit high school, she married one of them and set off with her new husband for California. He had a cousin who offered him a job with a construction firm near Bakersfield.

Ethel spent a normal adolescence going to school every day and getting average grades. She looked nearly the opposite of her striking sister. Ethel took much more after her mother, and she guessed it was because of her pudgy figure and her thick glasses that the boys in the school never paid much attention to her. It didn't bother her that much. She was perfectly content to pass the weekend hours sampling her mother's baked goods, or in front of the television with a half gallon of ice cream at her disposal.

Around the time when Ethel finished high school, Becky returned from California alone. Her husband had just begun serving a ten-year sentence at San Quentin on forgery charges. Rather than taking the chance of being implicated herself, Becky hastily decided to put the promised land behind her for a while. She got a job in a bar several towns away and rented a small apartment nearby, preferring the freedom of being on her own than living with her parents. Ethel later began her training in the dental office near the community college, and would frequently stop by her sister's place afterwards to catch up on lost time. They were happy with the each other's company, and the companionship they had missed since childhood.

It was through their renewed acquaintance that Ethel began having an interest in members of the opposite sex, which eventually led to her

112

meeting Wayne. And fortunately, she felt, her supportive family helped ease the tension with her new husband. Acknowledging the newlyweds' financial difficulties, her parents cheerfully offered them free room and board, and even took a liking to Wayne despite his difficult demeanor.

Ethel's parents had both lived to see the birth of Ethel's first child, but unfortunately, both had been called to their Maker while Ethel was pregnant with Junior. Her father went first, when his diseased lungs (the doctor described them as being blacker than the pavement he flattened) ceased to function correctly and ultimately squelched his already shortened breath. A few months later, Ethel returned from the store to find her mother stretched out on the kitchen floor, her overworked heart having succumbed to the immense burdens that her ample body demanded.

Of course, Ethel missed her parents. But Darlene occupied so much of her time and provided so much happiness, and Junior's demands shortly took up whatever time was left. So she gradually took their loss in stride and became accustomed to their absence as best she could. Becky gave up her apartment and moved into the house. The move provided the sisters with constant companionship and a stronger bond than they had ever experienced before.

Their relationship had continued for several more years until Ethel ended up in bed with her sister's boyfriend, which consequently separated them both physically and emotionally. Becky ended up returning to California where she reunited with her paroled husband. It wasn't until shortly before Wayne had decided to move to Indiana that the two sisters finally rectified their differences and began communicating again—although more than two-thirds of the continent still stood between them.

Ethel forced Crystal away from her breast and laid her down in the crib. Then she slipped the robe back on to her shoulders and tucked her aching breasts into the soft material. As she picked up the camera and snapped a quick shot of the two girls, she smelled the sweet, all-too-familiar odor of fresh, milky excrement begin to fill the room. She grimaced.

Suddenly an infant began whimpering. Ethel knew that before long the second one would join in the chorus. Putting the camera back down, Ethel prepared for the unpleasant task before her.

"Maybe it hadn't been all that bad at McDonalds," she thought aloud.

18

Wayne sat in the middle of his most recently completed project, a subterranean room he affectionately called "the shed." It was buried several yards from a corner of the garden, and until recently had been a cramped and musty hole in the ground. The shed could only be reached after passing through a couple of small, horizontal wooden doors just above the earth's surface, and then descending ten steep steps which were formed by decaying pieces of timber wedged firmly into the dark clay. Before, the walls had been lined with large chunks of stone, and the puddled floor carelessly covered by scraps of lumber and water-logged burlap. Once inside, it was difficult for Wayne to stand up straight without his head hitting the heavy support beams overhead. The roof was simply a thick, rusted slab of iron atop which the grass grew and helped camoflauged the room's presence.

Wayne didn't know what the room's original purpose was. He supposed at one time it could have housed a still or small cellar or something else hidden for a reason, even though when they had moved to the land there was no trace of a house that may have once stood over it. Since they had been on the property, the area had virtually been unused except to discard some of the building materials that were small enough to cart in a wheelbarrow.

Up until a couple of weeks before, it remained in disregard, while Wayne's own mental state was only slightly more ordered. Fortunately, the shock he received upon being told of the twins' birth had been relatively short-lived. He realized that, as with the pregnancy itself, there was nothing he could do to change the situation.

Wayne had done his best to adapt to the situation, but it had been so many years since he had been around babies that he now felt strange in their presence. One of the guys he worked with also became a new father just after Ethel had given birth, and all he could talk about was how cute the kid was and how he played with it all afternoon before rocking it to sleep at night. Wayne supposed that his co-worker's behavior was natural—after all, the guy was only about twenty-five years old. But Wayne also knew his circumstances were completely different, because he was nearly twice the guy's age and had been through it all a couple of times already.

The way Wayne saw it was that the years before a kid could talk or wipe its own ass were better left to the women. He could say "goo-goo ga-ga" to the twins, but he knew that his important advice and guidance could only come in a few years' time, when they began to understand the spoken language. The only course he figured he could take now was to accept the cards that had been dealt to him, and attempt to arrange them into a workable hand that might allow him to continue with his own temporary floundering career and goals.

At first it wasn't easy. He was still driving around in the back of the bank truck like a caged animal, and then coming home to a family who paid all their attention to the twins. He complained about his demotion to his boss, and although his boss showed some concern, he was unable to find anything else that might prove more challenging. So Wayne had continued in the cashier's position, even though his enthusiasm had waned to such a low point that he didn't even partake in his Saturday training sessions anymore. Instead, he tried to keep occupied in his free time by working several extra night shifts patrolling the school grounds. At least this passed the hours and boosted his income slightly.

But even with a few additional shifts, Wayne found it increasingly difficult to pay the bills at the end of the month. One baby was expensive, but two doubled the price of everything. And because they had no hand-me-downs, it meant extra expenditures for clothes, the crib, baby carriage, and things for them to play with. There were doctor's bills and boxes of diapers, whose prices always left him flabbergasted. As usual, there was the mortgage to pay on the property, as well as the electricity, gas, television, water, and telephone bills. And when the Fury decided to stop in the middle of the road one day and refused to start again, he found himself faced with another bill that dwarfed all the others put together.

Wayne knew that Ethel had to have a car for herself. So he ended up having the Fury towed to a junk yard, where he traded it for a beaten-up 1977 AMC Pacer that the owner said would last a few more years "around town." He didn't like the fact that he would now have to drive the Gremlin his wife drove, especially after being used to something that so perfectly resembled a police car. But he also knew that the financial strain on his family demanded it, and he had no choice but to say goodbye to his beloved cruiser.

When the twins were about seven weeks old, however, Wayne's future suddenly took a turn for the better.

Wayne was unexpectedly called to the security office and offered

115

a new job at a huge supermarket called Buy-Rite in Seymour, a good-sized town about twenty-five miles away. It was a new contract for Vanguard, and it called for two uniformed guards to make their presence felt in an effort to curb theft in the store. Wayne was appointed the head of the two-man team, and was given the added responsibilities of coaching whomever he was assigned to work with, as well as taking charge whenever an altercation might occur.

His new salary would surpass what he had been making before—even with the extra nights. But the demands would also be greater. He would have to be on his toes the entire day and show the store managers some definite results.

In a way, Wayne missed being around all the big money of the bank job and the situations that might have led to a possible shootout. But in the supermarket, he soon found that his enthusiasm for law enforcement returned with a vengeance. He once again began taking pride in his uniform and his physical appearance because he was giving the orders and calling the shots. He began viewing his assignment as one where his talents could shine while he further honed his craft, aspirations he had been deprived of in the previous months.

Every day he stopped several people as they attempted to leave the store without paying for the goods they concealed. He marched up and down the aisles of the supermarket relentlessly, making his presence known to people he suspected. Or he waited patiently up by the front doors, where he would collar suspects as they tried to get out of the store. Then he brought them into the back room to have a little fun.

Wayne's methods were generally things he'd picked up from police shows or movies that featured scenes in which the cops got results in their own secret ways. Much of that simply consisted of scaring the hell out of the culprits and breaking them down, often to tears and confessions of great remorse. Wayne's normal response was to sit quietly while the ''perp'' came out with bleeding heart stories or outright lies. More often than not, they would begin contradicting themselves within a few minutes. That was when Wayne got down to brass tacks.

Wayne had a police nightstick that he was fond of smashing on the table or the back of the thief's chair. Occasionally he made contact with the body if he particularly disliked the person. He never drew blood, but a little prod now and then certainly made them realize that he might if they didn't cooperate.

Of course, they never threatened to call the police for his violence, as he always planted the seed early on that he was a member of the force. And with his street cop's appearance, attitude, and savvy, he rarely had to leave a bruise to make them realize they were dealing with the real thing. After that, they usually began to shake and appeal to him with stammered pleas of mercy, as if they were facing God Himself on Judgment Day. Wayne would listen to them with contempt, then look at them despicably, take a couple of cheap Polaroid mug shots, and make them fill out a number of forms. Staring down at the criminal scum, he insinuated that the papers were confessions that would, of course, be used in their imminent trials. He let them know what kind of stiff jail sentence the judge (whom he claimed to be a personal friend) would hand down on Wayne's advice. And while he escorted them out of the store, he threatened that if he ever saw them again, he would make sure that they got longer sentences.

After working the new job a couple of weeks, however, he realized that he needed and rightly deserved a place where he could be on his own and unwind after a hard day's work. He wanted time away from the continuous noise and smell of his recent offspring. So he began the renovation of the dingy room outside by pouring cement into molds where the stairs lay, covering the walls with pieces of wood and burlap, and lowering the floor by a foot or so before resurfacing it with a couple of inches of concrete. He whitewashed the new walls and rusty ceiling, and ran a power line from the trailer that provided energy to the room's sixty or seventy square feet. The job only took him a couple of weeks. Because he had done it all himself and mostly used materials left over from his other work, the expense was minimal.

Wayne leaned back in a creaky wooden chair and rested his feet on the desk he had made with a piece of particle board placed on top of a couple of sawhorses. He read an article in a magazine taken from a stack of others that were scattered across the table's surface along with a few cans of beer. In front of him, a small television/video unit illuminated the room with gray, fuzzy snow. A few diagrams related to his work were tacked to the wall, as well as a framed photocopy of *The Law Enforcement Officer's Pledge*. The pledge was his Code, one that served as a constant reminder of the ten rules he always attempted to adhere to, things like avoiding favoritism, being loyal to God and country, acting as a model to youth, and keeping in good physical condition.

Wayne belched, threw the magazine on the table and popped the top on another can of beer. He leaned forward in his chair, returning its balance to all four legs. Then he reached past the magazines, grabbed a video cassette and popped it into the machine. He bought the VCR unit a few days before at a police auction, where the department sold all the confiscated, yet unclaimed items from the past year. He bought it not just because its price was so low, but because he also felt it would help him in his new work, which he was anxious to perfect.

The tape contained footage Wayne compiled from the different surveillance cameras in the store. There were six cameras whose cables led to a single monitoring unit located in the security room, ten or so feet above the shopping floor. The monitoring unit contained six small screens that correlated with each camera, but the screens were so small that it was difficult to notice anything but obvious movements by suspects. For this reason, he had recorded a three-hour tape of the action on the floor during the store's busiest hours. Now he hoped to pick up things that he'd perhaps been unable to detect on the tiny screens at work.

As if surveying dormant fish within a large tank, he stared at the tedious movement. As he watched, he jotted down notes on his pad and attempted to figure out which areas needed the most concentration, and where his assistant would be most useful. The switching cameras changed their perspective every five minutes or so, and he made copious notes. But none of the action he witnessed seemed out-of-the-ordinary.

After about an hour, however, Wayne was jostled as if he had just been pinched. Suddenly excited, he shot his short finger toward the rewind button and held it there for several seconds before letting the tape advance again, this time in slow motion.

There she was, he observed, the skinny woman in the ratty white coat and dirty, torn sneakers whom Wayne had suspected for nearly a week. He actually stopped her at the door once, yet he was unable to nail her for lack of evidence. She didn't look to be a day over twenty. But she always came into the supermarket with an entourage of three filthy young kids, pushing the smallest one around in the cart. He gazed at her now, standing in the meat aisle, pretending to read a package—a skill which he was sure she was incapable of—while occasionally looking around suspiciously for any stray eyes.

And then it happened: The customer next to her turned her back and the woman thrust the package into the coat of the youngster riding in the basket. Wayne paused the tape and viewed several other packages within the child's coat. What scum she was, he thought, involving her little urchin in criminal activity like that. He felt a flush of anger surge through his body and cursed himself for having allowed her to outsmart him before.

118

She wouldn't get away with it again, however, Wayne swore to himself. Touching the pencil to the tip of his tongue, he drew the pad closer and scribbled "disgusting woman with filthy children" under the descriptions of several other possible offenders.

He paused for a moment, then put his pencil to the paper again, this time with large capital letters next to his last notes that simply read "RETAL," shorthand for retaliate.

Wayne leaned back and took a sip of beer before setting the tape in motion again.

No one was above suspicion in the world Wayne Turner policed.

19

"Quit movin'! Your Momma's here!" Ethel hollered as Gladys reeled beneath her huge hand. "I'm just puttin' a new diaper on you for Christ's sake. Don't you wanna fresh Pamper?"

The girl rolled on her back and jerked her limbs playfully, grateful to be rid of the green shit that had covered her ass for the past half-hour. Ethel wiped her with a moist cloth and then covered her bottom with a clean, disposable diaper.

"Your Momma takes good care of you," she told the smiling infant while running her hand through her own hair and carelessly streaking it with a trail of feces. "You're just as clean and dry as your sister now."

Ethel raised the girl from the table and deposited her in the crib next to Crystal, then wiped her hands with the towel and sat down on the bed to rest. As she lit a cigarette, she glanced at her watch and remembered that she had to hurry. In less than three-quarters of an hour, she was due at the high school for a meeting with Darlene's guidance counselor. They were going to discuss the girl's current academic problems, over which her teachers were expressing concern.

It troubled Ethel. Even though Darlene had never been the best student, she had, at least, typically received average marks. During the past school year however, Darlene's grades began sliding. Her teachers claimed her decline stemmed from her inability to comprehend the concepts taught in the required math and science classes.

Ethel had to admit that she felt inept trying to help the girl. She didn't possess a very retentive memory either, and had certainly never been a whiz with facts or numbers. When she was in school, she had learned the basic things, like arithmetic and grammar, and consequently skimmed by. But many years had passed since she'd put the majority of things she'd learned into practice. So when Darlene began coming to her for help with subjects like algebra and biology, she was unable to provide any extra aid whatsoever.

Darlene's problem was one Ethel felt she could do without, because other facets of her life were beginning to come together. Physically, for example, she was beginning to feel a little better, largely due to the fact that the twins were now being bottle-fed rather than relying on her breasts for nourishment. They were becoming accustomed to the world outside the womb and were crying less than before, which gave Ethel some peace of mind. Of course, she was still awakened every night by their crying, but they normally quieted back down once they were attended to.

The main thing was that the twins didn't have to be observed or kept under guard constantly. Things like that were particularly important at times like this, when lugging two kids around would be impossible. With their advanced age, Ethel figured she'd have time to make it to the high school and back without them even knowing she'd been gone.

Ethel stamped out her cigarette and looked at her watch again. She realized that she had exactly thirty-four minutes to get herself ready and drive to the high school. She looked at the three wigs sitting on styrofoam heads atop her make-up table. After considering each briefly, she chose a straight, medium-length brown style and placed it on her head, folding her own oily hair underneath it.

She then dipped her hand into the foundation pot and began smoothing it over her face. She began with her high forehead, working it into the wrinkled area around her eyes and moving downward, across her fleshy cheeks and slightly protruding chin. She applied a bright red lipstick and light-blue eye shadow and mascara, then adorned her ears with a pair of large gold hoop earrings.

Walking over to the closet, Ethel put on a polyester shirt with a flower design and squeezed into a pair of brown stretch slacks. She chose a pair of white shoes and checked her reflection. After adjusting the wig slightly, she felt she looked respectable. She knew that was important. After all, any problem her daughter had could be a reflection of the family she came from.

After quickly checking to make sure the twins were asleep, Ethel hustled out to the kitchen and grabbed her pocketbook. As she swung it over her shoulder, she paused briefly to glimpse the remainder of a coffee cake the others had failed to finish for breakfast.

She'd been good that morning and resisted its temptation. But now, looking at its gooey frosting, delicate crust, and cream-cheese filling, her will was not as strong. Without hesitating further, she lunged toward the cake and scooped it up in a flash. She forced the entire piece into her mouth and then looked around guiltily, as if expecting some onlooker to ridicule her for her weakness.

121

The cake's sweet flavor ignited her taste buds like a match put to kerosene. She rapidly scooped up the rest of the crumbs with her stubby fingers. Manically, she ripped apart the box, licked the remnants of the cake's frosting from the plastic, and tapped what remained of the confectioner's sugar into her open mouth.

Feeling a sudden burst of energy, Ethel grabbed her bag and shot out the door toward the car, licking her white powdered lips contentedly between strides.

Ethel arrived at the high school about twenty minutes later and entered through the cafeteria doors facing the parking lot. She scurried toward the main section of the school and found her daughter already inside the guidance office. Darlene was talking to Mr. Harvey, a middle-aged man with a neatly trimmed beard and brown corduroy suit. Strung around his neck was a yellow bow-tie. Ethel introduced herself and pulled a chair up next to Darlene and struggled to squeeze into it.

Mr. Harvey spoke slowly and with an air of seriousness. He reiterated what he had told Darlene, shuffling some records in front of him and listing the classes in which she was receiving below-average grades.

"Darlene, I didn't know you were in danger of flunkin' English, too!" Ethel interrupted him. "Why didn't you ask me for some help in that?"

Darlene looked at her mother sheepishly and shrugged her shoulders before finally sinking back into her chair.

Ethel continued staring at her, deciding to continue so that Mr. Harvey would think she cared. "Answer me, Darlene!" she said. "You know Daddy and I are always there to give an extra hand with your problems."

The girl looked at her with a puzzled expression, heavily laden with skepticism. "But I asked you and you told me that you..."

"Darlene! Don't talk back to your mother," Ethel cut her off, shaking her head toward Mr. Harvey.

"Mrs. Turner," Mr. Harvey interjected. "There are many students who find adjusting to work on a high school level very difficult. It's not that they're any less intelligent than the others," he said, noisily clearing his throat, "but they just happen to put their knowledge to use in different ways."

"Oh, I see," Ethel said, responding as if a difficult theory had just clicked in her head.

"Now there's still the possibility that Darlene can still scrape by in a few of the classes," he added, fingering his beard gently. "But with a couple of others, her chances are highly improbable. So for this term I would probably advise Darlene to drop her Chemistry One course, as well as her Introduction to Trigonometry course, and use those periods in a study hall I can assign her, where she can at least work hard and pick up her remaining credits."

"Well that sounds like a good idea," Ethel said. "But as far as Darlene's high school diploma goes, won't this put her real far behind the rest of her class?"

"It will slightly," he said, glancing down at her records again and counting the units she had accumulated. "But rather than placing so much emphasis on things like that, I think it's more important that we try to discuss Darlene's plan for the upcoming year. And for that matter, her future."

Mr. Harvey suggested that instead of continuing her present studies the following term, Darlene might attend a technical school located about twenty miles away. There she could put her efforts into acquiring a practical skill, with which she could at least find work when she was finished. Her school hours would be more or less the same as before, even though more of her time would be spent being transported from one school to another. Mr. Harvey felt that Darlene could use the time on the bus to study her notes from the day before.

What they now had to decide, Mr. Harvey said more seriously, was a suitable course of study for Darlene to embark upon. He claimed that there were hundreds of possibilities for the taking, and began reading choices from a long list.

"That sounds like it might be interestin'," Darlene said when he had reached "medical office assistant." "It would be nice to help people."

Ethel glanced at her daughter and shook her head. "Oh Darlene, you don't wanna do that," she whined. "I don't think it would be very healthy being around sick people all the time."

Darlene made a face as Mr. Harvey continued with the other options that were open to her. The girl stopped him again when he'd reached "catering."

"I'm sure that if you were around food all day long you'd probably start to hate it," Ethel cut in. "Now just be quiet and let Mr. Harvey finish the choices, and then we can go back and see which one might be best for you."

"All right," Darlene said, "But I wouldn't mind learnin' how to cook some different foods."

"What else is there?" Ethel asked, facing the counselor and ignoring her daughter.

Mr. Harvey continued down the list, but after several seconds was interrupted again, this time by Ethel's loud voice.

"Now there's an area I could see you gettin' involved in," she said, suddenly turning to Darlene. "The beautician's field. Didn't you tell me you wanted to learn how to cut your own hair?"

"Yeah, but not all the time," Darlene drawled. She could remember when she tried to thin her hair with shears and cut out several large chunks of it instead. That had forced her to wear a hat to school for months. "That dressmakin' choice before sounded better to me."

"C'mon Darlene, you don't wanna be a seamstress," Ethel said with certainty. "You'd be cooped up in some little room all day long on your own, and that work just ain't very flatterin', believe me."

Mr. Harvey stared at Darlene. "The beautician's course is usually a very popular choice for girls your age," he piped in.

"There you go, Darlene," Ethel stated. "Wouldn't you like to learn how to do all that stuff to make people look nice?"

"I guess so," she said absently. "But let's see what the other choices are left first."

"Well if you like that one, what's the point in wastin' any more time?" Ethel said, glancing quickly at the counselor. "I'm sure Mr. Harvey is a very busy man."

"If Darlene isn't all that pleased with that choice, we can find something else," Mr. Harvey said.

"Darlene probably looks at it as haircuttin' and nothin' else," Ethel cut in, attempting to remain on the subject. "But that's not the only thing involved with it, is it?"

"Not at all," Mr. Harvey said, looking down again at his notes. "In addition to hair cutting there's...there's hair styling, removing, conditioning and coloring. And also, uh, manicure."

With each new field mentioned, Ethel became more and more excited. She knew she'd have a professional—or at least someone in serious training—at her immediate disposal. Indeed, Darlene could finally try to correct the mistakes she had already made, and at no charge to boot. With her new knowledge, Darlene would also be able to make Ethel's legs silky smooth and her nails long and beautiful. Ethel would finally get those lady-like things which had always been unavailable to her because of the high prices salons charged.

"Listen to him, honey!" Ethel insisted, glancing between Mr. Harvey and her daughter. "Wouldn't you like to learn how to do those things?"

"I guess so," she said hesitantly, unable to picture herself, a fat girl with glasses and acne, giving beauty tips.

"Well it's settled then," Ethel said, breathing out contentedly and then smiling broadly at the decision.

"Good," Mr. Harvey said, placing his pen to a form. "I'm sure you made the right choice."

"Yeah," Darlene responded without emotion, not so sure of herself as the others seemed to be.

20

The supermarket unfolded like a giant maze, its evenly spaced aisles extending in rectangular rows headed by towers of stacked sale items. The canned products, cartons, small boxes and plastic containers were stacked to capacity within the aisles, with large signs announcing the specials of the week. The dairy section ran along one wall, the meat counter along another, and the refrigerator and freezer cases were framed within glistening chrome against a third. The bread and deli sections sat near one of the front corners, while the manager's office rested near the entrance. Sandwiched between those, before the front wall of window-glass posted with the week's specials, were ten checkout counters.

Wayne Turner sat above it all in the back of the store, behind a small two-way mirror that concealed his presence. Even though nobody could see him, Wayne felt like a king holding court before his subjects. It wasn't that he owned the supermarket, but he did enforce the law inside—something he felt was nearly as important.

He wasn't the person who mopped up a broken bottle of ketchup from the floor, or argued with irate, out-of-work people about the validity of their food stamps. Nor was he the one who advised old ladies that bologna cost 99 cents a pound, or told some housewife that her coupons were out of date.

As head of security, Wayne was certainly above everybody else in more ways than his current logistic position. He wasn't dressed like the rest of their employees in their ill-fitting red, polyester smocks. He shared no role in ordering the merchandise, dealing with money, stocking the shelves or checking people out. From his clandestine position behind the TV monitors, he oversaw everything and made sure that the store's interests were met.

Wayne glanced down at his watch, saw that a half-hour remained on his break, and leaned back in his chair, stretching his short legs toward the simple wood table before him. Today had been a rather dull day, an ''off day'' as he referred to it. He hadn't caught any shoplifters or even been given ''the chill,'' the adrenaline rush that always accompanied the surveilance, trailing, and aprehension of a suspect. What was worse, though, was that he also spent a lot of time training a new guard the art and science of supermarket surveillance.

Wayne didn't mind training the young guys—after all, someone had to do it—but it always took his attention away from his own job of nabbing crooks.

It always seemed he was instructing; showing the others the ropes, teaching them about "key sections," or telling them what to look for in a thief instead. But all of this kept him from doing what he did best, which was trailing and getting the tingle. Then again, he knew that training was necessary. Wayne figured that it was better that the rookie pulled his first duty with a pro like himself, who not only knew what he was doing but excelled at his job.

Wayne leaned forward in the chair and scanned the immensity of the store. He looked for the new man, Duffy. Even though Duffy looked like he had just gotten out of high school, he was about twenty-five, with blond hair, red cheeks, and baby fat visible even beneath his uniform. He didn't seem to be the brightest guy, but at least he seemed eager. In Wayne's book, that was one essential quality for anyone who wanted to carry a badge.

Because of Duffy's enthusiasm, Wayne didn't take an immediate dislike to him, as he had to so many other "deputies" in the past. In fact, he was beginning to wonder if Duffy just might be that missing piece of the puzzle for an undercover supermarket surveillance team Wayne recently began thinking about. After all, with such a youthful appearance, he looked more like a dumb kid shopping for his grandmother than a cop. A perfect complement to his own hard presence. Only time would tell, but with some encouragement and continual reinforcement, the kid might eventually fit into his plans.

Wayne shifted his eyes toward the wall lined with many Polaroids of criminals he had apprehended over the past couple of months. Wayne believed that most people viewed shoplifters like these sorts, poor people who weaseled their way up and down the store aisles and loaded up their large overcoats with whatever would fit. There were a lot of people who operated that way, but they were also the easiest to catch because it was so obvious what they were up to, even to the untrained eye.

Over the past few months, Wayne had grown tired of busting this type of vermin. Sure, it was a collar and all, but he knew that the majority of thieves like that were hardened. They had probably never come into his supermarket before and would never come in again. They were transients, and there weren't many lessons you could teach a person like that.

It certainly wasn't that he felt sorry for them or any sort of compassion. After all, they were criminal scum who had broken the law and been caught. But it was obvious that they had been through the same thing a hundred times before. Wayne knew they would just end up going to another supermarket in the next town as soon as he turned them loose.

He certainly didn't let them get away lightly. But now, instead of giving them the full treatment in his office, he normally just took back the goods and threatened them quickly. He backed it all up with a casual uncovering of his holstered gun and a warning that the next time he wouldn't hesitate to use it to protect the store's property.

Wayne's tactics had proven successful. Even though he wasn't concentrating on them now, it seemed that those dirty, sneaky types were finally getting the message. It was as if through the grapevine they had heard that it wasn't a good idea to remove goods in the store surveilled by Wayne Turner.

Just a couple of days earlier, Wayne had observed a thief in action. Reacting immediately, Wayne made his way to the front door and, when the suspect tried to exit, he had blocked the perp's path and simply held out his hand, waving it in a gesture that silently said, "Gimme what you got motherfucker. Or else." The guy rapidly pulled out two chicken filets and stammered, "What are you doin' here? I thought today was your day off."

Wayne just smiled and flipped his hand like he was shooing away a fly, then replaced the warm styrofoam trays in the cold meat racks.

Those types didn't provide much challenge, but Wayne knew that in addition to the kind who stole because they were poor, there was also a second type of thief. This was the sneaky kind who worked in an office or gave the air of being educated. They looked trustworthy and above suspicion. They were likely to casually open the bag of cashews and eat them while strolling along, or change the prices on bottles of wine, or in some other way try to deceive the store by outsmarting the system.

Wayne now concentrated his efforts on this despicable breed, deceivers of the supermarket and society. It was the most common, yet often overlooked form of theft from the company. But it had the same impact; loss of revenue for the company, and loss of face for the guard.

Wayne took a bite out of a Twinkie and poked his tongue into the cream. He still couldn't locate Duffy, so he continued moving his eyes up and down the aisles. People weaved in, out, and between them, struggling to control their steel baskets, some filled to the top with groceries and others with small children.

128

He could see some people checking the prices in search of the cheapest product, others arguing about how many boxes to buy, and one squeezing every loaf of bread before throwing it back down. He observed a couple of long-haired guys ordering corn dogs from the hot foods counter, and a grossly overweight little girl standing before the ice cream freezers, almost drooling at the color pictures of frozen treats that adorned the boxes. In one of the aisles, a man knocked a jar of applesauce off the bottom shelf by accident and, seeing no one had noticed, hurried off as if he hadn't done it.

Business as usual in the supermarket, Wayne thought, driving his finger into and picking his nose. He stared down at the video monitors and saw nothing suspicious, so he looked back toward the floor and finally spied his deputy. Duffy stood over by the dairy section talking to an employee, who transferred cartons of milk from a plastic crate into the refrigerated bays.

Wayne took a pen and a pad from his pocket and made a note to tell Duffy that the security staff shouldn't mingle with the other employees of the store. A security guard needed concentration to perform his job well, and any sort of talk that didn't pertain to the specific chore at hand had to be considered extraneous and unprofessional.

The note to Duffy was not a big deal, but zooming in on what was occurring behind the boy was a different matter altogether. Wayne picked up a pair of binoculars and focused on the two long-haired hippies who were now standing in front of the yogurts and chomping down on their corn dogs. One of them was struggling to open a foil packet of mustard by holding it with his free hand and ripping the foil with his teeth. As some mustard squirted onto the floor, Wayne's blood began to boil. His deputy, Duffy, was standing right in front of them and jabbering to the dairy man as if nothing was happening!

Wayne looked at his watch. Ten minutes still remained of his break time. He knew that hot food was always paid for at the check-out counter, and he knew damn well what the hippies were trying to get away with.

Suddenly Duffy turned around and said something to them. Finally, Wayne thought, the kid caught on and was about to handle the situation himself. He couldn't hear what they were saying, but one of the hippies was motioning with his hand in the direction of the hot foods section on the other side of the store. Duffy appeared to be getting the information properly. Indeed, he looked as if he were going to deal with the situation on his own.

Wayne lowered the binoculars and sat on the edge of his seat, moving his eyes between the hippies and Duffy, who was now walking toward the deli girl. But when he raised the binoculars again, Wayne saw the girl give Duffy a corn dog. Then Duffy removed it from the plastic bag and bit into it!

Shifting back toward his suspects, Wayne saw the hippies throw their bags on the floor and head for the exit. He was still on his break, but he could take no more.

Wayne immediately responded to this challenge. He jumped up from his chair and grabbed the walkie-talkie from his belt.

"Duffy! One-Eleven in progress!" Wayne screamed into the mouthpiece. "Two dirty hippies moving toward the check-out! The ones you were talkin' to before! They must've dropped the bag on the floor that contained unpaid-for merchandise! A couple of corn dogs! Find the bag, Duffy! I'm headin' toward the door up front! Get on it Duffy!! Move!!!"

Wayne almost fell off the ladder as he backed himself down to the main floor. He ran through the swinging plastic doors of the storeroom and then walked hurriedly in front of the meat counter, checking the aisles for the hippies' whereabouts. Finally he spotted them near one of the check-outs, trying to decide which chocolate bar to buy.

In all the excitement, Wayne had begun to sweat. His uniform had become disheveled. He ran up the aisle, barking into the walkie-talkie. "Duffy! Get to the front of the store! Quick! They're gettin' ready to break! Get up here!" He bumped into one shopping cart and almost fell over, and then knocked a couple of little kids into a stack of Hi-C.

He finally reached the front door and stood with his arms folded just outside. He watched the hippies through the glass and then turned suddenly. Trying to appear nonchalant, he put on his mirror sunglasses.

"Duffy," he finally breathed easier into the walkie-talkie. "Get up here with that bag they threw on the floor. Move it! Now!"

The suspects were getting their change for the two candy bars they were buying. What food they lived on, Wayne thought. Corn dogs and chocolate. Wasn't that a typical diet for those pimply, dirty hippies?

Actually, Wayne didn't know if they were really dirty, but for one reason or another, he always referred to young people with long hair in this way. Maybe it had something to do with their smell of patchouli oil, or how their clothes always had holes torn in them, or that stoned look they always had in their eyes. He wasn't exactly sure.

But what really got on his nerves about them was the fact that their whole lifestyle seemed to be one big act. None of them *had* to walk around in ragged, unwashed clothes. They were just one big group of fakes, university students probably, who still got their money from Mom and Dad. And here they were walking into society's supermarket, thinking they could just eat whatever they want and let Buy-Rite foot the bill.

He saw Duffy hustling toward the door with the plastic bag at his side. Wayne knew that evidence was important—he needed it in order to make his accusation stick. Then he could teach those pseudo-hippies something in the back room. He was actually looking forward to it.

"Step over to the side and don't try to run!" Wayne yelled. "Security!" he added quickly, flashing his badge and immediately returning it to his pocket. He motioned the two hippies to follow him to the corner near the office.

They looked at each other suspiciously and followed Wayne over to a Pepsi machine next to the door. They were silent, although Wayne wasn't sure if it was because they knew they were guilty or because they were stoned.

"Gimme the bag," he said to Duffy, holding out his arm but not taking his eyes off the hippies. He grabbed it and handed it to one of them.

"Is this bag yours?" he asked, as the corners of his mouth formed a false smile. He knew he had them nailed.

The hippies examined it intently, and suddenly one shook his head. "No," he snickered. "It says here one corn dog. And we ordered two."

Confusion suddenly overtook Wayne's face and he stopped chewing his gum. He grabbed the bag and stared down at the label. Sure enough, it was for one corn dog at 69 cents, and he knew exactly whose it was.

Wayne crushed the plastic bag in his hands and glared at his deputy, who was swallowing the remains of his snack. He looked back at the hippies, who were trying to contain a laugh. Sighing disgustedly at them, Wayne shook his head and then hurried back into the store without saying another word.

If this Duffy kid was going to fit into his plans, he thought, he sure had a hell of a lot to learn.

21

Ethel sat on a metal lawn chair near the door, shaded somewhat by the fiberglass overhang that covered the trailer's small porch. Her bare feet rested in a small, water-filled tub. It wasn't even noon, yet the temperature had already risen to nearly ninety degrees. Ethel watched the baking soda run down her arm, carried away by the streams of sweat bubbling from her open pores. She had been bitten by a bee earlier that morning and had applied the baking soda to get some relief.

Ethel wiped some sweat from her brow and fanned herself with a magazine. She surveyed the area between where she sat and the garden, and watched the minute waves of heat swagger above the scorched grass. She was driven outside about an hour earlier because it was even hotter inside the trailer than it was outside. And because the fan was in the repair shop, she'd found the trailer's stifling, still air unbearable.

A loud burst of sound exploded through an open window and jostled Ethel. Junior had bought himself a stereo with the money he made from his new paper route, and he was letting the volume run loud. Ethel stood up abruptly and grimaced in pain, as her back muscles contracted wearily. She took a drag off her cigarette and walked inside. She staggered down the hallway, stopped in front of Junior's door and knocked loudly.

"Turn that down!" she yelled.

The door swung open and a wave of sound blew into her face. "What!?" he yelled, surprised to find her so close.

"Turn that down!" she repeated. "The twins are asleep and I want 'em stayin' that way. Why do you have to listen to that so loud anyway?"

"It's not loud!" Junior yelled defiantly.

Ethel put her hands on her hips and stared at the boy. His greasy hair hadn't been cut since spring, and now it hung limply around his pimple-covered face. "I can hear it outside for God's sake! So just turn it down like I said!"

"But the music don't sound as good when it's low," he huffed.

"Well put on the headphones then!" she retorted. "'Cause I don't want to deal with the girls in this heat. And I also don't want to have to tell you again!'' Ethel pulled on the cigarette and shook her head. ''And why don't you get your hair cut Junior? I think it looked much better when it was short.''

Junior sighed toward her. ''Oh give me a break, Mom!'' he blurted. ''You know I told you I was gonna let it grow, so just lay off it. All right?'' He closed the door in her face and a couple of seconds later she heard the volume lower slightly.

She quickly knocked on the door again. ''It's still too loud!'' she yelled.

''Jesus Christ!'' came his muffled voice above the music. ''I'll put on the headphones then! You happy?''

Several seconds later, the noise stopped immediately, and Ethel ground some stray cigarette ashes into the carpet with her foot. She walked into the family room and observed the tiny, inert bodies of Gladys and Crystal in their crib. They were now nearly six months old, so she had become accustomed to each one's particular habits and personalities. Ethel no longer had any difficulty whatsoever in telling them apart, although she knew her husband still had problems doing that.

Wayne's complete indifference toward the girls annoyed Ethel. She knew he was busy with his job at the supermarket, and she certainly appreciated the extra money he brought home each week. But the only thing Wayne ever did with the girls was glance at them and maybe rock their crib briefly before making some excuse to work in his garden, or take care of a few ''loose ends'' out in the shed.

Ethel grabbed a bottle of Tab from the refrigerator and returned outside, plopping her feet back into the water and staring over toward the subterranean room's hatch. She wondered what he had down there anyway. She had never seen its refurbished interior. In fact, as soon as he had begun transforming the area, Wayne made it clear that the space was off-limits to everyone including her. He claimed that it was his personal work and relaxation area—and his alone, and anyone else's presence would tarnish the atmosphere he had worked so hard to create.

Such ''laws'' pissed Ethel off, but she also had to admit that since Wayne had given himself an area to be alone in, his overall demeanor had improved dramatically. After all, Wayne's absence from the house led to fewer disagreements and arguments between them during the evening, something she certainly didn't miss.

In fact, Wayne's only gripe recently had been when Junior announced that he wasn't going to march in the Independence Day Parade with

133

the Boy Scouts. Junior said that he was embarrassed to be seen in the uniform in front of his school friends who, at age fifteen, now considered members of the Scouts to be sissies.

Always proud to see his son in the uniform with his sash of merit badges strapped over his chest, Wayne said that if Junior didn't march, it would be at least a year before he rode his bicycle either. In the end, the boy backed down and made the march, even though he walked the entire three miles with his lowered face obscured by his hat.

Disagreements like that weren't that big of a deal, and with Wayne happily occupied and out of her hair most of the time, Ethel finally had more time to get her body back into condition. But while reaching for the Tab bottle, she felt her gut rest against her bare, cellulite-puckered thighs, and was quickly reminded of all weight loss programs she had abandoned before.

Her first diets—the natural ones—failed miserably because they just made her crave the things she was deprived of even more. She'd go a day eating only lettuce and carrots, and then break into a cold sweat as she watched her children polish off an entire cake in front of the television. Once she even collapsed on the kichen table about an hour before eating her lunch ration of three tomatoes, two celery sticks and a couple of spoonfuls of low-fat cottage cheese. When she regained her energy, she ended up cheating, and wolfed down some beef jerky (which had fortunately renewed her strength). But Ethel also found herself deceiving her willpower nearly every day afterwards, which consequently led to more weight on her—and the scale. After a strenuous month of days filled with relentless suffering, cheating, and the guilt that followed, she finally threw in the towel and admitted defeat.

After that "natural" fiasco, Ethel looked more closely at the advertisements in the women's magazines she picked up every week at the checkout counter of the supermarket. She was especially drawn to certain claims that she could lose weight and continue to eat anything she wanted. She anxiously sent away for an introductory course.

A couple of weeks later she received a brown jar labelled "Re-Pile." She continued eating whatever she wanted and took the pills as advised. Yet after several weeks, the only physical change she noticed was in her yellower urine. Her weight loss was also negligible. So when the bottle was empty, she decided to switch to another brand that also arrived in the mail.

"Cal-Ban 9000" pills were developed at a university research center in Sweden by a doctor who promised quick results, but unfortunately, as with the other diet pills, the only change Ethel noticed after three weeks was in her own pocketbook. Fortunately, she received a free necklace made out of Chinese Faux Pearls that was offered with a six-week order, making her waste of money slightly easier to bear.

Finally, Ethel came to the conclusion that diet pills were of little benefit. She stopped using them, but found herself feeling more fatigued and lackadaisical than ever. She spent most of the day laying around and regressed to her bad habit of wolfing down whatever snacks lay about the house. She knew that the birth control pills she was taking again retained water and made her feel bloated, but she was also aware that they didn't force her to reach constantly for the cookie jar. Desperate to lessen her helpless binges, she finally decided to pay her doctor a visit to pick up something that might once again help her burn off the extra calories she took in.

She came away from her visit with a prescription for Preludin, which was supposed to stimulate her body with more energy. The doctor had also recommended an exercise program and strict, healthy diet. Ethel swore she would attempt to eat better and exercise. But even before leaving his office, she knew she'd never be able to stick to either program.

Ethel managed to make a personal vow to cut down on what she considered ''unnecessary'' sweets—the junk food she normally picked at before bedtime. But Ethel knew that any sort of exercise program was out of the question. One thing she had hated all her life was unnecessary physical exertion.

It was obvious that things like that weren't for Ethel anyway. A few years earlier, she attempted to perform some of the aerobics broadcasted on TV. But after less than two minutes, the only thing she experienced was a sharp spasm in her back that confined her to the armchair for nearly a week. Exercise of any sort just seemed so painful, and she knew she was under enough strain as it was without having to wear herself out in those ridiculous ways.

But Ethel had started her new prescription, and the pills certainly helped stimulate her. The only problem was that they only came in 25 mg. doses, one of which she was supposed to take four times a day.

Since it was summer, she spent more time sweating outside in the sun or inside the poorly ventilated trailer. Therefore, she found she only felt the effects an hour or so after taking the drug. So recently she began taking two pills at a time, instead of the prescribed one, and decreasing the time interval between doses. She felt her own doctoring finally provided her with enough energy to complete her demanding obligations, but that also led to another slight problem.

Ethel normally fell asleep several minutes after her head found a comfortable niche within her pillow. Now, because of the amphetamines controlling her nervous system, she tossed and turned for several hours. She was normally unsure if she had even dozed briefly before being awakened by the girls' cries for her attention.

So, for the past couple of weeks, Ethel added an occasional supplement to the three or four cans of beer she normally drank while watching TV at night—Valium. The combination enabled her once again to sink quickly into unconsciousness, and an extra Preludin in the morning helped relieve any trace of fatigue she might be burdened with.

Ethel didn't mind that she was going through a bottle of Preludin a week. What concerned her was the amount of calories in the beer she drank. It seemed to put back calories she burned while using the pills. Not only that, but whenever she drank, she also needed something nearby to snack on. Of course, her snacking consequently piled on additional pounds and left her where she started before trying any diet. She wondered if she'd ever be able to escape from the never-ending circle.

Hoisting herself from the lawn chair, Ethel brushed several circling bees away. She noticed the deep pink of her skin from sitting out in the sun. Indeed, the countless tiny blood vessels running along her pale arch seemed to connect the different-colored patches of skin like stitches. She picked up the hose and directed a cold stream toward the scorched area.

To hell with bee stings and sunburn, she thought. There were more important things to do. She began making a list. She'd go inside, clean the bathroom and vacuum the rugs. Then she'd paint her dry, chipped toenails, maybe iron some clothes, and then drive up to the high school to pick up Darlene, who was taking a couple of classes at summer school. After that, she thought she'd make lunch, spend some time playing with the twins, and then go to the supermarket to do the week's shopping. It was a lot she had to do, and she suddenly noticed the strength she had slowly drain away, just like the water dripping off her ankles and into the ground below her.

Glancing at her watch, she suddenly realized that her prescribed stimulant was nearly an hour overdue. No wonder she felt so weak.

Ethel rubbed her forearm against her sweaty brow and quickly took the Preludin jar from her pocket. To her surprise, she noticed it was marked "Valium" instead.

"Goddamn it!" she said out loud, upset at herself for having taken the wrong pills earlier. She trudged back into the house for a supplementary dose of the right ones.

22

A "tall boy" crashed against the metal garbage pail. Its noise bounced off the cement walls of the shed and reverberated through Wayne's head. As a rebuttal, he ripped the top off another beer and drained half its contents in one gulp, then reached for the cigarette burning against several other butts in the ashtray. A dense trail of smoke poured from the ashtray into the air, adding a thicker haze to the room's already stuffy interior.

Wayne was pissed off. For five months he had busted his ass in the supermarket, collaring between ten and fifteen thieves a week. Hell, he had made the store a veritable police zone, one that was sure to interdict anyone intent on shopping against the rules. Under his guidance, Duffy had actually come around and shown real progress too. Duffy had even taken the occasional "perp" into the back room himself for interrogation, using the proper tactics and techniques he had been taught. A few weeks ago, they even nailed a store employee who had been pilfering goods systematically. Several other part-time workers forfeited their jobs shortly thereafter because of the culprit's confessions.

Indeed, Wayne was given every indication that his work was valued and appreciated more and more as the months passed. Normally, at the end of the month, he'd meet with both the Vanguard boss, Mr. Knudsen, and Joe Schmidt, the manager of the supermarket, in the security room after his shift. They usually complimented him on his performance and listened to his new ideas with a keen interest in putting them into practice. But earlier in the evening, their meeting was unexpectedly cancelled, and Wayne was called to the Vanguard office instead to meet with Mr. Knudsen alone.

Wayne figured that they were going to move Duffy to another one of the chain's branches and introduce Wayne to a new trainee for Wayne to show the ropes. During the drive, Wayne even decided that it was high time he received a raise. He was confident that his performance fully warranted one. To his dismay, however, he never got the opportunity to make his demands.

"Gonna keep this short and sweet, Wayne. You just completed your last shift at Buy-Rite."

"What? I don't think I heard you right."

"Yeah, you did. Buy-Rite's no longer one of our contracts. The owner of the chain decided not to renew our agreement."

"But he's makin' more money than before because of..."

"Save it, Wayne. There's no use discussin' it. His reason is simple—finances. And he's bought out our contract and decided to monitor the stores by cheaper means."

"But I was saving them money."

"Yeah well, uh, I'm sure he appreciated that. But he also mentioned that he wanted to bring back some long-time customers who had apparently become intimidated by your, uh, strongarm presence."

"Strongarm presence?"

"That's how *he* described it, not *me*. But listen, because they broke the contract, we get severance payment out of 'em. And I'm gonna pass some of that on to you. So don't worry. In addition to everything else that's coming to you, I'm gonna give you two weeks extra pay."

"Two weeks pay?"

"That's right, two weeks, which I think is pretty generous, considerin' guys like Duffy are gonna get nothin'."

"And what about a new job?"

"Don't worry about that. I'll try to get you another contract ASAP. What I'd suggest now is that you take a little vacation. Take it easy, relax a little. And if you really want to work, I'll give you some hours patrolin' the schools or somethin'."

"Patrolin' the schools?"

"Look Wayne, that's all I got right now. Gimme a little time. I mean, c'mon! If you don't make money, I don't make money. I'll find you somethin'. What more can I say?"

Wayne took another long chug of the beer and stared at some of the mug shots in front of him on the wall. These were trophies of assholes he had nailed as he had permanently liberated the store from the nuisance of shoplifters.

All his work seemed so unappreciated now: But what really added insult to injury was the way Buy-Rite decided to handle the security situation.

In short, his boss explained, they planned to use his old office for accounting, and to replace his uniformed presence with plywood cut-outs of police officers in the "highest risk" areas. Wayne had seen models of a similar sort on the late news one night and had burst out laughing at their supposedly proven results. The facsimiles were life-size and depicted a generic cop with his hand in the air and a smile spread across his friendly face. The report came from some sociological study and claimed that the placement of these cut-outs in the aisles had "dramatically" lowered shoplifting. People subconsciously believed they were being observed, the report claimed, and therefore thought twice before attempting to shoplift.

What he didn't understand, however, was how sociologists and people in power positions, like the owners of supermarkets, could be so ignorant. Eliminating scum was Wayne's forte, and he knew damned well that any wrongdoer would not be slowed by such empty threats. After all, the photo dummy was standing there with a smile on his face, as if reminding a perp of one of his Sunday school lessons. The very least they could have done, he thought, was to have a facsimile of Wayne himself in a squatting position, gun drawn and aimed at a trouble spot.

Wayne crushed the beer can and whipped it toward the other empties. He shook a cigarette from the now half-empty pack and struck a match to it, searching briefly for its end before finally connecting. The cigarette felt awkward between his fingers, and when he sucked the smoke into his lungs, it burned.

After the meeting, he had bought cigarettes for the first time in years, reaching for their temporary consolation because of his frustration. It always went like that. The first time Wayne seriously took up smoking was shortly after being let go from his last job in Kentucky. For eight years he had punched the clock at the Atlas Receptacle Company, a firm that made steel barrels, trash cans, and buckets. Wayne worked as one of the ten welders who were employed as part of the assembly line during his entire stay. It was demanding work, but at that time it didn't bother him. It was far superior to his previous job in a plant manufacturing urinal cakes, whose smell constantly gave him headaches.

With Atlas, in fact, he never even took a sick day and normally put in additional overtime every week. He actually looked forward to pulling down the face mask and welding together two seams of cold steel. After several hours he'd become lost in that world, down on his knees, his mind cleared by the fiery hiss of the arc flame. It was easy to forget everything in the myriad sparks that erupted off the molten, rainbow surface and sprayed toward his concentrated eyes. He felt great, his body sweating, muscles taut, and mind relaxed.

But when recession began hurting industries all over the nation, the Appalachian area, as usual, was one of the first areas to feel the brunt of its effects. Steel mills laid off thousands of employees, and the price of raw materials subsequently rose, which, in turn, limited demand and affected more workers in related fields of work. State goverments began marking highway construction with plastic barrels filled with sand instead of the traditional steel barrels. Stores began stocking garbage cans of similar material.

Companies that adapted to the new market demand thrived, but the majority of these manufacturers—as was the case with Atlas—soon found their steel goods outdated. At first, they froze new hiring and weeded out positions through attrition in an effort to stay afloat. But when it was obvious that they would finally go under, everybody was sent a pink slip and final paycheck.

Even so, Wayne never allowed economic mismanagement or government fuck-ups to become a scapegoat for the problems he experienced. For two-and-a-half months, he went out every day looking for a new job. But when he finally realized that no openings would be forthcoming in the near future, he made a decision that eventually severed his ties with the area where he had been raised.

He knew that there was a union dispute in Lebanon, Virginia—not far from his hometown of Mercer. The Lambert Coal Company was paying men to fill in for the striking miners and drivers. Wayne's decision to return to the Appalachian corner of Virginia and take one of the posts had been strictly financial; he was broke and had both a family to support and a stack of unpaid bills. Because he knew the welfare of his own family was more important than anything else, and that good money was being paid for the substitutes, he decided to leave Ethel, Darlene, and Junior behind temporarily and find a solution to his cash-flow problems.

Decisions were normally like that with Wayne: impulsive and rash. He had never been one to deliberate endlessly over his problems. He rarely sought advice from others, or spent large periods of time considering his various options before deciding on the most logical one. That was the rationale of weak or mixed-up people, Wayne felt, and he had always prided himself on taking immediate action when a situation needed to be dealt with.

For two years he worked against union demands. When their dispute was finally settled, he returned to Kentucky, once again without a job. The economy hadn't perked up much around there, and frightening memories returned when he encountered the same scenes of violence he had seen in Virginia during a miner's strike in the Keavy area. With money problems creeping up on him once again and the economic and psychological depression starting to mount, he quickly devised a new game plan—one

141

that meant leaving the area forever.

Wayne decided on Indiana one day after returning from another unsuccesful job interview. He realized that if he lived in the Southeastern corner of the state he'd be within driving distance of Indianapolis and Cincinnati, even Louisville for that matter. Therefore his job prospects would dramatically improve without leaving a landscape that he was used to.

Just over a week later, he withdrew what remained in the bank and sold the house through a real estate agency. Then he found himself supervising the lowering of a second-hand mobile home on the new spread he'd just mortgaged, while the rest of the family sat in the parked car and looked on.

Wayne's search for work began with the same negative results he experienced during the preceding months. But after a couple of weeks, he was finally taken on as a night press operator in Indianapolis for the state's largest newspaper, *The Star*. It was there that Wayne got to know one of the security guards who, upon learning that Wayne had spent a couple of years in the service, mentioned that his firm was looking for qualified people to fill several positions.

The news interested Wayne. He had always held an interest in and respect for the law anyway. In fact, not long after Junior was born, he even considered applying to the state academy before finding out that he was not within the age brackets they required. That information had put a damper on his plans, and he soon suppressed his law enforcement urge beneath the more immediate concerns of bringing home the bacon for his family. Yet the guard's suggestion seemed to rekindle an extinguished spark within him, and the next day he paid a visit to the Tower Security office. Several days later, he received a job offer and immediately gave the printing company their required notice.

Shortly after completing a brief training period, Wayne was handed his first assignment. He felt good, content that his easy adjustment to his new career had proven that moving the family to a new state had been justified. The electricity and plumbing were finally connected to the trailer. The kids had settled into their new school. And Ethel seemed to like the new environment as much as her stomping grounds around Keavy. Wayne didn't mind that he was relegated to patroling building sites or electrical components factories at night, either, because deep down he knew he'd soon be moving up the ladder.

Which he did, thanks to the finesse and confidence he had

demonstrated on every assignment given to him. With the solid, diverse experience he quickly began accumulating, Wayne decided to push himself further, and became involved in more challenging fields of work. Tower's security spectrum was becoming too trivial for a man of his versatility, anyway. So after being offered the challenge of bank vigilance and more money with Vanguard, a neighboring firm, he promptly decided to switch his allegiance, and put the darkened, deserted warehouses behind him forever.

Wayne popped the top on another can of beer and lit a cigarette off the butt he held between his stubby fingers. He attempted to focus his eyes on the photos on the wall in front of him. Their blurred images began transforming, so that they now appeared to mock him by staring back, almost taunting him. "Look where all your training and extra hours got you, asshole," they seemed to be saying.

He abruptly stood up, thrust out his arm, and impetuously removed their ugly presence with several forceful strokes. Then he furiously ripped them into small pieces.

Wayne pulled hard on the cigarette. Closing his other hand like a vice around the shredded photos, he tried to suffocate whatever remained of their vile memory. He excelled in his work, he reminded himself, and was maybe even the best trigger man that Vanguard had ever employed. He knew no one else took their job as seriously as he, and when push came to shove, he was always ready to take control by whatever means necessary. A pro in every sense of the word.

But now, an *unappreciated* pro.

Wayne sat down and tried to regain his composure, empty his mind of its disillusion. He was aware that even though he was out of a job, his professional posture was essential for him to uphold, and he couldn't dwell on his misfortunes. That, after all, was something for weak people to occupy their time with.

What he really needed to do, he reckoned, was attempt to put his future back into perspective. Maybe something good would even come out of his being laid off, he thought. He would be assigned something that might provide an even greater challenge. That's what happened in the bank truck, when Wayne was promoted to "shotgun", and in the damn supermarket for that matter. There was no reason he couldn't bounce back again and attack his new position at full throttle.

In the meantime, he supposed he'd just have to pull a few night shifts at the schools and keep some extra money coming in. Maybe there was

143

even some sense in his boss's suggestion to take a few days off. He could use the time to unwind a little and put the past five months behind him.

Perhaps even a brief change of environment might help to clear his head, Wayne continued thinking. Since moving to Indiana, he hadn't even left the state. A little trip could get him away from his familiar surroundings and help him forget the recent past.

Wayne kicked around a few possibilities. He knew the Keavy area was out, because the only people they kept in contact with there were a few of Ethel's relatives whom he really didn't care to see. He figured he could maybe drive down to Nashville, the country music capital, a place that he'd long wanted to see. But a few days there would be pretty expensive, seeing as how he'd have to pay for the family to get into just about everything.

Something cheaper, Wayne thought, might be to spend a weekend out in some state park. He could relax and fish in peace, that was certain. But with the babies along for the trip, it would actually be a real pain in the ass. In any event, he didn't even have a tent, so that idea was scratched as well.

Wayne turned on the television and lit another cigarette. After flipping channels, he found a Cincinnati Reds game. That interested him because they were his favorite team. He put his feet up on the table and leaned back in his chair.

Even so, his mind drifted. The only other thing he could think of was to go back to Mercer, Virginia, where he'd been raised. He didn't like the idea of returning to his hometown, a small mining town nestled between Kentucky and West Virginia. In fact, he had grown to despise the area and its inhabitants with a passion. But if he returned, he thought, he would at least be able to see his mother again, the sole person in town to whom he still felt attached.

He wouldn't mind seeing her, he supposed, and not just because he knew she'd provide some sort of comfort in this unhappy time. Every time he spoke to her on the phone, he promised to visit soon with the rest of the family. But for a variety of reasons, those plans just never materialized. He knew that this was the perfect opportunity to go, but it wasn't exactly the change of scenery suited to real relaxation either.

When he drove a coal truck against the strike during his last months in the area, his siblings and friends abandoned him and even tried to kill him as the strike wore on. The dispute between union men and mine owners remained unresolved for two years. During that time, his mother had been the only person he knew who remained faithful, although he'd always been forced to meet with her secretly so as not to expose her to any violence meant for him. She didn't approve that he worked against the union's mandate. Her relatives and neighbors had worked in the pits for generations, and she constantly tried to persuade him to do something else. But, at the end of the day, she had at least never stopped calling him "son."

Wayne watched Dwight Gooden strike out the last Reds batter and flipped the television off. He sat in silence for a few minutes, slowly sipping the last can of the six pack and staring at the blank wall in front of him. His occasional phone conversations with his dear old mom were mostly filled with banter about the weather or other trivial matters. But she also made him aware that not long after he drove away from that part of Appalachia the last time, a lot of changes had taken place. He knew the coal company had been bought out, his brother had lost his job, his sister had left the state, and his mother had been moved to another home. He wasn't sure of the exact details, however, because his mother usually got side-tracked after several seconds and rambled on about other things. That didn't bother him all that much because he didn't give a shit about his siblings or their families anymore. They could go to hell and rot for all he cared.

His mother, however, would appreciate seeing him. And Wayne supposed a visit would relieve his own guilt for having continually raised her expectations with false promises. After all, he loved his mother and enjoyed her company and motherly warmth. And because she was pushing eighty and sounded increasingly senile over the phone, he wasn't sure for how many more years he would have left to see her alive.

Wayne dropped the end of a cigarette into his nearly empty can. Standing up, he stretched his arms above him and then hocked up a ball of mucus, savoring it for a few seconds before swallowing it. He'd call his mother the next day, he figured, and arrange a short visit the next weekend.

He wasn't entirely content about his vacation plans, but at least he knew it would give him some space and fresh air to see things more clearly.

23

The Gremlin moved slowly within the mountainous landscape, weaving its way through the sprawling desiduous trees in full Autumn glory. Their leaves splashed colorful clumps of red, yellow, and orange amongst the thick layer of soaring evergreens. A mass of clouds were strewn thickly across the sky in shades of gray. A few patches of blue peaked through the clouds, while a heavy mist danced precariously with the treetops lining the gorges beneath it. A sparkling fresh-water stream followed the twisting road, its powerful current flowing over the smooth rocks and splashing against the jagged granite banks. The bubbling noise of its relentless current created a natural symphony with the harmonious chirping of swarming birds overhead.

In contrast to his peaceful surroundings, tranquility was the furthest thing from Wayne Turner's mind. In fact, as every turn of the wheel drew him closer to his destination, a disconcerting tension took a firmer hold over his body. It began shortly after they left the gentle, rolling hills around his home in Indiana and entered the more masculine terrain of the Appalachian mountains. It continued to grow steadily as the car sped across the foothills of eastern Kentucky, and peaked when they finally crossed into the domineering expanses along the Virginia border.

Wayne supposed he had good reason to feel wound up. He hadn't driven this particular mountain route for nearly seven years, and when he made his last run on it in a coal truck after driving for almost two years against a strike, he was little more than a mental wreck. During that time, he survived constant physical threats, gunshots, obscene phone calls, heated provocation, and four nearly fatal accidents. Wayne left no friends and was considered an enemy and outcast by everyone in the area. His only sustaining force during that period was his knowledge that his wife, young daughter, and son were safe in another state, and they were being provided for with the money he made and sent home to them every weekend.

Wayne almost expected the Gremlin to be sabotaged in some way, as had been done in the past. He kept his eyes tight on the road, its surface barely covered by a thin and broken layer of old pavement laid around deep potholes. He passed the entrances to mining areas where he'd picked up and delivered coal, and their familiar settings brought back additional loathsome memories: throngs of angry strikers attempting to block his path, rocks crashing against his head, and windshields shattering in his face.

As the car pushed deeper into the hills, the frequent cascades spilled over the plush vegetation along the side of the road. They almost seemed to carry the same hideous filth of days gone by, stirring a feeling of disgust stronger than he had ever felt before. Wayne stared at an expanse of blackened land that covered the base of an otherwise green valley on the other side of the river. Its lack of vegetation made it appear cancerous.

"Look at that field over there," Wayne said, breaking a long silence and pointing out Darlene's partially opened window. "Do you see how the color of the soil is a weird-lookin' orange?"

"Yeah," Darlene said, observing the various shades of chipped, dull stone. "It looks like it's rusted."

Wayne grimaced and shook his head.

"Well that's exactly what it is," he spat. "Rust. And it's gonna be five hundred years before they ever grow somethin' again in that field. Strip mining's what done it. Plain destroyed the land round here."

The car twisted along the ascending roads, and Wayne tuned the radio to a country station. When he spoke to his mother on the phone and told her of his plans to visit, his only stipulation had been that no other family or kinfolk be present. He had no desire whatsoever to bridge the huge gap that remained between them. Her voice was faint and she seemed confused by his demands—as if she couldn't believe that his anger and hate still remained—but she finally told him that he had nothing to worry about. Just to make sure, he reminded her several times of his desire to visit her and her alone. He didn't hang up until he was fully content that she completely understood his request.

The prospect of spending six hours in a cramped car on curving roads with two screaming babies was downright depressing. Indeed, Wayne wasn't bothered in the least that the rest of his family didn't make the trip. Junior stayed at home with Ethel and the twins because he had soccer practice, but Darlene expressed a real interest in meeting her grandmother. Wayne believed she deserved the trip because she couldn't remember her grandmother from her few visits as a very young child.

Wayne hadn't told Darlene of his turbulent past in the area, and didn't have any intention to—he felt things like that weren't worth mentioning. It was all behind him and he believed more firmly than ever that

147

he had done the right thing by working. All he really wanted to do now was teach her what a big shithole the area was, in hopes that it would deter her from ever ending up in such a Godforsaken place.

After several more miles, Wayne pulled along the side of the road and stopped. In front of them was a weatherbeaten sign that was illegible to anyone who had never seen it before.

"What's it say?" Darlene asked, unable to decipher anything from the overgrown dirt road running up into the woods.

"It was a mine," Wayne responded. "Talbert Fork Number Three. But by the looks of it, it ain't been in operation for some time. Proba'ly just a big, ugly hole in the ground now. I s'pose it looks the same as Culvert Gap and all that land that was out on 201 near the old place in Keavy, you know, like some big meteorite hit it and just left a big hole. Can't build a house on it 'cause it would just flood out. And can't farm it neither 'cause it's just unhealthy soil. Proba'ly a quarter of the land around here is like that. Diseased. Destroyed. Gutted and left to die."

Darlene winced and shook her head. "Did you used to work there?"

Wayne was silent for a moment.

"Yeah, I did," he said solemnly. "A long time ago. There ain't a hell of a lot more to do around here but work at the mine. Most people work in some way with the coal, hard to avoid it. But when I left here the last time, back when you were about in the fourth grade, I said never again."

He opened the door and urinated next to the car, and then set the car back in motion. Before long they passed a hand-printed sign on the side of the road that read 'Grosries...3/8 mile'.

"Can we stop there and get a Coke?" Darlene blurted. "I'm real thirsty."

"Yeah, I wouldn't mind a drink myself," he answered, easing his foot from the accelerator.

Wayne didn't recognize the store when they reached it, but the "Millwall's General Goods" sign in front was familiar. The last time he was in George Millwall's store, then located just outside Trammel, the owner refused him credit and told him to do his business elsewhere. Treatment of that sort was something that Wayne had grown accustomed to. But he was surprised that such strong words came from George, who was always friendly and even extended credit to him. It was obvious that he was pressured into his policy by the strikers around him, rather than because of his own opinion regarding the strike. But it didn't make the snub any easier to stomach, nor his friendship with George worth keeping.

Wayne turned off the engine and handed his daughter some money, so she could make the purchase alone. But as soon as she entered the store, he thought that avoiding places that held nasty memories only added to his uneasiness about the area. He had learned through his police work that the only way to conquer fear was to face it or shoot at it. But since his service revolver was now several hundred miles away, he realized that only the first option was viable. He figured Millwall's was as good a place to begin as any, and after taking several deep breaths, he stepped out of the car.

Glancing through the store's screen door, Wayne saw a couple of unfamiliar men standing by a small wooden counter and talking to George, who was easy to recognize even though he'd shaved off his beard. His clean-shaven face looked more elliptical than before.

Wayne jerked the door open and walked in. He kept his head down and marched straight to the coolers against the back wall. As he checked the selection through the glass doors, he caught the reflection of the men at the counter staring toward him intently. The conversation had stopped and Wayne began to feel uncomfortable.

"Is it OK if we get these?" Darlene asked, appearing with a two-liter bottle of Mello Yello and a bag of cheese puffs.

"Yeah, but let's get out of here," Wayne whispered, grabbing the things from his daughter. He snatched a bag of Funyons from the snack rack before heading toward the counter. The men's eyes followed him coldly as he approached.

"Long time, no see, Wayne, " George finally spoke as he added up the items on a sheet of paper.

Wayne lowered his head and hid his eyes beneath the bill of his cap. "How much do I owe you?" he mumbled, ignoring the statement.

George paused momentarily, and stared at him with the others.

"Six sixty-four with the tax," he finally said. "Your brother Buddy come in here the other day. Brought in his five-year-old step-daughter. Cute little thing she is." He cleared his gums quickly and then stared in Darlene's direction. "This your girl here?" he asked.

"Yeah," Wayne said, handing him the money and glancing nervously at the other two men, who continued to glare blankly at him. "Gimme a pack of Marlboro too, will you?" he added, looking back down.

"So this is Buddy Turner's kid brother?" the man he didn't recognize broke in.

"Yeah," the other man said, forcefully spitting some tobacco into a cup he held under his mouth. "Didn't think he'd have the nerve to come back round here though."

George fumbled with the change, trying to get it right.

There was another splatter of tobacco. "I thought the asshole learned his lesson. Got the message loud and clear."

Wayne suddenly felt nervous. He wanted out of the store. Fast. "Hey Darlene," he barked to his daughter, who was leafing through a magazine. "Gimme a hand with this stuff, will you?"

Darlene sauntered over and grabbed the soda and the bags of chips, then walked out the door. Wayne grabbed the rest of the stuff and muscled the change into his pocket. Without another word, he quickly made for the door.

Wayne jammed the key into the ignition and pulled the car out of the lot rapidly. He breathed heavily and fumbled clumsily with the top of a beer before getting it open.

"Did you know those men in the store?" Darlene asked, taking a gulp from the pop bottle and staring at him. She was completely puzzled by his flushed face and jittery movements.

"Yeah, I used to know 'em," he answered quickly, reaching for the pack of cigarettes. "But then again, I knew a lot of people around here that I haven't thought of in years. You see, I left this area when I was about twenty 'cause I just couldn't see no future in it. I wanted to get away, and ended up goin' to the college in Keavy where I met your mother. I mean, I grew up around here, but I can't really say that I like it all that much. And those guys in the store, well, it's been so long I can't even remember their names."

He inhaled the cigarette deeply, and felt slightly calmer as the smoke penetrated his lungs.

"You see, people like that and most of the people around here, they never get away from this area, and they live in a pretty small world," Wayne continued. "They proba'ly never even been out of the state. They see the same people every day, day-in, day-out, and because of that, they remember everybody that goes in there. I mean, I proba'ly went in there twenty-five years ago and they still remember it. Just shows what a small world those guys live in. Hangin' round the general store all the time, doin' nothin'. I just prefer not to think about types like that."

He guzzled the rest of the beer and threw the empty out the window, bouncing it off a billboard that read "Floating Church Members Always Sink." After burping loudly, he turned toward his daughter and observed the nearly empty bag between her legs.

150

"Hey, you gonna eat all of those yourself, or you gonna give me some?" he prodded.

Darlene held the bag toward Wayne and he stuffed a handful of cheese puffs into his mouth. Above them the sun had broken through the clouds and cast a yellowish haze over the green mountains, giving the exposed rock face an unnatural glimmer.

"Hey, it says Mercer, 5 miles," Darlene said, pointing to a sign they were about to pass.

"Yeah, I know," Wayne said, reaching down for a beer and feeling another wave of nerves ease its way into his system.

* * *

A mid-morning shower fell on the aluminum roof of the mobile home, amplified within the darkened bedroom as if drummers were practicing a long, monotonous cadence overhead. Ethel was laying in bed, staring at the dim gray haze that eased its way through a pulled blind, barely illuminating the stuffy room's interior. A couple of fingers of one hand were buried within the overgrown thatch of her crotch, while the other hand roamed between one breast and the other, occasionally pausing to tweak a slightly aroused nipple. She was breathing in short gasps, enjoying the relaxing warmth that slowly extended throughout her prone bulk.

Moving her fingers more furtively against her lubricated organ, she felt a more intense sensation, not only within the tender tissue of her clitoris, but also within the deep confines of her mind. It felt as if a once-dim light were rapidly expanding into a deeply concentrated ball of fire. She closed her eyes and moaned softly, continuing to apply pressure and feeling the waves of ecstasy mounting within.

In front of the bed, the two infants laid on their stomachs within the blue vinyl crib. They were completely shrouded in the darkness of the stuffy room. A veil of dust and smoke hovered in a thick haze above them. One of them began to cry.

Ethel's hand suddenly lost its rhythm and she felt the electric current within her body discharge, as if somebody had pulled a plug. But despite the louder screams of both babies now, Ethel remained in bed and gradually caught her breath.

She had almost been there, she thought disappointedly, to the place

151

full of stars and energy that, for the past several years, she even had difficulty achieving with the motions of her own fingers.

Ethel had gone her entire pregnancy without sex. Since the twins' birth, Wayne had mounted her two or three times. She supposed she was pleased by his rare display of affection but, as had always been the case, she experienced absolutely nothing while he was outside or inside her. Afterwards, she usually felt she was little more than his sperm receptacle.

In a way, she figured she didn't have much right to expect more from her husband. She herself was repulsed by her naked image in the mirror and found it difficult to believe she could actually arouse anyone more intensely. She couldn't even bring herself to the lift-off point most of the time, and here she was alone in the house with no one preventing her.

Ethel noticed the crying again. No one, she reminded herself, except those two screaming twins.

Ethel's breathing had returned to normal. But although she thought she should feel relaxed and invigorated after spending the past hour in bed, her eyelids now felt heavier than a number of hours earlier, when she had made the rest of the family breakfast before seeing Wayne and Darlene off. She just couldn't understand it, because even with the extra rest, she felt more tired than before. It didn't matter if it was morning, afternoon or night, because nowadays she always felt fatigued.

For the past month, the place she'd really wanted to be was in bed, fast asleep and dreaming. Or at least in a place where she could relax and be unaware of what was going on around her. She figured that was a normal desire for a woman with such constant demands. But, even so, she reckoned that she'd have to consult another physician who could prescribe some new pills that would give her more energy. The pills she was on now just didn't seem to be doing their job, no matter how many she swallowed.

After lying still for a few more minutes, Ethel finally tossed the covers toward the floor, hoisted her huge body from the bed, and threw a pink robe over her round shoulders. After shoving her feet into her furry slippers, she ran her hands through her hair and then staggered toward her noisy offspring. Ethel lifted one out of the crib while telling the other one to shut up. She felt the dampness in her diaper and muttered an obscenity before pushing the crib out of the darkness and into the bright light of the kitchen.

After changing Crystal on the counter and repeating the process with Gladys, Ethel placed them both in a double high chair, wiped her hands on the dishtowel, and lit a cigarette. She looked at the clock. Junior would be home from school soon and she'd have to fix him lunch.

152

Normally Ethel made him lunch in the morning to take with him. But today he was attending school for only half a day. It wasn't for soccer practice as usual, but as punishment for having been caught smoking cigarettes with a few friends in the Boy's Room. The principal had called her on the phone and informed her of his misconduct on Monday, stating that her son would have to come to school every Saturday of the next month as part of his discipline.

Ethel was disappointed that she couldn't make the trip to see Wayne's mother. Even though she spoke to Grandma Turner occasionally on the phone and sent Christmas and birthday cards every year, the last time she had actually seen her was a couple of years before Wayne had returned to the mines. Back then, Grandma Turner's mind still functioned properly and her thoughts flowed clearly. That wasn't the case now, however. Sometimes she'd talk on the phone and, two minutes later, forget who she was even talking to. Even so, she was always kind and warm-hearted in her tone, and Ethel would have liked to go along and show off her family in its entirety.

Unfortunately, she knew the trip would just be too difficult with the little ones, not to mention a real drain on whatever energy she had left. She was happy that Darlene, however, was able to make the trip. Maybe a little traveling or the opportunity to see a place different from Greensburg or Westport would help broaden the girl's mind a little and give her some incentive to do better in school. In any event, she was glad that Wayne at least had a little company for the long trip, and would also have a token of familiar support once he was there.

One of the girls began crying again and Ethel opened the refrigerator, knowing this time she was more anxious for a feeding than a change of linen. She hoisted out a gallon jar with a generic label that simply read ''BABY FOOD,'' set it on the table, and then began shoving the brown goo sloppily toward both eager mouths.

Ethel recognized a few of the vegetables and a number of meat by-products on the ingredients label. But the majority of ingredients were written in that funny chemical language, many of which, she assumed, were some sort of vitamins that were supposed to be good for growing babies. In any event, the girls lapped it up with great enthusiasm, although nearly half of it dripped down their plastic bibs.

In between a couple of spoonfuls, Ethel decided to try the stuff for herself. She was surprised at how good it tasted and how easily it glided down her throat. It had the flavor of sweet soup—almost as if candied yams were

153

its mainstay—and the texture of a thick pudding. She soon found herself taking a mouthful for every one that the girls had.

When the twins finally began spitting out the majority of the continuous spoonfuls offered them, she screwed the lid back on the jar and replaced it in the fridge. But as she was about to close the door, she spotted the remainder of a saucepan of Hamburger Helper from the night before. She stared at it for several seconds, thinking that she'd reheat it as part of Junior's lunch. But the baby food she'd just eaten had primed her appetite. She could always make something else for him when he got home, she reckoned, and without passing another thought on the matter, she grabbed the pan and began wolfing its contents down.

When she finished, she threw the pan in the sink along with the other dirty dishes, wiped the kids mouths and carried them to the playpen in the family room. She flipped on the television and found cartoons on nearly every channel. So she picked up a magazine instead and began skimming through it. In between cigarettes, she yelled some nonsensical baby talk to her girls, one of whom stared back uncertainly while the other pounded a doll against the floor of the playpen.

Reading had the effect of a narcotic on Ethel, but just as she was about to succumb to the weight of her eyelids, she heard the front door open and realized her son was home.

"Hi Junior," she muttered as he entered the room.

"Wow, The Roadrunner!" he responded eagerly, sitting down in an armchair and focusing on the TV set. "Great!"

For half an hour, Junior laughed seemingly without pause, and when the coyote had been blown up for the final time and the credits rolled, he pushed himself back in the seat and ran his hand through his unruly red mane.

"Man, I thought I was gonna miss that this week with that stupid study hall," he said with a degree of relief. "I'm glad I got home in time for it."

"Well I'm hungry," Ethel said, pulling up one of the blinds and squinting toward the bright light outside.

"Me too," Junior yelled, moving toward the kitchen. "What do we got for lunch today?"

"Oh I thought we could have some hot dogs and a little macaroni and cheese," she said, following him out of the room. "You must have worked up quite an appetite with that extra duty at school."

"You've gotta be kiddin' me," he said, opening the refrigerator and removing the lid from a bottle of pop before slugging some down. "We didn't do anything except sit there for four hours doin' nothin'. The whole thing's just a big joke."

"But I thought the principal said he was going to have things for you to do there," she remarked.

"No way," the kid said. "He left after blowin' some hot air for about an hour and left some janitor to look after us. The whole thing's just a big waste of time."

"Well at least havin' to be there will teach you not to smoke at school again," Ethel said. She filled a pan with water and put it on the stove to boil while Junior ransacked the cabinets, finally hauling out a bag of potato chips that he ripped open.

"You know you shouldn't be eatin' those before your meal," she said, looking at him angrily and shaking her head. "Your lunch is gonna be ready in ten minutes or so, so leave 'em alone or you'll ruin your appetite."

Junior sighed and shoved a few more chips in his mouth before putting the bag away. He went to his room, and a couple of minutes later, returned with a magazine. Ethel measured out some milk and margarine for the macaroni and cheese. She sliced a number of hot dogs into the liquid and put it all in another saucepan to heat.

Easing over toward her son, Ethel looked over his shoulder and saw that he was reading another one of the music magazines he'd begun picking up recently. She peered down at some of the photos more closely and noticed a strong odor of cigarette smoke immersed within the boy's scraggly long hair.

"Junior!" she exclaimed. "I thought we'd agreed that you weren't gonna smoke anymore!"

"I know," he answered, flipping a page. "I'm not."

"Then why do you smell like a chimney then?"

He ignored her and continued staring at the photos.

"I'm askin' you a question, Wayne Junior!" Ethel said, raising her voice. "You know you promised me that if I didn't tell your father about you gettin' caught, you wouldn't mess around with cigarettes anymore. So answer me!"

Junior closed the magazine and stared at her for several seconds before pulling the hair to his nose.

"Well it must have been Mr. Simmons, John's dad, who gave us a ride home," he finally said. "That guy's like a chain-smoker and you can hardly even breathe in his car, even with the windows rolled down. I guess that's what it was.'' He shrugged his shoulders and looked toward his mother. ''Who knows?'' he added with a huff. ''Maybe it's from all the cigarettes you smoke round here.''

''Listen!'' she yelled quickly, waving a finger and taking a step toward him. ''I'm an adult. I know it's not good to smoke, but it just happens to be a bad habit that I'm in the process of phasin' out. You are still at school and you're not allowed to smoke there or in this house. That's the difference. So don't give me any wise answers!''

Ethel turned away abruptly and poured the pasta into a strainer, then dumped it into the hot milk mixture. Then she added the cheese packet and stirred it vigorously.

Junior looked toward her and shook his head.

''Relax already,'' he said calmly. ''I wasn't making any wise-cracks, for Christ's sake.''

Ethel wanted to mention something to him about swearing, but she bit her lip and plopped the lunch on two plates instead. She knew that he was right about her overreacting, but she also knew why. Because of the little cat nap that morning, she had neglected to take the tranquilizer she normally popped around ten in the morning. Was it any surprise, she asked herself, that she was a little bit edgy?

''I'm sorry,'' she finally said, placing the saucepan on the table. ''Just forget about it.''

They both began pushing the mush enthusiastically into their mouths. After clearing half his plate, Junior remarked, ''It's good this way.''

''How?'' Ethel murmured through a mouthful of food.

''With the hot dogs chopped up in the macaroni,'' he said. ''I like it when they have the cheese all over them.''

''I thought you would,'' Ethel said, smiling an open mouthful of food. ''I love this cheese powder too.''

Junior helped himself to another portion, breathing heavily between bites.

''How far away was it that Dad and Darlene were goin' anyway?'' he asked after a while.

''He thought about six hours,'' she answered, glancing at the clock. ''It would have been nice if you could have gone, too.''

''Yeah well, I wasn't really into goin' anyway.'' he said, belching. ''Hey Mom!'' he suddenly added as if having a brainstorm. ''John invited me to eat over his house tonight, and his dad said it was all right with him if I spent the night there, as long as it was all right with you. Can I?''

"Well I guess it would be all right," she said, reaching for her cigarettes. "I mean, I don't know if your father would approve if he knew about the trouble you had at school. But then again," she winked toward him, "I guess what he don't know, won't hurt him."

"Cool!" he said, carrying his plate over to the sink.

"But Junior," she said, igniting her smoke. "Let's just keep your stayin' over there a secret between us. OK?"

"Sure Mom," he said. It was just like with the secret pact they made when she had allowed him to go to James Dean's hometown without his father's knowledge. Opening the freezer door and reaching inside, he looked back at his mother.

"You wanna fudgecicle?" he asked.

"You bet!" she said, grabbing it with her free hand. Junior picked up his magazine and walked out of the room, leaving Ethel alone. She stared at the ice cream, whose freezing vapor evaporated into the air above it like the cigarette smoke from her other hand and, for a moment, was confused by which one she was going to pull toward her mouth first.

*　　*　　*

The town of Mercer hadn't changed any, except that now there were more stores boarded up than Wayne remembered. Father and daughter passed through a couple of stop signs and came to where a bakery thrift store once stood. The remaining structure consisted of a charred, hollow metal shell and broken glass. Who could expect to open a business in this shithole and keep it open? Wayne wondered.

All that was left in Mercer was a convenience store, a couple of churches and a small Piggly Wiggly supermarket, which had apparently put all the smaller shops out of business by placing everything under one roof and underpricing the competition.

Wayne eased the car along the side of the street where his mother now lived, checking each number before coming to a stop in front of 93. The building stood on a corner, and the sign above the door said Salvation Army Thrift Store. But the windows had been clouded by swirls of white paint and a note reading "Permanently Closed" was pasted on the door. He parked the car in front and turned to Darlene.

"This is it," he said.

"But it's all closed up," she responded.

"Yeah, even a damn Salvation Army has to shut down in this place," he grunted. "She must live up there, above it," he added, tossing his head in that direction.

Wayne and Darlene got out of the car and walked around and behind the store. A high wooden fence surrounded the area back there, and its heavy door was partially ajar. Pushing it open all the way, Wayne spotted a rickety wooden staircase leading up to the second floor. The building itself had once been white, but now was faded to a dull gray or brown, depending upon which parts of the peeling paint he looked at. The yellow grass that lay between them and the stairs looked as if it hadn't been cut for months, and the blinds in the closed windows upstairs were drawn shut. Except for the trampled path through the unmanageable growth, the place looked deserted.

They traipsed through the tall grass and climbed the stairs to the front door. Wayne knocked hard on the screen, hearing it rattle throughout the inside of the house. There was no answer. He knocked again and then yelled, "Momma...you there?"

Glancing behind him and across the street, Wayne could see an elderly couple, each one covered in a colorful afghan, rocking on a couple of chairs on their porch. The man smoked a pipe and the woman was knitting, and they both stared at him without expression. He recognized them from his boyhood. One of their sons had been a friend of his then. But that relationship, like the others, soured when Wayne returned to work.

He knocked on the ill-fitting door again and looked down at the paper he held in his hand to make sure he was at the right address. In that same moment Wayne heard the muffled sound of a toilet flushing inside. He spun around and pounded on the door with more force.

When Wayne pressed his face against the glass, he saw an elderly woman approaching from the shadows. Although quite thin, she waddled toward the door, covering only a couple inches with each step. Her one-piece nightdress was buttoned nearly to her neck. Her white hair was disheveled, and her eyes were like two licorice balls shoved into a skull. She cracked the door open slightly and stared blankly toward Wayne and Darlene.

"Wayne, is that you, son?" she asked. "I ain't got my glasses on and can't see proper. Is that you?"

"It's me, Momma," he said. "We finally got here. Darlene's here with me."

"Your wife?" she perked up, chewing her gum excitedly and extending her hand toward Darlene. "I wasn't sure if you was gonna be able to make it.''

Darlene stood confused and embarrassed, not sure what to do. She extended her hand uncertainly toward the old lady.

"No Momma. This is Darlene, my oldest girl. Ethel couldn't make it, 'cause she's back at home takin' care of the new twins. But thinkin' of you, she made a cake, and I got it out in the car.

He looked at Darlene, who stared back at him with her mouth hanging open. "Well don't just stand there!" he said, addressing her. "Say hello to your grandma.''

"Hi," she said automatically.

"Is it really you Wayne?'' his mother muttered. "You come back here? Lemme have a good look at you out in the light, son.''

Wayne held the door open for her and she waddled onto the porch. Her pursed lips formed a slight smile as best they could and she reached her hands up to his face, running her fingers across it. Wayne stood uncomfortably as she breathed heavily and gripped his flesh like a blind person trying to read a face.

"Oh Wayne honey,'' her voice broke. "It's good to have you back home again.''

He bent over and put his arms around her, looked toward Darlene's agape mouth, and then buried his face on his mother's shoulder. Behind his closed lids he could feel tears swelling, but he kept them closed until the sensation went away. Finally he stood up and looked down at his old dear, whose clear blue eyes were intensified by the moisture covering them.

"And this is my daughter Darlene, Momma,'' Wayne said proudly. "She's seventeen now and gettin' all grown up.''

His mother turned slowly toward Darlene and planted a kiss on her cheek before grabbing the back of her head and pulling her close. Wayne looked at the confused girl's face, which looked like a fish head as half of it was sandwiched against the old woman's head. Across the street, he glanced again at the old people, who were staring at the scene.

"Let's go inside, Momma,'' Wayne said, as he hastily looked away from the old neighbors and put his hand on his mother's shoulder. "I don't want you gettin' a chill out here in just your nightgown.''

The three entered the house, which didn't appear to have been aired for months. Although it was warmer than outside, the air was still and thick. A sofa with an old slip cover strewn across it sat in one corner next to a tattered armchair. Beside the sofa stood an overflowing floor ashtray. Against one wall was a fireplace topped by a mantle, upon which rested various trinkets the old woman had collected over the years. Among these were a couple of souvenir plates from neighboring states, an unshined bell, a one-eyed head carved out of a coconut, some dusty plastic flowers, and a few bottles of colorful pills. On the wall was a clock with a clapper, a picture of Jesus gesticulating, and a gold, spray-painted ceramic imprint of a child's hand that Wayne recognized as his own from childhood. The walls were covered with peeling, flowered wallpaper and the wooden floor topped by a well-worn braided rug.

"Sit down kids, sit down," the old woman said, gesturing toward the sofa. "It's so good to have you back home."

Wayne repeated his explanation of why Ethel and the other kids couldn't make it. His mother concentrated intently on every syllable, as if he were speaking a foreign language whose words occasionally brought familiar sounds but whose complete significance slipped comprehension.

"You mean this isn't your wife?" she finally said when he had stopped, pointing at Darlene.

"No," Wayne said curtly. "Look Momma, I brought some beer," he blurted, beginning to feel a need for one himself. "You want one? Or Darlene also has a bottle of pop. Get the bottle Darlene," he added, motioning toward her. "What would you like?"

"A beer," she said immediately. "Oh, I'd like to have a beer."

Wayne stood up and went to the kitchen to put the beer in the refrigerator. Opening the freezer door, he found its only contents were a thick layer of frost that prevented anything else from fitting in, and made the removal of the ice trays impossible. There was no stove, and the only cooking utility was a greasy microwave oven that stood atop the counter. The refrigerator had begun to rust on the outside and was nearly empty except for a half-eaten box of fried chicken and an open quart of milk. Opening the kitchen cabinets, he found them bare of food except for a few cans of soup and a half-eaten box of crackers. He grabbed a glass in the sink, rinsed it and made his way back to the room with a couple of cans.

"Who are you?" he heard his mother addressing his daughter as he rounded the corner.

Darlene, looking spooked, glanced up toward him and blurted, "Daddy, I'm gonna go out to the car and get the Funyons. I forgot 'em out there."

Wayne looked at his mother when they were alone and reiterated what he had already said a couple of times, this time more deliberately. "And the reason Ethel couldn't make it," he went on, "Is because the twins are real small and we both thought it wouldn't be a good idea to bring 'em.''

"But Wayne," she said. "I just saw Ethel before."

Wayne lit a cigarette and sat back in the chair. Was this really happening? he wondered. Was his mother really this senile? Why did she insist on believing that Darlene was his wife, not once or twice, but three times?

"Momma," Wayne began, opening the two cans and pouring one in the glass before handing it to his mother. "We brought some cake and we're gonna have a talk, eat some of it, maybe make a little supper and then go back home."

"Oh, that's nice," the old woman said, taking a sip of the beer. Half of her mouthful poured down the front of her nightdress as she spoke. Upon seeing Darlene return to the room she exclaimed: "I'm so glad that you and Ethel came to see me. But why didn't you bring your kids, son?"

Wayne sat back in the chair dejectedly, and the three of them sat in silence again.

After lighting another cigarette, he got up and said, "Darlene, why don't you tell your grandma what you're doin' in school. Tell her 'bout the new course you got. I'm sure she'd be interested in hearin' 'bout that."

Wayne walked through a curtain that separated the sitting room from the rest of the house. He relieved himself in the bathroom, and then began looking in the other rooms. One room, which he figured was once a bedroom, had a filthy cushion laying in the corner, next to which were some yellowed newspapers and a plastic dog bowl. In another corner were some dry, white feces interspersed with dark nuggets he guessed to be dog food. Near the window, several flies chased each other around aimlessly.

He shook his head, shut the door behind him, and entered what was obviously his mother's bedroom. As in the living room, all the furnishings were familiar: the iron-framed bed topped with a pink and black afghan, a rusted metal shoe rack, and a dusty wardrobe that held clothes probably not worn since Momma's youth. Pictures of horses and a painting of the crucifixion adorned the walls, and more dirty plastic flowers sat atop the bureau.

The only difference between the bedroom he now stood in and his parent's bedroom during his youth was that this one, instead of smelling of something warm and enticing, emanated the stench of elderly decay or, more to the point, the odor of approaching death.

His gaze shifted to some photographs resting on a layer of dusty white lace next to the plastic flowers on the bureau. Glancing at the first one,

161

Wayne saw the round, drawn face of his older sister, Pearl, topped with peroxide-blonde hair and overdone in make-up. She was standing next to a man he didn't recognize, and he wondered if it was a husband she'd managed to hang onto. By the time Wayne finished high school, Pearl already had five kids by three fathers. When he last spoke to her, she had birthed two more with the same man who fathered the last of the five.

Wayne really didn't care one way or the other now, because he really didn't give a shit about her or who the hell she waved her fat ass at. When he had returned to the area to work, the last thing she ever said to him was, "You are no longer my brother, and I'm never going to speak to you again in my life." That was it, just like that—and she had kept her promise. At the time, it hadn't affected him in the least. As soon as she said it, he said to himself that she was no longer his sister, either, and from that point on he began considering her in a similar way that she probably viewed the common law husbands of her children: distant and sour memories.

From the other room, Wayne heard his daughter mention something about the different hair conditioners she was learning about. He returned his concentration to the bureau and picked up another framed photo, this one of his father standing in the backyard behind the old house. It was the last photo of him. Several days after the photo was taken, while he was working on the roof, Wayne's father slipped and fell, and died instantly when he hit the ground.

In the photograph, Wayne's father, a gaunt man with graying hair and a three-day beard, was doing his best to smile for the camera. Yet somehow his eyes didn't quite focus on it. Behind him was the peak of the roof from which he fell, looming darkly, like some sort of strange omen. He never saw the photograph himself—in fact, no one did until several years later, when someone developed the film in the camera. Wayne had always found the photograph somewhat eerie, yet oddly compelling at the same time.

The photo next to it, however, utterly repelled Wayne. In fact, he hated it and had often threatened to rip it up. It was a portrait of himself, taken on the day of his high school graduation. He was wearing the traditional cap and gown, which all the boys draped over their shorts and t-shirts for the closing ceremony. Afterwards, some roving photographer had insisted on taking each graduates photo, and Wayne had been caught off-guard. His image was captured in a very unnatural way—so much so that when he had seen it for the first time, he hardly even recognized himself. He had a stupid, almost girlish smile on his face, and one eye was partially closed. His mother had insisted on having an enlargement made of the hideous thing, as proof to anyone who came to the house that at least one of her children had graduated from high school.

Wayne quickly placed the photo face-down on the dresser. Behind it, he saw a dusty picture of his older brother Buddy, probably taken about the last time Wayne saw him. In the photo, he was wearing a yellow miner's cap and throwing his chest out arrogantly through his open shirt. His face and neck were covered with black silt, although the base of his firm, muscled abdomen was white as a baby's ass. Beside him were a couple of his friends, all dressed similarly and smiling unnaturally. It all looked as though whoever took the picture had forced them to hold their expressions for several seconds before snapping the shutter.

Wayne recognized all of the other men. But one, who was resting his arm on Buddy's shoulder, brought back particularly deep, bitter feelings. Murphy was his name. Wayne and he went to high school together and played on the football team. Murphy was a running back and Wayne often blocked for him on the offensive line, although thinking about it now, he only remembered blocking for him at practice. The rest of the time, Wayne was delegated to the special teams as one of the many nameless players who comes on for kickoffs and punts. All that added up to was running down the field after the return man, trying to knock the hell out of him.

But their comaraderie on the football field was misleading, as Murphy ended up being an inseparable friend of Wayne's brother, Buddy. It was largely because of Murphy that Wayne had spent countless hours repairing upwards of 500 tires on his truck during the strike. That was the real Murphy, he thought, the one who the others at the mine nicknamed "Jack."

He got that tag because he was one of the striking miners who had a welding kit at home. Therefore, he assumed the responsibility of making "jackrocks," clusters of small spikes welded together to protrude in all directions, and laid out on the roads to bring the replacement trucks to a halt. Wayne knew that because his brother had told him about Jack. In fact, Buddy even helped Jack with the welding on a number of occasions to keep the replacements from getting through.

Wayne closed his eyes. He was in the truck again and his headlights reflected off the jackrocks' metallic surfaces. He could hear his brakes begin to screech, shifting the twenty thousand tons of coal forward and throwing the truck's center of gravity dangerously off balance. Suddenly the thunderous sound of multiple blowouts reverberated throughout the truck like artillery fire.

The steering wheel was immediately jerked from his hands. He struggled desperately to regain control of the wheel before finally locking on. The gears shifted downward. There was a nauseating rumble. Sparks flew in all directions. His momentum propelled him toward a rusted guardrail along an approaching curve. Two-thousand feet of rock face lay beyond it.

A car door slammed outside. Wayne was jarred back into the present. He could hear the unfamiliar voice of a woman yelling something about food and beer.

Wayne went to a window and cracked the blind. He heard the back door open, but from his vantage, all he could see was a thin blonde woman carrying a bag in one arm and a baby in the other. Trailing behind her on her way toward the stairs were two small kids. He didn't recognize any of them.

"Goddamn it!" he breathed, shutting the blind hastily.

"Wayne," he heard his mother softly call from the other room. "Got some company out here."

He strode quickly out of the room, but when he passed through the curtain, his mind went blank and he froze in his tracks. There, standing in front of him, surrounded by three kids and the woman, was his brother Buddy.

Wayne stood with his mouth open and gazed at him. His face was bloated. A huge stomach protruded between a stained t-shirt and a tight pair of jeans, which were unbuttoned at the waist to provide space for his enormous belly. His belly button was like a third eye, exposed and staring at him along with the others.

"Good to see you again, brother," Buddy said with a sly smile that exposed a half-empty set of blackened teeth. "It's been a long time."

Wayne stared at his brother coldly and then diverted his glare toward his mother.

"I thought I gave you explicit directions on the phone, Momma," he hissed.

"Well, I know, son," she said, realizing the mistake she may have made. "And I told Buddy what you done told me, but he said he'd really like to see you again."

"And it's the truth," Buddy said loudly, taking a step closer to him and sticking out his hand. Wayne reluctantly shook it, feeling something peculiar in his clasp. When he let go, he noticed that a few of his brother's fingers were missing, cut away at various lengths.

"Oh, it's nice," the old woman said, smiling absently in her chair. "I'm sure Daddy would be pleased."

Buddy interrupted his brother's staring at his disfigured hand by looking at it himself and fingering the stubs.

"Happened a few years ago on the Fourth of July," he said. "Blown to hell along with an M-80 I didn't let go of in time. Accident. Didn't realize the fuse was burnin' that quick and all of a sudden 'Ka-Pow!' Doctor told me I was lucky to come away with what I got left. He was right, I guess, 'cause I can still do jus' 'bout everythin' I used to 'cep flip somebody off with this hand." He laughed hard.

"I didn't know," Wayne said, ignoring the joke.

"I know you didn't," his brother said quickly. "There's lots of things happened round here that you don't know. You're a stranger round these parts now." Buddy's eyes narrowed, but a slight smile lightened his glare. "But you know you're still my brother," he added.

Wayne stared straight back at him, ignoring the fingers and studying instead the flabby face that had once, like the rest of Buddy's body, been taut. Buddy's face had been transformed to just an oversized ball of limp, red flesh topped by a John Deere cap. They still looked like brothers, Wayne thought, but he also was aware that type of resemblance was the weakest form of bond that blood could possibly draw. The bond with the person who stood in front of him, Wayne figured, was like a grain of sand along a coastline: Miniscule.

"This is my new old lady, Ronnie," Buddy broke in, gesturing toward the thin woman who stood next to him with a cigarette hanging between her lips. "And her two kids Stevie and Betty Lou, and our baby Tammy Rae." He grabbed the boy by the head and pulled him toward his leg. The boy tried unsuccessfully to squirm away. "My nice little family," he added with a crooked grin.

"Oh yeah," Wayne said, diverting his eyes toward his girl. "This is my daughter Darlene."

"Pleased to meet you Darlene," Buddy said loudly, holding out his deformed hand that the girl shook clumsily.

"Hey Buddy!" his wife broke in. "How's 'bout givin' me a beer already! I'm thirsty!"

"Sure," Buddy said, releasing the boy's head and removing the plastic lid from the container at his feet. "We got a whole case of it here. Everybody gets a beer, 'cep you kids. You run out to the kitchen and get yourself some pop."

165

The kids were moving to the kitchen before Buddy had even finished the sentence. He passed a beer to Wayne and Momma, then threw one to his wife.

"It's been too long since we all done this," he said, moving his eyes around the room.

His mother nodded her head and Ronnie grunted sarcastically. Buddy shook his can, popped the top and sprayed it toward the ceiling and then looked toward his brother while the foam ran down his arm.

"Wayne, it's good to have you back home," he said in a snide, dishonest tone.

Wayne mirrored the insincerity of his brother's smile, then popped the top on his beer, chugged it down in one go, and quickly reached for another.

Darlene went outside with the other kids to play in the backyard. After finishing another beer and taking a pill, Momma got up and went to her bedroom.

"I'm just gonna lay down a bit," she said. "Y'all go on and catch up with each other, and I'll see you in a little bit."

Wayne sat on one of the kitchen chairs he had dragged out to the sitting room, and Ronnie sat on the sofa next to her husband.

"We been out to the anti-nucular rally down in Marion earlier today," Buddy said, hustling his balls before taking another sip of brew. "They're buildin' a plant down there—a couple of big reactors—and a bunch of people were down there protestin' it."

The statement struck Wayne as odd. He didn't remember his brother being involved with some cause, let alone imagine he could be.

"What are you, turnin' into some sort of environmentalist or somethin'?" Wayne asked suspiciously.

"Hell no!", he responded, not believing that Wayne could have said such a thing.

"We was down there carryin' signs in favor of it!" Ronnie said flatly, looking at Wayne as if he were stupid.

"And throwin' a few rocks once and a while at them idiotic students protestin'," Buddy added, laughing. "Hell, I ain't for or against nucular power as far as it bein' a social issue goes. I couldn't care less, one way or the other. But what I do know is that power plant is gonna bring back some jobs into the area, and I already got my application in for one of 'em."

166

Even though they were within his reach, he signaled to his wife with his hand. "Hey baby," he said. "Pass me one of them beers, will you?"

Wayne was tiring of his brother's nice guy routine and, feeling his confidence return, decided to bring up their conflict in the past. After all, they hadn't spoken since that time and, even though he'd learned of the mine's closing, he figured he'd play a little game himself by feigning ignorance.

"What are you doin' lookin' for a job with the nuclear plant, when you're such a hot shot union man with Lambert's?"

Abruptly, Buddy's eyes narrowed and all the little lines that formed crevices around them deepened. He suddenly looked tough, like he once did.

"What did you just say?" he demanded slowly.

Even though Wayne knew that look and had once quivered when his brother stared him down, he found to his surprise that he wasn't even scared of Buddy anymore.

"You thinkin' about leavin' Lambert's?" he added forwardly.

"Leaving Lambert's!" Buddy yelled. "What the hell are you talkin' 'bout? I ain't been workin' there for four years now! Nobody has! The place shut down ages ago!"

"When'd it shut down?" Wayne continued calmly.

"Four years ago, man!" Buddy answered forcefully. "I thought I just told you that!" He stopped himself, took a deep breath and then continued in a calmer tone while glaring at his brother. "Hundreds of guys lost their jobs. I was one of the last to go, but I got the pink slip just like the rest. Times have been tough since."

"Wait a minute," Wayne stopped him. "Just when I left here, you guys signed a new contract and all, and Lambert's had agreed to most of your terms. What the hell happened to all that?"

"What happened?" Buddy pondered, as if anyone who hadn't heard the story was a fool. He looked around the room blindly and then returned his gaze to Wayne.

"What happened was; after we signed the new contract, things went real well for us for awhile. I mean shit, we'd all been out of work with the strike for almost two years, and we needed the goddamn money like a rabbit needs to make babies. So when we went back to work, all the money that we got went to payin' off all the bills and loans that'd been buildin' up. And after a few months, things were cool, back to normal. We'd signed a new contract and Lambert was makin' his profit and we were makin' ours. I mean, I was makin' a hundred and twenty-eight bucks a day ridin' the bulldozer. Jesus, all the kids were fed, didn't have holes in their clothes—times were good.''

"They sure were," Ronnie added. "My daddy even bought a new house. First one he ever owned hisself.''

"Those were the golden years," Buddy went on. "I bought me a new Dodge Charger, and I tell you, I got it stacked. I had a new huntin' rifle—a Remin'ton, new furniture, a satellite dish, even some jewelry for the wife.''

Buddy stopped himself abruptly and the sparkle in his eyes suddenly dulled as other memories came back to mind. "Of course, in other ways, things wasn't so golden," he burped. "A few personal things, uh, with the wife and the kids and...''

"Well keep goin' with the story about the mine!" Ronnie cut him off, not wanting to hear about his previous marriage again.

"I'm gettin' to that if you only gimme half a chance!" he yelled, looking at her coldly. "And gimme another beer!"

She handed him one and grabbed one herself and opened it. Wayne sat crushing his empty can. He finally stood up and reached across the table to the cans in front of her, eyeing her with disdain.

Buddy noticed the occurrence, and frowned at Ronnie.

"It would be nice if you had a few manners with my brother," Buddy said. "After all, he don't know you and I don't want him gettin' the wrong impression.''

Ronnie huffed and relit the stub of her hand rolled cigarette.

"Yeah...so...things were good," Buddy continued, annoyed with his wife's obstinacy. "For two years or so until the contract ran out again. Lambert wanted to renew it on the same terms, but we decided to strike again. The union, that is.''

"Weren't you makin' enough money as it was?" Wayne said, remembering the figure he had mentioned earlier.

"Yeah," Buddy said hesitantly. "But, you know, people's families got bigger and everybody had a little bit more to support. And that's what the UMW advised us to do anyway. That's the way it's done. You can't just settle at what you already achieved. You always got to push for more and make the boss remember where he's got to send some of his profit. To his workers, not his own pocket.''

"That guy had just bought a gold Cadillac and was sendin' his kids to some expensive private school up North," Ronnie added. "And I once saw his wife walkin' round town with a new fur coat.''

"That's right," Buddy said. "So it was obvious that it wasn't a very equal sharing of the wealth. And for that reason, we all walked out on him again."

"I see," Wayne muttered, the story beginning to sound familiar.

"And there it was, the same nasty thing all over again." Buddy paused and smiled lopsidedly toward Wayne. "But this time, Lambert tried a different approach. He didn't bring in any sca—any workers to work while the strike was going on. But he started layin' off people who hadn't been there for very long—say only a year or two.

"But the UMW still told us to hold out, and so we did. More months went by, and more pink slips were sent out—this time to people who had been there for five years or so. There were sympathy strikes in other states for us, but still, Lambert wouldn't reach our demands. So more people got their walkin' papers.

"So then, after about ten months, the guys who had been there for a long time started gettin' scared. Lambert said he'd keep everybody there who had been with him for six years and agreed to pay them what we had demanded. But he said in order to do that, all the others who had received their notices would have to go."

"Goddamn son of a bitch!" Ronnie hissed.

"And to tell you the truth, there were a lot of guys who were nearing their retirement age who began pushin' us to accept the terms. And I felt for them. And even though I didn't say it then, I think that's what we should have done. After all, those younger guys still had the gift of youth, they could've still gone out and found some kind of work or made the move out. But the UMW said no and so...we did too."

Buddy looked down sadly, introspectively, as if reliving one of those moments which could have been avoided—the kind that go on to alter the rest of a person's life, like a drunk-driving accident.

"So, when Lambert learned of our hard-line stance, he said he had no choice but to sell all his mining assets to a bigger company. And so that's what he did, and overnight we all became unemployed."

"And how about the new buyer?" Wayne asked.

"New buyer?" Buddy repeated, staring at his brother blankly. "No. A few guys, trained in certain areas, maybe ten-fifteen percent. But they was all educated guys brought into the area. The rest of us all became simple, out-of-work miners."

"My father included," Ronnie snarled. "After workin' his goddamn ass off for that guy for twenty-six years."

"Yeah, I wasn't as bad off as some guys," Buddy added despondently. "I'd only been there for nineteen myself. I still had a little bit of life left in me, at least."

They were silent for a moment.

"So what are you doin' now?" Wayne finally asked.

His brother looked up at him like a beaten dog.

"Whatever I can," Buddy responded. "I was workin' in a truck mine for a couple of years 'til it shut down, and picked up some seasonal work with the state. But that was only for a few months. And I did a little..."

"He never crossed the picket line though," Ronnie spat, looking spitefully toward Wayne.

Wayne sat back uncomfortably and looked down, enclosing himself for a moment within the silence of the room.

"I don't think that was called for, woman," Buddy whispered forcefully, between his clenched teeth. "I thought we said before that we weren't gonna mention anything about that."

"Yeah, well I know what you and everybody else says about your brother."

"Shut up!" Buddy screamed, drowning out the end of her sentence. "When I say somethin', I mean it!"

She glared hatefully at him and abruptly stood up, then marched hastily toward the kitchen. The sound of something being broken and a high-pitched obscenity filled the void of her absence. The baby started crying. Buddy ignored it, but was obviously containing himself.

He looked toward his brother, and when there eyes finally met, he said, "I'm sorry. I didn't want that to be brought up."

Wayne stared at his brother's bloodshot eyes, and then stood up and went off to the bathroom. When he returned, the baby was quiet again but Buddy babbled on, filling him in on what had been happening around the area. Wayne's brother kept on with his brother-buddy-pal shit, and at one point even said he was "happier than a fly in shit" to see him again.

Then he began talking about the rest of the family. It was conversation that Wayne continued to tolerate silently. Buddy said that Pearl was living in Winston-Salem, North Carolina, with a new husband who had a "good job" in some factory that made aspirin powders. Even though their sister was now forty-seven years old, she was expecting another child within a few months, adding to the nine she had already. Five of them still lived in the area and four of them now had children of their own.

"You know how she was livin' here with that husban' of hers?

170

Willy or whatever his name was? When you was drivin' the truck?" Buddy began again. "You know, the guy who was workin' with me at Lambert 22, the union guy?"

Wayne nodded his head slowly, as that bad memory came back as well. Buddy continued.

"Well, the guy took to drinkin' real bad. I mean, not like the rest of us, you know, a few beers after work and maybe tyin' one on the weekends. I mean, he started gettin' smashed every night of the goddamn week. And he wasn't just drinkin' beer like the rest of us. Oh sure, there was a lot of that, but he also started in full-time with the 'shine. Started goin' to work drunk and then started not showin' up at all. And you can't do that round here—you know that. There's six guys waitin' round for any job opportunity that comes up within fifty miles of here."

Buddy paused and took out a pouch of chewing tobacco and pried a wedge between his cheek and rotting teeth.

"So Pearl started comin' down on him harder at home. After all, she had five mouths to feed and clothe, in addition to lookin' after Momma, who'd been nice enough to let 'em move into her place to begin with. But he kept it up, and the more he drank, the more the others complained. And the more they complained, the more violent he got. He beat up Pearl real bad a couple of times—and I don't mean the normal kind of discipline that a woman gets when her man thinks she's gettin' a little out of line. I'm not talkin' 'bout black eyes and stuff. I'm talkin' broken bones. And I mean more than one."

"What a bastard," Ronnie said with a sigh.

"What are you talkin' 'bout?" Buddy snapped, stopping suddenly and looking at her sideways, annoyed that she had interrupted him. "You didn't even know the guy!"

"Yeah, well, what you was sayin' and all."

"Yeah," Buddy said and then paused, taking his eyes off his wife and returning them to Wayne. "What was I sayin' and all?"

He chuckled loudly but the others remained quiet, and he finally cleared his throat, spat into an empty can and continued.

"Anyway, she used to call me up and bitch about it all the time, 'bout what a bastard the guy was and how she was fearful for everyone in the house. But damn, I had enough problems of my own at the time. There was another strike goin' on, I had no money comin' in, one of my kids was sick, throwin' up every night and keepin' me up, creditors started takin' things away and hell, I was knee-high in shit myself. So I couldn't really deal with her problems, too.

"But one night, Momma called up in hysterics. And this time the guy didn't only beat up Pearl and a couple of the kids, but he also threatened Momma. So some friends and me came over and decided to inform the guy he'd gone too far and teach him a lesson.

"And when he got out of the hospital a couple of weeks later," he added coolly, finishing his can of beer, "I told him personally that he better stay away—forever."

"When was this?" Wayne asked.

"Damn," Buddy said scratching his head and looking toward his wife for help, before realizing she wouldn't know. "A few years after you left, I can't remember exactly. Somethin' like that."

Bored, Wayne grabbed another can from the table.

"Man, you been away from here for a long time. Jesus!" Buddy exclaimed, grabbing another beer too.

Ronnie moved to where the old woman had been sitting and flipped on a small black and white portable, obviously bored by her husband's stories as well. She looked to be between twenty and twenty-five—a bit young for his brother in any event, Wayne thought. She had stringy blond hair—which he guessed was unnatural—and couldn't have weighed more than ninety pounds. Every time she inhaled her cigarette, her gaunt cheeks puckered unpleasantly inward. When she reached out to change a channel, Wayne noticed a tattoo on her outer forearm.

"Where were we?" Buddy asked after checking the TV briefly.

"Pearl," Wayne said. "And you."

"Oh yeah...well...Pearl, you know Pearl," he laughed. "When she's in need of a man, she don't have too much trouble gettin' hooked up with one. Uh, she had another guy named Bill who must've lived here for a few years—although they weren't married, and believe it or not, she didn't have any kids with him. Must've been impotent, I guess, I don't know. But he had a job down in the deli department of a supermarket in Lebanon—he may have even been the manager—and Pearl got her welfare and food stamps seein' that they wasn't married still. I mean, financially they were all right, with Momma's social security comin' in too. And everybody liked the guy. I mean, we always asked each other, 'Why the hell hasn't Pearl had another kid with this guy?'. It was like, I don't know if the guy just didn't like bustin' his nuts with her, but whatever it was..."

The story was interrupted by Ronnie's oldest child, who ran in crying and screaming that Darlene—whom he referred to as "the fat girl''—had thrown him down on the ground.

Ronnie stood up and hissed, "That big fat bitch should know..."
before her husband cut her off.

"Jesus Christ, Jason!" Buddy yelled at the kid, beckoning him to
come over. "Shut up and quit cryin' or I'll give you somethin' to really cry
about!"

The kid was immediately silent. Buddy added menacingly, "Now
go back outside and leave us alone in here!" and then turned to his wife and
hollered, "And you too—watch your goddamn trap!"

Ronnie looked as if she was about to scream something at him, but
contained it by simply pursing her lips tighter and giving him the evil eye.
She moved her glare toward Wayne, who gave her a false smile.

"Where was I before?" Buddy asked.

"You tell me," Wayne mumbled.

Buddy paused and scratched his head.

"Oh yeah," he finally drawled. "That's right, with the nice guy
who had his nuts cut off." He smiled and shifted the chew from one cheek
to the other before continuing. "Bill, his name was, and those were crazy
times out there too. I tell you, it was like a goddamn orphanage, that house.
You'd go over there and none of the kids looked alike on account of they all
had different daddies. Pretty hard to keep up with all of 'em but uh...what
the hell, Bill came along and didn't mind the fact that there were all these
little bastards runnin' round, and we were all happy that Pearl had a guy who
seemed stable—financially and mentally—around the house.

"But one day he stayed home from work lookin' after the kids and
Pearl had gone visitin' some friend. And what happens when she gets home
but she walks into the kitchen and finds her new husband standin' in front
of her youngest daughter, with his pants down...movin' the girl's hand all
over his damn dick!

"Well, Pearl goes absolutely apeshit—understandable, and the
guy just says,'Pearl, you didn't see that. You didn't see nothin','' like tryin'
to make out she was imaginin' it and all. Up with the zipper and out with
the bullshit, you know? Anyway, she starts thinkin' she wasn't sure if she
had imagined it after all or not, 'cause she'd been on some strong medication
herself.

"And when she told me about it, hell, I didn't believe her neither.
I mean, the guy was nice and all and, as I said, pretty generous with the
money. And we all knew that sometimes Pearl came out with some pretty
strange things. Shit, I'd even left my kids over there with him a few times

and they got along real well with him.

"But anyway, she decides to check the guy out a little bit further anyway, some records and stuff. And it turns out the guy had been convicted of child molestin' twice before! I mean, she was right after all! No one couid believe it! So the authorities came out and they took the guy away."

Buddy brought an empty can up to his mouth and drooled some rancid saliva into it. "Damn, the guy obviously had somethin' the matter with him, but to tell you the truth, in other ways I think he was the best husban' Pearl ever had."

Out of the corner of his eye, Wayne had begun watching the television while his brother spoke. There were some music videos on, and Ronnie turned up the volume of one she recognized.

"Goddamn it!" Buddy screamed, annoyed that the TV was attracting all the attention in the room. "Turn that shit down before I make you turn it off altogether! I'm talkin' to my brother, for fuck's sake! You hear me?"

Ronnie turned it down without looking at her husband. Buddy breathed heavily and looked at her and then at Wayne.

"She's just like my first wife," Buddy said. "A discipline problem, kinda like a little kid."

Buddy sat back in the sofa and looked down at the floor for another beer. When he had found it, he muttered, "That's another story though. My ex-wife who...done me dirty."

"Yeah?" Wayne yawned, looking back from the television.

"Yeah," his brother said, appearing deep in thought. "And the worst thing about it is the way she done it." He seemed to be waiting for some response from his brother, but when none was forthcoming, he continued anyway.

"She ended up leavin' me for a friend of mine. A guy who was in the union with me, Stan Jenkins. You know him."

Wayne stared at his brother and nodded slowly.

"Oh yeah," he said, vaguely remembering the man.

"Not much to it," Buddy went on, rcmoving the waterlogged lump of chewing tobacco from his mouth and immediately reaching for the package of smoking tobacco on the table. "You work with a guy every day, go out drinkin' with him, fish with him sometimes, and invite him over for dinner. And what sort of thanks does he give you?"

He paused for Wayne to respond, but Wayne remained silent.

"He steals your wife," Buddy snarled, as if the answer was obvious, before repeating it for good measure: "He steals your *wife*."

Wayne covered his mouth to hide a yawn and Buddy, looking away, scratched the side of his face with his stumpy fingers and shook his head. "I mean, we was separated and all, but we was still legally married, we hadn't signed no papers or nothin'," he continued, looking back to Wayne. "But the weird thing is, when it happens, it's like you can't do nothin' about it. After all, he's like your best friend, right? And you're in a bar sayin' how much better you feel bein' out on your own again, talkin' about all the bullshit that you had to put up with the wife and the kids, and jokin' about some other pussy you got on the side, and how much better it is now. And all of a sudden, he's layin some lines on you about how he's in love, and how his lover is your wife, and how he never wanted what happened to happen, you know?

"And first you ain't sure this ain't another joke. I mean, you're sittin' in a bar and you been laughin' together all night long. But then he repeats what he just said and doesn't laugh, and you kind of look him in the eyes and know that he's serious, 'cause you know his serious look—you seen it before. And you think, 'Jesus Christ, what am I gonna do?' And you kind of sit there burnin' inside, your emotions ready to explode...and you're just about to let them go when you suddenly find...you can't.

"So you leave the bar, and it's a little like that song, you know, *My Wife Just Ran Off With My Best Friend—And I Sure Do Miss Him* or whatever the hell it's called. You drink some more on your own to forget, and then you go try to find that pussy you were talkin' 'bout earlier with your old friend...and you do. And you wake up in the mornin' and find that you're uh, layin' beside...your next wife."

Buddy suddenly looked toward Ronnie and burst out laughing, then winked and sent her a kiss. She regarded him without expression. She obviously missed the "funny" ending to his sad story. There she was, Wayne observed, hunched over in front of the TV, munching the nails of a hand that held a cigarette, pale, skinny, ignorant-looking.

Suddenly Wayne caught the lettering of her tattoo, that someone had obviously scratched in one drunken night with a needle, ink and a block of ice. It read "Live Free Or Die."

Wayne reached for another beer, and for the first time that day, laughed so hard he thought his insides were going to burst.

The small room was beginning to get stuffy with the smoke of continuous cigarettes, and Wayne stood up to open the window and clear the

175

air. Outside he saw the kids playing in the tiny yard; they had managed to trample most of the grass, so that it almost looked mowed.

Darlene stood between the others trying to intercept a ball that they passed back and forth between them. Her reactions were slow, and she normally thrust up her arms to stop the ball after it had already passed from one side to the other. Her glasses were drifting down her nose, and her hair, which hung in pigtails, moved in the same rhythm up and down as her large breasts beneath her sweatshirt.

The other kids throwing the ball looked about as scrawny as their mother. Their clothes were either too big or too small. Yet although the two boys had bruises on their faces and the young girl wore thick glasses, they looked relatively happy.

"They nice, ain't they?" Buddy mentioned, having moved behind Wayne's shoulder.

"Yeah," Wayne said without emotion, grimacing at his brother's foul, drunken breath that circled him like a threat.

"Sometimes I wish I was a kid again," Buddy added. "You know, no big problems to worry about, no need to think about what this month's check is gonna buy, how far it's gonna go. Never have to look at a price tag even."

Wayne looked over his shoulder at his brother's puffy face. What a sick individual he had become, he thought. He was an asshole before, for sure—but at least back then, Wayne figured, the guy had a little bit of self-respect. Now he was talking like a man about to be executed.

"Kids are crazy," Buddy rambled on. "Cryin' one minute and laughin' the next. All they need is to be sent outside and they're happy. Sometimes I'd like to just go outside and play and wait for Momma to call me in for supper."

Wayne moved himself away from his brother, who now looked like he was about to cry.

"What happened to the old place?" Wayne asked, changing the subject and sitting down again.

Buddy suddenly pulled himself together, and looked at Wayne unpleasantly for not appreciating his confession. He snapped back to his former self, eyes focused and body tense, as if he was ready to fight.

"I thought I told you that!" he whispered menacingly, awkwardly trying to regain the demeanor he'd displayed earlier in the afternoon. "The coal company done Momma dirty," he said. "Done us all dirty!"

Wayne remembered his brother mentioning that before, but somewhere he had gotten sidetracked—somewhere, he reckoned, on the way out of their mother's womb.

"You didn't tell me anything about that," he said, shaking his head.

"I must of started talkin' about somethin' else then," he drawled after a pause. "That's right. You wanted to know about Stan Jenkins."

Wayne hadn't asked him about Stan Jenkins, that was something he knew, because he hated Stan Jenkins, perhaps even more than he hated his brother. After all, Jenkins was sort of like his brother's henchman, who did whatever Buddy told him to do. Stan had made hundreds of threatening phone calls to Wayne, slashed his tires on countless occasions, and fired shots through the windows of Wayne's apartment numerous times from the security of the dark woods across the street.

There wasn't much Wayne could do about it at the time, because Jenkins wasn't normally on his own. There were always others nearby, doing the same things, always ready when his brother gave the word to move in against him.

All Wayne could do was call the police, who of course got there late—if they even responded at all. On the few times they did investigate, they certainly didn't have much sympathy for him. After all, these were the same guys who tied one on with his brother and Jenkins and Murphy and the rest down at the bar when they weren't on duty. So Wayne was forced to remain on his own, alone, trembling in his bed, trying to keep low and out of reach before the sun at least let him see what obstacles surrounded him.

He stared at his brother, who was contorting his face in a confused effort to remember what had been said and what he wanted to say.

"What about the old house?" Wayne asked again.

"Oh yeah...the house," he said slowly, rubbing the back of his neck. "Well the plain and the short of it is that the goddamn power company done took it away from Momma. Yeah, that's somethin' else you proba'ly don't know 'bout. Lambert ain't even in existence round here anymore. They sold out to the biggest goddamn coal corporation in the country. And when they sold that, they also sold all the assets they had, includin' all the land underneath the houses that their former employees leased.

"You see, Daddy paid a lease on the house all the while he was workin' for Lamberts, but he never actually owned it. And to the power company, the land underneath the house was a hell of a lot more valuable than the timber standin' upon it...or the people livin' within it," he blurted, as if having a brainstorm. "Our daddy came up in the old school, goin'

177

underground for coal. But they ain't hardly any places like that no more. It's all strip now, surface coal, and a person that's got a piece of land makes a good profit sellin' it out."

"Yeah, but that ain't nothin' new," Wayne said. "It was like that when I was here."

"Yeah well, I ain't sure how long you been away," Buddy retorted. "I can't even remember when you were here last."

Wayne reached down for another beer and tried to contain himself. Maybe Buddy had firebombed so many people's homes that he couldn't even remember he had done the same to his own brother. Maybe he couldn't remember threatening him with a nail studded baseball bat as he had inched the coal truck toward the mine entrance, shaking and fearing for his life. Maybe. But he doubted it.

"But before they moved all them people out of them houses that had been livin' there for decades, the power company made little allowances," Buddy rattled on. "Pitiful little gestures to try to keep right in everybody's eyes. And maybe the guy who came round givin' this pittance out felt sorry for Momma, or maybe a guy from Lambert put in a good word for her, seein' as how her husban' died fallin' off the roof. But in any event, they gave her enough to move into this place and pay the rent for awhile. I mean, imagine it, Pearl and all those kids and Momma squeezed in here!"

Wayne sat back and thought about it. It was becoming clearer to him just how ignorant his brother was. After all, the coal company didn't owe anybody anything, he felt. It was a business like any other. And really, because his father didn't have his accident while working, his mother wasn't entitled to collect any disability for his fatal slip. He remembered, when he was about fourteen or so, the man from Lambert's coming around and telling her exactly that.

But Lambert's let her stay in the house, seeing how her brother was already working for the company and probably figuring that her other son would, too. After all, what else was there to do in Mercer but mine? And he remembered his mother being grateful and almost crying when the man told her that, after having worried for days that everyone was going to get kicked out.

The coal company didn't owe them anything, he repeated silently. His mother had simply been blessed with kindness and good luck. His brother, Wayne concluded, was wrong again.

"You been out to see where the old place stood?" Buddy asked in a cracking voice, as if recalling another painful memory.

178

"No," Wayne responded dryly.

"I bulldozed it myself," he said, as if holding back a tear. "In forty-eight hours, that place was no longer the place where we grew up, but just another jagged line cuttin' across the hills that just kept gettin' deeper and deeper. First I ran across the piece of land where Daddy used to have his garden. 'Member them potatoes he used to grow?'' he stammered, his voice breaking.

Wayne's face was expressionless. He bug-eyed his brother without even sipping his beer.

"Then I knocked down that big oak tree where the tire used to hang, that swing. I knocked it down and remembered Pearl pushin' us round in it, and us laughin' when she fell off and almost broke her arm that time."

Buddy laughed with difficulty and then looked up toward Wayne, whose dour expression remained.

"You don't know how painful it was," he continued. "Like destroyin' all those past memories, wipin' them out with one quick pull on the throttle." His eyes tightened as he concentrated. "And then came the back porch, the beams snappin' like matchsticks, the lumber tossed up in the air, the dirt that was once the garden movin' into the kitchen. And then the foundation crumblin', the cement disintegratin' like powder, the roof comin' down, the huge steel wheels of the 'dozer drivin' into what was once the livin' room, where we used to sit round eatin' dinner. And then it was just a huge junk heap, doused with fuel and ignited...and I pulled that machine backwards and turned it off for a minute. And believe it or not, as I watched that smoke curlin' up toward the gray sky, I could almost hear the sounds of the happy family that once lived under that roof, talkin', playin', laughin'..."

His voice broke and he put his hand over his eyes, making a few wheezing noises as he held back the tears.

It was almost humorous for Wayne to see his brother in such a pathetic state. To keep from laughing, he had to divert his eyes from the sorry sight in front of him to *The Wheel Of Fortune* on the television to his side.

"Goddamn it!" his brother yelled, springing up from the chair toward Ronnie and bringing the back of his hand hard against her face. "I thought I told you to turn that shit off!"

She fell to the ground and looked up at him with an expression of fear and confusion. The veins in Buddy's neck bulged, and his enraged eyes burned into her.

"You didn't tell me to turn it off," she said meekly, looking plaintively up to her husband before her.

He rubbed his fingers over his closed eyelids slowly before focusing on her again.

"Get the fuck outside with the kids!" he whispered threateningly, shooting a half-finger toward the door.

Ronnie picked herself up quickly from the floor and scurried out the door, almost falling down the stairs as she exited the house. Wayne turned and went toward the bathroom, leaving his brother alone in the center of the room.

Buddy stood in the middle of the room, rolling his head back and forth. He was breathing heavily, as if he'd just had a sensational, deeply satisfying orgasm.

"Sometimes a damn woman gets on your nerves and you got to do somethin' about it," Buddy said flatly when Wayne returned to the room a few minutes later. He was breathing more easily now, as if nothing had happened. "Where's your old lady at anyway?" he asked. "Ethel, wasn't it?"

"Couldn't make it," Wayne said. "I got new twin daughters and she stayed at home lookin' after 'em."

Buddy leaned back in the chair and cracked his knuckles loudly. "You workin'?"

"Yeah."

Buddy reached across the table and shook a cigarette out of Wayne's pack. "Whatcha doin'?" he asked with a sideways glance.

"Security," Wayne responded, before adding quickly, "And surveillance."

"You know, I bought Momma a dog," Buddy said, lighting up. "To keep her company and also watch over the place. But it ran away a few weeks ago. Jumped over that damn fence somehow and never came back."

"Yeah," Wayne said. "I saw the room where it must've been sleepin'. Smelled like there'd been a dog in there."

"Yeah...well uh, she probably thinks that dog is gonna come back, and she wants to leave things the way they were for him. I mean, Momma ain't been all that well lately. Her mind just ain't functionin' the way it used to.

"I noticed," Wayne said, looking down.

"I mean, I been thinkin' of havin' her move in with us," Buddy

180

added, seeming to be searching for the correct words. "Our place is a little bit bigger than this and at least there'd be some people around to look after her. But, uh, thing is, I ain't workin' for the time bein' and, uh, we barely get enough money to put some grub on our own plates. So I was thinkin'..."

"That you wanna ask me to help out," Wayne interrupted him, already predicting the next part.

He looked up at Wayne suddenly, as if surprised at what he had said. "Well, you know," he said, shaking his head, "she's your mother too and, uh, the money she collects ain't even enough to pay for the pills the doctors prescribe her. Now Pearl..."

"How much you think she's gonna need?" Wayne interrupted him again.

"Well, I ain't really thought about it all that much," he said, obviously lying. "But maybe uh, a hundred dollars a month would help me, I mean her out a great deal. Pearl, bless her heart, sends some money now and again, and it was with that that Momma got the pills so she don't shake so much now. You should've seen her a year or so ago."

"And how about the money that she pays the rent with here?" Wayne said, eyeing his brother suspiciously.

"She don't pay rent here!" he said, offended at Wayne's tone. "I told you, the people at the coal company let her live here as a gesture. They own the building. They own the whole goddamn town, for Christ's sake. You know that! And I'm sure it's only a matter of time before they decide to rip down this place and dig up whatever's underneath it. Management's proba'ly changed again anyhow, they proba'ly forgot she's even here. It's only a matter of time before she'll get booted, I know it! So don't give me any shit like you think I'm gonna use that money for myself!"

Buddy looked at Wayne with a spiteful glare—a look that had been nearly constant on the rare occasions they saw each other when Wayne was driving the truck. Buddy began breathing more heavily, the beer on his breath filling the room again, and it somehow instilled fear in Wayne. It was a sensation that had so often overwhelmed him during those times.

"I wasn't assumin' that," Wayne lied, a knot forming in his throat. "I was just askin' a question, that's all."

"Look, I already told you that I was willin' to forget everything that went on between us years ago," Buddy said, pointing one of his finger-stubs at Wayne. "But anyway, what we're talkin' 'bout don't pertain to you and me anyway. We was talkin' about our beloved...mother."

"Yeah, well I got a family too," Wayne said, angry that he was getting suckered into this. "And had twins not long ago to boot. And it ain't like I'm makin' money to spare—you know what I mean?"

"Yeah, OK, you got a family too," he hissed. "But you have also been absent for a hell of a long time. And Momma, even with what she's been given, don't live for free. It's me and Pearl that's laid out the money—not you! We the ones who been goin' round short. Jesus, you're off and livin' in another goddamn state. I ain't even been out of this fuckin' area in my whole life!"

"Yeah, well that's because..." Wayne began, but stopped when his brother edged a bit closer toward him.

They both knew the reason well enough now. It was because Wayne had the brains to bail out. He had the foresight that his brother was obviously too stupid and pigheaded to have at the time. Buddy learned the slow and painful way instead: that he was living amidst a putrid corpse of land, controlled by a corporation that didn't give a shit about anybody. They didn't even use what was mined to fuel the area's economy but instead sent the product—and the profits—out to other states.

Wayne knew that the unions had started with the right intentions, but somewhere along the line had gotten a little greedy. After all, what independent coal company could afford to pay what the union men demanded? What independent company wouldn't have to sell out to the big boys? And which of the big boys would want to hire all those union men, with their salaries and attitudes?

"Look," Wayne began again. "I ain't been around here, you're right about that. And I haven't seen Momma neither, and I admit that seein' her now like this is...sad." He stared down at his hands and noticed his palms were sweating. "But, uh, I ain't had it easy neither. I mean, I been in and out of jobs too and frankly, I don't know if I can afford that kind of money."

"Well, don't worry about that figure I gave you," his brother said more enthusiastically, handing him another beer and opening one himself. "I was just mentionin' what...the *ideal* might be. I told you, Pearl sends what she can, and helped Momma out a lot when she was here. And I think..."

He stopped abruptly upon seeing their mother emerge from behind the curtain.

"Good mornin'!" she said yawning and focusing on the scene in front of her. "Where are the women and all the kids?"

"Shit," Buddy said in a low voice, annoyed at having been interrupted. "We'll talk more about this later, OK Wayne?" he added in a tobacco-stained whisper.

182

"They're outside playin', Momma," Wayne said, ignoring his brother. "Well, ain't it nice like this," the old woman drawled after regarding both her children several times. "Got both my boys back together again. Just like old times." Her eyes glowed magically, as if beholding a wonderful vision.

"Yeah, just like the old days," Buddy said, clearing his throat and smiling. "In fact, we was just sittin' here catchin' up on all those lost years, wasn't we Wayne?"

Wayne stared at his brother dumbly as he drew nearer.

"Yeah, about old memories and an agreement for the future." Buddy proclaimed, putting his arm around Wayne's shoulder.

"Oh, ain't that nice," the old woman beamed.

"Yeah, ain't it nice," Buddy said, smiling broadly at Wayne, whose silence was filled by the dull thud of Buddy's aluminum can toasting his in a ridiculous gesture of brotherhood.

* * *

Earlier in the afternoon, Junior rode his bicycle to Westport and met his friend at Eddie's Pizza. They had a couple of slices, played video games, and smoked some cigarettes. After that, they went to the Kone King for ice cream and played a couple more video games before moving on to Wal-Mart, where they took on the video machines there. Before they left, Junior bought a black t-shirt with a colorful heavy metal band's design on the front, and John bought a new album by a different group before they returned to John's house.

Even though it wasn't completely dark outside, every light in the small two story house was illuminated. Music soared out of the open windows and into the cool twilight air at frightening volume, giving the impression that the frail foundations of the tiny dwelling might crumble and bring the house down to the ground at any moment.

The two boys sat on the living room floor, their backs to armchairs. They drank glasses of beer while shouting back and forth to each other over the rumble of the stereo. The boys arrived at John's house about an hour before, wolfed down a couple of sandwiches, and then set out to do what they had agreed to during study hall that morning: to drink some beer and see

183

what happened.

"Man, could you believe that dick at the ice cream place today?" John yelled, lighting a cigarette. "He really pissed me off. I wasn't smokin' today or nothin'."

"Yeah, but he owns the place," Junior responded. "So he can do whatever the hell he wants."

"Yeah, but shit! It was two weeks ago that he kicked me out of there for smokin' a cigarette, when I was in there with Alicotti. Jesus, what's the big deal anyway? Everybody's always smokin' in there, and its the only place in town that's got the Corbus 666 game. And I love that thing, man! I mean, I only wanted to play the game for God's sake. I wasn't even gonna smoke. I shoulda kicked his ass!"

"I don't know," Junior said, unsure if he liked the taste of the beer in his hand but swallowing it down anyway. "He's a pretty big dude."

"Yeah, well he's just lucky that I'm pretty small then. I mean, I was right in the middle of the goddamn game—and with the best score I ever had—and that bastard just walks over and pulls the fuckin' plug right out of the goddamn wall. One second those lights were just flashin' in front of me like I was in another galaxy, and the next second the screen was all black. There were like forty-five more seconds left on that game, and I'm sure I would have broke the record."

"He should have at least given your money back."

"Yeah! But I mean he should've at least let me finish the game first before kickin' us out."

Junior imitated the owner's grumble. "You're banned from here. Get Out!"

"That guy is just a class A asshole," John said, standing up and shaking his head. He ran his hand through his long black hair as he looked in the mirror and then grabbed the glasses, disappearing into the kitchen for more beer.

When he returned, Junior was looking through a stack of albums. John placed the full glasses on the table.

"Did your mom give you any shit about comin' over here tonight?" John asked.

Junior smirked and blew some air out his mouth. "No way, man. My mom's pretty cool. She lets me do whatever I want most of the time. Unlike my stupid father."

John nodded and suddenly grabbed one of the records near the stereo, quickly taking it out of the sleeve.

184

"Some guy killed himself when he was listenin' to this song!"
John yelled excitedly while putting down the needle.

"What?" Junior yelled back, removing a cigarette from the pack
on the table.

"This song, man!" John screamed over the music. "Some guy was
listenin' to it and shot himself 'cause the music told him to do it!"

Junior stared cross-eyed toward the end of the cigarette dangling
from his lips before finally connecting a match to it.

"What the hell are you talkin' about?" he coughed.

"It's true!" John yelled. "My brother told me about it. There's
supposed to be some weird shit underneath the music or somethin' like
that."

"What do you mean, 'weird shit'?" Junior asked, drawing nearer.

John looked puzzled. "I don't know," he said. "I mean, I'm not
sure. Just listen."

They stood without speaking for a while. Before long each one was
crouching in front of a speaker, trying to hear some sort of secret message
within the music.

"All I can hear is the damn music," Junior said when the side
ended.

"Well maybe that song my brother was talkin' about wasn't on that
side," John said, scratching his head. "But I'm pretty sure it's somewhere
on this album. I mean, I don't know if the guy comes right out and says 'Kill
yourself!,' but it's like some kind of creepy voice that gets the idea across,
you know?"

Junior seemed impressed. "That's pretty cool, man," he said,
putting the needle down again.

"Yeah, my brother told me it was like devil worship or somethin'.
Like the band made some agreement with the devil that they would follow
him if he would give them success, you know, some kind of Satanist thing.
I don't know, like sellin' your soul to the devil or somethin'. All the heavy
metal groups are into it, you know, always singin' about Hell and stuff. It's
real big."

"Oh yeah, I heard about that."

"Hell, I guess if the devil said you could have anything you wanted
if you served him," John said anxiously, "it wouldn't be too bad a deal."

"Yeah, think of it," Junior added, finishing his glass. "All that
money and those girls in the videos. Damn!" He burped and brushed some
fallen cigarette ash further into the carpet.

"You feel anything off that beer yet?" his companion asked, changing the subject.

"I don't know," Junior said after thinking about it. "I ain't sure. What about you?"

"Not really," he said, moving toward the kitchen. "I think you're supposed to drink a lot. My dad's got a big jug of the stuff that he makes himself. I'm gonna go get us some more. He'll never know the difference."

Junior closed his eyes and mouthed some of the lyrics to a song he recognized. His stomach felt a little bloated and his head a little bit light, but in his mind he felt he could do just about anything. Like play the song blaring out of the speakers, even. He moved his head up and down to the noise that raced past him and bent back, stretching a chord on his air guitar to an imaginary stadium filled with thousands of screaming fans. When he opened his eyes again, they were gone, but his friend stood nearby headbanging to the final notes.

"I don't know," John said when the song ended, reaching for a large pitcher of beer he'd carried out. "I heard my dad tell some people that this stuff was really strong, but I don't really feel nothin' yet."

"Maybe we ought to drink it faster then," Junior suggested. "What time are your parents supposed to come home anyway?"

"I don't know," John responded casually, lighting another cigarette. "I think around midnight, so don't worry. We got plenty of time, man."

*   *   *

"Goddamn, I'm hungry!" Buddy yelled toward the kitchen where his wife and mother were preparing the meal. "Ain't it about time we ate?"

The room was partially in shadows, and outside the sharpness of the light was beginning to wane, as if a huge, muslin canvas had been draped across the sun. The kids had come in a few minutes earlier, and Darlene was now sitting in front of the TV watching some show, still breathing heavily and sweating from her rare afternoon of exercise. The other two kids were laying on the floor and looking through a comic book, further dirtying their already-soiled clothes. The coffee table between the brothers was littered with a few six packs of empty beer cans while both ashtrays overflowed onto the floor.

"Well damn, this is one helluva day in history, huh?" Buddy signaled Wayne with a flip of his head. "A family reunion of sorts. Ain't it somethin'?"

"Yeah, it sure is," Wayne said without enthusiasm, while eyeing his brother suspiciously. Even though there was less violent tension between him and Buddy as there had once been, there was still an angry distance that Wayne knew could never be shortened. He figured Buddy already knew that, but insisted on acting as if everything was all right between them—his only reason being the almightly dollar. If Buddy wasn't so desperate for money, Wayne knew, he wouldn't have given two shits about seeing his kid brother, "the scab." As far as Wayne was concerned, they still shared nothing in common except a dead father and senile mother.

"Food's all ready," his mother said feebly, waddling into the room. "And it looks real good."

"Man, it's about time," Buddy said. "I'm just about to starve to death. Get up off the floor kids. It's eatin' time."

They all made their way into the kitchen and squeezed themselves around a table that wasn't much bigger than a card table. Next to a pile of paper plates and plastic utensils sat a bowl of potato salad and a steaming pot of chicken and dumplings, recently removed from the microwave. Without waiting for the others to even grab their plates, Buddy heaped several spoonfuls of each onto his plate and began chowing down. Ronnie began dishing some out for her kids. After glaring at Ronnie condescendingly, Wayne stood up, grabbed another spoon from a drawer, and served some food to his mother.

"Oh, that's too much for me, Wayne honey," Momma said, smiling up at him.

"That's OK, Momma," Buddy murmured through a full mouth. "You just eat what you can and I'll take care of the rest." He laughed out loud, and called for another beer.

Wayne sank his fork toward the food on his plate, but after loading a few sauce covered dumplings into his mouth, he suddenly felt like spitting it out. The chicken was almost non-existent, and the dumplings were nothing more than giant clumps of flour that hadn't been stirred properly.

"It's my new recipe," Ronnie said proudly, finally beginning to eat herself. "Hope y'all like it."

Buddy burst out laughing. "And if you don't," he shouted, "they ain't nothin' else!"

The room was filled with the coarse sounds of feeding, much like that of pigs gnawing on their corn slops for the day. Momma finally broke through the commotion.

"It's got a particular flavor, Ronnie," she said kindly. "How'd you make it different?"

"Well, the recipe's real simple," she began, pouring a load of salt on top of what remained on her plate. "You just take a couple of cans of cream of chicken soup—cause the chicken's already in that—heat it up, add a bit of extra water and drop the dumplings in. Real cheap and easy." A look of self-satisfaction crossed her face, and she took another bite before adding more salt to her plate.

Wayne decided to leave what remained of the chicken and dumplings a la Ronnie on his plate and grabbed another couple spoonfuls of potato salad. There wasn't a hell of a lot she could do to cut corners with that, he thought.

When Buddy had finished eating, he belched loudly and lit a cigarette, exhaling it over the table as the others finished up.

"That sure was good, woman," he burped again.

Wayne pushed his plate away and stood up, crossing the kitchen to get the cake.

"It ain't a lot we got for dessert," he said, "But I didn't know there was gonna be so many people here."

"That's OK," Buddy said. "Long as it got sugar in it." He laughed. Darlene looked toward him and laughed too.

"It's awful small," Ronnie said, looking down at the cake Wayne had taken out of a plastic bag.

"Well, I didn't know *you* were gonna be here," he said flatly, staring at her coldly.

Momma wore a confused expression. "I told Buddy what you'd said Wayne, and he..."

"Surprise, surprise!" Buddy drowned her out, smirking. "The more, the merrier is what I always say!"

Wayne turned his back on everybody and began cutting the cake into tiny strips. He wasn't sure whose fault this whole horrendous visit had been: his mother's for letting the cat out of the bag, his brother's for inviting himself over, or his own for even coming in the first place.

He supposed he couldn't really blame his mother. After all, she hadn't told Buddy of his visit on purpose and was obviously a brick shy of a full load anyway. And if Wayne had known the others were going to be there and clog up the house with their presence, he certainly wouldn't have made the trip.

No, it was all his stupid brother's fault, Wayne reckoned. Buddy had succeeded only in putting his mother to sleep while boring everybody else with his idiotic stories—and begging for money, to boot. In addition to being an asshole, the guy was just a complete and total loser.

Darlene stood up and brought the thin slices of cake to the table. She served the first one to her grandmother.

"Ain't it nice she got manners," Momma told Wayne.

"Sure is," he said. Wayne smiled at his mother lovingly, momentarily forgetting the others around him in the heartwarming affection of her sweet, wrinkled face.

The kids had gone outside to play again. Their figures were barely illuminated by a dim outside light. The adults sat around the kitchen table drinking more beer. Momma was holding a box of chocolates out, offering one to everyone again.

"You're awful quiet, Wayne," she said, holding the opened box toward him. "Have another chocolate. It'll give you some energy."

Wayne searched for one with a nut and then popped it in his mouth.

The baby was crying in its crib and, after muttering "Shit," Ronnie walked over and picked him up and then sat back down at the kitchen table. She lit a cigarette, unbuttoned her shirt, pulled up her bra, and began breast-feeding the infant.

Buddy stared at her, annoyed.

"Do you have to do that here?" he asked.

"Well, we're talkin' here, so why not?" she responded, pushing her bony chest forward. "It ain't like none of us never seen a tit before."

"Oh, I'm so happy you're here, Wayne," Momma said, patting him on the arm. "You got a little vacation, do you son?"

"Yeah, I got a couple of days off."

"Wish I could say the same," Buddy said.

"Well, I think I'm gonna take the day off tomorrow," Ronnie added.

"You workin' now, honey?" Momma asked her through a yawn.

"Yeah, but it don't pay very much," she said dejectedly. "Just sellin' some old clothes and stuff on the side of the highway durin' the day when Buddy's tryin' to look for some work. I just put the stuff on the side of the car and hope somebody stops. Gotta watch over the kids most of the time though and make sure they don't get hit by no car." She laughed and pulled the baby in tighter to her pale, drawn breast. "But as soon as I stop feedin' this one, I'm gonna try to get me a job in the mines, or maybe down at that new nucular plant. I guess there's a bunch a different things I could proba'ly do. I mean, I might look skinny, but I'm real strong."

Wayne stared at her pathetically thin arms holding the baby against her small, deflated breast. She was hillbilly stock, he thought. Bad blood from deep in the mountains passed on from one beaten generation to the next in a downward, hopeless spiral. He knew her type—there were lots more like her all around the area. She'd probably whored her body with countless guys until one of her friends got pregnant and then thought she'd do the same.

And what had it gotten her in the end? A forty-seven-year-old divorced, violent, deformed, unemployed, and alcoholic husband. And her with that stupid tattoo! Wayne noticed the small baby mindlessly sucking on Ronnie's unhealthy-looking breast. Cigarette ashes fell on his head, and the drunken breath of his father surrounded him with the stench of stale beer. Wayne almost felt like throwing up.

Buddy grabbed the remaining cans and threw one to Wayne before giving one to his wife and opening his own.

"Hey Wayne!" he yelled from across the table. "Can you spot me for a couple of six packs?"

Wayne regarded his brother's puffy face, whose red eyes squinted while he concentrated on lighting another cigarette.

"Yeah!" his wife added. "I want some more goddamn beer!"

To his left, his mother had sunken in her chair and begun to doze, breathing noisily. She looked content.

"Sure," Wayne said after a pause, standing up and popping open his beer. "I might even buy us a case, seein' as what a good time we're havin'."

Buddy looked toward him with a broad smile and extended the can he held toward him. Wayne stepped over to their bent over mother and kissed the top of her head. She grunted slightly, but her eyes remained closed, twitching slightly as if she were lost in a confusing dream.

Wayne took a swig of the beer, swirled it around in his mouth, swallowed it, and then licked his gums. On the refrigerator he noticed a crudely rendered drawing of a flower stretching toward the sun. "Keep On Growing" was printed underneath it.

Behind him, Ronnie was disagreeing loudly with something her husband had brought up. As Wayne was about to open the door, she suddenly stopped. "Hey, maybe you can pick up a bag of potato chips at the store, too," she yelled. "The kids'd proba'ly like that."

"Yeah, and another pack of smokes," his brother added. "For the big kids."

"OK," Wayne said, without making eye contact and pushing open the screen. "Back in a minute."

Buddy shook another cigarette from his pack and returned to the disagreement with his wife. Wayne passed through the doorway and then closed it behind him, pleased that it immediately stifled their annoying voices.

"Hey Darlene!" he yelled toward his daughter who was about to kick a ball. "How about comin' with me to the store?"

"But we're in the middle of a game!" she yelled.

"Darlene, I said get over here!" he said firmly, pointing toward the ground in front of him. "Now!"

Dejectedly, Darlene kicked the ball once more and then ran over to him. She was all out of breath.

"Get in the car," he said.

The black sky was illuminated by what looked to be hundreds of white pinholes, whose brilliance was diminished only by the huge full moon. Darlene and Wayne batted several swarms of mosquitoes away from their faces as they walked toward the Gremlin in silence. The old people on the porch were no longer there, and the street was quiet apart from the sound of various night bugs.

Wayne fastened his seat belt and waited for his daughter to get inside. As soon as she had closed the door, he pulled off rapidly toward the craggy hills. The rough land seemed to consume the low-hanging moon slowly, as if somehow hoping that such shining lunar magnificence would restore some glimmer of life to its rotting carcass.

*   *   *

After splashing another shot of whiskey into her glass, Ethel sank into the soft cushions of the sofa, whose sticky, Naugahyde upholstery clung to her broad back like a second skin. She stared at the television, unsure if the blurred image in front of her was due to the set's bad reception or her own distorted vision.

191

She was watching a late-night, made-for-television movie which, like the other programs she had stared at throughout the night, didn't interest her very much. It had attractive stars and a believable story—things she thought essential in a good movie—but there was no romantic element involved in the plot. That disappointed her, since romance was normally what got her into the story.

Ethel reached for the ashtray in front of the chair and searched through its spent ash and charred filters in search of a butt with a puff or two left. She pulled one out and sparked it, quickly inhaling the foul-tasting remnant a number of times before throwing it back.

Ethel felt tense, in part because she had recently popped a couple of Preludins. But the main source of stress was her need for a cigarette. She smoked her last cigarette ten minutes earlier and wondered where the next one was going to come from.

It worried her, not only because she was addicted to nicotine, but also because she could have sworn that earlier in the day there were two almost-full packs on the kitchen table. She knew she smoked a lot, but she was certain that she hadn't worked her way through nearly forty already. After all, she'd dozed off a number of times in the afternoon. Moving the whiskey glass to her lips, she wondered if she was beginning to lose her mind.

In the corner of the room, the babies slept quietly. Their breathing was drowned out by the TV's exaggerated volume and Ethel's fingers tapping nervously against the chair. Reaching toward the table again, she picked up the large bowl of instant chocolate pudding and, for a temporary distraction, dug into what remained.

Ethel finished it off and immediately searched through the ashtray again for another butt. But she usually smoked them right down to the filter, so she was unable to find even one that was smokable. It pissed her off, because after eating something sweet, she desperately craved a smoke and the flavor of tar sweeping across her sugar-coated tongue.

Struggling off the sofa, Ethel made her way to the kitchen to look for the misplaced pack. She had already searched through all the likely places. Yet once again she re-opened the cabinets, checked the windowsills, and crawled uncomfortably on all fours along to the radiator. She even emptied the freezer, thinking she may have, for some unknown reason, left them in there when she had gotten out the hot dogs for lunch.

Ethel grew more frantic with her failure to find the pack. She rifled through the drawers of her bedroom, pulled back cutains, and even balanced herself precariously on a chair while searching the uppermost shelf of the closet. She walked back to the kitchen quickly, checking some additional places she had neglected before. Finally, she reached back into the freezer for the next best thing—a Fudgesicle.

Ethel sat down quickly and shoved the Fudgesicle into her mouth. She tried to calm herself down as she chewed, to think clearly. There were two packs earlier, she recalled, and now there was only one empty pack in the family room. She'd been wearing the robe all day and there were none in the pockets. The bedroom had been searched and...

Ethel's eyes moved toward the garbage can, and before she could even finish the thought, Ethel jumped up and rushed toward it. She threw its contents frantically around the room. Ethel pulled out empty soda bottles, a dog food can, grease-soaked paper towels, egg shells, and other remnants of the day's meals. Finally, she dumped another pile of cigarette butts from the day before onto the sticky floor. Unable to encounter any unspent tobacco, however, Ethel hastily replaced the trash back into its container.

Ethel's eyes widened joyously when she spotted half a discolored cigarette stuck to a margarine wrapper. Without hesitating, she shoved it between her lips and held a match to it, finally igniting what dry paper remained. She inhaled deeply and held the smoke in her lungs for as long as possible, and then exhaled quickly and took another drag.

When she finished, Ethel picked herself up from the floor. As if she were being controlled by an outside force, she grabbed a sedative from her secret hiding place behind the pots and pans. That's what she felt she needed most now—a Valium and a few more shots of hard liquor. That combination might at least knock her out and take her mind off the cancer sticks.

Ethel returned to the family room, sank back down into the sofa, and filled her glass. The TV movie didn't look any better, so she flipped through the channels, watching each for several seconds before returning to the original station. She swallowed more whiskey and once again eyed the ashtray, silently cursing the liquor for having renewed her desire to smoke. As she covered her stubby fingertips with gray ash, a thought suddenly raced into her mind.

"Junior!" Ethel yelled. Her outburst sent Ivy, her dog, sprawling onto the floor. Ethel abruptly stood up, thrusting her bulk toward the doorway and knocking over the ashtray. She pounded her feet toward Junior's room. That cunning son of hers had probably taken her cigarettes earlier in the afternoon, when she had dozed off.

Ethel flipped on the light and quickly scanned his bedroom. A few posters of sports stars and rock bands hung on the dark paneled walls, along with an American flag. Junior's bed was unmade, and dirty clothes were strewn across the floor. Even though the window was open, the room still smelled of stale sweat.

Ethel walked straight to the dresser and began poking her way through the drawers. But she found nothing but clothes, old baseball cards, and the other assorted junk she normally found on the rare occasion she cleaned Junior's room. After checking the pockets of his clothes on the floor, she hurriedly moved toward the closet. Inside there were sports equipment, some shoes, a couple of stinking pairs of sneakers, and a stack of school books and old magazines in the corner. She got down on her knees and began tossing them aside, but nowhere in between the multitudes of comic books or music magazines could she find what she wanted.

After putting everything back in order, Ethel stood up dejectedly and turned around. Her body swaggered while attempting to survey all the objects across the room. What the hell was she doing in there anyway? she wondered. If Junior had taken her cigarettes, he wouldn't have left them behind. He would probably be smoking them at this very moment with his friend.

Ethel belched loudly and shook her head. She was going to have to have a stern lecture with the sneaky bastard about taking her property.

Over the television's murmur, she heard one of the girls crying in the family room and traipsed back that way. She yanked the crying baby out of the crib and slung her against her chest, smothering the noise momentarily. Ethel clutched the girl's bottom. It was time to do her dirty work.

But she also felt a familiar object in the diaper, and suddenly her adrenalin soared.

Ethel rushed out to the kitchen table and undid the diaper. Indeed, there was the familiar red pack of Marlboros peeking out from a puddle of fresh green baby shit. She didn't even bother asking herself how they got there; instead, she ripped the box's top off, forced one into her mouth and lit up as fast as she could.

*　　*　　*

Wayne pulled his car into the first convenience store saw, about ten miles away. Once inside, he grabbed a large bag of sour-cream-and-onion potato chips, a cold two-liter bottle of cola, and a twelve pack of Milwaukee's

Best. He paid, left, then pulled the car back on the road. But instead of heading back the way he came, he turned in the opposite direction, toward Highway 58.

Darlene was sipping on the pop and munching some of the potato chips when they pulled onto the highway.

"How come you takin' such a long time to get back to Grandma's house?" she asked.

Wayne punched the gas to around sixty.

"I'm takin' such a long time to get back," he said, shaking out a cigarette and pushing in the lighter, "because I ain't goin' back to Grandma's house. That's why."

The girl chewed the chips loudly.

"Weren't you havin' a good time seein' your Momma again?" she asked after a few seconds.

"Yeah," Wayne said, shoving the glowing lighter back in its place. "It was nice seein' her, considerin' her condition and all. But what I objected to was the other people, who weren't supposed to be there in the first place. They're the reason we ain't goin' back."

"Well, your brother and his wife seemed a little bit..."

Wayne waved his hand and cut her off in mid-sentence.

"First of all, I don't ever want you callin' the man who was there my brother! I mean, technically he is, but really, we ain't anymore, if you can understand that."

Wayne popped a beer and took a long chug.

"I don't even want you callin' him Buddy," he added, "God forbid 'Uncle Buddy,' because that sounds like there's some sort of family tie there—which there certainly ain't. In fact, I don't even want you talkin' about him anymore at all. Got it?"

"I guess so," Darlene said, temporarily abstaining from the junk in the bag. "But ain't they gonna be surprised with you leavin' and us not even sayin' goodbye?"

"Sure they're gonna be surprised!" Wayne said proudly. He couldn't help but be pleased with the thought of his brother sitting around, waiting for him, desperately anticipating money and a fresh beer, his wife beginning to bitch, the baby starting to cry, and the little kids getting on his nerves.

"But I said goodbye to Grandma and she's definitely the only one in that house I care anything about."

"But I didn't get to," Darlene whined. "'cause I didn't even know

195

we were leavin' for good.''

"Well, don't worry about that!'' Wayne said firmly. "Come tomorrow morning, I ain't even sure she's gonna remember we were even there anyway. The truth is, I don't even want to talk about the whole matter anymore. Understand?''

Darlene took a large gulp of cola.

"Well, your Ma was a nice lady,'' she said, smiling. "And I still feel bad about not sayin' goodbye to her.''

Wayne turned slowly toward her. He was about to say, "What did I just tell you?'', but when he noticed the fat features of her barely illuminated face, he suddenly stopped himself. Darlene looked honest, caring and innocent, and there was really no point getting upset with her. She was a decent kid, Wayne knew, because he had instilled some good moral values in her while she was growing up. Like respecting her elders and doing what she was told, those sorts of things.

"Well, when we get home, you can write her a letter and tell her whatever else you want to say,'' he mentioned instead. "All right?''

"OK,'' Darlene said, smiling and reaching into the bag for more junk food.

As Wayne drove, he rolled his head in a slow circle trying to relieve the tightness within his upper back. Beside him, Darlene's hand remained in the bag of chips. She was no longer eating, but snoring. He still had between three and four hours of driving to go and, as the twisting miles of southeastern Kentucky slowly passed by, he was beginning to feel fatigued.

Ahead on his right, a little oasis of light sprang out of the darkness. A large neon sign near its entrance blinked "Flamingo Motel"..."American Owned And Operated"..."Cable TV"..."Singles from $16.95"..."Doubles from $24.95.'' The prices looked good and, after a quick decision, Wayne pulled the Gremlin onto the exit ramp just past it and drove into a darkened gas station next door. He nudged his daughter until she came out of her snooze.

"Listen,'' Wayne said. "We've still got a long way to go and my neck's pretty sore, so we're gonna stay at the motel over there.''

He pointed to the sign and then looked back to his daughter, who squinted back with sleep laden eyes.

"It costs a lot less for one person to stay than it does for two. So I want you to crouch down on the seat and put somethin' over your head so it looks like I'm alone. I'll go in and deal with the guy behind the desk.''

He got out of the car and opened the hatchback, removing the large yellow blanket that he'd last used to wrap the dead deer he'd hit with the car. A dry blood stain still covered most of it. With difficulty, his plump daughter squeezed herself between the seat and the dashboard, grunting and breathing hard as she inched her way downward until she couldn't move any further.

"Perfect," Wayne said, draping the blanket over her. "Now just stay there until I come back. You hear me?"

"Uh huh," came Darlene's hushed murmur, barely audible.

Wayne started the car again and pulled into the gravel lot, parking a few spaces away from the sign with an arrow underneath it that blinked "OF ICE." He flung open the screen door, whose greeting bells announced his entrance.

The room was brightly lit, and his eyes adjusted to some pictures on the wall. A couple of portraits of Loretta Lynn hung there, as did several others that seemed like images of Vietnamese people he had seen on the news, trying to paddle to America in little dinghies. The wallpaper was dark red with a gold pattern, and the room was filled with the sweet and sour aroma of Chinese cooking. Indeed, the motel seemed more like a Chinese restaurant than lodging.

A middle-aged Oriental man entered from behind a brightly colored curtain and propped his hands on the counter in front of him.

"Can I he'p you?" he asked with an odd accent.

"Yeah," Wayne said, cocking his head. "I want a room."

"OK, no probrem," the man said. "One person?"

"Yeah, a single."

The man slid a paper card and pen across the counter.

"You just have to fill out this card right here," he said.

Wayne covered the card with his hand.

"How much is it, first?" he asked suspiciously.

"$16.95. Just rike sign outside say. You see sign?"

"Yeah, but sometimes places advertise one thing and tell you another," Wayne said, picking up the pen.

"Not here," the attendant said quickly. "What we say, we do."

Wayne began filling in the registration form.

"The sign also says American-owned-and-operated," he mumbled.

"I American!" the man blurted. He glared at Wayne, annoyed at his insinuation. "Used to have green card. Not no more. Got me passport and identity papers, just rike you."

Wayne pushed the completed card toward him.

"You could have fooled me," he said, looking down coolly.

"OK," the attendant laughed forcefully while glancing at the details. "I need to see driver's ricense. You pay cash or charge?"

"Cash," Wayne answered, flipping his license and a twenty on the counter.

The man shuffled a few papers and then slid the change and room key across the counter.

"OK, Mr. Tanner," he said. "Room nine. Checkout time ereven."

Wayne stared at the attendant before finally grabbing the key. "And it's Turner," he said. "Not Tanner. Turner."

"Oh...I'm sorry," the attendant giggled, the flesh around his eyes contracting to the point where vision seemed impossible.

Wayne grabbed his receipt and made his way out. Printed along with the town—Booneville, Kentucky—was the name of the owner, L. Lin, and another picture of the famous singer. He scratched his head, wondering if the coal miner's daughter had something to do with the place, too.

Room 9 was barely larger than the double bed that stood in its center. From the top of the partially charred nightstand beside it, a lamp dimly illuminated its interior. Springing out from the brown paneling, a bolted metal arm supported a television.

Wayne closed the door and threw his and Darlene's bags on the graying shag carpet. He didn't like the fact that there was only one bed. After all, his daughter was no small girl and he really felt the need to stretch out. He had paid good money to spend the night in a rented accommodation, and he damn sure wanted to be comfortable. But he didn't think to consider that there would only be one bed in a single room.

Wayne flipped on the television and sat down on the end of the bed. He took off his shirt and grabbed a beer. Outside, he could hear Darlene slamming the door above the sounds of the highway. Soon her red face peered in the door.

"Well, get in already!" he whispered loudly to her. "Don't just stand out there. Someone might see you!"

"It's pretty small in here," she said, breathing heavily. "I always thought a motel room was bigger."

"Yeah, well your Daddy just saved us a few dollars. Just remember that!" Wayne snarled. "I don't particularly like the fact that the room is so tiny either, but it sure as hell beats sleepin' in the car."

"What time is it, anyway?" Darlene said, looking in the bathroom and frowning.

Wayne glanced at his digital watch and noticed that its battery had run out.

"I don't know," he answered, shaking his wrist. "It's got to be late."

Darlene yawned and slumped her weary body down on the bed.

"Well I'm tired," she said, taking off her glasses and rubbing her eyes. "I ran around a lot today."

Wayne began changing the channels while his daughter reached for the covers behind her, trying to get underneath. Finally he stopped at a channel broadcasting an old episode of Kojak. He drained his beer and opened a fresh can, then propped the pillow behind him. He glanced over at his daughter, whose shoes peeked out from the foot of the bed.

"Jesus, Darlene!" he said. "Get all the way under the covers and get comfortable, for God's sake!"

"Ain't you tired?" she asked drowsily, kicking off her shoes and straightening out the covers.

"A little bit," he responded, looking forward.

"Well I'm real tired," she said through a yawn. "So good night."

Wayne smiled as Kojak bellowed at his flunkies, Stavros and Sapperstein.

"Good night," he finally said absently.

Whoever had the room next door was also watching television, because Wayne could hear their set louder than he could hear his own. He was missing the end of Kojak for the adjacent noise of some documentary about animals in Africa. Wayne got up and raised the volume on his set, then got back on the bed and watched the rest of the show. When it ended, he opened another beer. It was warm, however, so Wayne got back up, grabbed the ice bucket from the bathroom, and went outside to find the machine.

When Wayne returned, he threw the cubes in the sink and wedged the remaining beers in between. Darlene had begun to snore, and he turned the channel rapidly through the infomercials, the only thing that seemed to be on.

But suddenly Wayne saw something that made him turn back.

199

He couldn't believe it at first, but on the screen in front of him, two people were fucking! Open mouthed, he stared for several seconds, until he recognized the actress, Tracy Lords. She was bent over and moaning, taking it from behind. He glanced at the sleeping form next to him and then back at the screen. Wayne got up, turned the volume down slightly, and then sat down on the edge of the bed to watch the couple's performance.

Wayne leered at the action intently. He liked pornographic movies—not because he was a pervert, but because he found the unclothed body of a well-built girl incredibly attractive. But unlike most sex magazines that featured the static, faked poses, X-rated movies proved that it all was really happening. Porno films allowed him to see the changing expressions on a girl's face, her moving body parts, and her ultimate submission to sexual pleasure. From the films, he'd also learned a great deal about different positions. Not that he actually put them into practice with Ethel, but fantasizing about them certainly helped pass the solitary hours in the shed.

The scene changed. Tracy was jogging with some buxom friends and they were talking about one of their university professors. Then Tracy went to his house and began discussing something with him. They were talking about some biology class she had with the guy. She was asking him about reproduction, a concept she said she didn't fully understand.

The couple moved into the bedroom so the professor could explain it better, and she took her clothes off. Embarrassed, he threw up his hands like that wasn't the type of lesson he had in mind. She began squirming on the bed and then she began touching herself, pleading with the professor to show her about the sexual act. She was a virgin and didn't know anything. He shook his head and began undoing his belt. He acted as if it was all against his will, simply for the purpose of education. He began his lesson by licking her vagina, explaining its different areas. There was a close-up. Tracy's hips wriggled beneath him. His tongue dashed in and out of her. The camera moved back. Tracy started sucking on the guy's huge dick while he continued his instruction.

Wayne turned back cautiously to make sure his daughter was asleep. He knew the film. He had borrowed it one night from a guy at Vanguard, who had a large porn collection. It was a pretty good movie, he remembered, but now he didn't feel completely at ease. Not only was the film showing a blow-job scene, which he never liked watching, but when he had seen it before, the circumstances had been different. He had been alone in the shed, not next to his sixteen-year-old daughter in a motel room, with an enlarged penis uncomfortably pressing against his leg.

Wayne stared back at the TV. Now Miss Lords was on her back, pleading with her teacher to continue his lesson by showing her how it was done. The professor reluctantly agreed. He pushed it in slowly at first, then increased the speed little by little. She was writhing beneath him. He was rolling his head backwards, and then suddenly pulled out, getting down on the bed and pulling her on top of him. They rejoined themselves and she grabbed his ankles. There was a close-up of their organs meeting. They were wet, red, healthy looking.

Wayne reached for his beer but, finding it empty, went to the sink to get another. When he returned, Tracy was leaving the house, fully dressed in her gym shorts and tank top, and the credits were running over the frozen frame. He watched them and was surprised to see that John Leslie had been the professor. He'd seen the guy's name so many times but just never seemed to recognize him on screen.

Then advertisements for the phone sex lines came on the screen. A fully clothed blonde with blown out hair was extending her voluptuous body across a blue satin sheet. ''When you're lonely and need a woman to talk to like only a woman can,'' she said seductively, ''you need 'Cum-Call'.'' 1-900-C-U-M-C-A-L-L flashed beneath her pretty, pouting face.

Wayne took off his trousers so that only his boxer shorts remained, and slipped between the sheets. While he had been up, Darlene had shifted her body so that she now took up more than half of the bed. He tried pulling the sheet up in an attempt to make her roll the other way, but she was so heavy that the flimsy material ripped next to her body.

He pushed her with his leg until she reacted.

''I was sleepin','' she said raising her head and glaring at him angrily.

''Well Jesus!'' he blurted. ''I can't even fit under the covers. Move over, will you?''

Darlene shifted her body over and squinted toward the TV screen. ''What you watchin'?'' she asked suspiciously.

''Nothin'. Just what's on,'' Wayne said, staring at another announcement.

She stared at the screen for a couple of minutes, propping her head up a little to see it better. ''Looks dirty,'' she stated, seemingly repulsed.

''It ain't dirty!'' Wayne said, looking toward her. ''It's just commercials. I'm having trouble sleepin' and it's about the only thing on. Just go back to sleep.''

''Well do you have to have the volume so loud?'' Darlene asked

201

him.

"Oh yeah," Wayne said, throwing back the covers. "The guy next door had his TV up real loud before, and I could hardly even hear what was on our TV."

He stood up and turned the volume down and flipped through talk shows and old re-runs that he didn't like. He stopped the channel on an episode of *The Rockford Files* and watched it for a minute, but he didn't really enjoy that show either. That private eye was a pussy, he thought. Wayne couldn't help feeling what he really wanted to watch was some more *real* pussy.

Looking back at his daughter, he saw that she had wrapped the pillow around her head and appeared to be asleep again. Flipping back to the adult channel, he saw that a new movie was beginning. He knew immediately by the look of it, although they hadn't shown any sex yet, that it was another X-Rated feature. The glossy colors dazzled before his eyes as barely covered women sauntered around a swimming pool, serving cocktails to some guy in a white suit who was obviously their pimp. He was on the telephone talking to some movie producer. And then they began: One of the girls removed her top and crouched down in from of the pimp, struggling to swallow his mammoth erection deep into her throat.

Wayne pulled the sheet over his body. He had never seen this movie before, but the actress going down on the guy looked really hot. She was standing up now, removing the bikini bottom and getting up onto a table next to the telephone. The camera zoomed in on her and Wayne blinked his eyes quickly a couple of times. Jesus Christ! he thought, concentrating on her. He couldn't believe it, but she'd removed all her pubic hair so that so that the huge flaps of her vulva hung down like two cupped hands, anticipating what was about to be delivered between them.

Wayne drained the rest of the beer and leaned back against the headboard. After dropping his hand beneath the sheet, he gently began massaging his crotch, keeping his eyes fixed upon the action flashing before him. He allowed his mind to sail toward their fantasy land, temporarily forgetting that his only true company was his daughter next to him and the rumbling of huge trucks cruising by on the highway outside.

24

WKSL was undoubtedly the biggest rock station in the Indianapolis area. But by looking at its headquarters from the outside, you'd never guess it. The station was located in a mobile home a few miles off Interstate 65, next to a single lane gravel road that seemed to go absolutely nowhere. A six-foot chain-link fence surrounded about an acre of overgrown property, upon which the trailer, a huge antenna, and transmitter stood. The land was interrupted only by a gate surrounding the dirt clearing where employees parked. The trailer itself was precariously balanced upon multiple pillars of cinder blocks and concrete-filled barrels. It had several large windows running along its sides between thick strips of artificial wood panneling.

Inside, the ceiling was covered with the type of square, white industrial tiles common to office buildings and schools. The rooms were lit by four fluorescent bulbs. The floor was lined with orange indoor/outdoor carpet that was badly soiled in the areas most heavily traveled. Equipment for recording commercials and spots was bolted in a U-shape at one end of the trailer. At the other end—just past a small bathroom and behind a closed door—lay the control room, from which music was broadcast twenty-four hours a day. Running against one of the long walls, in between the two technical areas, were a couple of desks and file cabinets. Beside these were a couple of small tables piled high with books and cassettes.

Wayne Turner sat behind a table in the corner, leaning his chair against the outer bathroom wall. He smoked a cigarette and flipped through a catologue of fishing equipment. Through the flimsy partition behind him, he could barely hear the muffled sounds of whatever song was currently on the air. So he adjusted the cotton balls in his ears in an attempt to completely eradicate the noise.

It was his second week on the job, an assignment Wayne had been given not long after returning from his unpleasant visit to Virginia. His duties were simple. Basically, all he had to do was guard the expensive equipment and provide security for the night-shift DJ, who was usually the only other person in the trailer during these hours. Once an hour or so, Wayne had to walk outside to make sure the gate was locked. At all times, however, he had to be ready to deal with any persons intent on creating some disturbance that might jeapordize the broadcast—an opportunity that still hadn't knocked.

The job's demands were well below what Wayne had proven he was capable of handling in the past. Mr. Knudsen, his boss, assured him that it was strictly an interim position, until something more along his lines turned up. Wayne decided to take it for the time being. Because the job called for a guard to be present between ten and six every night of the week, it would at least give him steady hours and enable him to collect a lot of overtime.

The graveyard shift forced him to rearrange his schedule, but it didn't bother him very much. He had already harvested the last of his crops for the year, and didn't have much to fill his daytime hours with anyway. He also figured he'd at least be able to get seven or eight straight hours of shut-eye without being bothered in the middle of the night by the twins either. Ethel could deal with them in the other room while he slept undisturbed in his bedroom during the day.

The control room door popped open and, following a wave of loud music, the late-night DJ named Timmo strode into the room. His long blonde hair was pushed under a red bandana, and he wore a slow growing, patchy beard. Wayne watched him walk to the coffee machine and pour a cup, then stare at himself in the mirror over the machine, pout his lips and smile.

"Pot's real fresh," Wayne mumbled from the hidden corner.

Timmo dropped the cup of coffee on the carpet and turned abruptly.

"Jesus!" he gasped, shaking his head. "You scared the shit out of me. I didn't know you were here yet."

"I got here at ten o'clock," Wayne said, bringing the chair down to four legs and pointing to his watch. "Just like every night. On time."

Timmo picked his cup off the floor and rubbed the spilt liquid beneath his boot.

"You want a cup?" he asked.

"Yeah, all right," Wayne said, closing the catologue in front of him. "But I'll get it. You proba'ly got to change the next record or somethin' important like that."

"No, it's OK," he said, gesturing reassuringly with his hand. "Tonight I'm just playing album sides. You want milk?"

"All right," Wayne responded, leaning back in his chair again.

"You know you can turn on the monitor on that shelf if you want," Timmo said, motioning with his head to a small speaker behind him. "It would at least give you something to listen to."

"No thanks," Wayne said, quickly shrugging off the suggestion. "I don't really like the kind of music that they play here, you know, with all that noise. I prefer a song when I can hear the lyrics and uh...it tells a story."

"This music does say something," Timmo said. He heaped a couple of plastic teaspoons of Cremora into the styrofoam cup before handing it to Wayne. "This group is talking about the Vietnam War and stuff like that. You should listen."

Wayne smirked and turned away briefly.

"Those ain't exactly the kinds of things I'm talkin' 'bout," he said.

"Well I think you should," Timmo said, blowing into his cup. "I mean, this group was talking about all the stuff that was happening in the country during that time. And I think what they were saying was right."

"What do you mean?"

"I mean they were protesting, man. They were telling the truth about all the shit America was doing."

"Wait a minute," Wayne said, putting up his hand. "Just what are you referrin' to, exactly?"

"The war," he said firmly. "Something we never should have even been involved in in the first place."

Wayne held up both hands, puzzled by the DJ's stance. "Hang on!" he commanded. "How old are you anyway?"

"Twenty-three," Timmo said, almost proudly.

"Well, for your information," Wayne said condescendingly, "you proba'ly couldn't even count backwards when all that was happenin', if for that matter you were even born yet. So how can you tell me that we never should have gotten involved in that in the first place?"

"It wasn't a situation that was threatening America directly, now was it?"

"At the time, it was," Wayne said firmly. "But of course you wouldn't know about that. You've just heard about the aftermath. Now I happened to be about your age when all that was happenin'."

"If I had been your age back then," Timmo said proudly, "I would have been in San Francisco with all the other people, protesting the war and dancing in the streets."

"Yeah, well, that's where you're naive. Because back then, there weren't nearly as many people against the war as they make out now. It was a trivial minority, thank God. And a lot of the fakes who said the same things you're sayin' now were just gettin' their spaced-out ideas from drugs anyway."

205

Timmo looked at him as if he were crazy.

"You're not gonna tell me that you still think that war was a good idea, are you?" he blurted.

"You're damn right I am!" Wayne said sternly. "And I'm proud to say that I was ready to go and serve my country and strengthen its dedication to freeeedom!"

"Oh man," Timmo said, rolling his eyes.

"And I also knew a lot of people who fought courageously over there and lost their lives. And they were protectin' principles they valued enough to have risked their lives for."

"What principles?" Timmo yelled back, angered.

"Principles of democracy!" Wayne shot back. "Fightin' for people to have it as good as we have it here. To have freedom of choice."

"But wait a minute," Timmo said, taking a sip of coffee and holding up a hand defensively. "I disagree."

"What do you mean, you disagree?"

"I mean, uh, the people over there had their own lives and it didn't have anything to do with us. It wasn't like the Communists were threatening us."

"Yeah, but they would have been if it wasn't for the US military presence. That's how those things go, just like dominoes. First one country gets taken over, then the next follows. Don't you know anything about history?"

"Yeah, but listen to this song right now," Timmo said, trying to regain control of the argument. "They're talking about Kent State."

"Well I didn't go to Kent State..."

"Well there you go," Timmo interrupted him. "Four innocent students shot down in cold..."

"But I would have if I had gotten the call," Wayne cut him off. "Damn right! I was in the National Guard myself and felt for those guys that fired those rounds. What they needed at the time was support, not criticism. They were actin' under government orders."

"I can't believe you just said that," Timmo said, looking at Wayne in confusion.

"You better believe it!" Wayne said firmly. "'Cause the majority of the American people think the same way as me.

"And I want to tell you somethin' else. For years the goddamn leftists have been sayin' that we lost the Vietnam War—almost like they're proud of the fact that America is on the way down. But the thing is, if America hadn't been involved in Vietnam and thrown a wrench into the Communist plan for a world takeover, the Polish people would still be dressin' in those gray clothes and toein' the Red Line. So the way I see it, with democracy now beginning to spread through those pinko countries, we've come out the big winners.''

Timmo had a sour look on his face. ''But how about all the guys who fought over there and got real fucked up, the ones who the government just turns their back on now?''

Wayne leaned back in his chair and put his hands behind his head, filling the room with the rank smell from his moist armpits.

''I guess a few of them need some help,'' he said, looking down the length of the trailer. ''But not as many as a lot of liberal journalists make out. I mean for the most part, the people who deserve compensation get it, although unfortunately there's a hell of a lot of fakes who claim that they've been psychologically damaged by the war too.

''But really, what they're doin' is just beggin' for that type of government handout, 'cause it pays more than welfare. And I'll tell you somethin' else that you don't hear about. There's a whole hell of a lot more men who fought and have taken everything to do with the war in stride, and gone on to do somethin' with themselves, instead of just bitchin' about it and blamin' the government for their fucked-up lives.

''And another thing,'' Wayne continued before Timmo could speak. ''I am sick and tired of those ridiculous movies comin' out about the goddamn war, starrin' those stupid rich brats who don't know the first thing about it but just do it because it's popular and the liberals love it. And then as soon as the camera stops rollin', they just go back and live their spoiled lives in Hollywood, sittin' around a swimmin' pool and takin' cocaine. Stuff like that just makes me sick.''

''Personally, I think those movies tell it like it was,'' Timmo said. ''And realistically.''

''Well, that's your right to think however you want,'' Wayne pointed out, ''even though it's pretty damn stupid to think that way. And you should just be thankful that you have that privilege in this country,'' he added. ''You might get shot in another country if you said things like that.''

''Huh?'' Timmo said, shrugging off Wayne's words. ''I think you're just caught up in some sort of conservative power trip.''

''Call it whatever you want,'' Wayne said, staring at him sternly. ''But one of these days you're gonna realize that playtime ends and that it's time for show and tell. As an officer of the law, I learned that a long time

207

ago.''

"What do you mean, 'officer of the law'?" Timmo blurted, smiling sarcastically. "You're just a security guard at a radio station!"

"Hey listen!" Wayne yelled. He stood up abruptly, angry at Timmo's insult. "You don't know anything about me. Who's to say I'm not just moonlightin' in this shithole? You see my uniform! You see my badge! You see my gun! So just who the hell do you think you're dealin' with?"

Timmo took a step back hesitantly.

"Just calm down!" he said, holding up his hands. "Take it easy!"

"I'm always in control!" Wayne barked, trying to regain his composure. "That's part of my job."

"Yeah well, I think I better get back to my job," Timmo said, shaking his head and obviously wanting to get away. "I've got to flip this album over."

"Sure," Wayne said calmly. He heard the control room door close around the corner.

Wayne stared down at his watch and saw that it was nearly eleven o'clock. He realized that he had to get back to his job as well.

After all, he hadn't checked the lock on the gate for nearly an hour.

25

Peeking through the oven door, Ethel ran her tongue over her lips. The chocolate cream cheese brownies she was baking for her weekly card game were forming the thin top crust that let her know they were nearly done. For the past half-hour their billowing aroma sailed through the air and masked the kitchen's usual sticky odor. This had only served to ignite her taste buds and cause her stomach to growl continuously in anticipation of their gooey richness.

Ethel took her eyes away from the heavenly sight and quickly reached into her pocket. She swallowed a couple of her new prescription diet pills, in hopes that the double dose would ensure that she didn't blow her diet so early in the day. Ethel picked them up several weeks ago when she visited her doctor and complained that the Preludins were not strong enough. The doctor sent her away with a prescription for Didrex to take their place.

With these new new pills, she noticed a definite rise in her energy level and decline in her drowsiness. But Ethel still found herself hovering around the two-forty mark every morning on the scale. She felt sad that her weight problem remained the number-one bane of her life, for even though she was eating less than before, she just wasn't shedding any pounds.

Ethel read something recently about liposuction and its proven results with such stars as Kenny Rogers. Because of that, she had a real desire to give it a go herself, but she also knew the cost of the operation was far beyond her budget. As far as removing the flab that riddled her body was concerned, she just didn't know where to turn. No matter how many pills she took, she just couldn't repress her appetite enough to avoid food completely. She was becoming convinced that the only way to get rid of her excess weight was by getting a knife and slicing it off.

Ethel walked into the family room and glanced at her sleeping babies. The TV drew her eyes to a program coming on, Clayton Tillman's *Profiting Through God*. Ethel checked her watch and realized that her first soap opera was still nearly a half-hour away. She walked back to the kitchen and peeked in the oven. She saw that the sides of the brownies were beginning to pull away from the pan, so she quickly yanked the pan out and laid them on the counter.

Ethel wanted to save the entire pan for her friends but, after staring at the steaming brownies for several seconds, she decided to try one—just to make sure they were presentable. She grabbed a spatula and dropped a huge, moist chunk onto a plate.

Ethel carried the plate into the family room and plopped down on the couch next to the dog. On the TV, a black woman named Roxy was talking about some problem she had with arthritis, which caused her joints to swell and forced her to take ten large pills a day to ease the pain in her hands.

"And then one morning Reverend Tillman said, 'Put your hand up on the screen,'" Roxy said. "And all that day I kept feelin' a tinglin' sensation, and after that I left it alone. And now I don't have to take them pills no more and the pain is gone."

"Vowing to God through success in life has drawn Roxy closer to the Lord," a voice bellowed over her image. "And she has been able to step out of the circle of blackness and into the circle of blessing."

"Makin' a pledge and vowin' was my first step out of the situation I was in," Roxy added. "That was my first step out of it. And I continue to vow and listen to Reverend Tillman and obey Reverend Tillman. Since then, me and my family been on trips, we done things we never done before. We've had those extra things for our children, I been able to buy extra things for them to keep them happy. So all in all, Reverend Tillman's been a God-sent blessin' to my family. I tell my husban', I tell my son a lot of times—it's like Christmas-time all year long when you learn the principle and do like he says. You just got to have belief and willpower and confidence in yourself...and in him."

The brownies were so good that Ethel swallowed the last bite down without even chewing. While listening to Roxy's story of her successful turnaround, she licked her fingers dejectedly, disgusted by her own lack of self-restraint. She passed gas, then reached across the table for a cigarette.

As the double dose she'd taken earlier was now taking control of her nervous system, her hands began to shake. She felt like a person with a nervous disorder as she brought a match to the cigarette end. In an attempt to alleviate the jitters, she washed down a Valium with leftover warm beer resting on the coffee table.

Clayton Tillman appeared on the screen and began saying a prayer, his normal introduction to his sermon. Although she occasionally caught the tail-end of his show, Ethel usually didn't like religious programs. She did, however, find the Reverend a very pleasant man to look at and very exciting to listen to. He was in his mid-forties, had a full head of dark brown hair turning gray at the temples and a deeply tanned face that almost looked to be sculpted from wax. He always wore nice suits and ties, and had several large rings that sparkled against the studio lights. Sometimes she felt he was the most attractive man on television.

"Roxy...let go...of her problems," Reverend Tillman began slowly, coming out of a short prayer. "That's what she did when she made that vow. That was her act of faith—letting go! And God...just honors it and brings miracles...But you've got to do what takes faith. I just sense, right this moment, that God by his love has sent me...to you."

He pointed his finger at the camera, and from Ethel's angle, he seemed to be pointing directly at her.

"I have several letters here," he went on, shuffling through some papers and beginning to read one. "Dear Brother Clay. Thank you so much...I made a vow, a five hundred dollar vow. I was on welfare when I made it, and you taught me how to step out in faith one day, step out of the problem as I was watchin' your program. Since then God has blessed me with transportation. God blessed me to get off welfare. I also received the exact job I was prayin' for. I now have a new truck. I know it was all because of the vow I made to God."

Reverend Tillman looked up at the camera and smiled.

"Truly he will open the windows of heaven and pour out blessings that we don't have room enough to receive," he said, before beginning to pray. "Thank you Lord...Thank you Lord...Thank you Lord for what you do! You said you'd give us seed to sow and...bread to eat and would multiply our seed. And you said you would forgive us for our doubt and unbelief. Forgive us for trustin' what we have which brings so much turmoil. That's a part of the problem. It's trustin' what you have instead of what God has. That's having gods before You."

Suddenly he opened his eyes and stared into the camera intently. "And if you make a vow, you'll see how quickly you're gonna have favor where you had no favor with certain people. You're going to begin to develop a level of favor. This is the way it happens, do you see? You're spirit just changes its...its flavor and...and...and people become attracted to you and want to help you and they want to be a blessin' to you. And why? Because you let go!"

He was getting more excited as he spoke, and the camera began zooming in on his beautifully crafted features.

211

"I want you to call me right now," he demanded, "and tell our prayer minister what your need is. We're going to agree with you. And then I want you to make a Thanksgiving vow of faith and just pay it every week—just pay it. As God prospers he'll begin to give you seed to sow. Just every week put what you can in there. It's like keepin' a pump primed. Don't drink the water before you prime the pump! It takes faith!"

Ethel lit a cigarette and watched the phone number flash across the screen. She suddenly wondered if the handsome Reverend could hold a solution to her weight and financial problems.

"Enlarge your world!" he yelled. "Don't let others limit the size of your world! For just as I created the world through faith, I've given you the measure of faith to create your world and the kind of world you want to live in. For I will expand thy waters as you strengthen your stance. And I will increase the fruits of your righteousness. 'Help me advance my kingdom,' sayeth the Lord. 'And I will cause the things that you need. For do I not even know when a little sparrow falls to the ground? Are not the very hairs of your head counted by me?' 'Are not you much more valuable than a little sparrow?' sayeth the Lord.

Oh, you're much more valuable to me than a little sparrow. For I touched you, I've called you, I'm strengthening you, I'm helping you today to let go! For other gods are dead. And they cannot speak and they cannot supply!"

He paused for a moment, gathered his vision and nodded his head toward the camera knowingly.

"There's a homemaker out there," he said. "You've got a big family but not enough money to enjoy the things you want. God wants you to make a vow too. That's God giving you the word."

Ethel leaned forward in her chair and snubbed out her cigarette prematurely, amazed at how the Reverend spoke directly to her.

"And then there's a woman who said, 'God, if this is really you, speak to me again.'"

Ethel's jaw suddenly dropped.

Clayton Tillman paused and stared at the camera. The combination of hot studio lights and excitement carried away a layer of his make-up in constant streams of perspiration.

"He's spoken to you so many times, but your ears have become dull of hearing!" the evangelist began again. "You need someone to teach you again, the first articles and principles of God! You yourself were a follower. You served God, but your ears became so dull that everything just became traditional to you.

"Listen! I'm talkin' to a faith person right now!" he yelled. "Prosperity is real and it's for God's children! It's not for the devil! Those new cars, those parkin' lots are not for the devil's offspring. They're for God's children! He sayeth I want to make you prosper and be in health."

Ethel nodded her head in agreement. Her eyes refused to blink. Clayton Tillman drove on.

"Those four lepers, they said, 'Why sit we here until we die? If we go back with that bunch of unbelievers,'—where they were eating each other's kids and killin' each other in Sumeria—they said, 'We'll die back there with that bunch of doubters and unbelievers. If we sit right here where we are, we'll die here, but if we go forward, we might just live.'

"And do you know what happened? They went forward and God caused the enemy to flee in terror and the enemy left behind everything he'd been holdin' back from Sumeria, and they walked into the midst of riches! Jehosephat, when he did what God said to do, it took him three days to carry away the spoils! Psalm 68:12, it says that Jesus divides the spoils with the strong, and he wants to spoil the principalities in powers through *you* today!"

The sound of an organ grew louder in the background and the Reverend began talking even faster.

"I've got thirty seconds before we go off the air!" he said excitedly. "And there's a lot of people out there who are sufferin' in pain, just like Roxy was. There's someone that walks with a limp, another person who has a nervous twitch, and someone else who has another physical ailment of some sort. I want you to put whatever is causin' you grief up against the screen right now, and then I want you to mail a prayer card and a letter with a financial vow. Just put what you can into it. Always, just put enough that you feel it. If you can put it all at once, do it!"

Ethel jumped off the sofa and threw her body around the TV, almost knocking it over. Pressing her stomach forcefully into the glass, she closed her eyes and listened to Clayton Tillman's emotional prayer.

"Father, in Jesus' name I pray for those who are seeking solutions to their problems. God, You said pray, and You would tell us what You wanted, which is what we want. Pay our vows and we would decree a thing and you would shine a light on our path. God, you said it would be established unto us. I agree with my viewers, Lord. Help them to get what they want and deserve."

When the music finally died out and a new program began, Ethel

213

stepped back from the screen hesitantly and ran her hands across her belly, amazed at how the electricity enveloped within her shirt made her arm hair stand on end and her fat stomach tingle.

Ethel sank back into the sofa and closed her eyes. Even though she had no intention of paying a vow, she thought she may have just experienced a miracle.

26

The alarm jerked Wayne out of the dark, dreamless void that had enclosed him since his head made contact with the pillow seven hours earlier. He threw the covers from his body and quickly sat up, adjusting his eyes to the gray December light that broke dimly through the unveiled window. He leaned over to one side and grunted loudly as he passed a reverberating wind through the cheeks of his ass. Then he yawned with an exaggerated gesture, closing his mouth around the stale flavors of cigarettes and beer.

Wayne picked up a pair of trousers from the floor and stepped into them, and then pulled a flannel shirt over his bulky chest. Walking out of the bedroom, he heard the muffled noise of abrasive music coming from his son's bedroom. Before he entered the bathroom, he took a few steps toward the kitchen and saw his wife hunched over the sink washing something.

"Ethel!" Wayne yelled toward her. "Make me some coffee!"

Wayne veered back into the bathroom. He closed the door behind him, then urinated forcefully and farted several more times. He cleared his throat loudly and hocked a couple of quids into the sink. Then he splashed some water on his face and covered it with a layer of shaving cream, which he immediately cleared with rapid, efficient strokes of his disposable razor. After removing the excess foam with a towel, he sunk his hand into a jar of hair tonic and slapped it onto his scalp. Wayne rubbed it over the bare surface and matted back what hair remained on his sides. Then he licked a dollop of toothpaste straight from the tube, swished it around his mouth briefly, and swallowed it down.

Wayne went into the kitchen next, and greeted his wife by asking, "Do you have that coffee?"

"Just a minute," she said, turning toward him. "I just made a fresh pot and I'm waitin' for the machine to stop drippin'." She glanced at the coffee maker and then back at him. "Did you sleep well?" she asked.

"Like usual," he said through a yawn while moving over to the twins' crib and staring down at them dumbly. "Although proba'ly not as well as they seem to be," he added.

"They've only been like that for the past hour or so," Ethel said, pouring the coffee into a cup and handing it to him. "They were a real pain in the ass all mornin'. And to make things worse, somethin' happened to the refrigerator and it's leakin' all over the floor. You need to have a look at it to see what's wrong. I couldn't figure it out myself."

Wayne stared over at the floor in front of the refrigerator and saw that it was covered with a thin layer of greenish liquid. He shook his head at the mess and then looked at his wife as if the problem were her fault.

"Do me a favor, Ethel," he said. "I just got up, so at least give me a chance to finish my coffee before layin' ''fix-it'' shit on me."

"All right," she said, annoyed by his tone. "But I didn't say for you to do it right this minute. I was just tellin' you what happened."

"Well how 'bout making me somethin' to eat instead of bitchin' at me," Wayne said as he shuffled through some mail on the table. "Do we have any doughnuts?"

Ethel remembered finishing off the box earlier that morning while watching her first soap opera. She grabbed a sponge and began to wipe up the liquid from the floor.

"No," she said. "The kids ate the rest of them before school. I'll make you a sandwich as soon as I clean this up."

Wayne glanced briefly at the letters, most addressed to "occupant," before crumbling them into a ball and throwing them toward the garbage. The last letter he opened was the only one addressed to him, and he recognized it as the phone bill. He glanced at the amount due and frowned, and then unfolded the paper to see the itemized record of calls. One in particular puzzled him.

"What the hell is this about a collect call from Bakersfield, California?" Wayne yelled.

"What's that?" Ethel said, lifting herself off the floor with difficulty.

"It's on the damn phone bill right here," he said, pointing down at the sheet of paper in his hand. "On October twenty-eighth, somebody called here collect from Bakersfield to the tune of forty-six dollars and eighty-three cents."

Ethel threw the sponge in the sink and wiped off her hands. For a moment she didn't answer.

"Oh that must have been Becky," she finally said, opening a jar of Cheese Whiz and spreading it on a couple of slices of white bread. "Didn't I tell you about that?"

216

"No, you didn't!" Wayne said angrily. "And what I want to know right now is why the hell you accepted the charges!"

"She's my sister, for Christ's sake!" Ethel said, impetuously handing him the sandwich. "And she happened to be goin' through a difficult period last month. She needed to talk to somebody."

Wayne dipped the sandwich into his coffee and took a bite.

"Couldn't she have talked to one of her friends out there?" he asked, annoyed at Becky's nerve.

"Listen Wayne," she said. "You don't know the story, but it was very complicated and there were reasons why she called here. But that doesn't really have anything to do with it. The important thing is that she's my family—the closest relative I got left too. Now you may have turned your back on your family—and that's your right—but I still like to keep in touch. And if that means that once in a blue moon she calls here collect, then that's the way it is."

"You just better change that to 'that's the way it was'," Wayne yelled. "Because there's a lot of cheaper ways to maintain family contact than over the phone. What's the matter with the US Mail, for God's sake? That serves the same function for less than a few dimes."

"Well, sometimes things need to be dealt with immediately," Ethel said, pouring herself a cup of coffee. "Isn't that what *you* always say? The night she called, her new husband had thrown her and all her stuff out of the house and threatened to shoot her if she tried to get back in. She needed to talk to someone she could trust."

Wayne tried to imagine what could have caused the poor guy that married Becky to have such a violent reaction. He was sure it stemmed from her screwing around behind her husband's back. After all, that was Becky's usual style, and he knew firsthand of the scores of men she had drunkenly brought home when they subdivided the house in Keavy. On countless occasions, he was awakened in the middle of the night by the grunts and groans passing through the paper-thin wall their bedrooms shared. He would listen to the pathetic conversation of Becky and her lover afterwards, followed shortly by more drunken moans as they fucked again. It had made him sick then, and the thought of it now turned his stomach once more.

"Well, to be honest," Wayne finally hissed, "I don't give two shits about why she called. All I know is that I don't want to be the one to pay for someone else's personal fuck-ups, which it looks like I'm gonna be forced to do this time. But from now on, I'm tellin' you," he pointed his finger at Ethel, "not even someone claimin' to be Jesus gets through on that line

217

without payin' for the call himself!''

"All right!" Ethel yelled, feeling her blood pressure rise. "You've made your point already!"

"Yeah, well, I just wanna make sure that it's sunken into that thick skull of yours!" Wayne huffed, and walked over to the refrigerator.

Ethel hastily grabbed some plates from the dishwasher and placed them loudly in the cabinets.

"And by the way, there's somethin' else I want to talk to you about," she said, turning around to face him. "And that's money for some Christmas presents. You know it's only two weeks away and you haven't given me any cash to buy things with."

"Maybe I haven't given you any money," he said calmly, putting his cup on the counter, "because there isn't any money to give—especially now, with this outrageous phone bill. You should have thought about that before you accepted the charges."

"I thought we said we weren't gonna talk about that anymore!" Ethel yelled as she grabbed a bag of Fritos off the counter and dipped her hand into it. "That's somethin' that you found out about just now. So quit tryin' to avoid the subject!"

"I ain't avoidin' the subject!" Wayne yelled back. "I'm just tellin' it like it is! You know the shift I'm workin' now isn't as well-paid as the one I had last year. And also, we've had two more mouths to feed for the past eight months. So this year we're just gonna have to make some sacrifices."

"Now just a minute, Wayne!" Ethel screeched. "There's some things that the kids need that I purposely haven't bought, thinkin' that I'd give it to 'em for Christmas instead."

"Well I don't see any reason why this year Darlene and Junior can't help out a little with the Christmas gifts. I mean they're both workin', and I don't think it's right that whatever gifts they decide to give gets put on my credit card. You know what we agreed on last year when that bill came and nearly floored me."

Ethel remembered it, and also recalled hearing about it for several months afterwards.

"But I'm not talkin' about them," Ethel said, spitting out some chips as she spoke. "I'm talkin' more about the twins. Crystal and Gladys need clothes and other things. It's not like they can do with hand-me-downs like Junior did with Darlene's stuff. They need some new stuff. And I also want to buy a baby carriage so I can at least move them around 'cause they're gettin' heavier every day. I mean, it's not like there's only one."

218

"I already give you most of the money I bring home every week to take care of those things," Wayne said, shirking off her concern. "I would of thought you'd put a little bit aside each week for things like that."

"You must be jokin'!" she said angrily. "I do all I can with what you give me. What happened to the man who said he was goin' to make enough money to support the expandin' family?"

"What happened," Wayne spat, annoyed at her obstinacy and snatching the nearly empty chip bag from her hand, "was that he didn't know his wife was going to spend most of the money on junk food that she ended up wolfin' down herself, or worthless pills she thought was gonna take the pounds off. I mean, look at it in here!" he yelled, opening a cabinet and staring at the half-filled shelves. "It's almost empty!"

Wayne paused and did a quick double take on a stack of cans with the same label. "And what the hell is all this corned beef hash for?" he added.

"Look!" Ethel shouted, stepping in front of him and slamming the cabinet shut. "I do the shoppin' here. And this week there happened to be a sale on corned beef hash. I would think you would appreciate me tryin' to make our money go a little bit further. What do you expect me to get with the money you been bringin' home lately anyway, filet mignon? Don't blame me! Maybe you should pester your boss a little bit more for another job, or at least put in some extra hours instead of sleepin' all day long."

"Hey!" Wayne yelled and grabbed her fleshy arm. "Don't tell me what I should be doin', because that's somethin' you obviously don't understand! I'm a professional and a veteran on the Vanguard force, and when you're in a position like mine, you don't beg and scrape for whatever odd job comes along. That's what a rookie or a desperate amateur does! When you're in my situation, you wait patiently until somethin' arises that suits your qualifications. And you can bet when the boss gives me the word, I'll be all over it like a fly on shit."

"Well, you know you've been waitin' for this 'new position' for three or four months now," Ethel said. She shook him off and reached for a cigarette before heading toward the bathroom. "And things ain't like they used to be. You can't do anything about the past, you know."

Wayne silently watched her leave the room and turned to look at the twins. He was about to make a rebuttal when his wife walked back in the room, but his words were stifled when the outside door swung open and Darlene pushed her way through.

Wayne stared at her dumbfounded. "What the hell have you done to your hair?'' he asked.

''Why Darlene,'' Ethel said, stepping in front of Wayne and staring at her daughter's new permanent. ''You look fantastic!''

''Do you really think it looks good?'' she asked timidly.

''Do I think it looks good?'' Ethel said as she ran her hands through the curls. ''I think it looks great!''

''I didn't have enough time at school to leave the gel on for as long as I should have,'' she said with a shy smile. ''But I think it was long enough to get the idea.''

''I think you left it on for the perfect time,'' Ethel commented, poking her hand at a clump of straight hair near her daughter's neck. ''Although maybe you missed a little bit here. But you can't even see it unless you're real close.''

''I haven't gotten used to it yet,'' Darlene said.

Ethel turned to her husband and said, ''Don't you think it looks nice, Wayne?''

Wayne had a strange look on his face, somewhere between confusion and laughter.

''I think I preferred it the way it was before,'' he finally said.

''A man doesn't know about these things,'' Ethel quickly cut in. ''I mean, it looks so natural. In fact, if I didn't know you, I would have thought you always had curly hair.''

Junior's door suddenly burst open, and the entire house was filled with the noise he was listening to.

''Hey Mom!'' he said, walking into the kitchen. ''Did you find that library book I asked you about yet?''

''No, I didn't,'' she replied. ''I guess you must have left it somewhere else.''

''Well, I guess it's lost then,'' he said, scratching his head. ''So can you give me the money to replace it?''

''How much is it gonna be?'' she asked while a cigarette dangled between her lips.

''Ten bucks,'' Junior said. He saw Darlene hunched over the babies and scowled. ''What the hell did she do to her hair?''

''Watch your language, Junior!'' Wayne said from behind him. ''And what's this about borrowin' money from your mother?''

Junior turned around quickly. He hadn't been aware of his father's presence and was annoyed with himself for having brought up financial matters in front of him.

"It's a library book that the librarian's been hasslin' me about 'cause it's been due for two-and-a-half months," Junior complained. "I don't know what happened to it."

"Why don't you replace it yourself?" Wayne said, staring at his son's pimply face. "You've got a job, and you lost the book."

"Yeah, but I don't get paid until the end of the month," he said. "And the stupid librarian has been on my case for the past week."

"Let's talk about this later, guys," Ethel said, moving between the two of them. "I don't want the babies woken up."

"No, let's talk about this now!" Wayne stood up and yelled. "But first, turn off that goddamn music because I can't even hear myself think."

As if on cue to Wayne's final word, Gladys suddenly burst out with a high-pitched wail. Along with Junior's music, her crying filled the room with a dissonant wall of noise. Crystal's added sobs soon brought the noise to fever pitch.

"Now look what you've done!" Ethel shouted as she moved toward the crib. She eyed her husband contemptuously. "Did you have to cause such a commotion over a stupid library book?"

Wayne stared back at her angrily and then shifted his eyes to Darlene, whose expression echoed that of her mother. Then he turned his head toward his son, who smirked.

"Oh Jesus Christ!" Wayne hissed, rolling his eyes and blowing some air loudly from his mouth. He pushed his son forcefully out of the way and stomped through a fresh puddle near the refrigerator. Hastily, he swung the door open, stared at Ethel spitefully for a few seconds, and finally slammed the door shut.

The noise behind him was quickly stifled, and Wayne rapidly made a beeline for the comforting solitude of his shed.

PART THREE

27

Ethel picked up the cards and looked at her two friends, who were seated around the small card table in Tina's living room. "Who's turn is it to deal?" she asked.

"I dealt the last hand," Miriam said, shrugging her shoulders.

"So that means it's your turn," Tina reminded Ethel.

Ethel looked across the table at the others and squinted.

"Yeah, that sounds right," she finally said, grabbing the cards and beginning to shuffle.

Miriam lit a cigarette and arranged her winnings, a stack of nickels, in front of her.

"How are the twins doin'?" she asked Ethel. "They still got them colds?"

"No, they're back to normal now," she said, skimming the cards across the table and sniffing, "although I think I caught a little bit of it myself. It must've been that change in temperature when it snowed last weekend."

"You got Darlene lookin' after 'em this afternoon?" Tina asked.

"Yeah," Ethel responded as she placed the deck at her side and sized up her hand. "It's real good, 'cause she's started this work program with the technical school, and a couple of days a week she does a kind of internship at a beauty salon in Westport. It's in the morning, so she's got a couple of afternoons off a week. That gives me a little bit more free time."

"Which salon's she workin' in?" Miriam asked, discarding a couple of cards.

"Mario's," Ethel answered, as she threw out three cards. "You know, that little one in the Piggly Wiggly Shoppin' Center."

"Oh yeah, I know the one," Tina said. She shifted her hand around. "I never been but I hear he does real good work. Does he have Darlene cuttin' hair too?"

"Not yet," Ethel said as she lit a cigarette. "Hopefully she'll be startin' that soon, but for the moment all she's doin' is washin' hair and sweepin' up the remnants layin' on the floor."

"Well Mario should let her have a go with the scissors," Miriam said. She pushed a few nickels toward the center of the table. "Because judgin' by the work she's done on your hair, she looks like she's got some real talent."

"Do you really think it looks nice?" Ethel asked as she fingered her tight curls.

"Yeah," Tina remarked. "And a lot of women don't look good with permanents."

Ethel smiled. "Well thanks," she said, pushing two nickels to the table's center. "But Wayne doesn't seem to like the way it looks."

"I don't think Wayne likes the way anything looks," Tina said. She looked at her cards and folded.

Ethel laughed nervously and suddenly exhaled a cloud of cigarette smoke. "I suppose you got a point there Tina. It's hard gettin' a nice word out of him nowadays."

"From what you always say, Ethel," Miriam added, "it's been like that for a hell of a long time, not just nowadays."

Ethel placed a pair of sevens next to Miriam's pair of fours and pulled the change in the middle of the table toward her.

"Yeah well, he's just depressed about his job." she said with a sniff.

"Hell, he was depressed about his job when he screamed at me!" Tina snapped. She adjusted her squat frame on the chair. "And that was a year ago!"

"Yeah, you're right," Ethel said as she shook her head and stubbed out her cigarette. "And I'm gettin' tired of his moods all the time too. Not that I see him all that much anymore. He either seems to be sleepin' or doin' somethin' out in his shed. I mean, we haven't even slept together for a few months."

"I don't know if I could deal with that," Tina remarked. She gathered the cards together and began to shuffle. "Sometimes Roy and I go a week without makin' it, or ten days at the most, but a few months...that's terrible, Ethel."

"When I said 'slept together' Tina," Ethel said as she lit another cigarette, "I meant in the same bed at the same time. I mean, with his night shift, he ain't there when I go to bed and sleeps during the day when I got other things to do. But with regards to what you're talkin' about, I could proba'ly count on one hand the number of times we made love together since I got pregnant with the girls almost two years ago."

"What!?" her friends yelled in unison.

"That's right," Ethel said. She stared down and shook her head, embarrassed by her own admission. "It's not normal, is it?" she added and looked back up shyly.

"Are you kiddin'?" Miriam howled.

"That man is an absolute monster!" Tina said vehemently.

"I mean, that's unbelievable Ethel," Miriam continued, shaking her head. "A woman deserves a little comfort like that, and it's the man's responsibility to give it to her."

Tina flipped a few cards across the table. "I've listened to plenty of men complainin' about their so called 'right,' but I never heard of a young woman like yourself that was deprived of it like that."

Ethel made a weak attempt to defend her husband's behavior. "Well, I guess with the twins and all he's got a shaky feelin' when it comes to us makin' love."

Tina huffed and shook her head. "The way I see it, the way he treats you is just...cruel."

Ethel checked her new cards and frowned. "Well, the way I see it, I just don't really see him changin' his ways."

Miriam shook her head and sighed.

"Have you ever thought of havin' an affair, Ethel?" she asked matter-of-factly as she glanced at her hand.

Ethel contained a laugh. "An affair? Yeah, well...not recently, I guess."

"If I were you, I would," Tina said.

Ethel took a long hit off her cigarette.

"Well I once had an affair," she said with an exhale. "But that was a long time ago and it caused me a hell of a lot of problems. Like a trip to an abortion clinic and a huge argument with my sister that separated us for a few years, seein' it was her boyfriend who came onto me."

"Well, that's different," Miriam said, folding her cards. "You shouldn't of been messin' round with family. That always gets you in a heap of problems."

"Seein' the horrible situation you're in, honey," Tina said, "I'm sure I'd be considerin' another one."

Ethel tossed her hand on the table and smirked. "Even if I was considerin' it," she said, "I got the twins to think about." She paused as she considered her babies as an excuse. "And anyway, I don't think anyone would be very attracted to a plump mother of four like myself."

Miriam looked at her as if she were crazy.

"What are you talkin' 'bout?" she laughed as she pulled a few nickels toward her side. "There's lots of men who like their women a bit large. And what middle-aged woman around now hasn't had kids anyway?"

"I'm gonna go out to the kitchen and get us a little snack," Tina interrupted them. "Maybe a little break will get my luck back, 'cause I haven't won a hand since the first one. You girls keep talkin'. I can hear you through the door."

"Don't forget about those no-bake fudge cookies I brought," Ethel called to her, pointing toward the foil-covered plate on the coffee table.

Miriam quickly pulled a cigarette out of her pack. "Now Ethel, I'm gonna give you a little bit of advice," she began, eyeing Ethel intently. "You know this guy I've been seein' lately, named Scott, that I've told y'all about."

"Yeah," Ethel said as she pulled a kleenex from her pocket and blew her nose.

"I met him through a computer datin' service in Indianapolis that guarantees complete privacy. And I tell you, since meetin' him, I've been a hell of a lot happier. I mean he's married and all, but that suits me fine, 'cause I ain't lookin' for another husband anyway. And he don't want to divorce his wife, neither, 'cause he's got a family and all that he cares about. And he says he loves her anyway."

Ethel looked at her sarcastically. "So what's he screwin' around on her for, then?"

Miriam flipped some ashes into an empty beer can and placed her elbows on the table. "Well, it seems that she's a little bit of a prude when it comes to sex. I mean, he loves her for her other qualities, but, like everybody, he feels a physical urge that she won't allow him to express anymore." She smiled and added, "So we see each other once a week or so and spend a few very enjoyable hours together."

Ethel rolled her eyes and reached for a cigarette. "Yeah, but Miriam, look at yourself," she said. "You're a very attractive woman who I'm sure has no problem findin' a man. I wouldn't have the first idea about where to get a man like the one you got."

"That's the advice I just told you about before," Miriam insisted, running her hand through her hair. "I didn't meet Scott in a bar or somethin' like that. Meetin' someone there is the key to failure, believe me. I learned that with my other marriages. I met Scott through this datin' service in Indianapolis. You just give them some personal details and a photograph and they find someone in the area they think matches you."

"But I thought those datin' services were just for singles," Tina said as she returned to the room for a moment.

"They *used to be* just for singles," Miriam corrected her, "until they all started going out of business and finally realized that more married people were lookin' for friends than single people were. And the singles proba'ly all seemed like a bunch of losers or perverts, anyway—you know, lonely hearts."

"But don't things like that cost a lot of money?" Tina asked. She placed a tray of various cookies, a pot of coffee and nearly empty pint of whiskey on the table.

"Well, that's the thing," Miriam said as she stubbed out her cigarette. "You have to pay a hundred dollars, or something like that, to subscribe, but the computer they've got really seems to work well, and Scott was on the first list of names they sent me."

Ethel shook her head and reached for one of her cookies.

"There you go," she said dejectedly. "Where would I come up with that kind of money?"

Tina began pouring the coffee. "It does seem like a lot of money," she commented.

"Well, I guess if it takes a little money to find some happiness," Miriam said while splashing some whiskey into her coffee, "it's worth it."

"Yeah, but I barely get enough from Wayne as it is to put food on the table and clothe the kids," Ethel whined. She pushed another cookie into her mouth. "Without even considerin' a little extra. I mean, you should've seen the Christmas we had this year. I had to get everything from the Goodwill store, including a baby carriage that's actually made for triplets."

"Oh, it must of been that woman's I used to see up in Hope," Tina said. "Those three kids were so cute."

"Oh yeah, I saw them the other day down at the Wal-Mart," Miriam added. "They were all dressed in the same clothes and looked real adorable."

Ethel frowned and drove another cookie toward her mouth.

"That'll be the day when I get the money to get Gladys and Crystal wearin' the same thing," she huffed.

"Look Ethel," Tina said as she reached for a cup of coffee. "If a little bit of money is standin' between you and your happiness, I could see what I got put aside and try to help you a little. I just don't want to see you sufferin' anymore. And I say that as a friend."

"Listen girls," Miriam said. "I think I can put in somethin', too, over the next few weeks." She blew into her coffee and took a small sip. "In fact, if the money brought you a little joy," she added, "I wouldn't even care about gettin' it back."

"Right," Tina said, nodding her head in agreement. "You got enough problems with that monster husband of yours without worryin' about a little money you owe your friends."

"Well I appreciate it," Ethel said. She looked at the others and smiled. "But there's no way I can get to Indianapolis and deal with that computer and stuff anyway, so we just better forget about the whole idea right now and just let it be a nice little fantasy."

"It sure sounds excitin'," Tina said seductively. "A secret rendezvous with some handsome stranger. Just like that TV movie we were talkin' 'bout before."

"Look Ethel," Miriam said as she lit another cigarette. "I go to Indianapolis about every week to see Scott, and if you want, I'll get all the papers together for you and bring them next week for you to fill out. You just get a nice photograph of yourself, and then I'll take everything to the office and deal with all the paperwork. In fact, I'll even use my post office box as the address. That way you don't have to worry about anything. It'll be real confidential, just between us, and I'll just give you the letters when they arrive and we can deal with all that here."

"Oooh, this is gettin' excitin'," Tina crooned. She winked at Ethel and raised and lowered her eyebrows suggestively.

Ethel smiled timidly at the glowing faces around her. "I must admit it's got my juices runnin' a little bit, too," she sighed. She splashed some whiskey into her coffee.

"There you go," Miriam smiled. She rubbed Ethel affectionately on the shoulder.

"I can hardly wait to see what happens," Tina smiled, then poured more coffee into their cups.

"We'll know before long," Miriam added. "And I'm sure we're all gonna be jealous."

Ethel thrust her hand out nervously for another cookie and nodded her head automatically with her friends. She did her best to smile. The prospect of a lover was certainly stimulating, but the fact that it might soon become a reality left her feeling suddenly unsure.

In fact, it scared her shitless.

28

Wayne stepped out of the light snow and into the brightly lit interior of the Waffle House. He paused at the door and surveyed the neon-lit interior as if he owned it. There were several sleepy-eyed couples at some of the tables, and a counter staggered by men hunched over their plates as if drugged by the thick, greasy odor of bacon, sausage and fried dough that bubbled on the grill in front of them. After pouring some batter into a waffle iron and covering it with a handful of crushed pecans, the cook, a new guy who looked to be Mexican, yawned and then sucked some of the splashed mix from his fingers.

Wayne shuffled across the recently polished floor toward a vacant corner booth and slid himself in, carefully placing his cap and police scanner on the table top.

"Hey Louise," he said to the waitress. "How you doin'?"

The middle-aged waitress smiled warmly at him.

"Oh, hey there, Wayne," she replied. "Be bringin' your coffee over in just a minute."

"Take your time," Wayne said confidently as she moved away. "Don't want you movin' too fast for me." He felt impressed with his sense of style and smiled at the couple next to him. They continued eating without looking up.

Wayne took off his damp coat and placed it on the seat next to him. Coming to the Waffle House was a fairly new habit, one he developed shortly after beginning the security shift at the radio station. Sitting in the warm, bright interior provided him a relaxing alternative to the hustle and confusion of his own home. There the twins were typically crying, Ethel was yelling, and Junior and Darlene were hurrying to get dressed before streaking out the door to catch the school bus. Living with all that chaos was in complete contradiction to what he wanted to do.

What made the Waffle House even more convenient was the fact that Wayne now found it the perfect spot to pass the couple of hours between his Vanguard shift at the radio station, which ended at six, and his part-time job, where he had to be at eight o'clock. He took on the new job, a cashier at the Sinclair Mini-Mart, shortly after the New Year. The holidays had, as usual, wiped out all Wayne's savings, and because Ethel continued to complain that she didn't have enough to provide the family with the things they needed, he decided to find a second job. He figured the job was just a temporary thing to supplement his income until something else at Vanguard turned up, which he knew would be soon. Three day shifts a week at the convenience store at least give him a little financial breathing room.

Wayne also liked passing his free time in the Waffle House because of Louise. Unlike the other men, who sat at the counter and followed her constantly with hungry stares, he wasn't attracted to her physically. She wasn't what he considered his type. She was thin, lacked any hint of curves no matter what angle you caught her from, and had short blonde hair parted in the middle. She also had the habit of constantly chewing on a toothpick.

What appealed to him more than her looks, however, was the special treatment she always gave him. He knew that in some restaurants, policemen didn't have to pay for what they ordered. The restaurant staff liked to have a man in blue around while it was dark outside. Normally though, that was reserved for the state police, whose shiny cruisers, parked auspiciously in front of the door, helped defray the possibility of a robbery.

But even though Wayne wasn't an actual policeman, Louise had treated him as one from the start. For the first couple of weeks, she referred to him as Officer Turner as his polished bronze name tag read. She talked to him, but questioned him only vaguely about his work. Wayne finally told her to call him by his first name. He said that he was involved with surveillance, for which he used an unmarked car—the Gremlin. He quickly added that he was unable to tell her anything else about his "assignment" because of "police code." The explanation satisfied her, and from then on he didn't spend a cent in the joint except for the quarter or two tip he always threw on the table before leaving.

Louise approached his table and placed a steaming cup of coffee in front of him.

"How things been on your beat?" she asked.

"Quiet," he answered nonchalantly while rubbing his moustache. "Being an officer of the law might sound excitin', Louise, but that's the way it is a lot of the time."

"Well, it's been pretty busy in here tonight, for some reason," she said. "And my feet are killin' me." She put the empty coffee pot on the table and stared out one of the plate glass windows in front. "Look at that little dog out there," she said, pointing to the car parked nearby. "He's cute."

Wayne looked out the window and saw a chihuahua strapped into what looked to be a customized high chair. It was barking furiously, with its snarling head pressed up against the windshield. Not exactly "cute" in Wayne's book.

"Poor little thing, left all alone," Louise added, shaking her head and taking out her pad. "You want the usual to eat?" she asked, taking a pencil from behind her ear.

Wayne took his eyes off the chihuahua and sat back pensively. After a couple of seconds, he nodded his head. "Yeah, two eggs over easy always does me just fine."

The customers at the table next to his asked for more coffee and Louise moved off toward the machine to get a fresh pot.

"Lemme know if you want somethin' else, Wayne," she shouted over her shoulder. "We got other things, you know. And I wouldn't want to see a law officer too hungry to catch criminals."

A content, confident grin crossed Wayne's face. Now everyone present knew just who he was, and that he was a preferred customer—somehow more important than the others.

Wayne ripped open a packet of sugar and dumped it into his cup. He stirred it blindly as he watched Louise give the order to the cook.

A message suddenly barked from the police scanner, drawing a number of curious stares toward his table. Wayne immediately sat up attentively, listening carefully to the coded blurb. Feeling the call was not of a criminal nature, he turned the radio off and placed it on the seat while looking at the other customer's gleaming reflections in the window.

"What was that call all about?" Louise asked him inquisitively from behind, filling his coffee cup and looking down curiously at the radio.

"Oh, nothin' to involve me," Wayne said, leaning himself back and throwing a leg up on the bench seat, facing her more openly. "Just a call for a paramedic out in Jackson County. Heart attack victim."

Louise crossed her arms and laughed, regarding Wayne as if he were some sort of genius. "I don't know how you understan' all that stuff. It just sounds like a bunch of static to me."

The truth was it sounded like a bunch of static to Wayne most of the time as well. But with the help of several books he had sent away for, the hours listening to the scanner in the shed, and the pages of notebooks he had filled trying to figure the jargon out, he finally began to recognize the most typical calls. He knew the last call had been for something in Jackson county, but the nature of the call was beyond his pale of knowledge.

231

"Well, when you're involved in the field I am," he commented coolly, "it starts to become like a second language...just like English probably is to your cook over there."

Louise looked toward the grill and then back at Wayne, whom she smiled at while shaking her head.

"Sometimes I can't even understan' what he's sayin'," she whispered.

Wayne moved closer to her and shifted his eyes toward the cook.

"He's legal, ain't he?" he whispered back.

She looked at Wayne and then at the cook and then back to Wayne, appearing confused.

"I guess he is," she finally said softly. "He lives over in the trailer park next door with his wife and six kids." She hesitated as if trying to remember something. "I think that's what he told me anyway," she added.

Suddenly the door of the restaurant swung open forcefully. Three state troopers entered and slid into a booth near the cash register.

"You're in awful late tonight!" Louise yelled to them while moving toward the coffee machine.

"Yeah, we had to back up some of the county guys out at the Four Seasons Mall earlier," one of them said. "An attempted armed robbery of the night receipts at Belk's. Had every cop in the area out there."

"Anybody get hurt?" Louise asked, approaching them with the pot and some cups.

"None of us," another cop said. "But we sent two of them to the morgue. Put the other one down too."

"Well, thank God for that," she said, shaking her head and filling their cups.

"Yeah, it was pretty hairy for a half-hour or so," the third cop said. "They were experienced with their firearms. But we used ours better," he added coolly, fingering his mirror shades closer to his eyes.

"I'm surprised Officer Turner wasn't out there with you guys," Louise said, looking over at Wayne's table. "I never seen y'all in together. Do y'all know each other?"

The two cops with their backs to him turned around, and Wayne suddenly found four sets of eyes staring at him blankly.

He nodded his head in their direction, suddenly feeling as if he were shrinking under the force of their gaze.

"Officers," he finally muttered with a nod of his head, his voice higher than usual.

They nodded back in unison, suspiciously.

"No, he's not with us," one of them finally said, looking back at Louise.

"You security?" another one asked Wayne.

Wayne cleared his throat uncomfortably.

"Surveillance," he said, looking away.

Louise looked confused. "I thought you said all the officers were called out there," she said, looking back down at the troopers.

"Yeah, all the policemen," one of them said. "Not..."

"Order!" the cook called loudly, grabbing Louise's attention. She turned around and went to the counter to retrieve it, and the troopers returned to talking among themselves.

A few seconds later, Louise placed the food in front of Wayne.

"I guess that undercover stuff keeps you away from the action," she said.

"Yeah," Wayne muttered softly, looking away, embarrassed. But before they exchanged any more words, Louise hustled over to another table.

Wayne ate slowly. He kept his eyes down on the plate in front of him, pushing the food into his mouth mechanically. He felt a knot forming in his gut as he eavesdropped on the troopers' conversation, which described the night's exciting events in painful detail. All the while, he felt humiliated in their presence.

After all, what they had been involved in several hours earlier was what he dreamed about participating in night after night, during the long hours alone at the radio station. Here they were, guns drawn, shooting it out with a few scumbags amidst the excitement of spinning sirens and powerful floodlights. Meanwhile, he walked around some vacant lot in the middle of nowhere, hearing only his own footsteps and the damn cadence of those stupid crickets.

Louise returned and topped off his cup.

"Don't look so depressed," she said consolingly. "There'll be other nights."

"Yeah, I guess so," he said dejectedly, pushing half an egg around the bacon grease before finally putting it in his mouth.

"What else can I get you to eat?"

Wayne looked down at his watch and saw that he still had an hour to kill, but felt uncomfortable around the state troopers. It might be better to leave before they asked him anymore embarrassing questions and humiliated him further, he thought.

"Nothin'," he said, reaching for his coat. "It's about time I be gettin' back to work."

"Now look, Wayne!" she said, placing her hands on her hips defiantly. "I'm not gonna have you goin' back on the beat with no food in your stomach. I'll get you a couple of sausage-and-egg biscuits and you can take them on the road with you. All right?"

Wayne looked into her pleasant blue eyes and smiled.

"Well, all right," he said, moving himself out of the booth. "If you insist."

As Louise dashed off toward the grill, Wayne put on his cap, slipped the radio into his pocket and strode quickly past the troopers without looking at them. Finding shelter in the men's room, he closed the cubicle behind him and sat down on the toilet.

When he returned to the restaurant, he nervously busied himself by absently punching the buttons on the cigarette machine. All the while, he kept his back toward the other uniformed men. Before long, Louise hustled over to the machine and handed a bag to him.

"There you go, Officer Turner," she said with a wink. "Be careful out there."

"Thank you, Louise," Wayne mumbled, grabbing the bag and looking down. "'Preciate it."

Wayne glanced up shyly and smiled, and then turned quickly, making his way out the door. He stared enviously at the three shiny cruisers and shuffled his feet heavily across the sand and slush of the parking lot.

Once inside the Gremlin, the comforting, appetizing warmth of the food bag between his legs made him feel better. But as he looked down and noticed his Mini-Mart uniform on the passenger seat beside him, the feeling seemed to drain out of him and disappear, just like what he'd flushed down the toilet a few minutes earlier.

29

"I don't know about this joint, man," Junior said, forcing out the last few words through a cough. "It doesn't really taste like pot."

"It's pot, man," Fred responded while taking the roach and inhaling noisily. "Believe me."

"I don't think it tastes that much like pot either," John mentioned.

"But I'm kind of gettin' a buzz from it. Who'd you get it from, anyway?"

"From my cousin," Fred muttered through slightly parted lips. "He knows some guys that deal a lot."

John reached for the roach. "What kind is it?" he asked.

"I think he told me it was from Colombia," Fred answered, exhaling a trail of smoke.

"Oh yeah, Colombia," Junior said, rolling his eyes. "Columbia, South Carolina, more like it."

"Hey listen, man!" Fred shot back. "My cousin wouldn't rip me off, man. He told me himself that this was primo quality. And he knows."

Junior reached for the joint and deeply inhaled the smoke. "Well, I still don't think it tastes very good, but I guess it works all right," he offered.

The three teenagers sat on large rocks in the middle of the woods, several miles outside Westport. As was their custom on Saturday night, Junior and John hitchhiked separately into town earlier and met at a monument that commemorated the town's combat casualties from every American war. They walked together to Gunther's Delicatessen and, along the way, met another guy they knew from school—Fred. Neither John nor Junior hung around Fred that much. But when they heard he had some pot, they invited him along. The trio waited around for half an hour outside the deli and got turned down by several people. Finally, they got someone to buy them beer with their pooled money.

Because none of their parents had gone out for the night, they were forced to head out of town and find a secluded spot. They wanted to be sure that no cops came snooping around and gave them shit for being under age and drinking. It was nothing new to them. Occasionally they sat around some deserted building in the rain or were forced to endure other inclement weather. But conditions like that were really superfluous to the chore that always faced them: to finish the alcohol, listen to some music on John's portable radio, and then raise a little hell.

Junior wrapped his arms around his pudgy torso.

"Jesus Christ, it's cold out here!" he said, shivering.

"No shit!" John said, tucking his chin under his coat. "I can't even feel my toes. How many degrees you think it is?"

"It's got to be around ten or fifteen," Fred responded, rubbing his hands together rapidly. "But I bet the goddamn wind chill makes it below zero."

John reached an ungloved hand to the can beside him and swallowed some of it down.

"We should have gotten whiskey or something that would've at least warmed us up," he said.

"I said that before, didn't I?" Junior said, taking a sip of his chilled beer.

"Yeah, but whiskey costs a lot of money," John said. "And besides, the last time we tried to get a bottle, we spent three hours outside the package store and nobody would buy us booze. We're lucky we got my brother's friend to buy us this so fast tonight."

"Yeah, well next time the weather's like this," Junior said through chattering teeth, "we try the package store again. Because my goddamn beer is startin' to freeze, and this is only my third one."

"We should build a fire or somethin'," John muttered.

"Well you're the damn Boy Scout," Fred snickered. "Why don't you do it?"

Junior stood up and looked at him angrily.

"I quit the Boy Scouts two months ago," he hissed. "So don't give me any of your shit. Why don't you do it?"

"What's the big fuckin' deal," John said, getting off the rock and grabbing a couple of sticks from the ground. "I don't know if we're gonna get it goin' anyway 'cause this stuff is so goddamn wet."

The three boys wedged their cans in the snow, ripped off some small branches and grabbed all the wood laying on the ground nearby. After breaking up the sticks into foot long sections, Junior cleared some snow off the ground and arranged the wood in a tee-pee shape, shoving the paper bag that had held the beer beneath them. After several false starts, the flames finally began to grow in unison. As the timber cracked, the three of them hunched over it.

"That's more like it," John said, holding his hands inches from the flame. "All we need is a few girls out here to keep the rest of us warm."

"Yeah, I wouldn't mind having Donna Addoniro sucking on my dick right now," Fred said. "That would warm the rest of me up, that's for sure."

"I don't know," Junior said, shaking his head. "I think I'd rather have Julie Dinkham's lips around my schlong."

Fred jetted some air out of his nostrils.

"No way," he disagreed. "Addo's the best."

"Yeah, well I'd take Sue Mantewski over both of them," John remarked, holding a cigarette to the flame while unknowingly melting some of his glove as he did. "That chick's got an unbelievable ass."

"Yeah, but she don't put out," Junior added quickly, grabbing his beer and taking a large gulp. "Bill Klein went out with her for three months and didn't even get tit."

"Yeah, well that's just because Bill Klein is a pussy," Fred huffed.

John shook his head and winced.

"Sometimes I feel like beatin' the shit out of that guy," he hissed.

"You should, man!" Fred said. "We should all kick the shit out of him! He wouldn't even give me the answers to the math homework yesterday!"

"Whose class is that?" Junior asked.

"That old fucker, Mr. Courtin," Fred responded, shaking his head. "I've already got like seven incomplete homework assignments."

"Well you should talk to Ted Cook then," Junior suggested. "He ripped off the teacher's book and it's got all the answers in the back."

Fred stared at him dumbly and scowled.

"Oh man, I wish I'd known that before," he said despondently.

"Will you guys drink this goddamn beer?" John interrupted them, popping open a can. "If we're gonna go knock over a few mailboxes, we should drink faster. I'm already on my fourth."

The other two rapidly finished the cans they held, and threw them off into the darkness of the woods.

"Gimme another one," Fred blurted, breathing heavily.

"Hey turn this song up!" Junior yelled, keying in on the noise coming from the small radio. "This is that new Metallica song."

"Excellent!" Fred yelled, reaching for the volume control and opening another beer. "I can't wait until they come to Indianapolis, man!"

"My brother told me they've got a huge light show this year!" John yelled excitedly while vocalizing some guitar chords. "Better than the last time."

"That guy Lars is an ace drummer, man!" Junior shouted while imitating an extended roll.

The three boys began pounding their heads in unison and continued until the song began to fade out.

"Jesus Christ! I hate this pussy shit!" Fred groaned loudly as the song segued into some slow ballad. "What station is this anyway?"

"KSL," Junior answered. "They always do this shit. I wish we had a phone right now so we could call 'em up and give 'em a bunch of shit like last week, and tell 'em to play Slayer or somethin'."

"You should just give your father a few records to take to the station," John suggested, examining some hair that the fire had singed earlier. "Maybe that new Megadeth album."

Junior was poking a stick into the fire.

"Oh yeah, sure," he said sarcastically.

"Well, he works there, don't he?" John continued.

"Yeah, but not exactly with the music," Junior answered. He pushed a small log over, sending a hail of sparks into the air.

"Maybe he can get us some free tickets for the concert, then!" Fred said excitedly.

"No way," Junior responded dourly while shaking his head. "He's just their measly security guard."

"He probably knows the DJs and stuff!" Fred persisted. "They're givin' away free tickets all the time! He could proba'ly get us some!"

Junior spit into the fire.

"I don't think so," he drawled. "He told me he hardly ever talks to the DJs anyway."

"It would save us some money if he could get us in," John said.

"Yeah, but you know my father," Junior said dejectedly as he watched his breath dissolve into the smoke of the fire. "He's just an asshole."

"Gimme another beer," Fred yelled, tossing his can into the woods.

John watched the can drop solidly into the wet snow about ten feet away.

"What the hell did you do that for?" he asked, annoyed. "You didn't even finish that one yet."

"Yeah," Junior said, noticing as well. "That must have been half-full."

Fred nervously shook a cigarette out of his pack.

"There was like one sip left in there," he voiced, casually shrugging off their accusations.

"A sip is a sip," John said. He pushed his boot closer to the fire and watched the steam rise off it.

"Well I got to get up tomorrow at like seven o'clock," Fred said defensively. "I got to serve at the eight o'clock church service."

Junior began to laugh.

"And you were making fun of me for bein' in Boy Scouts," he said with an undertone of sarcasm. "You're a damn acolyte!"

"I'm gonna quit as soon as my father lets me," he attempted to excuse himself. "I mean, I almost got kicked out last week."

"How come?" John quizzed him, piling some more wood on the fire.

"Well, last Saturday night me and Rob Harvey drank like a six-pack of Tall Boys each, and were listenin' to a bunch of music and stuff in my house, 'cause my parents went to some Lion's Club social. We were playin' guitars and shit along with the record player and when we finished the beer, I raided my parent's liquor cabinet and we had a huge glass of Southern Comfort. I mean, I was feelin' excellent, and we decided to go into the woods near my house and try to find this fort that Steve Atkins and Don McRoy made out there. I mean, it's pretty cool. They've got carpeting on the walls and the floor and its pretty warm, even though its all wet."

Junior shook his beer and then swallowed some down.

"Oh yeah, I've heard about that place," he remarked.

"Yeah, it's pretty cool," Fred said, pausing to inhale his cigarette. "But anyway, we finally found it, and they had a few bottles of wine down there. And we ended up drinkin' that and listenin' to music, and when we finally left, we could hardly find our way out of the woods 'cause we were fucked up and didn't have a flashlight or nothin'. And we were bumpin' into trees and branches and fallin' down and pukin' and shit. But we finally got back to the road and I saw my parents' car was parked out in the front. So before we went in, we sat down on the driveway next door and tried to straighten out a little, but before we did, we both ended up fallin' asleep right there on the damn driveway."

"Oh man!" John laughed, his pimples glowing like match-heads against the light of the fire.

"And the next thing I know," Fred continued, "was the next-door neighbor is shakin' me and I'm starin' straight into his headlights. So he helps us up and brings us to my house, wakes up my mother and tells her that he found us passed out on the driveway. I mean I could hardly even hear what he was sayin' 'cause I was so fucked up, and I just headed straight for the bed without sayin' anything.''

"What happened to Harvey?'' Junior questioned.

"He ended up staggerin' home,'' Fred said. "He said he couldn't wake me up or anything. I think he thought I was dead. But that's not the end of it.''

He paused to light a cigarette.

"After that, my damn father wakes me up at seven the next mornin' and reminds me that I got to serve at the eight o'clock church service. So I get out of bed with this huge hangover, and he drives me to the church and I go in and put the robe on and stuff and do the procession and all that. And I'm sittin' there up in the front, strugglin' to keep my eyes open and tryin' to deal with this poundin' in my head and all of a sudden it's time for communion, which I'm supposed to help out with.''

Fred shook his head and frowned before going on.

"And if you're helpin' out with communion, you got to take it first, you know? So I get down on my knees with one of the ministers—trying to remain in control—and took a mouthful of wine from the chalice. And when I stood up, I just felt this sweat comin' out of my face and this heat rushin' my body, and I felt like I was gonna pass out or somethin'. But I somehow managed to get behind the altar and start refillin' the chalice and wafers as the other people began comin' up and takin' communion. But I was still sweatin' bullets, and my hands started shakin' and the whole church started spinnin' before me.''

"So what'd you do?'' Junior asked excitedly.

Fred looked toward the fire and shook his head.

"I just started to pray,'' he said flatly. "And right in the middle of it, I felt it comin', and I just ducked down behind the altar and lifted the fabric coverin' it and puked like a motherfucker underneath.''

"Goddamn!'' Junior yelled, coughing out some smoke.

"And what did the minister say?'' John pumped Fred.

"Nothin''' Fred said, shaking his head, as if suddenly realizing the horror of it all. "Cause when I came up, they were still serving the people at the communion rail, and I just acted as if nothin' happened. I don't think anyone saw me, but man, I felt a hell of a lot better after pukin'.''

Junior and John were laughing hard.

"It's a miracle!" John muttered in between gasps.

"Yeah, well I guess it sounds funny now," Fred said straight-faced. "But it wasn't that funny at the time."

"Oh, man!" Junior exclaimed, holding his sides. "Ask the Lord and He will provide!"

Slowly Fred began to join in their laughter.

"I don't know what they're gonna say this week though," he said, finishing off his can and shaking it to the others to prove it was empty. "I just hope the janitor cleaned it up or somethin'."

"Me too!" Junior howled, pounding the fire with a stick and sending a stream of sparks into the starless sky overhead.

30

Wayne was seated at a small round table in a big country hot spot, surrounded by smiling photographs of famous music stars. Beer splashed from people's mugs as they boogied to the country sounds blaring from a small stage up front. A barmaid who looked like Reba McIntire pounded a beer down on his table and winked at him.

Looking back toward the band, Wayne did a quick double-take before realizing that one of his heroes had joined the group on stage. It was none other than Waylon Jennings, the outlaw, recording star, and living legend, and there he was in front of Wayne—beard, cowboy hat, long brown hair, and tobacco-stained smile pulling it all together. He was singing a one of Wayne's favorites—hell, Wayne loved all of the Big W's stuff.

Suddenly, Wayne was somewhere else. Maybe in the back room; he wasn't sure. And who was next to him but the man himself, surrounded by lots of beautiful women.

Suddenly the crowd separated under Waylon's command, as if he were Moses parting the Red Sea. The luminary entertainer approached Wayne—actually singled him out. Next thing Wayne knew, they were talking to each other, just Waylon and Wayne, and hugging each other like they were good buddies or something.

The scene switched and they were outside. Waylon was handing Wayne a guitar and he was holding on to it. It was a token of their friendship, and goddamn if it wasn't the same one he'd just been playing on stage.

Some lights flashed quickly, and Waylon began drifting off in the distance, just as fast as he'd arrived. He pulled out in a huge white limousine. As he left, his weatherbeaten hand formed a wave that got smaller and smaller until it disappeared over the crest of the neon-lit horizon.

Wayne was suddenly shaken out of his dream by a hand nudging him firmly on the shoulder. Jerking his head up from the table that rested before him, he slowly brought the face of one of the other security guards into focus and frowned.

''I been waitin' for you out on the floor for the last fifteen minutes!'' the upset guard said. ''I didn't know where you were and it's time for my break!''

"Oh, shit," Wayne said, rubbing his eyes and staring at the dull walls of the dingy room. "I guess I fell asleep. I was havin' some dream that I met Waylon Jennings."

"Yeah, well congratulations!" the other guard said sarcastically, sitting down and kicking his feet up on the other side of the table.

"Just take fifteen minutes extra now," Wayne said casually, adjusting his hat in the mirror. "No problem with that my way."

The other guard set the alarm on his watch and pulled his hat down low.

"OK," he said, closing his eyes and smiling. "Maybe I'm gonna dream about Nina Hartley and she's gonna give me somethin' else."

Wayne stared at him, thought about Nina, the porno star, and laughed.

"Just hope it ain't herpes or somethin'," he cracked, flipping off the light and closing the door behind him.

He walked into the exhibition center of the Indiana State Fair Grounds, whose expansive ceiling amplified the voices of thousands of eager visitors into a loud, deafening hum. He was there to work security at the country music exhibition, an extra assignment he'd taken on a week-and-a-half ago.

The extra money from the shift came in handy, but his motive for taking the job was not solely financial. At the Fair Grounds, Wayne also knew he'd have the opportunity to walk amidst the relics of stars he had listened to since he was a kid, which excited him greatly.

Unfortunately. the assignment required that he worked an extra four to six hours a day, in addition to his duties at the radio station and Mini-Mart. The job called for him and about twenty others to patrol the floor of the exhibition center and make sure that nobody touched the exhibits or got too close. Since most of the exhibits were roped off anyway, he didn't have to be on his toes constantly. But he had to keep moving and remind people once in a while to look with their eyes, not their hands.

As he had done on each of the preceding days, Wayne walked slowly by the exhibits. He paused in front of each exhibit and stared at it carefully before moving onto the next. He saw Gene Autry's hat, a pair of boots that Will Rogers had worn, and a complete suit—adorned with sequins and tassels—that Webb Pierce had first performed in at the Grand Ole Opry. Continuing along, he saw a yellow dress that Patsy Cline had worn before she died in the plane crash; one of Hank Snow's guitars, and a pair of running shoes Willie Nelson had played the Texas Jam in.

Moving into another room, he saw a girl about Darlene's age staring with a confused expression at an old car that stood before her.

"That is history," Wayne told her in a fatherly tone. "Not just musical history," he moved closer, "but genuine American folklore. You can go to some museums and see fossils, and others to see bullets from the Civil War, but where else in the world are you gonna see somethin' like that?"

He pointed to the black automobile, in whose back seat one steamy night Hank Williams had passed from this world into another while enroute to a concert. Wayne leaned against the barricade surrounding the car and stared intently for several seconds. He lowered his head, as if paying some sort of silent respect to the man who had once penetrated the depths of his heart and actually made him cry.

"He was only twenty-nine years old when he died," he said sadly, looking beside him again. But instead of seeing the innocent image of the girl before, he unexpectedly found himself staring into the contorted face of some teenage boy with long brown, greasy hair.

"What do you mean 'when he died?'," the kid said arrogantly, "I saw him in concert on TV a few weeks ago and he was great!"

Wayne straightened his body and stared in horror at the kid.

"That was Hank Williams Jr.!" he quickly corrected him. Wayne recalled watching some of the mediocre concert himself.

The kid looked at the sign and read the small print under "Hank William's Cadillac" before looking back at Wayne.

A confused expression crossed his pimpled face. "Was that Bocephus's father or somethin'?" he asked. "I ain't never heard of the guy."

Wayne looked at the kid with scorn.

"That's right, sonny," he said, talking down to him. "The greatest country music singer that ever lived."

The kid took a step back and squinted, like he thought Wayne was full of shit.

"Well, you obviously haven't heard these guys," he said. He pointed both thumbs toward his t-shirt, which was covered with a colorful logo reading "38 Special."

Wayne looked strangely at the kid, who cocked back his head and started singing some inane lyrics right in front of Hank's old Cadillac. He felt like punching the boy, but instead Wayne just stared into his tightened, red eyes with contempt.

"Are you stoned or somethin'?" Wayne finally asked, frowning. The kid suddenly stopped and blew some air from between his chapped lips.

"No, I'm not stoned," he said, beginning to laugh. "Their new album is real good, man. You should hear it."

"I wouldn't listen to that crap if you paid me!" Wayne barked. "And from here on, you just make sure you read the fine print underneath all these exhibits and maybe you'll learn somethin'. Because really, no one today comes close to any of the legends, you understand?"

"Oh yeah," the kid said sarcastically. "And the next thing you're gonna tell me is that this twangy country garbage is better than Molly Hatchet—or even Lynyrd Skynyrd."

Wayne didn't feel like wasting his breath on the moron anymore so, instead of responding, he simply shook his head sadly and walked the other way. The dumb kid was a waste product, Wayne felt, who was probably doomed because of his own stupidity.

But what bothered Wayne most was that he felt his own son was in the same boat, exhibiting his immaturity by having no respect for the people who had learned some of life's realities through experience—and certainly could teach him something. People like Wayne himself, his own father.

Attempting to take his mind off the unpleasant subject, he looked around a room devoted to the man in black, Johnny Cash, before moving into another room where one of Elvis Presley's cars stood atop a platform. It was a pink Studebaker whose highly polished surface constantly reflected the flashes of onlookers' cameras. The information panel informed viewers that it had shuttled The King around while he was in Hollywood making *Charro*.

Even though the car drew the most spectators, it was Wayne's least favorite exhibit in the hall. To him, it didn't matter if the guy was from the South, or that he had made a couple of average country albums. Wayne simply didn't feel Elvis belonged at a country-and-western exhibition, amidst the other luminaries who were dedicated to that field. It pissed him off, actually, because in addition to the fact that he had never liked Elvis, this exhibit just took all the attention away from the other exhibits that Wayne felt were much more valuable.

Wayne continued his beat. He told a hysterical fan in front of the car to keep her voice down, then walked into another room. There he glanced quickly at Ferlin Husky's guitar, Johnny Paycheck's belt buckle, and Marty Robbins' hat. Just before leaving the room and furthering his rounds, he told a spectator not to breathe on the glass case that housed several of George Strait's rings.

He strolled past a wax figure of Barbara Mandrell, facsimiles of the plaques depicting the Country Music Hall Of Fame's inductees and a comprehensive history of the Carter Family. He paused briefly to watch several minutes of a film clip showing one of Crystal Gayle's early television appearances.

On one of the other TV monitors, he saw a recording of a Randy Travis concert. Randy crooned for the camera and smiled widely to his female fans in the front row. He'd been popular for a few years, but Wayne had never liked him because he thought he was a just George Jones copy, except not as good. But the real reason he disliked the Travis kid was because he'd seen published reports in the newspapers at the Mini-Mart that claimed that he was gay. Wayne felt that was an unnatural betrayal of basic decency that slammed the door on what little respect he had ever allowed for the guy.

The video's volume sailed away as Wayne stepped into another section of the arena. He came upon rows of stalls selling various souvenirs. At the first one, shelf after shelf was lined with memorabilia, all adorned with Conway Twitty's face. Postcards caught the man in scores of different poses, and posters of him covered every inch of wall space. There were Conway Twitty cigarette lighters, key chains, ash trays, glasses, vases, can openers, bottles of shampoo, and even boxes of condoms embossed with his gleaming image.

Wayne wasn't a big fan of Conway Twitty. In fact, he didn't like him at all. About ten seconds was all he could tolerate of being bombarded with thousands of sets of Conway's beaming eyes and perfect white teeth.

At the next stall Wayne saw the same items, only this time they were covered with smiling portraits of Tanya Tucker. He didn't like her very much, either, because he considered her a slut. So he promptly moved on and passed by the next stall.

This time he was confronted by an array of similar items, but with a variety of stars' faces embellishing each one. He picked up two items and admired them: a George Jones coffee mug and a knife sheath with an autograph of David Allen Coe etched into it, which he considered buying. But he decided against it and continued along souvenir row.

At the next stall he saw something he decided to buy—a leather wallet with Dolly Parton's face and her two most famous assets burned into it.

Even though Wayne wasn't a big fan of her music, he did like the way she looked. He often thought that she was the ideal woman, who possessed the ideal body. She was big—huge even. Yet she was also slender, unlike his wife, Ethel, who was simply huge all over. He had never bought any of Dolly's records, but he had purchased a number of glossy pictures that accentuated her buxom figure. Wayne tacked them up in the shed, next to the suspect photos and other material related to his police work.

During his long hours out there alone, Wayne occasionally closed his eyes and imagined Dolly and him having a secret rendezvous somewhere off in the woods. She would be naked, of course. And she would be waving her long fingernails suggestively, beckoning him to join her in the cool lake in the wilderness. They'd roll around on the long, damp grass along its edge for a while, and then swim together to the middle. They would eventually make love as the moon glistened brilliantly off Dolly's milky white breasts. Afterwards, they'd swim back hand-in-hand to the shore, where Dolly would towel him dry, then tell him how good he was before they got into it again. It was always like that with Dolly in the shed. With Wayne, she just always seemed to want more.

He paid for the billfold and made another quick round of the rooms to keep people in line. Wayne checked his watch and saw that two hours still remained before the exhibit permanently closed. He walked over to the corner of one room, where he decided to take a quick break. He sat down, extracted his old wallet from his back pocket, and transferred everything into the new one. He discarded the old wallet in the garbage can, and ran his fingers gently over the painted surface of the new one.

Wayne carefully eased it into his front pocket and smiled, pleased by the thought that Dolly's joyous face now rode close to his action.

31

An early April rain splashed against the half-rusted body of a gray AMC Pacer. The car sat in the corner of a Motel 6 parking lot, surrounded by puddle-filled potholes. Inside, Ethel was hunched over the steering wheel. She pressed her hefty body toward the continuous stream of warm air that blew toward her from the heater. Even though she wasn't really cold, Ethel still felt a chill deep inside that caused her to tremble slightly. She tried to alleviate the sensation by sitting back and wrapping her sweaty palms around her thick torso.

As every minute passed, Ethel grew more impatient. She checked her watch: one forty-two, then opted for a cigarette in place of another Moon Pie to relieve her anxiety. During the past hour, Ethel had nearly finished off the whole box of Moon Pies.

Ethel replaced the lighter in the dashboard and abruptly turned on the windshield wipers. She stared through the foggy glass around her, desperately hoping to see the car somewhere within her view. Instead, she observed the same five cars and two trucks that were there when she arrived fifteen minutes earlier. She took a deep drag off the cigarette and began nervously tapping the fingers of her free hand on the wheel, in rhythm with the swing of the windshield wipers.

Ethel had changed her mind frequently the past few months. But at last she decided to follow her friends' advice and give the dating service they suggested a try. She searched through a box of photos tucked away in the closet and finally found one taken many years before. It was the only one she felt did her true appearance some justice.

With Miriam Tanner's help, Ethel filled in the forms. They answered the questions by exaggerating her good points and playing down the others. As they had promised, her friends took care of most of the cost, and Miriam brought the application to Indianapolis, where it was entered into the computer.

At their card game a few weeks later, Miriam arrived with a broad smile on her face. She carried a brown, sealed envelope addressed to Ethel Beck, a pseudonym they agreed Ethel should use.

Anxiously, the women gathered around Ethel as she tore open the envelope and stared at its contents. A computer printout and photographs of several suitable male candidates were enclosed. Ethel decided to make a date with one near the end of the list—a fifty-two-year-old native of Huntington, Indiana named Kenneth Blanton. The photograph showed a man who looked slightly younger, with dark, medium-length hair parted on the side and pulled across a high forehead. He wore aviator glasses and a short, neatly trimmed beard and mustache that surrounded a pleasant smile.

Ethel filled in a few more forms and gave the envelope back to Miriam who, a couple of weeks later, came to Tina's house with yet another brown envelope. Its contents included more information and a phone number. As her friends egged her on, Ethel nervously picked up the phone and dialed the number.

"Hello," a voice answered warmly.

"Hello," Ethel said hesitantly. "Can I speak to Kenneth Blanton, please?"

"Speaking."

"I got your number," Ethel began, "from the printout the agency gave me."

"Well it was very nice of you to call, Ethel," Kenneth said warmly. "How are you today?"

"Oh, I'm a little bit nervous, Kenneth, I guess," Ethel giggled.

"Well that's understandable, Ethel, seeing it's the first time we've spoken," Kenneth said reassuringly. "But first things first. Kenneth sounds so formal. So from now on, I want you to call me Ken."

Ethel soon found herself relaxed while listening to Ken's pleasant tone. He seemed like a genuine person, and Ethel felt he sounded honest. They chatted for several minutes, and then agreed to meet for coffee the next week to get to know each other better. For Ethel, it was also a chance to see if a more substantial relationship was worth pursuing.

Ethel told Darlene to look after the babies while she went shopping. She then ran to her car and drove to a meeting place in Greensburg. She had no problem recognizing Ken once she was inside the International House of Pancakes; he looked exactly as he appeared in the photograph.

Ken didn't bat an eye at the fact that Ethel didn't resemble her picture very much. He even mentioned that she looked prettier in person than her photograph suggested. Ethel suddenly found herself developing a passionate interest in the man.

For an hour they spoke virtually non-stop about their interests and reasons for seeking a new friendship. Ken told her that he was an industrial tool salesman who traveled all over the southeastern part of the state, visiting factories and hardware stores every day and demonstrating the latest tools of their trades. He told her that he had been married for twenty-six years, but two years ago, his wife had died of leukemia after suffering for nearly ten months. He had two grown children who lived in different parts of the country, and he was now seeking a new lease on life that he felt a new friendship might offer.

Ethel merely repeated what her friends had suggested almost verbatim. She told him that she was a divorced mother of three, her youngest child being seven years old. She mentioned that she worked part-time as a file clerk at a shipping warehouse, and that she, too, was seeking a new person who might shed a little bit of light on her monotonous days.

During the next week, Ethel saw even less of her husband than before. Three days a week he was at the Sinclair Mini-Mart and wanted to sleep immediately upon returning home. Wayne barely managed a few words to her when he got up, before dashing out the door to his job at the radio station. But when Ethel completed her chores around the house and sat in front of the television, she found her mind continually drifting to her upcoming lunch date with Ken, upon which they had mutually agreed and for which he had happily offered to pay.

They met at Captain Jack's Sea Shack the following week. Ken, looking even more handsome than before in his checked blazer and Sansabelt slacks, greeted her with a bunch of fresh flowers. They both ordered the jumbo seafood platter, which included a small piece of lobster, something Ethel had never tasted before. Once again, they talked continuously.

Ken's character was nearly opposite that of her husband's. Ken was patient with her and hung onto nearly every one of her words as though he were truly interested. And unlike Wayne, he spoke with soft, reassuring words that made her feel that at least she had something more to offer than the ability to perform things that were expected of her.

Almost regretfully, Ken informed Ethel that he had made a vow, shortly after his wife died, that he would never marry again for respect of her memory. He claimed that it was only right that she know, and insisted that he wasn't merely looking for a substitute in Ethel. He just wanted to be honest with Ethel right from the beginning.

Ethel blushed, and for the first time reached her hand out and covered his. She explained to him that she certainly wasn't looking for a new husband, either, and she complimented him on his honesty. She added that a similar thought had crossed her mind, but that she was unsure about it herself. They continued holding hands for the rest of their meal, and Ethel felt a tinge of electricity soar through her body now and again when their legs met underneath the table. At times when she stared into his smiling eyes, exaggerated through the aviator lenses, she felt as if she were in another world—free, attractive, and desired.

She carried her newfound self-confidence secretly at home. But at their card game, her friends complimented her on her rekindled humor and cheerful spirit. They listened intently as she told them of the sensations she'd felt during her latest meetings with Ken. Ethel's friends insisted that she take precautions to avoid an unfortunate accident, though; they reminded her that pregnancy would take the magic away from their secret coupling and return them to the real world in a hurry.

Ethel rubbed the condensation off the window again and stared at a second-floor window of the motel. They ended up inside that room the week before, after an abbreviated rendezvous at the Cuckoo Clock Lounge in Columbus. They had met earlier that day, and after a couple of quick cocktails, Ken drew her close and looked deeply into her eyes.

"I'd like to show how much I care for you in a more private place," he whispered.

Ethel finally heard the words she had dreamed about for the past few weeks. She hurriedly threw her coat on and actually led him to the door by the hand. They drove straight to the Motel 6 and had soon found themselves enclosed within the privacy of a dark room. Their mouths locked, and they embraced and wrestled frantically upon the bed, feeling the revealed touch of heated skin underneath their clothes.

A red Chevrolet Nova pulled into the lot and Ethel watched it draw nearer. She felt her adrenaline soar as she spotted Ken's figure behind the wheel. He stepped out quickly and held an umbrella over her door. After a short kiss and brief visit to the office, the two lovers soon found themselves in a room much like the last one they'd shared. They wrapped their bodies around each other, melting together, Ken's passionate kisses covering Ethel's face in a flurry of passion. Their clothes dropped to the floor and piled on top of each other, much like their bodies on the bed. Before long Ken climbed atop her, and Ethel found herself begging for his entry.

But unlike the first time they had been naked together, something wasn't quite right. When Ethel reached down and attempted to direct his cock into her spread orifice, she found herself holding a limp tube of sagging

251

flesh that simply bent against her moist cavern. She fumbled with it unsuccessfully for several minutes, rubbing its head against her clitoris. That motion sent shallow waves racing throughout her skull, but it didn't quite get her to the point she had arrived at the week before, when she'd actually felt herself flying.

Ken suddenly rolled off her and backed off.

"I'm sorry, Ethel," he said dejectedly.

Ethel followed him, holding on to his flaccid prick like a preoccupied dog on a leash being jerked away by its master.

"What's the matter, Honey?" she asked, pulling her body toward him and continuing to work her hand gently.

"I don't know," he said, reaching up and rubbing the back of her neck. "And I want you so bad."

"Well, just give it a little time," Ethel said, reassuringly. "Maybe I'm not doin' my job properly."

"No, it ain't you sweetheart," Ken said, lowering his face to his hands. "I guess I should have told you about this last week. I've had a little problem with this once in a while in the past. I got the desire in my heart, but my body just doesn't seem to respond sometimes because it can't make this...desire...happen."

Ethel pulled her body up closer to his.

"Why didn't you just say so, baby?" she said, smiling warmly. "If you want to make love with the lights on, that's all right with me."

"Well, it's not exactly that," Ken smiled, rubbing his hand across her flabby thigh. "I mean, when I'm on top of you, I can picture in my mind what's happenin'—us making love. But I just can't feel it like it's right there, if you know what I mean. It's like I just can't see it."

"Well maybe it's just the position we're usin'," Ethel said, hoisting her thigh with difficulty on top of his. "I mean we could try somethin' else where you can see me more. From behind or somethin'."

"Oh, Ethel," he said, rubbing his hand across her face. "You're so sweet. But this is something I just got to..."

"Just tell me, Ken!" Ethel interrupted him, grabbing his hand and looking at him sincerely. "Whatever you want me to do, just tell me!"

Ken took Ethel's hand between his and stared at her lovingly.

"I've got this...thing," he began. "I don't know where it started, but I've had it all my life. I mean, it probably came from when I was in the service and looked at magazines and stuff to fulfill my needs during those long periods out at sea. But I just find I can't express my feelings properly without seein' some sort of picture of what it is I'm making love to.''

"Do you mean you have to look at a magazine or somethin' before you can get an erection?'' Ethel asked, confused by the thought.

"No, no, it's not that," Ken said, nervously laughing at her insinuation. "I haven't looked at one of those magazines since I was discharged. I mean, that kind of voyeurism is...''

"Dirty?'' Ethel interrupted him as he paused to search for the correct word.

Ken looked up at her and smiled.

"Well, I was gonna say educational...I mean, once things are right between a couple that loves each other. You know, about learnin' new positions and stuff.''

"Yeah, I suppose so," Ethel said, unsure.

"But it's different if the picture happens to be of the person you're with," Ken added quickly, with more optimism. "Then it's not perverted, 'cause your sharin' the moment with the person in the photograph.''

Ethel rubbed her fingers through his lacquered hair, and thought she felt it give slightly. She was confused by what he was saying.

"Did you used take pictures of your wife?'' she asked timidly.

Ken frowned and dropped his head.

"Let's not bring my deceased wife into this, Ethel," he said softly, after a pause. "She's nothin' but a cherished memory, bless her soul. But what matters now is you and I. And its only because of the deep trust I feel with you that I've even got the courage to mention it. I mean, I think I'd just die of shame if this were to ever go beyond you and me.''

"I'm sorry Ken," Ethel said, upset with herself for having brought up such a painful topic. "You don't ever have to worry about me tellin' anybody about what happens between us. But I'm just not sure if I'm followin' exactly what you're sayin'. Do you want to take a picture of me or somethin'? I mean, you don't even have a camera.''

Ken grazed his hand over the electric part of Ethel's thigh near her groin, a gesture that made her quiver.

"I've got one in the bag," he said, looking back down as if ashamed to admit it. "But I wouldn't want to do anything that you wouldn't be willing to allow." He paused and moved his body closer to hers. "All I do know is I that want to make love to you so bad...for our bodies to join together atop these very sheets and experience an unrelinquished feeling of joy.''

Ethel stared beyond his caring, sincere face to a landscape painting bolted to the wall. She wasn't sure if she liked the idea of being photographed

253

in a provocative position, but what she did know was that the sensuous movement of his hand coupled with his last words had sent a heat flash surging through her loins, and that she was desperate to have its spark ignited once again.

"Well, if that's what you need sweetheart," she finally breathed, moving her mouth closer to his. "You just position me however the hell you want and let me take care of the rest."

32

When Wayne entered the kitchen, he saw Darlene sitting in the family room curled up on the sofa and watching television. The playpen was pulled up next to the chair, and the two infants were staring off inquisitively in different directions. The room smelled like baby shit.

"Where's your mother?" he asked her.

Darlene jerked her head quickly toward him, so engrossed in the TV show that she had been unaware of his presence.

"Oh, hi Daddy," she said. "You scared me."

"Hi," he responded unenthusiastically. "Where the hell is your mother?"

"She's over at her friend's house playin' cards," Darlene said, looking back toward the TV. "She said she was gonna come back around five."

Wayne looked at his watch and saw that it was still over an hour away.

"I thought her bridge game was on Tuesday," he said, frowning.

"It is," Darlene muttered. "But they've also started playin' on Thursday, too."

Wayne walked over to the refrigerator and pulled out a package of bologna and a jar of mayonnaise. He sat down at the table to fix a sandwich, pissed off that he had to do this himself. He'd just have to tell Ethel to switch the time of her card game so that she could be there when he got home. Here he was working sixteen hours a day and, when he returned, she was off playing cards. He felt the least he deserved was to have something waiting for him when he came in the door.

Wayne made another sandwich and walked over to the window, observing his garden through the glass. Because he had less free time than in years past, it was smaller than usual, and the plants appeared to be slow to sprout. He stared glumly at its lack of progress, then frowned when he noticed the poison sumac near the wall had begun spreading around the base of his corn stalks.

"Where's Junior?" he called to his daughter.

"I don't know," she responded while rattling something at one of the twins. "He's proba'ly still at school."

"You know I told him to get rid of that sumac last weekend," he said, coming into the room and tickling one of the infants. "And he still hasn't done it."

"Can you move, Daddy?" Darlene asked, adjusting her large body on the seat. "You're blockin' my view."

Wayne slowly shifted his frame to the other side of the playpen and began making some faces at the other girl.

"What is this garbage you're watchin' anyway?" he said, staring up at the screen.

"It's not garbage!" she said, scowling at him. "It's one of those talk shows. Today they're talkin' about people that had sex change operations and got married afterwards."

Wayne grunted and stared at the television, only to see some freak who used to be named Daniel but who was now Danielle.

"That person is sick," he said, disgusted. "And I don't know if you should be watchin' this."

"Oh, c'mon Daddy!" she said, shaking her head toward him. "I'll be eighteen years old next month. And it's daytime television, for God's sake!"

Wayne stared back at the screen. His face was twisted with repulsion.

"Yeah, well, that girl...or guy...or whatever the hell it is, is a very, very sick person," he finally said. "And you'd think whoever ran the networks could think of somethin' more beneficial to put on instead of this trash. I mean, that just goes against nature. Next thing you know..."

"Dad, will you please be quiet!" Darlene interrupted him. "I can't even hear what they're sayin'!"

Wayne loudly rattled a toy close to the face of one of the twins. But instead of smiling playfully, as she'd done before, she began crying.

"Oh Jesus!" Wayne hissed, throwing down the toy.

"Now look what you've done!" Darlene spat irately. She reached into the playpen and grabbed the scared girl. "I asked you nicely to be quiet, didn't I?"

"Don't worry," Wayne said, slightly annoyed with her tone. "It's not a big deal. You just shut Gladys up and I'll leave the room."

She pushed the girl against her breast and rocked her gently.

"It's Crystal, not Gladys," she said, returning her eyes to the television.

"All right, Crystal, then," Wayne said, rolling his eyes. He felt embarrassed by his error and tried to defend himself. "I mean, they're identical twins for God's sake! Sometimes mistakes can be made."

Darlene was too engrossed in the program again to listen, so Wayne returned to the kitchen and reached into the refrigerator for a jar of pickles. He washed them down with a glass of milk. Wayne moved to put his boots on and go do a little work in the garden. Maybe he'd even get rid of the sumac himself.

Wayne moved down the hallway, pausing at his son's open door and gazing at the mess inside. He entered the room and picked up some of Junior's clothes off the floor and threw them into a corner. He noticed the stale smell of dirt and perspiration that weighed down the air in the room. Wayne opened the window and, as he stepped backwards, felt something on the floor crack beneath his weight.

Wayne reached down, threw a dirty t-shirt into the corner, and lifted a framed picture from the floor that had rested beneath the t-shirt. The shattered glass that had covered the photo dropped onto the matted black carpet. He dumped the rest of the glass into a wastebasket and sat down on the bed to view the image he had stepped on.

It was a faded newspaper clipping of Junior and Ethel standing out in the backyard of their house. Junior was so small that he only reached the second rung of a fence beside them. Ethel had her hand on his shoulder and was smiling proudly, and Junior was staring into the camera suspiciously while clutching his father's old .22-caliber rifle in front of him.

The photo was taken about eight years ago, when they lived in Kentucky and Wayne was away working for the coal company in Virginia. A few days before the newspaper man came around to take the photo, Ethel was at home looking after the kids as usual. While cooking dinner, she had heard a continued noise near the garage and gone outside with a frying pan to investigate. She told the children to get the family's gun. While checking the side of the house, Ethel was confronted unexpectedly by a man with a blue bandana covering his face. She immediately tried to run, but the man grabbed her around the neck and put a knife to her throat.

As she struggled to loosen the man's grip, Junior suddenly appeared with the rifle and told the assailant to let his mother go. The man tightened his grip around Ethel and told the boy to drop his weapon. But instead of obeying his demands, Junior responded by cocking the gun. The man apparently believed the little boy was actually going to shoot him, and loosened his grip on Ethel. As she broke away, the man turned and disappeared running down the road.

Ethel called the police and, an hour or so later, a man matching the description of the criminal was arrested not far from their home. There was a story about the incident along with the photograph in the local newspaper, and the article stated that Junior's gutsy behavior had probably saved the rest of the family's lives. Wayne smiled at the image and remembered how proud he was that his son had reacted so swiftly under pressure. Even though the gun was unloaded because Junior hadn't had time to find the shells, he had responded just as Wayne had instructed him to do in the face of danger.

Wayne wiped the dust off the top of the frame and put the photo on the bed beside him. He suddenly felt depressed. The memory made him realize just how much his son's character and attitude had changed. Where he had once been an obedient, respectful child, he was now an insubordinate, unruly teenager.

Wayne figured Junior's defiant behavior probably began a couple of years ago, when he got his paper route. Junior had extra money to spend on himself and was no longer completely dependendent on the small allowance Wayne gave him. Junior began going into town on his own to waste his money on video games with his friends, instead of playing the one Wayne had given him. After several heated arguments with Wayne, Junior quit the Boy Scouts—he claimed he "just wasn't into it" anymore. It annoyed Wayne at the time because he knew the values the Boy Scouts promoted were important to a growing kid. But in the end, Wayne figured that Junior's participation on some of the sports teams at school would at least add to the valuable experience he picked up during his years with the Scouts. So Wayne finally decided to encourage him in those activities instead.

Junior had been a decent athlete until he bought his stereo and began throwing all his money away on horrible records. After that, he refused to get his hair cut. He claimed long hair was now the style that all his friends had, and that he didn't want to look like a nerd. Shortly thereafter, Junior started smoking and, when Wayne caught him out back, he punished the boy severely—which certainly taught him not to smoke around the house. But Junior continued smoking near school, and the third time he got caught, he was kicked off the baseball team. Fortunately, Wayne convinced the coach to reconsider his decision, and Junior was allowed to practice with the team again.

But just two weeks ago, Junior was suspended from school along with two other friends for pulling a fire alarm. The kid just didn't know where to draw the line, Wayne felt. Even though Wayne took away Junior's stereo and assigned him additional chores around the house, Wayne really didn't have time to play the enforcer any longer, as he had in the past. Everything had changed because of the additional hours he was forced to take on at the Mini-Mart in order to make ends meet.

Ethel assured Wayne that she was making sure his word was upheld at home, although her ability to control Junior was becoming highly suspect as well. Just a couple of weeks ago, while Ethel sat on her fat ass in front of the TV, Wayne came in from the shed and smelled cigarette smoke coming from Junior's room. Wayne was forced to deal with the situation himself. After smashing a couple of his son's records, he yelled at Ethel for letting Junior get away with things right under her nose. She feigned ignorance, but the event just confirmed Wayne's suspicion that she let the kid do whatever he wanted.

Wayne stared at the posters covering his son's walls. The sports stars that once hung there had been completely replaced by the hideous grins and lewd gestures of rock stars. He stared at these "people." Their skinny bodies were wrapped in studded black leather. They stuck their tongues out and handled their instruments as if they were sex organs. Scantily clad women stood beside some of them, monsters from some vision of Armageddon behind others, and a few pictured musicians whose gender Wayne was completely unsure of. It reminded him of the defects on the program Darlene was watching.

But it wasn't until Wayne's gaze fell on the poster directly in front of him that he felt the sudden need to react. It showed a long-haired urchin with crooked teeth and warts all over his face holding up his middle finger arrogantly, defiantly. Printed beneath it in bold, gothic lettering were three words Wayne couldn't bear: "FUCK THE LAW!"

Wayne sprang from the bed and tore the poster from the wall with one quick sweep of his hand. He felt satisfied with his action, so he quickly reached for another poster and pulled it down just as easily. Taking a step to the side, Wayne yanked another one down. He felt joyous at the sensation of crumbling such garbage within his powerful clasp, and he soon found himself moving along the walls as if in a frenzy, reaching up with both hands and ripping down everything in sight.

When Wayne had finished, he stared at the blank walls surrounding him. He breathed forcefully for a moment, trying to get his breath back. He picked up the portrait of Junior and Ethel from the bed, hung it on a nail sticking out from the wall and stepped back to admire his redecorating touch.

Wayne retrieved all the crumpled posters from the floor and crushed them against his chest. He closed the bedroom door behind him and headed toward the garbage cans outside.

"That little bastard will learn his lesson this time," he thought as he smiled contentedly.

33

Although all her peers seemed to think Darlene was friendly and had a nice smile, she had never been very successful with boys. As sad as that was for her, she didn't really blame guys for never asking her out on dates. All she had to do was look at her high school yearbook to see why. Her fat, round face was surrounded by overgrown, frizzy, dark brown hair, and her widely spaced eyes were covered by a steel-rimmed pair of glasses. She even admitted it herself: She was an ugly duckling.

Calvin Smith was not what one would consider very good-looking, either. He was about half a foot taller than Darlene and weighed a lot less. His medium-length, greasy brown hair was usually matted to his head because he rarely seemed to wash it. He wore thick, black-framed glasses that were fastened together with tape on one side. Whether he was standing or sitting, his head was always directed toward the floor, and he wore the same pair of dirty overalls every day that he had clearly outgrown.

Darlene had seen Calvin at the Jennings County Technical School a number of times and knew that he was studying tractor mechanics. They never spoke to each other until a pair of mutual friends set them up on a blind date. On that occasion, the two couples went bowling together. Although Calvin wasn't very forthcoming, Darlene made some small conversation with him. She learned that he lived a few towns away and had a part-time job on a pig farm, where every day after school he'd prepare the mush for the hungry hogs. He was planning to join the army as soon as he turned eighteen in July. He seemed like a nice enough guy, whose sporadic conversation was probably due to his shyness—something Darlene certainly could understand, since she felt exactly the same way most of the time.

In the weeks that followed, Calvin didn't speak to her again, and Darlene finally figured that he was probably embarrassed about getting outbowled by Darlene in the first two games. She figured it was only natural that a boy would be embarrassed by losing to a girl, let alone in front of friends. So Darlene didn't blame Calvin for not talking to her. It bugged her that she had been so stupid; after all, she should have told him that she had bowled every Saturday for years as a kid.

As the weeks rolled by, she didn't get the chance to let Calvin know how she felt, or to apologize for the bowling oversight. The senior prom was drawing near and all her friends started talking about their plans for that evening. Darlene began to fear that she was once again going to be excluded from the school's social activities because of her inability to attract a date. It troubled her, because what she longed for was a steady boyfriend that she could talk to her friends about, instead of constantly being an outsider to their conversations.

Darlene knew she'd finish her beautician's course before long and, therefore, her schooling. Then it would be summer. And while her friends went out with their boyfriends or got married—as several already had plans to do—she'd be alone, sweating it out with the old ladies at Mario's or looking after her sisters. It wasn't a very bright prospect for the future. Yet Darlene thought it would at least be bearable if she had a steady guy and the hope of a baby of her own to pamper and play with.

She heard from her mutual friend that Calvin hadn't asked anybody to go with him to the prom. Darlene realized that he wasn't going to ask her himself, so she finally worked up the guts to call the only boy she had ever gone out with. When she finally asked Calvin to go to the dance, he made a few nervous excuses. But, with Darlene's encouragement, he finally agreed to go.

Although Darlene was very inexperienced at dating, she had plenty of opportunities between her beauty classes to hear about the adventures that many of her friends shared with boys. And through those stories, she learned vicariously what a boy really wanted out of a girl. It was one thing if a girl was pretty or had a fantastic personality, but another thing altogether if she hadn't been blessed with those things. She figured that most boys didn't give a hoot if a girl was a nice person, or knew how to do a manicure, or had a pretty smile. They were primarily interested in one thing—sex—and if they got that, they would most likely stick around.

At the same time, she also told herself that being overweight did have two advantages, and both of these graced her chest. She was well aware that she had the biggest chest measurement among her friends. But she always looked at her breasts as nothing more than two huge mounds that lay like lopsided pillows in front of her barreled torso, not something that boys dreamed about getting their hands on. When she finally came to that realization, she knew that if Calvin Smith were to be her boyfriend, she'd have to attract him in a way he desired. Darlene rapidly devised a plan for seducing her prom date.

With her mother's help, Darlene made a chiffon dress for the evening. She was careful not to make it too loose, as she normally wore her clothing. On the day of the dance, she had Mario himself work on her hair and another friend do her make-up. Before leaving the house, she doused her body with nearly a whole bottle of Avon perfume and dressed carefully.

But after Calvin drove her to the high school auditorium where the dance took place, her attempt to attract his attention didn't go very well. They both stood in the shadows, and Calvin expressed more interest in the snacks and punch than in Darlene. When she encouraged him to dance, he just shrugged his shoulders and refused. He claimed that he didn't know how to dance and would feel stupid if he even tried.

When the dance finally ended, the couples made their way out to the cars for the drive back home. As they made their way along the familiar roads leading back to her house, Darlene felt more disheartened. She felt as if she hadn't made any progress with the mission she had set out to accomplish. Here they were about to begin the summer, and she hadn't even kissed the guy she was already envisioning as her steady boyfriend.

As he pulled his borrowed pick-up truck to the foot of her driveway, Darlene suggested that they go on a bit further and talk a little more. It wasn't even midnight yet, she explained, and she didn't feel like going home yet. They drove on and he parked near an old dumping ground. As they talked, Darlene casually attempted to shift herself next to him. They talked for over an hour, and while Calvin maintained his distance, Darlene hung on to his every word and waited. That moment she had dreamed about was close, she just knew. They were about to undertake that uncomfortable pause, and their mouths would draw closer and closer together before finally making contact. The moment's electricity would bring to an end the nervousness, anxiety, and inhibition that separated them now.

After Calvin checked his watch and mentioned it was getting late, that moment came at last, although not exactly as she had envisioned it. What really happened was that Darlene simply thrust her massive chest against him, muscled his head closer to hers, and planted a huge, sloppy kiss somewhere around his left nostril. At first his head jerked back as if in self-defense, but gradually he succumbed to her assault. Darlene felt Calvin's hand touch her breast at the same moment that their tongues finally connected.

As she twisted her body on the seat, she heard her tight dress rip somewhere over the hip. The position pulled the dress even tighter over her chest, which distressed her. She knew that Calvin was trying to get his strong hands on her huge breasts, which was exactly where she wanted them. So with a quick jerk, she ripped the material that covered her bait, simultaneously struggling to raise her body toward his face. Beneath her, she heard him struggle—perhaps for his breath—and squirm in an attempt to escape. But she held on tight and pulled him in the opposite direction, so that he was on top of her. At that, he responded in the manner she wanted. Darlene was content that, at last, some of the animal noises filling the front seat of the pick-up weren't coming from herself alone.

She leaned back on the seat and pulled up her dress, then muscled him on top of her. Calvin unfastened his trousers rapidly, which convinced Darlene how much he wanted her, loved her even. She moved one leg toward the dashboard, held him tight, and let him do the rest.

It was all over in less than thirty seconds, and then the truck was enveloped in complete silence. She didn't feel much of anything, except for a slight cramp around her hip. But as Calvin moved his body off of hers, Darlene felt the slimy fluid between her legs and smiled. She had him, she thought: someone to love. And she had never felt so good in all her life.

34

Wayne parked across the street from a low-rent building and stared up at a fourth-story window. He double-checked the address, then nodded his head and coolly stamped out a cigarette in the car's ashtray. He got out, casually crossed the street, entered the building, and walked up the stairs as if he had done so a hundred times before. He reached the top floor, stared down the drab hallway, and made his way toward its only source of light—a dirt-covered window at the end. Through the thin walls lining the hallway, he heard a wave of sound combining music, television banter and foreign dialects. When he reached the final door, he knocked hard.

A woman who looked like a hooker poked her fat nose through the barely opened door and, upon seeing him, attempted to slam the door shut. Wayne took a quick step back and landed a kick in the middle of its metal surface, which sprung it open and sent the woman flying in the same direction. He entered the apartment and was faced by another door, a thinner one made of wood. Without even pausing, he reared back, fired a punch at it, and broke it clean off its hinges; it fell in splinters to the ground.

In the corner of the room, Wayne saw the little cretin he was there to detain—a bastard who had borrowed bond money from a loan company and then skipped bail. The guy was obviously frightened. As terror overtook his beady eyes and saliva ran off his puffy lips, he looked like a cornered animal before an unconquerable foe. The bail jumper quickly reached for the nearest object, a wooden chair, and heaved it in Wayne's direction. Wayne deflected the chair effortlessly. The fugitive then made for the window, but before he reached it, Wayne was all over him.

Wayne grabbed him by the belt and the scruff of the neck and heaved him across the room, where the guy bounced like a rag doll off the wall and onto the floor. Before he could get up, Wayne had him again and threw him toward another wall. Wayne could hear the whore screaming behind him, but he didn't stop. As the urchin attempted to get up off the floor, Wayne sent a kick to his stomach, which doubled him over, and then another to his face, which sent him reeling backwards.

The scumbag lay in a crumpled mass, gasping for breath and

beginning to spit up blood. Wayne grabbed him by the hair and brought him to his feet, and led the shithead out the door and to justice.

The sound of the news ticker machine printing out reports jarred the would-be bounty hunter back to reality. Wayne lifted his head from the desktop and adjusted his eyes to the things on it: a couple of styrofoam coffee cups, a magazine, and a half-filled ashtray. He stared at a cigarette he must have lit just before falling asleep; its form was still intact, although its contents had burned entirely. From the control room he could hear the muffled sound of some horrendous song.

Wayne rubbed the back of his neck and checked his watch. He had slept through one of his rounds, and another one was upon him. Yawning, he picked up one of the cups and walked over to the coffee machine where he filled it and stirred in some creamer. He checked some late-night sports results on the news machine, then walked the length of the trailer, toward a stack of duplicate albums used for production purposes. He began looking through them. Halfway through, he decided to stop, though. He couldn't find one he recognized, and he didn't want to waste more of his time by looking at the ridiculous photos that graced their covers.

Wayne tossed the cup into the garbage, unlocked the door, and stepped outside. A few stars peaked through the haze-covered sky, and above a thick silhouette of pine trees, he could see a nearly full moon. He walked slowly along the pothole-riddled driveway, waving his arms around to dry out his armpits. When he reached the gate, Wayne directed his flashlight beam at the metal chains wrapped tightly around the steel bars and saw it was secured as usual.

Wayne lit a cigarette and stared back at the trailer. He could see the silhouette of the female DJ moving behind the curtains in the area where he normally sat.

She'd taken over Timmo's shift a couple of months before, but since then, Wayne hadn't spoken to her much at all because she didn't seem to like the fact that he was there. He found it strange that the only time she'd come out of the control room was when he'd gone out to make his rounds. After all, he always greeted her with a smile and was polite to her. He even made a few suggestions about the type of music she might play to pick up more listeners. But she shrugged off his advice, just like the other DJ. Wayne just couldn't get it into their thick skulls that country music was where it's at.

Wayne trampled through the overgrown grass along the fence and felt its dampness seeping through a hole in his shoe. The sound of crickets and other night insects filled the still air with a shrill symphony. Wayne added to their noise by whistling his off-key version of the melody from one of his favorite Merle Haggard songs. In the distance, the weak moonlight reflected dimly off a small pond, and he could barely make out a muskrat leaving the bank and entering the water. He watched its body cross through the still, black pond until it finally disappeared behind thick underbrush. Wayne flipped his cigarette in its direction before making his way back to the trailer.

Once inside, he poured himself another cup of coffee and turned on a radio that sat on top of a filing cabinet. He tuned it to a station that he liked, leaned back in his chair, picked up a detective magazine, and flipped through it for a story he hadn't read. While reading some of the headlines, a smile suddenly crossed his face as he thought about his apprehension of the bail-skipper earlier in his dream. But the abbreviated image disappeared as he realized that it was all just a fantasy. That depressed him, because it seemed that the only recent excitement in his life came through daydreams that shot in and out of his groggy mind as he passed his boring work hours at the radio station.

Wayne stared down at a black-and-white photograph and shook his head. A tough-looking cop was leading a handcuffed con into the courtroom for his trial. The cop eyed the criminal that he had collared with disgust. Skimming through the article, Wayne read several quotes from the lawman that detailed the procedures used in apprehending this piece of filth. Turning the page, Wayne saw another photo of the same cop seated behind the wheel of his cruiser. His name was underneath along with the quote, "He helped bring the vicious perp to justice."

Wayne abruptly threw the magazine on the table and dejectedly reached for a smoke.

For years, Wayne had envisioned his own face gracing the pages of *Detective Dragnet, Official Detective,* or even *Detective Files.* But it now appeared as if that dream was moving further and further away from his grasp. While the others put their lives on the line and grabbed the headlines, he sat on his ass in a stuffy trailer, smoking cigarettes, drinking coffee, and checking to make sure a chain-link fence was locked. No one except employees had ever pulled their cars up to the gate since he had been there, and he couldn't even remember the last time he had been involved in some sort of altercation, let alone taken his gun from his holster. It just seemed that his current life was one big bore.

Yet that was Wayne's reality because Vanguard still hadn't come through with what they had promised. He was offered a job patrolling the entrances of large office buildings in Indianapolis, as well as the opportunity to return to the back of the bank truck. But the thought of going back to that stuffy metal box on wheels was like taking a huge step backwards. In fact, Wayne really didn't think it was any better than sitting around at the radio station every night—which at least was not far from home and enabled him to work extra hours at the Mini-Mart.

Having to make ends meet by working as a cashier at the convenience store was especially degrading. Just the year before, Wayne was in charge of security for an entire supermarket that was twenty times the size of the Mini-Mart. Now, instead of watching over a huge expanse of floor space and merchandise as though it were his, he was relegated to standing behind a tiny counter and punching a cash register for little kids who came in to buy candy. To make matters worse, he had to wear a stupid green-and-white uniform and endure the ridiculous small talk of his fellow employees—people he couldn't even say he commanded.

In spite of his unhappiness, Wayne felt there wasn't much he could do except remain with the two demeaning jobs. After all, the small paychecks from both jobs were essential to making ends meet. Fortunately, Junior had found an extra job on weekends washing dishes at a restaurant, so at least he could help out with a few dollars for food. Darlene continued giving part of what little money she brought home as well. But even with their additional, if minimal contributions, he still found himself falling behind more than ever and unable to purchase even something small for himself once in a while. Just that afternoon he received the electric bill, and the amount due stunned him. And then there were the usual medical bills for the twins, increased car insurance, payments for the appliances, his wife's medication...the list just went on and on.

Wayne knew he couldn't put a stop to the constant influx of bills; all that he could do, he figured, was try to keep abreast of the debts, to keep his head above water and continue to struggle to keep afloat. He supposed he would call Vanguard later in the day and try to pick up a few more shifts doing whatever they had available, which meant that his free time would be brought down to little more than sleeping.

Wayne rubbed his tired eyes and shook his head at the prospect. He stood up and walked the length of the trailer several times, pausing occasionally to stare at the common objects laying upon the table tops. He had studied these things often, but had learned nothing further for all his concentration. Inside the control room, he heard the DJ clear her throat and then speak to her audience with a smooth voice before starting another record.

Wayne returned to the coffee machine, poured himself another cup, and reassumed his position at the table. He stared straight forward, and between the curtains, he saw that the sky had begun its gradual shift from black to gray—the beginning of a new day. For many people it also signified some sort of hope, or a new beginning, or another chance.

But not for Wayne. All it meant for him was that one shift was about to end, and another about to begin.

35

"Make sure you don't have the temperature too high!" Ethel yelled across the room to her eldest daughter.

Darlene continued ironing in the opposite corner of the kitchen.

"You know that polyester blend can't take as much heat as pure cotton," Ethel reminded her.

"I know," Darlene said. She checked the temperature gauge, just to make sure. "I learned that lesson last week, when I burnt one of Daddy's shirts."

"That was such a shame," Ethel said, pulling a few clean plates from the dishwasher and shaking her head. "He just bought that the week before, too."

"I know," Darlene answered despondently. "He told me that about a hundred times."

"Well, don't worry," Ethel said over the clang of the silverware. "He'll get over it in time, just like he did with that shirt I spilt bleach onto and stained real bad." She looked over at Darlene and then at an orange-and-yellow-print shirt her daughter was folding. "Where'd you get that blouse, anyway?" she asked.

"Ain't it nice?" Darlene smiled, rubbing the material between her fingers. "I got it at the Wal-Mart the other day after work. Unfortunately, it was the last one they had in my size or I would've bought another one."

Ethel put some glasses onto a shelf.

"Well, there should be some sales in a couple of months, once the winter stuff starts comin' out," she said. "Maybe you can find somethin' else you like, then."

"I hope so," she said as she ran the iron over the material. "'Cause I wouldn't mind havin' a new pants suit, or somethin' to try to find a better job in."

Ethel rinsed off the breakfast plates and loaded them into the machine. "What happened to that job you went for yesterday, anyway? The one in the old folks' home?"

Darlene exhaled noisily. "They said they were just lookin' for someone to work a few hours every afternoon doin' little stuff around the place, like emptyin' bedpans and helpin' some of the patients eat their food. So if I took that job, I'd have to give up workin' at the beauty parlor. And even though I'm only workin' twenty-five hours a week there, it is what I'm trained in, so I guess I'd rather stay at the job I got."

"I just don't know what's the matter with them at Mario's," Ethel said, wiping her hands. "You do such good work on my hair all the time, and you really should be doin' more than just washin' people's hair. He should have you workin' every day. Which reminds me," she added as she lit a cigarette. "My friend Tina told me she'd like to have you cut her hair over at her place some day next week."

"Great!" Darlene said. She put the iron down and reached for another garment. "What does she want to have done?"

"I think she wants to have a perm of some sort," Ethel said. "And maybe have a few blonde streaks put in. You know, the kind of hairstyle like lots of women have nowadays. I think it'll look real good on her, too."

"Well, at least I'll get to practice on somebody," Darlene said, pleased with the prospect. "Now that I don't have people at the school to practice on anymore, I think I'm gettin' a little bit rusty."

"Keep your spirits up, honey," Ethel said, tossing some old circulars into the garbage. "If Mario has any sense, he'll start givin' you some more responsibility pretty soon. And if he doesn't, I'm sure you'll find another job in a place where your talents are appreciated."

Darlene looked down and grunted, not quite as optimistic as her mother.

"Yeah," Darlene said after a pause. "Just like I'm gonna get a boyfriend, too."

"Oh c'mon, Darlene," Ethel said, moving toward her. "Just what are you talkin' about? You've only been out on one date, for God's sake."

"Two," Darlene corrected her.

"Well, two then," Ethel said, rubbing her on the shoulder. "What was his name, anyway? Floyd or somethin'?"

"Calvin," Darlene muttered. "Calvin Smith. And he went off and joined the army."

"Well, I'm sure you'll see him when he comes back home."

"No, I won't," Darlene said quickly. "'Cause he didn't even call me before he left. And when I finally called him, the phone was disconnected. So I found out where he lived and went over there myself to see him, and whoever was livin' there now told me his parents moved out to New

Mexico or somethin'. So I guess I'll never see him again."

"He sounds like a jerk to me, then," Ethel said flatly. "And if he couldn't appreciate your qualities," she continued reassuringly, "then it's just his loss. I mean, there's a lot more fish in the pond than one little snapper. Right?"

Darlene lowered her head and began biting her lower lip. She knew that what her mother was saying made sense, but she just couldn't bring herself around to thinking the same way. After all, she'd given the guy exactly what she thought would bring him closer to her but, in the end, it hadn't gotten her what she wanted. Her chances of finding a husband, she felt, were about as good as the likelihood of Mario giving her a full-time job at the salon. She just didn't seem to be cut out for either of them.

"I guess so," she finally said feebly, stretching a dress over the ironing board.

"There you go!" Ethel encouraged her.

Darlene looked at her mother and smiled.

"Yeah," she said, as she wiped a tear away from her eye. "But I just wish somethin' would come along soon that would bring a little joy into my life."

"Don't worry, Darlene," Ethel said. "It will, believe me. Just be patient. Rome wasn't built in a day, you know."

Darlene pulled another garment over the ironing board and smiled warmly.

"Thanks, Momma," she said.

"Don't mention it, honey," Ethel said. "That's what mothers' are for anyway. You'll know that someday."

"I hope so," Darlene said, picking up the iron again and dragging it over a dress.

Ethel picked up a couple of toys from the floor, wiped off the table, and unloaded the washing machine. She kicked open the outside door, then carried the basket of wet clothes across the grass until she reached the clothes line. Above her, clouds were scattered across a deep blue sky like huge, unraveled cotton balls. The sun stood high above them, providing a pleasant warmth rather than the oppressive humidity she had grown so weary of during the summer.

Ethel glanced at her watch. She felt a vague fuse of excitement begin to burn through her body, for in just a couple of hours, she would meet the man who had become her permanent lover. She experienced the sensation whenever she thought about Ken during the week, but on

Thursdays, it was always intensified. Its binding tension ultimately culminated in an explosion of sexual pleasure in one of the rooms at the Motel 6, where they always met.

Ken always took several photographs of Ethel so he could perform. Sometimes he spiced things up even more by bringing a costume for her to wear or a little prop, like a sexual gadget of some sort. His little quirks made her a little uncomfortable at first. But as she became more accustomed to his desires, she gradually began to find the photographic sessions incredibly erotic—an additional stimulation that added to her orgasmic ecstasy as well.

Throughout the hot summer, they made love two or three times an afternoon. With each additional session they shared, the amount of time they spent naked, twisting fervently on the damp sheets, grew longer as the periods of communication during their recovery periods grew shorter.

Ethel didn't mind the fact that they didn't exchange that much personal information. She didn't want to feel a strong emotional attachment to her lover, anyway. After all, she had no desire to leave her family behind. Likewise, Ken had his commitment to his deceased wife, so their relationship seemed ideal. Even so, she had to pinch herself once in a while to be reminded that it was all happening to her because, in a way, she couldn't imagine why such an eligible widower like Ken would be so attracted to her enormous physique.

What she did know was that she sure as hell enjoyed Ken's narrow fingers grazing across her tingling flesh and certainly didn't want it to stop. For a couple of hours a week, she felt like a desired woman, and then she'd kiss her Romeo goodbye and return to her normal life at home. At times, she just couldn't envision her life being any better; she could play the mother of young children, the housewife, the knowledgeable parent, the middle-aged woman, and the whore. It was like everything she could ever wish for, wrapped into one.

There were only two drawbacks to the whole situation: She had to increase her intake of Valium and other medications just to calm her anticipatory jitters; and, her husband occasionally wanted a little bit of nookie himself. As always, he chose a time that was convenient to him only, like while she was engrossed with one of her evening television programs or doing something like changing the twins' diapers.

Fortunately, she was usually able to somehow get around the unpleasant encounter. But sometimes she had to acknowledge the vows she had taken at the altar, and follow him into the darkened room to let him have his way. At times he would attempt to caress her and be as passionate as he was capable of being. But, because he was never even able to bring her past the stage of slight lubrication, she'd just end up laying back and pretending she was at the motel room. It was only by doing that that she felt it possible to experience even the slightest form of pleasure.

Then it would suddenly be over, and Wayne would jump up and throw on his trousers and make his way out to work. And she would be left on the bed, thinking of Ken. Ken and his camera.

"Ken," she said out loud, rubbing her lips.

"Momma!" Darlene yelled excitedly from the kitchen door, suddenly sidetracking her thoughts. "Get in here quick! Gladys just said somethin'!"

Ethel clipped the last sheet to the line and ran toward the house with the basket.

"What did she say?" she called, entering the family room.

"Listen!" Darlene said, her eyes smiling broadly behind her glasses. "She talked for the first time!"

Ethel squatted down in front of the multi-colored playpen and stared at the identical twins.

"What'd you say?" she whispered to Gladys. "Tell your momma!"

Gladys looked back and forth at the two figures hunched in front of her with a confused expression. Then she slammed her hands down on a rubber ball and made a string of unintelligible noises similar to those her sister made. But suddenly from the nonsense, a word crept from between her spit-covered lips that nearly floored Ethel.

"Food!" the infant yelled. "Food!"

Ethel's mouth hung open as she stared at the girl, but her chapped lips finally began to arrange themselves in the form of a smile.

"Food!" Crystal suddenly imitated her sister while pounding on the side of the playpen. "Food!"

Darlene burst out laughing.

"Ain't it funny," she said while rubbing both girls' finger-length hair. "I can tell right now. They're gonna be just like their momma!"

"Yeah, just like their momma," Ethel smiled while picking Gladys up. "So let's give them exactly what they want," she added, delighted with the prospect of a little snack herself.

36

The Tender Trap was a small, private club that had the appearance of an old speakeasy, with red-and-black-velvet covered walls and a low ceiling from which numerous red Chinese lanterns hung. A long bar stood against one wall and, opposite it, on the other side of the room, a small wooden stage rose about a foot above the floor. Scattered around the rest of the room were numerous circular tables, half of which were occupied by an entirely male clientele.

Wayne sat at a table about ten feet from the stage and smoked a cigar. A waitress had just asked him again if he wanted to buy a drink but, as before, he told her he wasn't thirsty yet. Again, she reacted with an annoyed look.

Wayne was not in the habit of smoking cigars, but then, he was in an unusually good mood. He figured he deserved the luxury of a Swisher Sweet because it finally seemed as if something was going right for him after over a year of disappointment and frustration.

Several weeks before, Wayne applied for a job as a corrections officer. Just a couple of hours ago, he was interviewed and given a physical at the State Corrections Office on the other side of Indianapolis. His interview had gone well, and he felt an instant and immediate rapport with his interviewers. They seemed impressed by his quick, confident responses and desire to become part of their team, and assured him that within a month, they would be back in contact. They even told him to be prepared to leave his other jobs at short notice—a hint that he would soon be hired, he reckoned.

The job opening came to Wayne's attention about a month and a half earlier. He saw it advertised in the classified section of the paper he read while whittling away his time at the radio station. The ad called for men between the ages of eighteen and forty-five with a handgun license and some sort of corrections-related experience. Wayne had lost faith that Vanguard would find him anything better in the near future, so he decided to send away for an application. When he received it, he completed it and sent it back the same day.

The prospect of new work eased the monotony of his sixteen-hour work days. Wayne knew that with his experience and qualifications, he was a virtual shoo-in for a job as a prison guard. Instead of staring at the walls of the radio station, he began reading every book the public library had dealing with criminal justice and the prison system. He re-read all the back issues of the detective magazines he had stored in the shed. As he gained new knowledge and re-evaluated what he already knew, he found his passion and ambitions for criminal justice returning. The only thing that puzzled him was why it had taken him so long to pursue his true vocation.

Over the past five years, Wayne had worn his badge proudly and done his utmost to live up to the "commandments" of *The Law Enforcement Officer's Pledge*. But it wasn't until recently that he came to the conclusion that only a slight minority of free people represented a threat to society's norms. Sure, every now and again, somebody broke the law, but they didn't typically cause any sort of permanent damage.

In the penitentiary, however, it was a completely different story. Within those four walls, society's defects were housed. They were the dangerous ones, who would kill you as soon as look at you. And they were the ones who had to be kept in line and learn their lessons the hard way, who had to pay for the grief and suffering they had recklessly caused innocent people. If they didn't learn, they had to be punished until they did, and the state stood four-square behind you in that mission. The penitentiary was exactly where Wayne saw his future, and that knowledge provided him with a deep, abiding sense of satisfaction like none he had ever experienced before.

It was because he felt so relaxed that Wayne now sat in The Tender Trap. He was anxiously awaiting a show he had seen advertised in a store where he had bought a cowboy hat after leaving his interview. The flyer announced a special week-long engagement of afternoon shows by Tiffany Lynn, the famous porn star. She was making her appearance on stage as part of her tour of strip clubs all across America. Since Wayne was in the area, and because he felt he deserved a little diversion, he drove to the club and forked over the seven-dollar admission without even thinking about it. After all, Tiffany Lynn had provided him with a lot of entertainment over the years, and he figured he wouldn't mind seeing his favorite porn star in the flesh at least once in his life.

Wayne lit another cigar and noticed that most of the tables were now occupied. Suddenly, the lights were brought down. One by one over five minute intervals, a series of girls took the stage and danced to a song played by a DJ in the back of the club. The music boomed from the speakers, and its rhythm compelled each girl to spin around and prance atop the stage. Each girl gradually removed her top, gyrated her hips with more energy, and shook her breasts around more fervently. The younger-looking ones didn't have to do anymore than that, and they frequently caught tips from the men near the stage in the waistbands of their g-strings. But as the show went on, the cock-teasers were replaced by older, more-weathered women, most of whom looked like they had been around the block a few times. They weren't much to look at, but they made up for their physical inadequacies by being daring. They bent over and flashed their wares openly, for this was the only way they would collect any tips at all.

When the last dancer finished, the girls began mingling in the audience to solicit more tips. Wayne shrugged them off, but finally coughed up a few quarters to a skinny woman with a hare lip who insisted on bumping and grinding her crotch near his face. When she finally sauntered off, another waitress approached him for a drink. But as before, Wayne refused their hard-sell tactics.

As the women repeated their rounds and asked for more tips, Wayne decided to avoid them by heading for the bathroom. When he returned to his seat, the lights were dim again, and as he glanced toward the stage, she was suddenly there.

Tiffany Lynn, in person. Her bronzed, statuesque body set off by a hot-pink bikini bottom pulled high over her perfectly formed hips. She was topless, and she smiled confidently. In fact, she looked even better than she did in her films. She wiggled her hips, then brought her hand down over her crotch and rubbed the thin material while saleciously sliding her practiced tongue in, out, and around her glossy lips.

Then she was down on the floor and arching her back, provocatively cupping her perfectly rounded breasts as the sensuous groans of a love song pulsated through her throbbing body and drove its shameless flesh further.

Like a python, Tiffany oozed in her sensuous, oiled body, sliding along the floor and gradually contorting her figure until she was on her knees. As she seductively licked her fingertips and tweaked her erect, maroon nipples, she slowly rose, then reached one hand inside the thin cloth of the bikini. She rubbed it suggestively several times. From where he sat, Wayne could hear her groaning over the loud music, and he felt the tension within his stiff member mounting against his fly. He eagerly anticipated her next step, but as she was just about to bring the material down, the song

277

suddenly faded out and the stage went black.

When the lights came back up several moments later, Tiffany Lynn, the shining star, was gone.

A voice blared over the speakers, informing the spectators that the show was over. There were several shouts of disapproval, but gradually all the guys in the crowd began piling out. Wayne followed them, agitated that Tiffany hadn't shown more and put on a real show, as she did in her movies, as he had expected. For a seven-dollar entry fee, he reckoned, something like that was certainly called for.

The crowd bottlenecked at the door and, when Wayne finally passed through it, he saw the now-fully clothed star standing in the foyer behind a thin white rope. In front of her, a white-haired man in a tuxedo was taking pictures of the starlet next to her fans. Standing alongside both of them was another guy with a lot of cash in his hands.

"Five bucks for a picture next to your favorite star!" he barked repeatedly. The barker caught Wayne's eye and winked at him.

Wayne stopped and glared angrily at the man. He was furious at what he was witnessing. After all, Tiffany didn't even take her bottom off! The other girls had flashed a little, and they probably weren't getting a tenth of the money she was. Who the hell did she think she was, he asked himself—some sort of goddess?

Hell no, he reckoned, as he glanced at the glossy lips that had sucked hundreds, if not thousands of pricks without shame. In the end, she was nothing but a conniving, capricious little nobody who thought she was some kind of queen.

"Only five bucks!" the barker continued, beaming his attention toward the others. "A pittance for your picture beside a classy lady like Miss Lynn!"

Wayne looked scornfully toward the star, who was smiling falsely for a photo with some kid. He looked like a college student who had never been laid in his life. Wayne shook his head and frowned, then pushed his way through the crowd and made his way out the door. He decided that he'd never watch another Tiffany Lynn movie again. The girl he once viewed as a star and a good actress had turned out to be nothing but a phony and a whore.

The streets were congested with the rush-hour traffic of thousands of commuters. As the Gremlin crept slowly toward the highway entrance, Wayne decided to make a slight detour and take another road heading east toward Dunlop, where one of the state's maximum security prisons was located. He figured that institution was the one where he would most likely be assigned, and he wanted to have a close look at it before he began working there. There was still another hour or so of daylight remaining, so he figured he could make some useful observations and take his mind off the load of shit he was just subjected to.

Wayne drove rapidly across the flat, straight roads that cut through thousands of acres of corn and wheat fields. Their monotony was broken occasionally by pig farms that lay along the route. A half an hour later, he saw an arrow-shaped sign bearing the prison's name and turned his car onto the road. He crossed through a small wooded area. When he arrived at the top of a small slope, he saw the looming, octagonal edifice, which sprung up from the flat fields surrounding it like a majestic cathedral. A huge floodlight revolved atop one of the taller structures within the walls, providing stark contrast against the thick, gray sky like a resilient star. Beside it, an American flag flapped proudly in the gentle wind.

Wayne was astonished. He thought it was one of the most beautiful sights he had ever seen. He felt his adrenaline beginning to flow and noticed the familiar odor of his own sweat fill the stuffy interior of his car. He sped forward and watched its form grow larger. He felt increasingly anxious to be next to it.

He drove by the main entrance, which was fenced off and heavily guarded. He continued on toward the other side of the structure and finally parked on the edge of a field, about a hundred yards away. Beside him, a farmer transversed his fields, tilling the spent earth methodically with a tractor. The plow's blades ruptured the dried, harvested stalks and pushed them deep into the soil, creating evenly spaced, geometric patterns from the upturned mulch.

Wayne lit another cigar and sat on the hood of his Gremlin, staring awestruck toward his future workplace. Its impenetrable red-brick walls were about twenty-five feet high, which effectively denied even the slightest glimpse into its private world. Only a jagged outline of the main cell block's roof and the domes of two different-sized water towers stood out from the walls. Polished barbed wire ran in continuous, identical circles atop the building's narrow lip, occasionally highlighted by the revolving beam reflecting off its shiny steel. The effect briefly gave the impression that the wire was alive with electrical current. Guard towers were placed strategically at each point of the octagon and, from his position, Wayne could see the silhouettes of attentive guards within several of them. Aside from the

279

distant hum of the tractor, the only sound breaking the silence was that of the facility's generator system, which filled the air with a gentle stream of white smoke and a continuous, comforting buzz.

Wayne adjusted the cowboy hat on his head and wondered what position he would be assigned within the fortified complex. He figured he would probably start out on the cell block, responsible for keeping all the inmates in line. He imagined himself walking the line along one of the tiers, running a truncheon against the iron bars of each cell. He would delight in waking up the convicted murderers, rapists, and other scum, and he'd laugh when they complained. Maybe he'd even put in a bad report on them just for the hell of it. If they didn't acknowledge that he was The Man, he'd simply take away some of their privileges, like their radios or yard time. Or if anyone gave him any lip, he'd just slam them down in solitary for a few days. And if one of them had the balls to continue behaving insubordinately under the rule of Wayne's iron hand, maybe a cracked head and a couple weeks in the hole would teach them just who they could and couldn't fuck around with.

Mixing it up with the incarcerated vermin and keeping them in line was probably where he'd start his career. But he didn't think that it would take very long to demonstrate to the administration that he was capable of more demanding work. Eventually he'd be transferred to one of the guard towers, where he could look down upon the inmates. With a high-powered rifle propped up beside him, in full view of all the inmates, he'd survey the area below him just as he had in the supermarket. He'd pick up the scent of trouble before any altercations broke out, and he'd keep the safety off his rifle, maybe even let the word get around that he was just itching to pull its trigger. And if someone tried to escape or, God forbid, a riot broke out, Big Wayne Turner would shoot to kill.

Additional lights suddenly slammed on to compensate for the approaching darkness. The outer walls were illuminated like a historic monument. Wayne removed his mirror shades and stared at the penitentiary. He wondered what the execution chamber within the structure looked like. He'd seen pictures of some in various magazines: the sturdy chair within a stark room—cold, ominous, waiting. For some reason, he thought that it would smell of musty leather, and told himself that one day he wanted to be inside there, pulling the switch.

Wayne ran his hand casually over his crotch and felt his dick harden through the worn material—just as it had a couple of hours earlier at the strip club, when Tiffany Lynn had taken the stage. He rubbed it gently and smiled, confident that before long he would indeed reach his goal.

37

"Why don't we just go home and I'll fix us somethin' to eat," Ethel said as Wayne steered the Gremlin into the parking lot. "We're spendin' enough money as it is, with the car bill and all. Maybe we should try to save a little."

"Don't worry about it," Wayne said. He turned and smiled at her as he steered the car into a parking space.

They had just dropped the Pacer off at a garage in town because Junior had driven the car over a curb while practicing for his road test with Ethel the week before. The garage had given Wayne a $215 estimate for replacing the tie-rod. But the expensive repair drew no complaints from Wayne now; this afternoon he had something important he wanted to tell his wife that completely overwhelmed his usual financial preoccupation. In fact, he'd decided to make a little celebration out of it, even if it meant spending a little extra money. Upon leaving the garage, Wayne drove straight to Hardees, an appropriate spot for sharing his news. After all, they both loved the food there and the place was having a promotion on fish burgers that week.

In the back of the car, the two baby girls were strapped into their car seats. They seemed anesthetized by the car's motion.

Wayne reached into his wallet and pulled out a five-dollar bill.

"Now you just go in there and get us a few fish burgers," he said. "And when you come back out, I got somethin' to tell you that's gonna make you happy."

Ethel glanced toward him with a puzzled look on her face.

"What is it?" she asked.

"What did I just say?" Wayne said, rolling his eyes. "Just get the food first and then I'll tell you." Wayne grabbed Ethel's hand and stuck the money into her sweaty palm.

Ethel continued to stare at him suspiciously, but she eventually got out of the car and headed toward the restaurant. When her husband loudly reminded her to get extra tartar sauce, she turned back briefly and nodded her head.

When Wayne saw Ethel enter the restaurant, he took a plain brown envelope out of his jacket pocket and stared at his name and address printed on the front. Wayne found it laying amidst the junk mail when he returned home from the Mini-Mart earlier that afternoon. He knew at once that it was the letter from the Corrections Department he had been anxiously anticipating for the past month. The letter informed him that after careful consideration, the placement committee had decided to assign him to the correctional facility in Windsor, about thirty miles northeast of Indianapolis, and that his training period was to commence at the beginning of November.

Wayne smiled smugly as he skimmed over the letter again. In only two weeks he would be issued another badge and uniform—this time the official brown uniform of the state of Indiana. He would immediately begin adding to his already extensive knowledge of criminal justice within the prison itself. At the end of the week, he'd give his notice to Vanguard and work until the end of the month. Maybe he'd throw in the towel at the Mini-Mart a few days before that, and take advantage of the free time by tending to a few things around the house that had been neglected. He stared out the window at a pumpkin stand across the street. Maybe he'd even buy a couple and carve them up as Halloween entertainment for the twins.

The door swung open and Ethel sank into the passenger seat.

"Did you get the extra tartar?" Wayne immediately asked her.

"Yes I did," she responded. Ethel opened the bag, poked her nose into it, and deeply inhaled the escaping fishy odor. She handed him a fish burger. "Now what is this big surprise you were talkin' about?"

Wayne handed her the letter and winked.

"Read it before you eat," he said. "'Cause I don't want you gettin' any greasy fingerprints on it. I'm thinkin' about gettin' it framed."

"What is it?" she asked. "A letter sayin' you won the lottery or somethin'?"

Wayne smiled and sighed heavily.

"Just read it," he said.

A confused expression crossed Ethel's face as she looked up at the envelope.

"State Corrections Department?" she said, puzzled. "When did you decide to apply for that?"

"A couple of months ago," Wayne smiled, exposing a mouthful of food. "I didn't tell you about it 'cause I wanted to wait 'til I knew for sure. And now you're holdin' the proof in your hands."

Ethel stared back at the letter and continued to read, silently pronouncing every word with her lips.

"But it says here that you're startin' at the Windsor facility," she stopped again. "And that's about eighty miles away."

"Yeah, I know," Wayne said. He wiped his hands on a napkin and grabbed the letter as he chewed. "All the spaces over at the Max must be full, but I'm sure I'll be movin' in there before long. This is a startin' point, and you got to begin somewhere—training, you know? I mean, I don't really like the fact that it's in the minimum security unit, 'cause from what I hear, it's almost like a country club over there in Windsor. Lots of guys in for white collar crime—embezzlement, forgery, pussy stuff like that. Lots of privileges, no trouble—boring, by the sound of it. But I would think that some older guards nearin' their retirement would want to be transferred over there, seein' what an easy ride it is. And believe me, they won't have to twist my arm to get me to work in the big house as soon as they give the word."

Ethel unwrapped a fish burger and took a bite.

"What's the salary?" she asked.

Wayne tore an edge off the roll and handed a piece to one of the girls, as if he were feeding an animal at the zoo.

"Less than I'm makin' now," he said, making a face at the infant. "But unlike now, every year it goes up."

Ethel reached into the bag for some fries and stuffed them into her mouth.

"How much less?" she asked, concerned.

"Just less," Wayne responded bluntly. "So it just means we're gonna have to make a few more sacrifices, that's all there is to it. And maybe Darlene is gonna have to make a real effort at findin' a better payin' job and Junior's gonna have to cough up a bit more, too—especially with this goddamn car bill."

Ethel felt a pit growing in her stomach. She put the sandwich down on her lap. She was not happy about his new plan and suddenly lost her appetite. What worried her most was that Wayne's new job might require a change in her own lifestyle, which she had grown very used to.

"But Wayne," she said. "How are you gonna work an extra job to pay the other bills if you got such a long way to commute every day?"

Wayne ignored his wife's concern and dangled another piece of bread in front of the other girl's face instead.

"Your daddy's gonna be a big prison guard," he addressed the smiling infant in a baby voice. "He's gonna make you proud."

"Did you hear what I just said?" Ethel asked.

283

Wayne reached into the bag and pushed some fries into his mouth.

"Yes, Ethel, I heard exactly what you said," he finally drawled, facing her. "And I'm gonna tell you right now that I don't want to hear anything else about it. Maybe you can even go out and get a part-time job again a couple of days a week while one of your card-playin' friends looks after the babies in their free time—which they seem to have plenty of, anyway."

Ethel shifted on the seat and pushed a straw through the plastic top of her drink.

"That's ridiculous Wayne," she said, shrugging off his suggestion. "You know I barely got enough time to do things around the house now as it is."

"Well, you seem to have enough time to play cards a couple of times a week."

Ethel started to correct him—she only played once a week—but, wisely, she held her tongue.

"I don't think a few hours a week of socializin' is to much to ask for," she finally said. "And I think you're gettin' off the main subject anyway."

An annoyed look crossed Wayne's face. He stared at her angrily.

"Ethel," he stated firmly. "I'm gonna say this once, and once only. In two weeks I'm beginnin' a new career within the state penal system. And I want to make this perfectly clear right now: I am not gonna work an extra job anymore. It's against the state contract anyway, so get used to the idea pronto. At the end of the month, I'm saying goodbye to Vanguard and Mini-Mart forever, and we'll just have to make do with what we have. Tighten a few screws, so to speak. It's as simple as that."

"But Wayne, we barely have enough now to..."

"But nothing!" Wayne interrupted her, holding up his hand.

"Listen Wayne," Ethel said as she reached for a cigarette. "I've got somethin' important to tell you."

"No, you listen, Ethel! With the stress I'm gonna be faced with at the prison, not to even mention the commute, there's no way I'm gonna be able to work another job. So I just want you to get that into your head right now and not mention anything else about it!"

"It's not about the jail job for God's sake!" Ethel looked away obstinately.

"Don't say 'jail job', Ethel!" Wayne said, as if he'd just been insulted. "The 'prison' is where I'm gonna be, with convicted felons, not in some little small town jail with people awaitin' trial or sleepin' one off. There's a big difference, so give me a bit of respect, for God's sake."

"All right, prison then!" she yelled, reaching toward the dashboard and shaking a cigarette from the pack. "But will you just listen to me for a minute?"

Wayne stuck his hand in the bag and searched around for what spilled french fries remained.

"All right," he said. "As long as we got that clear, tell me whatever you want."

Ethel lit the cigarette and inhaled deeply.

"I been meanin' to tell you about somethin' I found out a couple of days ago," she finally said. "But I just haven't known how to do it."

Wayne suddenly stopped chewing and jerked his head toward her.

"Don't tell me that Junior has been screwin' up at school again," he said, recalling the news from a month ago that his son had been caught making a pipe in his metal shop class. (Junior insisted that it was for tobacco but Wayne knew better than to believe the little liar anymore.)

"No," Ethel said, looking down. "This has nothin' to do with Junior."

"Well, it better not!" Wayne said, enraged. "'Cause if his stereo bein' taken away doesn't teach him a lesson, military school will. I promised him that much."

Ethel bit one of her chipped fingernails and then examined it.

"It concerns the result of a medical test," she said flatly.

Wayne stared at her suspiciously and then reached his hand toward her stomach, slowly grazing his hand over the familiar flab and pinching it.

"You're not gonna tell me you're pregnant again, are you?" he blurted as he glared at her.

Ethel did her best to smile, then shook her head slowly and looked away.

"No Wayne, I'm not pregnant," she said.

"Well, thank God for that," he said. Wayne took his hand from her belly and breathed a sigh of relief.

"Darlene is."

38

Farmers in Eastern Indiana were boasting that their recent harvest was the best in over a decade. But as Wayne dug up the roots of the dead stalks that remained in his garden, nothing seemed further from the truth. This year's crop had yielded less produce than ever for him. In fact, his late vegetables never even reached full maturity.

He knew at least one of the reasons was his own neglect. With all the twelve and sixteen-hour days he had put in over the past year to keep his family afloat, he just couldn't find the time to take care of the garden like he used to. Consequently, they suffered, and their failure to produce simply meant that he would be faced with a larger vegetable bill over the winter. Another unexpected expense, he thought, as he pulled the rake through the soil forcefully.

The chilly autumn wind whistled across the base of the fire and chewed its way through the embers of burning stalks. The gust fed the density of the red-and-yellow angular flames and sent a thick stream of smoke curling lazily into the dark sky overhead. Wayne heaved another stack of refuse on the fire, which momentarily crushed some of the flickering light.

Wayne listened to the rotted stems hiss as they heated up. He stared off toward the trailer, now fully illuminated in context with the approaching darkness. Through the undrawn curtains of the front door, he could see Darlene applying some rollers to his wife's hair. Both of them were laughing and seemed happy. As his daughter turned slightly to her side, he thought he detected a slight hint of the life growing within her.

Learning of Darlene's pregnancy undeniably shocked the hell out of Wayne. He didn't even realize that she was going out with boys, let alone that she had reached the stage of messing around. After all, she was always sitting on her ass in front of the TV, playing with the twins, or she was off at the salon sweeping up the floor. He figured the inane talk shows she watched were about as close to a sexual experience as she had ever come.

But as he tried to come to terms with the unexpected news a few weeks ago, while staring out the car window and listening to his wife dig into another fish burger at Hardees, a thought crossed his mind that made him view the situation in a different light. Instead of viewing Darlene's pregnancy as a huge mistake—like Ethel's had been over two years earlier—he thought he could simply begin making preparations for a wedding and finally relieve himself of the financial burden when he gave Darlene away at the altar. It would mean one less mouth to feed and worry about. It suddenly seemed as if the unexpected news had been timed perfectly, just as he was about to take on a new job and receive a pay cut.

"The only problem with that, Wayne," Ethel quickly shattered his plans between bites, "is that Darlene doesn't know where the father of the baby is. He's gone off to boot camp somewhere, and Darlene doesn't know where."

"I'll go straight to his parents, then," Wayne threatened.

"They don't live around here no more, Wayne," Ethel continued. "They moved somewhere out west."

"I'll get the little bastard one way or another."

"Don't get yourself too worked up, Wayne," Ethel shook her head. "Darlene told me it wasn't even his fault. It was all her idea and doin'. Happened the night of the senior prom."

Wayne suddenly felt like the little boy with his finger in the dyke. What was worse was he could visualize the cracks getting bigger and bigger, until finally the water was surging through, carrying him and his plans further away than he ever could have imagined.

Wayne was speechless. But he also began to realize that, even though he had always been against it, an abortion was the only logical solution to their predicament.

"That's gonna be hard, Wayne," Ethel said, shaking her head.

"Sure it will, but that's the way it's gonna have to be."

Ethel paused. "It can't be like that," she said.

"It will be like that," Wayne affirmed.

"No it won't," Ethel cut back. "'Cause when the doctor down at the clinic confirmed that Darlene was pregnant, he also said the life inside her was too far advanced to remove."

It all seemed like a bad dream that continued to get worse. And as Wayne rested his closed eyes against the steering wheel and listened to his wife repeat herself above the crying of the twins in the back seat, it was as if he were watching the events of the past dissolve behind him and the prospect of his future flood out in the distance, the destructive forces too great to halt. It was as if something as murky and viscous as molten lava were beginning to solidify around his dreams, suffocating the life in them so

287

completely that it seemed they never existed in the first place. Right there in the Hardee's parking lot, he almost felt like he was dying.

Wayne pulled the rake through the lumpy soil and ripped up the roots of his corn plants. As with most of the disappointments he had experienced in his life, he ended up surrendering his own goals to the situation at hand. And once again, the situation wasn't of his own making, but for the mistakes that created it, he was paying the price.

What bothered him most was that now his sacrifices were not only financial ones, but career ones as well. After all, it was because Darlene was pregnant that he was not making the drive home from the penitentiary at this very moment.

Turning down the job offer from the state was the most painful decision Wayne had ever made, but considering the circumstances he was faced with, he knew it was his only choice. Darlene finally consented to his demands that her baby be given up for adoption upon delivery, but he knew that before long she would also have to give up her job. Her meager pay at least took care of certain necessities. And Wayne simply came to the conclusion that the money the Department of Corrections had offered him would not cover his reworked budget. What they paid was more appropriate for a single man or one just beginning a family. For someone already bogged down by other financial worries, it just wasn't enough.

Wayne knew that in a couple of years he would once again be in a position to afford a pay cut. But what was unbearable was the certainty that he would never be presented with the opportunity for employment within the corrections system again. By the time applications were solicited next year, he would be over the age limit, anyway, and therefore he wouldn't be eligible for the job. It was as simple as that: He would never strut up and down the cell block as he had dreamed. Instead, he seemed destined to remain a prisoner of his own family. Forever.

A gust of wind swept across the yard, carrying a cloud of gray smoke into Wayne's path. He turned his back on the fire and wiped his watery eyes, then stared at the trailer again. Through the window, he saw Darlene holding up a mirror to Ethel's smiling face, now surrounded by a voluminous auburn-colored perm. Appalled at her ridiculously hideous appearance, Wayne threw down his rake in disgust and heaved a final stack of crumpled stalks on the fire before making his way toward the shed.

Once inside, he sat down before his desk and lit a cigarette. He just wanted to unwind a little before heading off to the radio station for another shift at the monotonous job he was forced to keep. Unfortunately, there wasn't much in his work area anymore that provided him with entertainment. He had to hock his television and VCR in order to help pay for the Pacer's repairs, and reading detective magazines or tactics publications only depressed him, now that he was unable to picture himself amid the action realistically. For the past week, the only material strewn across his desk had been all his bills, a constant reminder of his financial instability.

Even though he was not exhaling, Wayne could see his breath. The small heater that raised the temperature the winter before was something else he was forced to hock recently. But in spite of the cold, Wayne still preferred the confines of the chilly, damp shed to the comfort and warmth of his own home.

Fact was, Wayne no longer felt at home when he was in his own home. He had felt that way for some time. Of course, he slept inside the trailer and ate some meals there, and knew damn well that without his paychecks the four walls wouldn't even exist. But all that he ever seemed to be confronted with during what little free time he had there were the problems and gripes of the others. Or worse, their complete ambivalence toward his presence. His family just seemed to prefer that he wasn't there.

Wayne could picture them now, sitting around in front of the television, engrossed in some ridiculous sitcom. Ethel was smoking a cigarette and dozing off, Darlene had her hand sunken in a box of Bugles, and Junior probably had that indifferent stare glazed across his face. He figured the twins were asleep or, if not, loudly demanding the attention of their caretakers. The whole situation was sickening, he thought, as he stamped out his cigarette. In a word, pathetic.

It hadn't always been like that though, Wayne recalled, as he removed the top from a nearly empty pint of whiskey and took a sip. And it didn't even seem that long ago that he enjoyed being around all of them. Shortly after moving to Indiana, they cooked burgers on the grill and ate on the picnic table in the backyard, or strung up a badminton net and played all afternoon. He used to play catch with his son nearly every weekend, and sometimes even take him down to the batting cages or to the school field to shag fly balls. Or he'd take the kids to the miniature golf course in town, or to the bowling alley. Their first year there, he even took the whole family to see the Indy 500.

Wayne smiled, remembering the time they went swimming at a nearby lake, where he encouraged Darlene to dunk her brother in the water. She must have weighed about forty pounds more than him at the time, and as the boy pleaded toward the shore for her to stop, Wayne just continued to

289

egg his daughter on. When Junior finally escaped her grip, he swam to the shore frantically and nearly collapsed into the outstretched arms of Ethel, who was laughing even harder than Wayne while witnessing the scene.

Those were the fun years, Wayne thought, when the kids listened to what he said without question. When they enjoyed going to school and got good grades. When they did work around the house without being told twice. When they obeyed and followed directions to the tee. When they only watched TV on Saturday morning and played outside afterwards. When they were young.

Wayne thought about how all those good memories were now buried behind him forever. Back then, he never would have imagined in a million years that his sweet, innocent daughter would end up spreading her legs for any Tom, Dick, or Harry that came along—and would soon be giving birth to a bastard. Or that his athletic, responsible son would end up getting suspended from school and involved with illegal drugs. Or that his faithful, reliable wife would forget to use birth control and bring twins into the world, and then turn into a lazy pill addict. Or that he, Wayne Turner, the ruthless and diligent lawman, would be putting in sixteen hour days at a rock station and Mini-Mart in order to pay for all of their mistakes.

Lighting another cigarette, Wayne became upset that his mind had wandered back to such unpleasant thoughts. He reached underneath the table and grabbed a cheap sex magazine he found near the dumpster at the Mini-Mart that afternoon. He ran his finger across its waterlogged cover and placed his feet up on the table, loosening his belt when he felt comfortable.

It had been almost two months since he had messed with Ethel. Nowadays, she always seemed to come up with some sort of excuse to postpone sex. Most recently, she told him that her gynecologist suggested a weaker pill that retained less water and might help her shed a few pounds, and that he had advised her to abstain from sex for a month or so until her body adapted to the new dosage. Before that it had been something else—he couldn't even remember what. In any event, she just didn't seem to want it very much anymore.

As he flipped through the glossy pages and stared at the provocative photos, Wayne felt the pressure beginning to mount against his fly and finally extracted his own penis, enjoying its sense of power within his hand. One woman reclined on a motorcycle seat and stretched her legs out onto the handlebars while another spread her vulva and lowered herself toward her lover's outstretched tongue. They all seemed like they were having fun, releasing themselves and enjoying it, and to add to his own pleasure, Wayne skimmed through a few articles while massaging his balls.

He began turning the pages more quickly, leering at the models briefly before moving on. Woman after woman exposed herself shamelessly, and as he brought his gaze to their most private parts, he began jerking his hand passionately. He could feel that launch nearing.

Wayne flipped the pages rapidly again. He stopped briefly at a series of photos depicting a grossly fat woman reclining on a bed and inserting various sex objects into her vagina.

Wayne abruptly stopped moving his hand and could almost feel the blood diverting itself from his groin and redirecting its path through the rest of his body. The warmth that had just flushed his entire body suddenly seeped out his pores in the form of a putrid-smelling sweat.

The woman's face in front of him was partially hidden by the immensity of her breasts, but he could see enough to recognize exactly who it was. Wayne felt weak as his mind slammed into overdrive, the thoughts racing through his head too fast to comprehend. He saw himself lost within a huge, dark void, the same place he found himself when he learned that his daughter was pregnant.

But this time he didn't feel like he was dying. He felt something even worse.

39

"What's a baptism supposed to be for, anyway?" Darlene asked. She stared across the table at her mother, who was sandwiching a onion ring between the roll and meat of a hamburger.

Ethel thought about the question briefly as she devoured half the burger with one bite.

"Well, I guess it's supposed to make the children members of the faith," she finally said. "Isn't that right?" Ethel directed the question toward her husband.

Wayne sat uncomfortably on the edge of the bench-seat, looking out the window. He stared across the snow-covered parking lot toward the Gremlin. He noticed that a hole had begun to eat its way through one of the rust patches below the car's front door. As he chewed his burger, he wondered how much the technical school would charge him to patch it up.

Ethel stopped chewing her burger and stared at him, annoyed by his lack of response.

"Wayne, I just said somethin' to you!" she said, raising her voice. "You haven't been listenin' to me all mornin'!"

Wayne turned from the window and looked at his wife.

"What?" he said.

"Darlene wanted to know about the baptism," she said, dipping her burger into a mound of ketchup on the paper plate. "It's to make the kids members, isn't it?"

Wayne slid his ass around so that he looked more part of the group.

"Yeah," he said, reaching for an onion ring. "But it's also to forgive them for the sins of their parents." He stared directly at Ethel.

Ethel shoved the rest of the burger into her mouth. She glanced at Wayne, then locked eyes with him. He seemed to be implying something deeper than his obvious words, but she couldn't be sure.

"That's right," she finally said, shifting her glance toward Darlene. "You see, they're brought into the world innocent. I knew there was some other reason. I just couldn't remember it."

For the first time since the twins were born, all the Turners were eating out together. They were crowded around an imitation wood table at a new White Castle in Westport. This fast-food place had just opened up that weekend in a vacated Long John Silver restaurant that had been boarded up for nearly a year. As an inaugural special, they offered five-cent hamburgers during the lunch hour, and the sparkling blue-and-white-tiled interior was packed with townsfolk eager to try the small, square burgers. A line of shivering customers stretched from the counter to just outside the entrance, so that the door constantly remained open and ventilated the interior of the hazy restaurant with an uncomfortable, chilly draft.

An hour ago, the family attended a service at the Tree of Life Church, where the twins were baptized. Ethel and the kids normally went to the church only on Christmas Eve, but it was the first time Wayne had set foot in a church since Junior was baptized a decade and a half ago.

It wasn't that Wayne didn't believe in God—he did. He just found the whole service boring and drawn out, basically a rehash of things he already knew. Consequently, he promptly fell asleep as soon as the baptism was over. He was shaken from his slumber by the shrill voices of the sopranos as the choir made their exiting procession past him.

"Get away from my plate!" Darlene shouted, slapping her brother's hand. "These are my burgers!"

"But I'm still hungry," Junior whined, and gave her a dirty look. "I knew I should have gotten more. It takes like four of these to equal even one over at the bowlin' alley."

"I think these are pretty good," Ethel said, handing a french fry to each of the twins. "They almost melt in your mouth."

"Hey Dad, can you go get some more?" Junior shouted across the table.

"I don't want anymore," he responded, hunching over the couple that remained on his plate, as if protecting them. "If you want some more, go get 'em yourself."

Junior pulled some pennies from his pocket and frowned.

"Well how about giving me some money then," he said.

Wayne stared at him and shoved another bite into his mouth, chewing it noisily.

"Why don't you pay for them yourself? You got a job," he muttered.

"Oh, for God's sake, Wayne!" Ethel said, heedlessly spitting part of her mouthful into Crystal's face. "They're only five cents each!"

"Exactly," Wayne said, turning toward her. "It's not like it's gonna break his bank account, neither."

"Do we have to argue right here in this nice restaurant?" Ethel said, looking annoyed, back and forth, between the two males. "Gladys and Crystal have just been baptized. We should all be celebratin', not nickel-and-dimin'." She reached into her pocketbook and handed a couple of quarters to Junior. "And while you're at it," Ethel yelled over her shoulder as he moved toward the line. "Maybe you can get a couple of extra ones so we can bring 'em home."

Wayne looked at his wife disapprovingly and then gathered up the remaining crumbs of the onion rings. After belching loudly, he squeezed himself out of the booth. Wanting to stretch his cramped legs a little, he walked over by the counter and looked through a glass partition where a cook was busily preparing the food. It was a curious sight, because unlike most fast-food restaurants he had ever been in, the burgers at White Castle were made in a different way. Instead of grilling the burger and placing it on a roll that had been toasted seperately, they did both operations at the same time—actually frying the burger in the roll.

Hundreds of burgers lined the grill, and the cook's actions were so fast that Wayne suddenly felt dizzy staring down at the little squares of meat and bread. It was like a constantly moving chess board: New squares replaced the old, one second changing and the next second the same as before. The onions hissed, the meat spit its boiling fat, the bread soaked up the grease and the cook pressed them all together into a completed whole ready for consumption, over and over again.

And for some reason, Wayne couldn't take his eyes off of the repeated movements. It almost felt as if he had been hypnotized.

He wasn't sure how many hundreds of burgers he observed being prepared, but Wayne's trance was cut short when he was poked from behind. He spun around and saw the strange image of his son, who was loudly slurping a drink.

"You ready to go yet?" the boy asked obstinately. "We've been waitin' for you."

Wayne rubbed his eyes and glanced quickly back at the grill, whose activity was distorted by his own reflection in the glass. He wondered why the hell he had been staring at it for so long.

"You get a couple more burgers?" he finally said, looking back at his son.

"No," Junior answered, removing the top from the cup and stirring the liquid with the straw. "I got a milkshake instead."

Father and son waited by the door without exchanging another word. Over at the table, Ethel stood and wiped off Crystal's mouth as a cigarette dangled from her mouth. Darlene was holding the other girl as she struggled to pull her coat over her expanded girth. Another family immediately slipped into their empty seats.

"Did you get those other burgers, Junior?" Ethel asked him when she finally made her way to the exit.

Junior slurped the milkshake noisily.

"No," he said, licking the straw and tossing the cup toward the garbage can. "I only had enough money for that."

"Hey Wayne, how about gettin' in the line and gettin' a few more then," she said, throwing her cigarette on the floor. "The special's only on for another hour or so."

Wayne sighed angrily.

"You must be kiddin'," he said, gawking at her and shaking his head. "Your selfish son blew that chance for you when he decided to spend all the money on himself."

"Oh c'mon, Wayne!" Ethel pleaded. "I got a couple of bucks..."

"Out!" he suddenly interrupted her. Wayne grabbed his wife by the arm and forced her from the premises, with the rest of the family in tow.

A light snow began to fall, covering the roads with a thin, virgin layer of white powder. The Gremlin rode low to the ground, bogged down by the weight of the six and a half people stuffed within its tiny interior. As the car made a turn at an intersection, it skidded toward the curb, thrusting its occupants to one side, then the other. Wayne skillfully brought the vehicle back under control.

"What are you tryin' to do, kill us all?" Ethel yelled at him from the back seat. "You know this car don't have snow tires on it. Slow down, for Christ's sake!"

Wayne looked at her over his shoulder.

"You leave the drivin' to me, Ethel," he sneered. "And don't tell me how to do my job. We're goin' slow enough as it is."

"I wish we could've gotten a big box of the burgers to bring home and freeze," Darlene said, bouncing one of the babies on her knee. "They say you can just put them in the microwave for a few seconds and they taste pretty much like in the restaurant."

"I know, Darlene," Ethel said, poking the back of her son's head.

295

"Your brother could've gotten us some more. It would of saved me makin' dinner tonight."

Junior knocked her hand away.

"Gimme a break!" he hissed. "You didn't even act like you wanted 'em that bad before. Dad should have gotten some more anyway. He could've gotten in line instead of just standin' there watchin' the burgers bein' cooked like some zombie."

Wayne stared at his son with disdain briefly, then responded by letting out a long, voluminous fart.

"That's disgustin'!" Darlene yelled from the back seat.

Wayne caught her repulsed face in the rear view mirror and farted again.

Ethel punched her husband on the back of the shoulder.

"Cut it out, Wayne!" she said. "You might think it's funny but the rest of us don't!"

"Jesus Christ, it stinks!" Junior screamed, rolling down his window hurriedly. "It smells like rotten onions or somethin'!"

"Goddamn it, Junior!" Ethel yelled, holding up her arms to protect herself from the sudden draft. "Put that window back up right now! Do you want the twins to catch a cold or somethin'?"

Junior kept it down and leaned his face toward the fresh air.

"You just can't smell it as much back there," his voice trailed off with the wind. "It's a lot worse up here."

"I don't care!" Ethel continued. "I don't want you catching a cold, neither. You can't afford to miss any more days at school. You've already been absent about ten times this year, and Christmas vacation is still two weeks away."

"Yeah, well, I don't really care," Junior responded as he brought his head back in and rolled up the window. "Because I'm thinkin' about quittin' school after this quarter is done with anyway."

"Don't say stupid things, Junior," Ethel responded. "You're only sixteen years old, for God's sake."

"Exactly," Junior said, turning around to face her. "You can quit school when you're sixteen."

"With your parents permission," Wayne interrupted him. "And believe me, I will never give you permission to quit school."

"I don't see why not," he hissed. He ignored his father and turned to face his more receptive mother. "I'm probably gonna end up gettin' kicked out anyway, seein' how all the teachers have it out against me. And

296

besides, The Country Kitchen said they'd gimme a full-time job whenever I wanted it. I wouldn't mind makin' some more money anyway, and gettin' a motorcycle or somethin'."

Wayne eased the Gremlin around another curve and wiped off the fogged windshield with his hand. What an asshole his son was, he thought, to have no greater ambition than to be a faceless moron who wipes the grease off plates at some filthy little family restaurant. His son's lack of ambition reinforced what Wayne had believed for the past year: His son was a complete and total loser. He flipped on the radio and turned the dial until it landed upon a soothing, country number, hoping it might take his mind off the disagreeable subject.

"That baptism today sure was nice," Darlene said, making the sign of the cross on Crystal's forehead. "I wouldn't mind standin' next to the minister with my own baby doin' that."

"Well, you can just stop thinkin' about that right now," Wayne blurted from the front. "At least with the baby you're carryin' right now anyway, 'cause that's gonna be up to the pair of responsible people that adopt it. Not you."

"Yeah, well, I been thinkin' that maybe it's not that good of an idea to give the baby away," she said quietly. "I mean, I've had it now for almost seven months and I'm gettin' pretty attached to it. I talk to it at night and everything. I've even started pickin' some names out for it."

Wayne caught her face in the mirror.

"Darlene," he began, "I would appreciate it if you just erased those ideas from your head and never thought about them again. We made an agreement before that we just can't afford the kid. But it's not only that, 'cause I'm thinkin' about your interests, too. I mean, how the hell are you gonna find another man when you got this little baby to worry about all the time? What single man is gonna wanna deal with that?"

"Oh c'mon, Wayne," Ethel said, lighting a cigarette. "Half the marriages nowadays end in divorce, and there's lots of single parents with children that get married again. I don't think Darlene would have any trouble attractin' another man with the child."

Wayne glanced over his shoulder and stared at his wife disdainfully.

"N-O Ethel," he said firmly. "And don't start."

Ethel adjusted Gladys on her lap and turned to Darlene.

"Men just don't understand how attached women become to the children they're carryin'," she said. "Takin' it away is like takin' all your hopes and dreams away.'' She rubbed her daughter's belly and winked at her. ''Don't worry honey,'' she added softly. ''I ain't gonna let your daddy give that little, sweet thing away.''

Wayne covered up their hushed conversation by turning the radio up. He had already made his decision and didn't want to go over worn ground anymore.

''Do we have to listen to this?'' Junior moaned, pushing the hair that covered his face behind his ears. ''I hate country music more than anything.''

''Well I don't care,'' Wayne said, flipping on the wipers to clear the snow. ''Because this is my car and this is what I wanna listen to. So shut up!''

Darlene's eclipsed voice could be heard softly from behind.

''I just want to keep this baby,'' she moaned.

''Hey Wayne!'' Ethel yelled from the back seat. ''We won't even have to pay for clothes when Darlene has her baby 'cause we already got plenty of hand-me-downs that the twins are growin' out of.''

''Can you at least turn that crap down!'' Junior protested from the side.

''Which, speaking of clothes, reminds me,'' Ethel continued. ''They've got a big pre-Christmas sale on over at Wal-Mart. I wouldn't mind gettin' started on my Christmas shoppin' before the big rush starts. Do you think we could swing over there later on and pick up a few things?''

Wayne looked into the rear-view mirror and saw his wife's fat face splashing over its sides. She was picking her nose and running her tongue along her front teeth, trying to clean them. Wayne took his eyes off the ugly sight and directed his eyes back at the road, seeing his mailbox in the distance.

He didn't respond to his wife's question. His mind was suddenly overwhelmed with another train of thought.

40

Wayne glanced up at the clock. It was just past six o'clock.

He wasn't sure how long it had been exactly, but he guessed eight or nine hours must have passed before he finally decided to call the police. He had hung up the phone only a couple of minutes ago, and his conversation was brief. He didn't even give his name: In a calm voice, he simply gave the operator his address and said there had been a shooting. Then he hung up the phone and reached into the refrigerator for another beer.

Wayne now sat in the kitchen in his bleach-stained, blue security guard outfit. He was casually smoking a cigarette and staring out the window at the snow-covered yard. The bare branches of the trees cast shadows, which shortened as the sun began its slow ascent into the charcoal-gray sky. The blinking lights of the Christmas tree in the family room provided a sporadic splash of color to the otherwise dimly-lit kitchen. The silence surrounding him was periodically broken when a drop of water seeped out of the leaky faucet and crashed against the metal sink basin. Resting on the table in front of him was an overflowing ashtray, a couple of dirty plates, several empty beer cans, and his empty .38 caliber service revolver.

Last night, after the sun disappeared, Wayne awoke from a short nap. He dressed for work as usual, taking special care to shine his shoes and make sure that his uniform looked just right. He clipped his fingernails, combed his hair in place and even polished his badge. After that, he took six bullets from the closet and pushed them into the cylinders of the revolver. Before leaving the bedroom, he had checked his appearance in the mirror. Everything was in place.

Wayne then made his way out to the family room.

As usual, he found them all sitting in front of the television. And as the adrenaline flowed through his body and surged toward his trigger finger, he thought he heard one of them yell something before the hammering outbursts began. But he couldn't even recall who he shot at first.

What Wayne did know was that within a minute, it was all over. His ears were echoing each of the six rounds that had raced from the barrel of the gun. It didn't matter that he hadn't had any shooting practice in almost two years because at such close range, even a mere beginner could have hit every mark with one eye closed. And slowly, through the blue haze of spent gunfire, he began to see all his family members either sprawled across the floor or thrust back against their chairs. Their bodies were splattered with expanding blood stains.

Completely still. Strangely silent. Obviously dead.

Wayne left the room, and didn't return to survey the scene. Instead, he stayed several yards away in the kitchen, periodically glancing through the Sunday paper, casually smoking a cigarette or drinking a beer. He cooked himself a few fried eggs at one point, and even dozed briefly once or twice, when his eyelids grew too heavy to hold open.

Even though there were still bullets in the bedroom, Wayne never once during the wee hours of the morning considered turning the weapon on himself. That was a coward's solution, he thought, a person who couldn't come to terms with what they had done and own up to it. Certainly not him, he knew, because while sitting alone and busying himself with everyday activities, Wayne began to see his future more clearly than ever.

He knew that the police would eventually slap the handcuffs on him and lead him away from his trailer, forever. He also knew that he wouldn't say a word when they asked him questions. He had a motive, that was clear enough to him, and that was all that mattered. At the trial he would plead guilty to every single charge brought against him, and when his death sentence was handed down, he wouldn't argue it.

He imagined the other inmates on death row, counting the days before they would make that last solitary walk, awaking in their sleep every night, shaking, cold, scared, and hoping to delay their execution date or get their sentence commuted altogether. And as they filed petition after petition to save their lives, Wayne wouldn't make even the slightest protest at all. He'd simply await the day. He imagined the other inmates would treat him with scorn because he would be a threat to their attempts to stay alive. That thought pleased him, because he knew that once he was executed, it would pave the way for the others to follow.

But there was another reason why Wayne wanted to calmly wait for the morning they led him to the death room. That had to do with the man who would pull the final switch, the man standing in the shadows, the executioner. Wayne certainly didn't want to deprive that lawman of his duty and privilege, as it had been denied him.

In the distance, Wayne could hear the faint wail of a siren sailing over the trees and toward his trailer. He felt relaxed, confident that he had done the right thing. He lit another cigarette, kicked his feet up onto the table, and calmly waited for the police to arrive and do their job.